29

W9-CKL-064

THE WINDOW OF TIME

THE WINDOW OF TIME
A Novel of Suspense

William A. Thau

iUniverse, Inc.
New York Bloomington

The Window of Time

iUniverse books may be ordered through booksellers or by contacting:

iUniverse
1663 Liberty Drive
Bloomington, IN 47403
www.iuniverse.com
1-800-Authors (1-800-288-4677)

Because of the dynamic nature of the Internet, any Web addresses or links contained in this book
may have changed since publication and may no longer be valid. The views expressed in this work
are solely those of the author and do not necessarily reflect the views of the publisher, and the
publisher hereby disclaims any responsibility for them.

ISBN: 978-1-4502-2589-2 (pbk)
ISBN: 978-1-4502-2590-8 (cloth)
ISBN: 978-1-4502-2591-5 (ebook)

Printed in the United States of America

iUniverse rev. date: 10/6/10

To Jane, my eternal love and inspiration.

I heartily accept the motto - "That government is best which governs least;" and I should like to see it acted up to more rapidly and systematically. Carried out, it finally amounts to this, which I also believe, - "That government is best which governs not at all;" and when men are prepared for it, that will be the kind of government which they will have.

Henry David Thoreau
On the Duty of Civil Disobedience - 1849

Anarchism holds that one thing, namely government is bad and should be abolished.

Emma Goldman - 1901

We should war with relentless efficiency not only against anarchists, but against all active and passive sympathizers with anarchists. Moreover, every scoundrel like Hearst and his satellites who for whatever purposes appeals to and inflames evil human passion, has made himself an accessory before the fact to every crime of this nature .

Theodore Roosevelt,
in a letter to Henry Cabot Lodge,
September 9, 1901

Time will explain it all. It needs no questioning before it speaks.

-Aelous in the Odyssey
8th Century, BC

PROLOGUE

▼

Hampton Roads, Virginia - 1907

It was his brainchild. Theodore Roosevelt had brought to the White House a deep conviction that only through a strong navy could a nation project its power abroad. In his tenure, American shipyards had turned out eleven new battleships to give the navy awesome battle capabilities, but the fleet was known as the Atlantic Fleet and was concentrated only on the East Coast. There were but a handful of smaller ships on duty in the Pacific. Hostilities with Japan seemed probable; the Japanese navy dominated the Pacific and posed a substantial threat to the Philippines. The Japanese, only the year before, had annihilated the Russian fleet in the Russo-Japanese War. His own commanders had reluctantly concluded the Philippines would have to be abandoned if Japan attacked. Yet Congress opposed him.

Leading senators, including the chairman of the Naval Appropriations Committee, refused to support him in his efforts in the Pacific because it would weaken naval defenses in the Atlantic. In defiance of Congress, he secretly ordered the American fleet to proceed to the Pacific. The Atlantic battleship fleet had been assembled in Hampton Roads in June for what, he had said, was to honor the Jamestown Exposition. But rumors had spread wildly that he planned to send it to the West Coast. The official announcement was later made – the fleet's orders were to sail on a "practice cruise" to rendezvous with the small Pacific fleet in Baja, California. Congress threatened to withhold money for this "cruise", worried that it would compromise the defense of the East Coast, but he was belligerent. He dared Congress to stop him - he already had the money.

What no one knew except his admirals was that he intended that the fleet circumvent the globe. Other nations had sent small squadrons, often with disastrous results, but this was the first attempt by any country to send an entire battle fleet. It would be a grand pageant to demonstrate to the world American sea power, and on the fleets' return in almost fourteen months, it would be a fitting end to his administration. The scope of such an operation was unprecedented in history, and it would involve the entire operational capability of the American navy. With their hulls painted white except for the gilded scrollwork with a red, white and blue banner on their bows, the ships would become known in history as the Great White Fleet. The magnificent fleet was Theodore Roosevelt's creation, a lasting monument to his obsessive dedication to restoring America's place in the world.

The rain had stopped, and the heavy fog hung chilly and damp around him as he stood alone on the presidential yacht known as the *Mayflower*. His keen, searching eyes swept the bay, looking for signs of the spectacle he knew was soon to arrive. His wife and an official party were twenty feet away, chatting in low voices. For two days, an Atlantic storm had churned the waves and threatened the display that had been so carefully planned by the navy for its commander-in-chief. A cold west wind blew across the hull; looking up, he saw the dark clouds slowly begin to dissipate. As hard as he tried, he couldn't erase from his thoughts his deception of Congress and the enormous risk he had undertaken. Behind him, unaware of what he had planned, the noiseless throngs of sightseers held tightly to their gas lanterns that eerily reflected off the now still waters of Hampton Roads.

One hundred yards to his left, concealed in the shadows, was another yacht. It had not been there long. Neither Roosevelt nor the others on his boat were looking in its direction. The man watching him had come for a single reason, not to see the sight that had attracted the crowds, but to kill him. His eyes peered anxiously back and forth for assurance that he had not been seen, but his intended victim had his concentration elsewhere and failed to notice the stranger on the nearby yacht or his murderous intent.

For Roosevelt, this was one of the great moments of his presidency. For the man on the nearby yacht watching him, it was the culmination of a plan that had been painstakingly set in motion over a year ago. Suddenly, the crowd began to roar as the band struck up *The Girl I Left Behind Me*. Over the horizon, at 8:00 AM on December 16, 1907, sixteen gleaming white battleships of the Atlantic Battle Fleet appeared one by one, led by the USS Connecticut as their flagship. The squadron was manned by fourteen thousand sailors and was a striking display of American sea power.

Their journey of over forty-three thousand miles was about to begin. As the Connecticut steamed past, its sailors stood at rigid salute while its big guns began to boom. The President returned their salutes with a tip of his top hat. At the same moment, the man watching him raised a high-powered Lee-Enfield Mark III rifle and brought him within its sights. The explosion of the rifle coincided perfectly with the firing of the ships' massive cannons.

PART I

CHAPTER ONE

▼

Buffalo, New York – 1901

Each day, tens of thousands of people from all over the world lined up at the front gates eager to see the amazing scientific achievements that would change the course of American history. It was a miracle. That was all they could think when they first saw the sea of color and fantastic shapes, illuminated by tens of thousands of electric light bulbs. It was the Pan-American Exposition of 1901 in Buffalo, New York. The buildings at the expo were constructed according to the Spanish renaissance motif, painted in bright pastel colors and covered with the colorful lights. At night, the fairgrounds lit up the entire sky and could be seen for miles. By the time it closed its gates, over eleven million people had visited its buildings.

Somewhere in that multitude, in early September, a young man held a .32 caliber revolver concealed in his pocket. He was twenty-eight years old, of slim build, and wore a small brown mustache on his pale face. He roamed the exhibitions with only mild interest and was curiously unimpressed. Drifting from display to display, he walked the grounds with a growing anger at everything he saw. Convinced that the government was intent on exploiting workers like him, he raged within himself that something had to be done to break the bonds of poverty imposed on the destitute people of America. He was Leon Franz Czolgosz, the son of Polish immigrants. And soon, this disturbed loner who was a disciple of the anarchist movement and an avid follower of its radical spokesperson, Emma Goldman, would take action to accomplish that goal. In July, Czolgosz had visited Goldman in her home and spoke again with her later as she caught a train. Her passionate speeches had "set him on fire".

On the morning of September 6, President William McKinley visited Niagra Falls and returned to the exposition for a speech and scheduled reception in his honor. He was guarded by the Secret Service, Buffalo detectives and eleven soldiers, all of whom had been alerted to watch the crowd. McKinley, flanked by his advisors, stood and shook hands with persons waiting in a long line. Among those was Czolgosz. All those watching missed him.

After several minutes, the President was approached by Czolgosz, his "bandaged" hand extended forward to greet the man who had just won a second term in office. The President smiled back, but when he reached for the extended hand, he suddenly became aware of a small pistol clutched there. Without warning, two shots were fired point-blank into the President.

The President was rushed to the operating room at the exposition's emergency hospital to have the bullets removed. Ironically, the operating room had no electricity even though the exteriors of many of the exposition's buildings were extravagantly covered with thousands of light bulbs. Doctors were forced to use a pan to reflect sunlight onto the operating table as they treated the President and attempted to remove the single bullet that remained in his body. The newly developed X-ray machine, which might have helped find the bullet, was on display at the exposition. Oddly, no one thought to use it to save McKinley's life. Unable to find the bullet, the doctors left it in his body and closed up the wound.

At that time, there was general agreement that the President would survive. In the following days, the inventor of the X-ray machine, Thomas Edison, arranged for a machine to be delivered from his shop in New Jersey to the home of the exposition's director where the President was convalescing. It also was never used. Appearing to slowly recover, the President lay ill at the director's home for over a week. He subsequently went into shock and died of his wounds at 2:15 AM on

September 14, 1901. The official cause of death was listed as gangrene of both walls of the stomach and pancreas following the gunshot wounds. He was the third U.S. president to have been murdered in a brief span of thirty-five years.

Meanwhile, in Chicago, another drama was taking place. A middle-aged woman sitting in police headquarters was carefully guarded by several prison matrons. A cold and defiant look was on her thin, chiseled face. The room was gripped in a grim silence as minutes passed without anyone uttering a word. With a slow determination, the woman turned and spoke to one of the matrons. "Suppose the President is dead. Thousands die every day, yet no one cries for them. Why should anyone shed a tear over this man?"

For her insensitive words, all she received were blank stares of disbelief. Suddenly, a patrolman burst into the room, shouting, "All the flags are being lowered. The President must be dead!" The woman sat unmoved. A police matron began to curse the woman. "Have you no heart – no sorrow for this man and his family?" she screamed.

"I tell you, I don't care." The response was cold and flat. An icy glare went from the woman's eyes to those of the matron. The woman, Emma Goldman, was being held for the assassination of President William McKinley. A search of Emma Goldman's flat that day revealed a box, implicating the owner of one of the country's largest shipping lines. The police were perplexed as to why such a man would be involved in an assassination of the President until they read the letters found in the box. She vehemently denied knowing anything about them, and further denied that she had ever known the man, Matthew Stanton, but the box told a different story.

The hand-written engraved letters it contained spoke of Stanton's hatred of McKinley because of the invasion of the Philippines and the President's unwillingness to bring the conflict to an end. McKinley's America was an imperialistic nation, a nation that Stanton could not tolerate. His sympathy with the anarchists who shot the Prince of Wales and the King of Italy was well documented. Though Stanton would prosper from the emergence of international trade, the letters portrayed a man who saw a convergence of economic and political forces determined to silence the voice of the individual. For him and the loose affiliation called anarchists, the complete destruction of imperialistic America was the only solution to bring about a just country. And the letters confirmed that his anger and zealotry would lead to bloodshed, and gave witness to his willingness to finance that bloodshed. The evidence was damning.

Within hours, a manhunt unlike any seen since the murder of Abraham Lincoln was set in motion. After an intense search, it was found that Stanton had disappeared. When questioned, his employees described him as a ghost, rarely seen and uncommunicative. His competitors had harsher words. They described him as a cunning fox, willing to destroy his enemies as he saw fit, and as a plotter and a radical in both his methods and schemes. He constantly got the better of them, and none were surprised that he might be involved in killing the President. When asked about his appearance, the most that anyone could say was that he was tall, about six feet, was heavily bearded with dark brown hair, and had cold piercing eyes.

There were no pictures of him because he refused to be photographed. His company, Far East Shipping, dealt in freight to and from the Philippines and the Far East. To those who knew him, he was Mr. Stanton, and most thought his first name was Matthew or Matt. They could give little information about his background, except that he either came from an extremely wealthy family or had made his millions on his own, and that he had no wife, children or other family. He was a loner, but at the same time one of the wealthiest tycoons in America.

*   *   *   *

Three days later, at 3:30 in the afternoon, a man who was about to become the 26th president of the United States stood in the drawing room of the home of Ansley Wilcox in Buffalo, New York. Before him was a federal judge who would administer the oath of office. Around him stood several members of the deceased President's cabinet, including Secretary of War Elihu Root. Elihu Root would stay. His formidable power of analysis, his creative genius in discovering solutions to problems, and his disciplined attention to detail had captured Roosevelt's admiration years before. He would oversee the search for McKinley's killers. And it was Root who would get the battleships that Roosevelt needed for an imperial America.

His eyes moist with tears, Theodore Roosevelt took the oath and declared his aim to continue unbroken the policies of President McKinley. Deep within himself, though, he felt a certain satisfaction that an assassin's bullet had now given him the supreme power he had always craved. He intended to make good use of it.

The day before, he had arrived from Albany and paid his respects to the memory of the murdered McKinley at the Milburn residence. As he passed many of McKinley's relatives who were standing on the lawn, he tipped his high silk hat in respect. He inquired for Mrs. McKinley, but saw neither her nor the body of her husband. Returning to his carriage, he ordered that the Secret Service and police be discharged from further escort duty, declaring that he would not "establish the precedent of going about guarded." That was a decision he would live to regret.

CHAPTER TWO

▼

Philadelphia, Pennsylvania – 1901

It was a wide, quiet street blanketed by heavy, freezing snow. There were only a few houses, barely visible through the snow flurries, protected by high walls and wrought-iron gates. In Philadelphia, it was a place where the very rich lived--not those who had recently acquired a lot of money, but those whose fortunes had been passed through family members for decades. A little faded, it was nevertheless very conscious of its status as one of the prominent addresses in this status-conscious city.

A large three-storied gray stone house sat in the middle of the block, so far back that it could barely be seen from the street. It had a graceful classical façade, the work of one of Philadelphia's finest architects. In front of the house was a cobblestone courtyard surrounded by large, empty urns. The courtyard was protected from passersby with a pair of tall iron gates topped by a gilded crest of oak leaves with a coronet.

She stood alone staring out a second floor window, oblivious to the cold, blustery wind that drew patterns of white across the landscape below. Her only thought was to escape. Turning to the bed, she finished packing the open suitcase and then pulled a heavy wool scarf around her neck. Picking up her fur coat, she returned to the window where she saw a horse and enclosed carriage, illuminated by the soft light of a gas streetlamp, pull through the gates and come to a halt at the canopy sheltering the front door.

Putting on her wool coat trimmed in fur and a broad-brimmed hat, very stylish for the times, she stopped for a moment to take a deep breath. She shuddered at the thought of him. Without regard to the bitter weather outside, she had no choice. She had to leave. If she didn't, her married name would turn into a death sentence. How had she surrendered all her joy? She knew her past and childhood had not been the reason; her father had encouraged her academic and artistic talents. But he had died years ago; it was her husband's obsessive control that was at the root of her deepest fears. Within twenty-four hours she will have disappeared.

Reflecting on her past, she thought of how her family had moved to New York in 1880, when she was a young schoolgirl. Her father, a struggling banker, had died that year, leaving behind enormous debts. His wife and two children were destitute. For years, they lived in near poverty, but by the time she reached adolescence, her startling beauty had come to the attention of several artists, and she was able to find work as an artist's model. Soon she was modeling for some of the most distinguished artists of the day. She rapidly became one of the most in-demand models, making enough money to support her unemployed mother and brother.

Alyssa had become seductively beautiful with long, wavy auburn hair, a perfectly shaped face, and a slender, shapely figure. She had become the "it" girl who everyone wanted to see, including Clayton Harding. Harding was a descendant of a railroad tycoon, was one of the most desirable and wealthiest bachelors in New York, and was insane. His mellow behavior around strangers was a subterfuge for his violently irrational behavior in private and his uncontrollable rages of jealousy. His secret life was unknown to Alyssa and her mother, and it was her mother who had set her eyes on young Clayton as their only hope for wealth and stature.

Alyssa, at the age of twenty-four, refused his offer of marriage, and her mother was enraged. The next day, her mother was hospitalized with what *she* diagnosed as a heart attack. Giving in to her mother's "dying wish", Alyssa married Harding in 1896 and set off for a honeymoon in Europe. It wasn't long before she realized he was a cocaine addict and a sadist who subjected her to severe whippings. She wanted to leave, but he put her under twenty-four hour guard and kept her in constant fear for her life.

She was held as a prisoner in her own home, prevented from modeling or any outside relationships, and was carefully watched on the few occasions when she was permitted to step out. His insane jealously had, even on those few times, led to violent bursts of anger. Her life had become a living hell. And then suddenly, she had an opportunity to escape. His mother had died, and he gone to Newport. A sympathetic guard offered Alyssa a way out – for a price. She had little money of her own, but Clayton had showered her with expensive jewelry. A diamond broach was all she needed for the guard. He jumped at the opportunity.

Now it was time to leave. She picked up her suitcase and walked quickly from the bedroom, quietly descended the winding staircase, and opened the door to a furious blast of freezing air. The driver of the carriage leaned down and opened the passenger door, and then reached for her suitcase and placed it next to him. She climbed in and closed the door, letting out a deep sigh of relief that she had made it this far. Laying her head back, she closed her eyes and felt the soothing protection of the carriage. Pulling the collar of her coat up around her face, she was comforted by the thought that soon no one could find her.

Arriving at the train station, she allowed the driver to help her out of the carriage and then opened her handbag and handed him the exact fare. After a moment's hesitation, she added a large tip, which prompted him to carry her luggage inside the station. Thirty minutes later, she was sitting in the quiet confines of the Pullman car of the Pennsylvania Railroad, destined for Chicago.

CHAPTER THREE

▼

The Train

He had boarded the train at a small town in northern Pennsylvania. There were now ten other people in the car. The lights were dim and the passengers rested quietly, reading or trying to sleep, seemingly unaware of him. A very pretty young woman, who had boarded in Philadelphia, sat near the front of the car. Behind him, near the back of the car, were three men who caught his attention, each separated by several seats from the others. They weren't travelers. Their darting eyes and their whispered conversations told him they were looking for someone. It was soon apparent to him that it was the woman who had their attention. Her name was Alyssa Coolidge. He overheard her speak it at the station.

The conductor opened the back door as he entered the car, bringing with him a blast of cold air. Several times he added fuel to the cast-iron stove. The woman turned and looked back, briefly at him, then at the conductor, and then with an expression of worry at the three men. Her dark auburn hair was thick around her face, highlighting eyes that were a startling luminous blue. She was a young woman, not over thirty, and wore a crisp high-necked white ruffled blouse with a soft beige jacket and a long flaring matching skirt. Her skin was soft and creamy, and a diamond-encrusted necklace hung around her neck. She was an unforgettable beauty.

He found himself staring at her, and she caught his stare with her bold eyes. She had a graceful way about her; he knew she was a woman who had been around men and was comfortable in dealing with them. When the conductor approached, she gave him her ticket and instructions on how her luggage should be placed in the baggage car. Turning to wipe the moisture from her window, she looked only at her reflection, realizing the countryside was invisible from the car. The train steamed ahead as if it were sailing through an endless tunnel. The clanking of the rails was only background noise to him as his mind was again occupied by the plan for his disappearance.

In another time, at another place, he would have approached her. But now, it was impossible. As the train began its ascent up a steep incline, he mentally prepared for his exit at the scheduled stop eight hours from now, where he would disappear into the blackness of the night. He had actually ceased to exist a month ago, when he put his affairs in order and assumed the name of a long-deceased acquaintance. His only real friend and confidante, Robert Longbourne, had agreed to handle his affairs and make his wealth readily available when he needed it. They had established special codes for transfers of money and property. He had also deposited money in bank accounts under his new name which would be easily accessible to him, and had written checks to close all his present accounts. Then he shipped some personal belongings to different addresses where he expected to be.

Longbourne would not deceive him; others would. It was Longbourne who told him federal investigators and the police were coming to arrest him, and that overwhelming evidence of his guilt had been planted against him. In the midst of the frenzy to find the anarchists who murdered McKinley, he had no choice but to leave. For over a month, he had remained hidden in a remote cabin in the Catskill Mountains, waiting for the hysteria to pass so that he could clear his name. That hadn't happened, and he knew now that he had to do something.

His thoughts briefly drifted from Longbourne and returned to his current life and the people he would never miss. They used him for their purposes, and he in turn for his. He called them friends, but he never regarded them in that way. He had always avoided close relationships. In his early years, he learned that to trust people was to put his life at risk. He would never do that again.

Many thought they knew him well, but in truth they knew little about him. He had never been married; in fact, he had steadfastly avoided it. The few women he had become close to regarded him as distant – an uncaring, hard man. The heavy beard and the dark eyes, eyes that were always studying people and that missed little, didn't help that perception. The beard was now gone, but the eyes remained.

He watched the woman as she stood up and walked to the next car, a Pullman dining car. She was tall, slender, and very fashionable. Her hourglass shape came from a corseted small waist and a body that was padded in the hips, bosom and sleeves to exaggerate her curvaceous figure. His eyes softened as they followed her, but his expression hardened as one of the men in the back of the car, who had been feigning sleep, rose to follow her. As the man passed by him, he stood up, stretched, and also walked to the dining car.

She sat alone, staring at the small glowing lantern on the table, while the other man sat three tables away, staring at her. As he walked up to her, she lifted her eyes as if to ask, "What do you want?", but instead asked for the time. He pulled out a small, gold engraved pocket watch, pressed the stem and said, "Half past eight." She smiled and said, "It's very beautiful."

"A gift. Thank you." Easing himself into the chair across from her, he asked, "Do you mind?"

"I do mind. I'd rather be alone."

Ignoring her request, he hesitated for several seconds. "You look worried."

"You didn't hear me. Please leave."

He offered no response and remained seated, studying her alarmed expression. Looking away, she said under her breath, "I'm being followed." Turning back to him, her face was pale. "Are you one of them?"

He was startled. "Who?"

"The men hired by my husband to bring me back." She looked down, rubbing her hands together. Shaking her head, she whispered, "It won't work, not this time."

Staring into her blue eyes, he said, "I'm not one of them, and I hope it doesn't work."

"Then who are you?"

"Just someone heading west. And you?"

She studied him for a moment. Thick brown hair, about six feet tall, dark brown eyes, and a remarkably handsome face. Speaking in a very low voice, she said, "If you won't give me your name, how can I trust you?"

He smiled. "It's not a secret; I don't have occasion to say it much. It's William Lawrence." He noticed no wedding ring.

She placed both hands on the table, thinking his answer was very strange. "Do you want to tell me why?"

"Not particularly."

She pulled her hands back. "Are you wanted for something?"

"What?"

"Mr. Lawrence, what's wrong?"

He ignored her question. "Where are you going?"

"As far as this train will take me."

"Chicago? This train ends there." He then turned and signaled the waiter. When he approached the table, Lawrence asked her, "Would you like something to drink?"

She nervously answered, "Champagne, please."

Turning to the waiter, he said, "And I'll have scotch on the rocks." Looking back at her, he studied her as she attempted to smooth non-existent wrinkles from the table cloth. "Are you in some kind of trouble?"

She averted her eyes and stared out the window. "My husband."

"Your husband? I don't see a wedding ring?"

"I removed it. Do you see that man at the table in front of you?"

Narrowing his eyes in the low light, he saw a man hunched over three tables away.

"He's one of them."

Eyeing her suspiciously, he sat back and thought to himself that he had to get up and leave, now. But he didn't.

She mumbled under her breath. "He swore I'd never get away. They'll never bring me back – he'll have to kill me first."

Accepting his drink from the waiter, he took a long, slow sip. "For a woman being hunted, you don't seem very frightened."

She shook her head. "I've been terrified every day of my life since I realized what a beast he is. Those men – he sent them. But they won't stop me."

"A beast? Who in the hell is your husband?"

"My husband is Clayton Harding."

"The Clayton H. Harding from Philadelphia?"

"I'm afraid so."

"And you're Alyssa Harding. You know he's insane! He'll never let you go, and he will kill you. Why in the hell would you marry him?"

Taking a deep breath, she sipped her champagne and noticed they were climbing steadily through the mountains. Soon, the train would begin its long, steep grade as they sped toward Chicago. Seeing his reflection in the window, she said without turning to look at him, "My name is now Alyssa Coolidge – my maiden name. You asked why I married him. I had no choice; my mother forced me into it. She took away my happiness in her lust for money. I married him because of her, because without him we would have been struggling in the streets of New York. She was horrified at that prospect, and frankly, so was I. It's done, and now she's dead. I suppose I had warnings enough, but I was young and had no idea how violent he could be. If I hadn't decided to leave him several weeks ago, I'd be dead."

"Those three men, how do you possibly expect to escape them?"

"I've planned for that. In Chicago, I have a friend who'll help. I won't be there very long. When I leave, I'll go far away; he'll never find me after that."

Silence engulfed him for several moments. He had faced odds like that before, but he had been willing to strike back, even to kill when it was necessary. He felt that familiar anger and torment rising in him again. Men were dead who misunderstood his civility, his sense of fairness, and his reserved demeanor as a sign of weakness. She wasn't like him. He would not hesitate to resort to violence – she would. It was his way of life, but not hers. He was cold and calculating; the world had given him no chance to be otherwise. She was soft and demure.

Taking another long sip of his scotch, he felt the burning sensation drift down his throat and into his chest. Looking at her as one would look at a lamb headed for slaughter, he said bluntly with little feeling, "You don't stand a chance. If they felt you could escape in Chicago, they would have taken you by now. There's no one here to help you. The police won't stop Clayton Harding and his $60 million from getting his wife back. Do you have any money?"

With a shaky voice, she answered, "I have jewelry. And there is my friend." She noticed the doubt in his eyes. Challenging him, she said softly, "About there being no one on this train to help me, there is you."

"No, there's not. I have my own problems. When I get off this train, I intend to disappear."

She gazed at his well-tailored suit and elegant appearance. "You? You don't look like a man who would want to disappear."

His expression hardened. "There are men looking for me. I need some time."

She gasped, her hand instinctively covering her mouth. "Who are they?"

"You don't need to know that. I've done nothing wrong." Stopping to take another drink, he said, "You don't have to be afraid of me. Just keep this between us."

She relaxed a little. "I have no intention of saying anything to anyone." She paused, lifting her eyebrows. "Where will you go?"

"Like you, far away."

He stood up and motioned for the check. Turning back, he said, "Forget we ever met. I hope your friend in Chicago can help you." Giving the waiter three dollars, he began walking back to his seat as the train slowed to a stop at a small town in Illinois. She stood up, watching him leave and thinking he was the strangest man she had ever met. Reaching down to pick up her purse, she felt a gun pressed into her back and a rough hand cover her mouth to stifle her scream. Terrified, she was dragged to the door as the train slowed to a stop.

Hearing the commotion, Lawrence turned to see her struggle. The left hand of her assailant held a small pistol. Glancing out the window, he saw that the other two men had left the train and were waiting at the steps.

Silently cursing himself, he rushed to the end of the car and slammed his fist into the head of the attacker. With his other hand, he wrenched the pistol out of the man's hand. In a state of shock, Alyssa turned to see him just as her assailant fell to his knees. Lawrence jerked Alyssa behind him and kicked the man violently in the face, breaking his nose and causing a spurt of blood. He then grabbed the assailant and shoved him down the metal stairs onto the concrete platform. With little time to react, the other men could only watch as the train began to move, pick up speed and disappear into the night.

Wide-eyed, she whispered, "Thank you."

Holding her hand, he pulled her back down the aisle to a table. "We're getting off at the next stop."

In a daze, she mumbled, "I have to go to Chicago."

"You can't stay on this train. They'll be waiting for you. I'll get you there some other way."

CHAPTER FOUR

———————————▼———————————

Columbus, Ohio

The Chittenden Hotel had just been rebuilt from the ruins of the hotel that had burned down in the great fire of 1893. The smell of the new carpeting and paint permeated the building. They checked in at two in the morning and were given rooms on separate floors. Exhausted, Alyssa lay awake in the darkness long after she had said good night to William. It had been one of the most terrifying days of her life. While Clayton was away, she thought she could escape. She had slipped away from *that* house, believing the bribed guard would allow her to disappear from the horror that had dominated her life. But Clayton had somehow known, and she had been followed. What would have happened if that stranger . . . ?

He wasn't a stranger, not now. He had very dark eyes, fine eyes, set well apart, and a striking face, not a face you'd forget. What had he done? What was he running from? She knew she couldn't stay with him. Men were looking for him, he had said. When he was found, they would find her, and Clayton would put her through hell. She would leave, early in the morning, without him. With plenty of money, she would find her friend. She would hide in Chicago until the arrangements were made, and then she would disappear forever.

At 6:00 AM she was awakened with a knock on the door. Room service brought her breakfast of oatmeal and juice, and with it the *Columbus Gazette*. Sitting down to the small table, she suddenly stopped breathing. The headline was bold: *Nationwide Manhunt Continues for McKinley's Killers*. Underneath it was a name, Matthew Stanton, and a sketch of a heavily bearded man and a description – about six feet tall, dark brown eyes, and thick brown hair. He was the owner of Far East Shipping, the largest carrier of trade from America to the Philippines, Japan and China. The article said that while he was a wealthy industrialist, he was also a loner, a radical, and a supporter of the anarchist movement. The police were certain that he had planned and financed the murder of the President. Not only had damning correspondence been found, but a search of Czolgosz's hotel room disclosed five thousand dollars in large bills, hidden under the bed. On the day of the assassination, records showed that five thousand dollars had been withdrawn in cash from Stanton's bank account.

She stared at the picture, gripped with fear. Those eyes and that hair! She knew – Lawrence was Stanton. Panic set in. She nervously got dressed, quickly packed her suitcase, and grabbed her purse. Before she could touch the door knob, there was another knock. *Please be room service*, she prayed to herself. Opening the door, she saw it was him.

Smiling, he asked, "Did you sleep well?"

Unable to speak, she nodded. Then, with a shaky voice, "I must leave, now."

As she was trying to edge past him in the doorway, he saw the newspaper on the table. "What's wrong?"

"Please let me go." When he blocked her way, she blurted out, "You're Matthew Stanton, aren't you? And you had the President killed!"

"No, I didn't do that. I'm innocent!"

Speaking with a trembling voice, she said, "You didn't deny it – you are Matthew Stanton! The paper says you arranged for the killing of the President. That you're an anarchist. Read it – it's all there. They're looking for you everywhere." Stopping to catch her breath, she pushed him away with her hands. "Why would you do that? What is the matter with you?"

He tried to place a hand on her shoulder, and she again pushed him away. "You're not listening to me - I didn't do anything, and I'm not an anarchist. It's all lies." She backed away, and he knew she didn't believe him. In desperation, he asked, "What will you do? Will you tell them?"

"I don't know," she whispered.

"Please, give me a little time. Just a couple of days."

She squeezed by him and rushed down the hall. His mind was frozen. He watched her leave, unable to react. Suddenly, without conscious thought, he ran after her. He found her in the lobby, waiting for a carriage, and was met by her horrified gasp when he appeared. "Alyssa, please wait, just for a moment." She silently stared at him, and his first thought was that she would yell for the police. The doorman, sensing she was in trouble, stopped him with his hand and turned to her. "Are you all right, miss?"

Lawrence pushed the hand away. "She's all right. One minute, please." Moving past the doorman, he walked over to her. "Alyssa, I'm not going to stop you, but if you leave, we'll never see each other again. Dammit, I told you I've done nothing wrong. Where will you be?"

Holding her hand up to stop him, she screamed, "No. Stay away from me!"

Retreating, he backed into the wall. "Don't believe what you read. I'll find you someday, but you need to know I'll be looking for you."

The doorman stepped in between them. "Sir, the lady has asked that you leave her alone. If you don't, I'll call the police." Turning to her, he said her carriage had arrived. He picked up her luggage, and she followed him. Lawrence stepped outside and watched her go, in silence. Turning back, she said, "Don't ever try to find me!" She avoided his stare and entered the carriage. As it drove off, he stood in the bitter cold for several minutes, asking himself, "Why now?" And then his thoughts turned to the scene they had made and the several people who were now staring at him.

Alyssa rode in stunned silence along the bumpy roads of Columbus leading to the train station. The carriage was enclosed and well sealed, but in the intense cold it offered little warmth. Shivering, she pulled her fur collar tightly around her face, terrified at the thought that she had just encountered the man accused of murdering McKinley. She wanted to tell the police, but that was impossible. Clayton would know. The Pinkerton Detective Agency was on his payroll; her picture would be widely circulated. But she was the only one, *anywhere*, who could identify Lawrence as Stanton. Then suddenly another thought entered her mind – what if he were innocent? Three of the last five presidents had been assassinated. People were hysterical. But why was he running? Her mind was twisting so rapidly she felt as if she were going mad. Closing her eyes to calm the voices in her head, his face appeared. She had known him for less than twenty-four hours, but it seemed like a lifetime. He had saved her on the train. What if she had been wrong? What if he were the one she had been searching for her entire life?

*   *   *   *

It was dark and cool inside the church. He was surrounded by statues of the Virgin Mary, with the Christ child in her arms, and saints. The images were painted and gilded with crowns and paste jewels that glimmered in the dim light, and there was a pervading smell of mildew and incense. Empty at ten in the morning, it was the last place anyone would look for him.

An aging priest sat in the confessional, watching him with suspicion. The priest had a large bald patch on the top of his head, surrounded by wisps of white hair, and wore wire-rim glasses that clung to the end of his nose. He saw that the man didn't kneel, but instead sat low in a back pew staring at the door. He was well dressed but looked as if he had slept in his clothes. He wasn't there to pray. Something was very wrong. Pulling the curtain slowly back, the priest stepped out of the booth and walked over to him. Unaware of the priest's presence, he looked up with a startled expression.

The priest spoke in a low voice. "Why are you here? This church is a place of thanksgiving, peace and prayer. You're not a member. There's nothing for you here."

"Father, I'm a Roman Catholic. Please don't turn me away."

The priest sat next to him and shook his head. "I know when a man's in trouble. You're not listening to me. This church will not protect you. I don't know what you've done, but you can't stay here. Our president has been shot. Everyone in our community has been warned by the police of strangers. This is not a shelter."

Lawrence stood up. "Father, will you take thirty minutes and listen to me? It could change your life – and mine. Refuse me, and there will be a price to pay, I assure you."

The priest stepped back, alarmed. "I'll call the police if you don't leave."

Lawrence regretted his last remark. "Five thousand dollars, a gift to your church, if you'll help me. I promise you, in the name of Christ Jesus, that it's legal and you'll have nothing to fear."

Inhaling deeply, the priest looked around. The church was empty. Five thousand dollars! The cost of the new school. "Thirty minutes, in my office, and then you leave. Is that agreed?"

"You have my word, Father."

"And you can pay me the money then?"

"Yes, I can do that."

Nodding, the priest pointed to the left. "My office is in the building next door."

Kneeling to pray, Lawrence said, "Father, you go ahead. Give me a moment longer here." After the priest had gone, Lawrence stood and walked hurriedly to the door of the sacristy, knocked softly, and, after finding it empty, entered. Moments later, dressed in the white collar and black suit of a priest, he walked out of the church to a waiting carriage. The old priest sat alone in his office, wondering what had happened to the stranger – and the five thousand dollars for his new school.

CHAPTER FIVE

—————————▼—————————

Chicago, Illinois

Why would he want to do it? What would possess a wealthy industrialist to plot to kill the President? Henry McDermott, a graying, craggy-faced, overweight lieutenant in the Chicago Police Department, pondered that question as he studied the letters found in Emma Goldman's flat. Across the table, his wiry partner Danny Stroud shook his head. "Why the hell do you think people do things? They're nuts. Two more presidents murdered since Lincoln. You tell me what this world's coming to?"

McDermott opened another file. "Did you read this?"

Stroud hesitated while he took a puff on his cigar, blowing a cloud of smoke in McDermott's direction. "What are you looking at?"

McDermott rubbed his eyes. It was ten o'clock in the evening. "He was an abandoned orphan. How in the hell does a man like that get to be a wealthy tycoon? It doesn't make sense."

Stroud pushed back his black wire-rimmed glasses, his attention focused on McDermott.

"I'm reading the federal investigators' report. They talked to people who knew him and got a lot of mixed stories. But two and two makes four. This report says he was abandoned when he was ten years old – both parents killed. Then this guy they called Berg picks him out of the gutter, raises him and sets up a trust for an education at Harvard?"

"What the hell? Harvard? Who is Berg?"

McDermott flipped through some pages. "Says here he *was* a union organizer. Went up against some of the big boys, including Carnegie. So one night they grab him, beat his brains out with lead pipes, and then shoot him like a rag doll." Turning the page, McDermott's eyes went wide. "You ain't gonna believe this. The kid was there and saw it all."

"Why didn't they kill him?"

"I'm sure they wished they had. I don't think they ever saw him. While these goons are looking at what used to be Berg, this kid draws a gun, calm as hell, and shoots all five of them."

"Guns aren't that accurate. No way he shoots all five."

"It doesn't say how good he was then, but this report says he was a master marksman. He was a hunter, Africa and places like that, and he didn't miss."

"How much time did he serve?"

McDermott smiled. "Not one damn day. They let him off. Said it was justifiable homicide."

"That kid had balls."

"Yeah, and he evidently still does. He graduated from Harvard at the top of his class, and ten years later owned a shipping company."

Stroud stood up, leaned across the table, and twirled the file 180 degrees. "How in the hell does that happen?"

"Hey," McDermott said with his arms raised, "this is America."

Stroud looked at him in disgust. "I'm an American, but I don't own a goddamn shipping company."

McDermott laughed. "And you didn't graduate from Harvard either. Some people are just lucky as hell." He sat back and read the account again. It was all beginning to make sense. A self-made millionaire, but a loner, who has a hatred for the rich. Narrowing his eyes, he looked up at Stroud. "It's late. Let's go home. I want the Commissioner to know about this. Tomorrow we talk to him and then we go after that son-of-a-bitch."

Stroud stood up, stretched, and grabbed his coat. "Yeah. There's always tomorrow. McKinley died over a month ago. Stanton disappeared into thin air a week later. And nobody knows a damn thing. Maybe he's dead."

McDermott joined him at the door. "He's not dead. Use your brain. Follow the money. He can't live on nothing. Someone's helping him. Let's find that someone. I've sent a telegram to the feds. We'll have some names very soon, you can count on that."

*   *   *   *

A thousand trains a day came and left Chicago. Those trains brought huge numbers of people who had never seen a great city before. They were strangers, young people looking for jobs, tourists, and many others stopping in America's second busiest station on their way to somewhere else. Matthew Stanton, dressed as a priest, stepped off the Illinois Central the next morning, carrying a large suitcase. He would not have attracted attention in normal times, but today was different. The Chicago police had stationed thirty officers to watch for him.

It took time, but pictures had been drawn and circulated of what he looked like with a beard, and what he might look like without one. There were rumors that he had been in Columbus, Ohio, and had left from there on a train to Chicago. He was affluent, and that gave the officers a different perspective of the man they were hunting. Matthew Stanton would have an expensive leather suitcase, would be well-dressed, and would be tall.

Before walking thirty feet after leaving the train, he was stopped by two officers. Pulling him aside, one of the officers asked for identification. Startled by the request, he asked, "Why?"

Studying him carefully, the younger officer said, "Father, we're looking for a man about your height and build." Looking down at his expensive shoes and case, and then at his ill-fitting suit, the officer commented, "You seem to be very prosperous for a man of the cloth."

Lawrence smiled. "Oh yes, that. A gift of my parents. You see, my father is Harold Lawrence, the owner of the Olympic."

Both officers were confused. One said, "The Olympic?"

"The hotel in San Francisco. He insists that I enjoy a few of the fine things of life. Even though I entered the priesthood, I can't turn my back on a wealthy father." He reached into his wallet and removed a card and handed it to the officer. "I'm afraid that's the best I can do."

With questioning eyes, the officer asked, "With all that money, he couldn't buy you a suit that fit?"

Lawrence shrugged and smiled weakly. "An awful tailor."

Looking suspiciously at the card, the officer read, "Father William Lawrence, Church of Our Savior, San Francisco, California." Turning, he handed it to the other officer, whispering something Lawrence couldn't understand. Turning back, he asked, "And where might you be going, Father?"

"Home, of course."

"And that would be . . . ."

"San Francisco."

"Yes, of course. Do you have a ticket?"

"Not yet, but if you'll step out of my way, I'll have one soon."

"Wait one minute." They stepped back and spoke quietly to each other while Lawrence took a deep breath and said a silent prayer. "Father, we're only doing our job, but we have to look into your suitcase."

Lawrence's expression turned to anger. "This is an insult to the Church and to me. You would have me open my suitcase here, on this concrete walkway? Do you have a search warrant?"

The older officer hesitated and held up his hand to the younger one. "It's all right, Father. You can go. Have a safe trip."

As he walked away, Lawrence looked back to see the older officer staring at him while the younger one was writing on a pad. At the ticket window, he purchased a seat in a private compartment on the Union Pacific to San Francisco, and then entered a nearby coffee shop where he sat and watched the ticket agent. Within minutes, the officers appeared and talked to the agent. After they left, Lawrence walked casually to another agent and purchased a seat on a train bound for Washington, D.C.

CHAPTER SIX

───────▼───────

New York City

They had been waiting for over thirty minutes. The four New York and Chicago detectives had been joined by the federal investigator, Charlie Wilcox. Wilcox was a heavy-set, partially bald man of average height. He had just celebrated his forty-second birthday. A carefully manicured, heavy black mustache softened his elongated face, sharp nose and dark gray eyes. He had been a cop for over ten years and then joined the federal investigative force. He could pass as a salesman, but looks were deceiving. There was nothing ordinary about him. His abilities as a detective were legendary. He was relentless in everything he did; a perfectionist that drove his co-workers crazy. Many truly believed he never slept.

Wilcox's darting, piercing eyes missed very little. Theodore Roosevelt had heard of him and had insisted that he lead the police investigation to find McKinley's killers. Wilcox also fulfilled a vital function for the President – he was his liaison with police departments and other federal agencies involved in the search for the killers. They had the shooter, but the investigators knew there were other anarchists involved. All the evidence pointed to a conspiracy. Wilcox had gone so far as to investigate the members of McKinley's cabinet, a move that had made some members furious and others very nervous. Those investigated by him often formed an early revulsion to his rude personality and tactics, and that pleased him. He was not in the business of making friends.

Rubbing his forehead, Wilcox looked at the closed door and mumbled, "This is bullshit. Two more minutes and I break the damn door down."

The four detectives seated looked at him in amazement and then at each other as if to ask, "Who in the hell is this guy?" But they remained silent.

The offices of Far East Shipping on West 57th were not what they had expected. Sparse in appearance and decorated with little money or thought, they looked more like the offices of a cheap wholesaler than a major shipping company. A lone secretary sat twenty feet from them, sifting through piles of correspondence. On several occasions she raised her pale face, devoid of makeup, and looked with empty eyes at the waiting officers. Her graying hair was wrapped tightly in a bun, and she wore a washed-out maroon cotton dress with shoulder pads and no jewelry. She knew why they were there and inwardly delighted at the agitation they expressed at their long wait.

The door behind her eventually opened to expose a short man in his late sixties, whose gray hair was parted neatly in the center and mouth was tight with tension. Behind his silver framed glasses, his dark brown eyes flashed with anger. With a total lack of apology, he said to the waiting officers, "You want to see me?" In unison they stood and waited for Wilcox to speak. Nodding, he replied, "In your office."

Robert Longbourne turned and led them into a small office that was in total disarray; papers and files were strewn in every corner. He walked behind an old oak writing table and sat in a tall swivel leather chair. Only two chairs were available on the opposite side. "Sorry, but three of you will have to stand." Wilcox and McDermott took the two chairs. Allowing his eyes to roam the room, stopping to look with quiet amusement at the standing officers, Longbourne said with a sweep of his hand, "Gentlemen, as you can see, I'm a very busy man. I'll give you five minutes."

Wilcox took a deep breath and glared at him. "Like hell you will. If you'd rather talk at police headquarters, Mr. Longbourne, that's fine with us. But we're not leaving until you've told us what we came here for."

"And that is . . . ."

"Where's your boss, Matthew Stanton?"

"I have no earthly idea. You must know – Mr. Stanton is a very secretive person. Even I don't have access to his whereabouts."

"You know this man planned the murder of McKinley. If you fail to cooperate in any way, I swear to God you'll spend your life in prison as an accomplice to murder."

Longbourne was unmoved. Turning in his chair to glance out the window at the cold, overcast day, he said, "He's guilty of nothing!" Turning back around, he pointed at Wilcox. "You have nothing except manufactured evidence that isn't worth shit. I've known Mr. Stanton for over ten years. He doesn't give a damn about politics and wouldn't know an anarchist if he saw one. For that matter, neither would any of you."

McDermott butted in, shaking his index finger. "Have you seen those damn letters he wrote? He's guilty as hell, and you, Mr. Longbourne, are in the wrong place at the wrong time. You'd better be careful. You're skating on very thin ice."

Longbourne slammed his fist on the desk. "Are you threatening me? Are you that damn stupid? You're being manipulated; someone is playing games with you. Are you so dumb you can't see that?"

Wilcox could barely hold his temper. Glaring at McDermott, he motioned him with his hand to step back and be quiet. He then took a deep breath and looked calmly at Longbourne. "If you're so sure he's innocent, have your boss turn himself in. We'll listen to him."

"And then hang him? You want a scapegoat. Not in your dreams will that happen." Standing, he said, "Now if you'll excuse me, I've got better things to do."

Wilcox was furious. "Get your affairs in order. You're looking at jail time, Mr. Longbourne."

"I'll tell my attorneys you said that. Now get your ass out of here." When they had left, Longbourne pulled a white handkerchief from his pocket and wiped the sweat from his brow. Staring out the window, he leaned back and called for his secretary.

*   *   *   *

At Chicago police headquarters two hours later, Commissioner Jay Neeley sat alone in his closed office, his chair back with his feet on the desk. On his lap was a report he had just received from the Secret Service. After six weeks, the bullet that the doctors had failed to remove from McKinley had finally been examined. No one had thought to do it before. He stared at the findings with a cigarette dangling from his mouth, his eyes wide in disbelief. The bullet was from a .38 caliber gun. He removed the cigarette, stubbed it out and closed his eyes, thinking back to the two shots fired by Czolgosz into McKinley. They had been from a .32 caliber revolver. It didn't make sense – two shots by one man but two different bullets. He pulled his feet off the desk and stood up. They weren't from the same gun. The first bullet had been recovered immediately after the shooting, and it was a .32 caliber. Maybe Czolgosz fired only one shot into the McKinley. But witnesses said there were two shots fired by Czolgosz. The thought suddenly crossed his mind - *Could there have been another shooter?*

"Miss Evans," he shouted. "Get McDermott in here."

Sitting on the edge of his desk, Neeley twisted the ends of his handle-bar mustache while he waited. Where in the hell was McDermott? Neeley had been commissioner under two mayors, and before then had served as police chief for eight years. He had grown up as a boxer and became a policeman out of financial necessity. He was tough and tough minded, and was never known for his patience. It was his wife, Dorothy, who brought out his soft side. She never ceased to remind him of what a pushover he was with his boys. His days were filled with gangsters, murderers and prostitutes, but his nights and weekends were for his kids. Three boys, all boxers and all tough, and he loved them. "Miss Evans," he shouted again, "get McDermott in here."

A crack in the door appeared, and she reported that McDermott had not returned. "Do you want someone else?" she asked.

"Yeah, get someone up here from ballistics."

Within minutes, Walter Hines stood at the doorway. Neeley motioned him in and Hines was greeted with one word, "Sit." Neeley then tossed the report across his desk. "What do you make of this?"

Hines opened the file and let out a deep breath. "Where did this come from?"

"Washington, but that's unimportant. See what it says about the bullet taken out of McKinley – a .38 caliber."

"So?"

"So, our shooter had a .32 caliber revolver. How does this happen?"

Hines rubbed his chin. "They must have made a mistake. That's impossible, unless . . . ."

"Unless what?"

"Unless Czolgosz had another gun."

"Not a chance. The pistol was wrapped in a bandage around his hand. No way he had two guns. And there was no mistake."

"Something's not right here. Could someone have switched the bullets?"

Neeley smiled. "You're right that something's wrong, but why in the hell would anyone switch the bullets? This came from the Secret Service." Pausing, Neeley lit a cigarette and blew a ring of smoke. The door opened and McDermott walked in. Narrowing his eyes, Neeley asked, "What's the news?"

McDermott plopped down in a second chair and loosened his tie. "This guy Longbourne's a son-of-a-bitch. All he said was that Stanton was framed and we're a bunch of . . . idiots."

"Are we?"

"Hell no! You saw the letters."

"Yeah, I saw them. Do me a favor. Describe the room where McKinley was shot."

McDermott rubbed his forehead, silently trying to get his thoughts together. "It was just a room, a big room."

"Come on, McDermott, you stood in it. Give me something better than that."

"Like what?"

"How long have you been a detective?"

"Ten years. What's that got to do with anything?"

Neeley shook his head and shifted on the edge of his desk. "Ten years and just a room? Detective, was there a balcony?"

McDermott looked embarrassed. "Now that you mention it, there was."

"And who was standing there when the shots were fired?"

Hines looked at Neeley as if to ask, "Where's all this going?"

Ignoring him, Neeley said, "Answer the question."

"In all due respect, sir, how the hell should I know? I wasn't there when it happened."

"So you didn't talk to witnesses?"

"You know I did."

Neeley was becoming irritated, his eyes bearing down on McDermott. "Are you telling me that you didn't ask anyone about the balcony?"

Defensively, McDermott said, "No one did. It wasn't important. Czolgosz shot McKinley on the main floor."

Neeley put out his cigarette and lit another. "So you're saying, detective, that you know exactly what happened at that moment."

"Yes, sir, there's no question about that."

Turning to Hines, Neeley said, "Give him the report."

McDermott took it and skimmed through the two pages. His look of confusion said it all. "Damn it," Neeley exploded, "look at what it says about the bullet removed from McKinley. It was a .38 caliber. The shooter's gun was a .32. Doesn't that want to make you think about the balcony?" He took a long drag on his cigarette, waiting for an answer.

McDermott's eyes widened. "You're not saying you think there was someone else?"

"Think of it this way," Neeley said. "If there was a second shooter, where would he be? Not in the line to see McKinley – the guards subdued everyone near him when he was shot. McKinley was surrounded by his people. There were hundreds of people on the ground floor. No one could get off another shot in that crowd. It had to be from above, *if* there was someone else. Here's what I want you to do. Get a search warrant and go over every inch of Stanton's offices and home. Find me a pistol that matches that .38 slug. Can you do that?"

McDermott was on his feet. "Yes, sir, we'll find that gun."

Neeley stopped him. "*If* he did it and was dumb enough to keep the gun."

A look a surprise crept into McDermott's eyes. "What do you mean *if*? You know he did it. Read the letters."

"McDermott, I'm too old for this. Does it make sense to you that a man who graduates at the top of his Harvard class writes damning letters to the country's top anarchist telling her he's planning to assassinate the President? And then she stores the letters in a box in her closet? Emma Goldman denies she ever saw them - or that she ever knew him. No one's ever seen them together."

"And you believe *her*? We've checked the letters. It's his handwriting. And he paid Czolgosz the five thousand dollars."

Neeley smiled slightly and shook his head. "His handwriting or the world's best forger? And you don't know that he paid Czolgosz – that's nothing but circumstantial evidence." McDermott was dumbstruck at that comment. Neeley heard him mumble to himself, "Stanton's dirty; no way he didn't do it."

Walking McDermott and Hines to the door, Neeley opened it and turned back to McDermott. "You're so damned certain Goldman's lying and Stanton wrote the letters, prove it to me. Find that gun."

Neeley turned to go back into his office and then spun around. Speaking in a loud voice to McDermott, who had made it half-way down the hall, he said, "And, McDermott, while you're at it, find out who might want to frame Matthew Stanton. He might be our second shooter."

CHAPTER SEVEN

▼

Chicago, Illinois

On the day Clayton Harding had planned to kill her, Alyssa Coolidge stepped down from a Chicago trolley and into a waiting carriage. Chester Willingham was waiting inside. Grabbing his left hand with both of hers, she whispered, "Thank you, thank you, thank you." He smiled back through his heavy white beard in appreciation. Dressed elegantly in a dark navy, high-button suit, with a vest and crimson silk tie, he exemplified the high fashion of the Gilded Age.

"You made it. I wasn't sure you would," he said in a deep, resonant voice. "We have some celebrating to do."

The carriage rocked gently in the blustery wind that swept Michigan Avenue as they headed for his home. She looked at him with soft blue eyes. "I was terrified," she admitted. "I believed he would try to kill me. Do you have any idea of what he put me through?"

"Calm down, Alyssa. You're safe. With what I've read about him, I can only imagine the horror you've lived through. Did my man take good care of you?"

Stopping to catch her breath, she nodded. "When he stepped aboard the train and flashed his badge, I knew I was saved. How did he manage to impersonate a federal marshal?"

Willingham laughed. "He didn't impersonate anyone. He was a federal marshal."

She didn't hear him. Her mind was numb. She mumbled, "I tried once before to escape. I actually got as far as the train station. It was one of those times when he wasn't watching me closely. I remember thinking, *I have no plan.* He was miles away. I thought it would work, but it was crazy. It wasn't logical. I was alone and helpless. His men showed up at the station, and I was lost. It was one of the most terrifying moments of my life." Staring into his eyes, she breathed, "I've dreamed of this moment for years. I never thought I could get away. But you made it happen – and you've taken such a risk. He has people everywhere. Chester, I can't stay here long. He knows you, and you won't be safe."

"He only knows I was your agent before you got married. I was then in New York. How can he know where I am now? Dreams can only become nightmares if you let them. Alyssa, you're not thinking clearly. You need rest. Stay with me for awhile; then we'll decide where you should go."

She laid her head back with her eyes closed, and suddenly felt a shiver run through her body. She felt relieved, but could he find her? She knew the answer, and it terrified her. Willingham sensed what she was thinking and placed a gentle hand on hers. The remainder of their journey was in silence.

Traveling along the opulent Prairie Avenue streetscape was reminiscent to Alyssa of the wealthy European city streets she had visited on her honeymoon with Clayton. Many of the grand homes were ostentatious in their appearance and size and were owned by the urban elite of Chicago, men like George Pullman and Marshal Field. The spectacle of them brought back terrifying memories of the house in Philadelphia where she had been confined for five long years. As the carriage pulled to a stop, she looked out to see a three-story Georgian residence with a soft pink brick veneer. It was not a house to be feared.

Chester Willingham's wife had died years before, and he lived alone except for a housekeeper. She met them at the door and ushered Alyssa into a large drawing room decorated with draperies and carpets of deep reds and blues. The fashionable Victorian furniture was draped in satin and velour fabrics, with gold fringe hanging from all lampshades and draperies. While beautiful, she felt the room was dark and mirrored her feeling of being suffocated. "Do you like it?"

She snapped out of her spell to see Willingham standing against a tall row of bookcases. "Yes, yes of course I do. Do you mind if I go to my bedroom to freshen-up a little and rest?"

He studied her with a worried look on his face. "Are you all right?"

Leaning back against the wall, she closed her eyes. "I don't know. Give me a little time."

"My housekeeper has taken your bag to the second floor. You'll be staying in the first bedroom on the left. Come down when you feel like it."

Her bedroom was no different than the drawing room: dark blues and reds, but it was quiet and secure. The sun had gone down, and a slight freezing drizzle was beginning to fall, bringing fog into the night air. She looked out the window to see the gas street lamps being lit, and then lay down on the bed without removing her clothes. Her thoughts floated and drifted as she tried to focus on pleasant memories. A face appeared that she couldn't seem to get out of her mind. William Lawrence, or was it Matthew Stanton? What was it about him that continually haunted her? It wasn't like Clayton – those thoughts petrified her. It was a sensation, something about his smile and the way he had treated her. She knew she was attracted to him, but she also knew she would never see him again. What he had done, or what they said he had done, was unspeakable. Yet she had now come to believe he was innocent. How she wished she had told him that in Columbus. He had begged her to believe him, but she couldn't – not then. She put her hands over her eyes, trying to forget him. It was impossible, and it was also too late.

She dozed for several minutes and then awoke with a start. Staring at the ceiling, she numbly tried to focus on where she was. She got up, walked over to the wash basin, and splashed cold water on her face. The mirror over the basin reflected sad eyes and a tired complexion. She stood there staring at herself. Behind her reflection was the streetlamp and the fog. Turning to change clothes and unpack, she froze. There was something else. With a slight tremor, she walked to the window. Below, silhouetted against the light, was the figure of a man. And he was looking directly at her. She gasped and then turned away, whispering, "Please no, God."

Her heart beating wildly, she rushed down the staircase into the arms of Willingham. "Alyssa, you're shaking. What is it?"

Stammering, she mumbled, "Oh my God, he found me."

"Clayton?"

"Yes. He has a man watching me under the lamp across the street."

Willingham looked at her with an expression asking for forgiveness. "I should have told you. I'm so terribly sorry. That's my man. He's a Pinkerton detective I hired to watch the house. Please forgive me for not telling you."

CHAPTER EIGHT

▼

Philadelphia, Pennsylvania

A furious anger engulfed him. He had to keep his hands out of sight because they shook with the force of it. She wasn't dead. She'd cheated him. The anger twisted his insides into knots. Ten thousand dollars was what he had paid – a small fortune to them. They had found her; the telegram had said they would kill her today. Then a later telegram said she had escaped. That would cost them. With deceit and cunning, she had left him. No one, ever, had left Clayton Harding, and no one would ever be allowed to enjoy her beauty as he had. She would be dead! He would find others who were more competent. The Pinkertons – they wouldn't kill her, but they would find her. They owed him. She was in Chicago with another man – he knew it. He would kill them both.

The two men sitting across from him were startled by his wild eyes and erratic behavior. He was crazy, but they would do what he asked. He paid them well. They had worked for men like Gould and Carnegie. Union busters and thugs, they had been called. They had no scruples, and crippling men to keep open the factories of the wealthy industrialists was what they did. Killing a woman was different. He hadn't asked them to do it, but they knew he would.

Violent and paranoid almost since birth (his mother had claimed his problems had started in the womb), Clayton had spent his childhood bouncing from private school to private school in Philadelphia, never doing well. He was described by his teachers as unintelligent and a troublemaker. But as the son of Edwin Harding, he was granted admission to the finest universities, four of them, where he put forth little effort. He was an embarrassment to his father, but his mother always stood by his side. Many thought she was also mad. He went on long drinking binges, and would be expelled by one university only to be accepted by another.

Until Alyssa, his life had been cockfights and romancing young women. But he was not entirely worthless; he had been credited with the invention of the speedball, an injected combination of morphine, heroin, and cocaine. After his many expulsions, he developed a hobby of "studying" chorus girls and models. That stopped when he first saw Alyssa Coolidge. She quickly became the target of his crazed obsession with women. He soon came calling, bearing gifts and money. His wooing was ceaseless, and her mother became his greatest worshipper. He was handsome and also charming, when he wanted to be. When her mother had been hospitalized for presumed heart problems, he visited her almost daily, making her believe he was one of her most ardent admirers.

Over the course of a year, Harding remained enraptured with Alyssa. He never allowed her to see his dark side, and eventually, with her mother's constant prodding, wore her down. Under duress, she married him at the age of twenty-four, only to find he never loved her and that she had become a captive to his insane jealousy. Now he had pronounced her death sentence.

Fidgeting with a gold pen on his desk, he stared at them with the frenzied eyes of a madman. "She's in Chicago. Find her and kill her." Throwing the pen across the room, making them both duck, he screamed, "And kill the man she's with."

The man named Turk removed a cigar from his mouth and looked at him with mild disgust. He slowly exhaled the smoke, pointing the burning tip of the cigar at him. "We hurt people; we don't murder them. This will cost you a bundle."

"I don't care what it costs. Tell me your price. I want them killed!"

The other man, a heavy set balding man in his thirties who was known as Monk, leaned his square face into Turk's and whispered, "What do we ask for?"

Holding up the cigar, he turned to Harding. "Twenty grand, take it or leave it. You want two killings, that's what it'll cost you."

Rage swept into Harding's eyes. His face became a bloated red. "Do it, do it, do it!" Pausing for a breath, he watched them stand to leave. "One more thing," he said in a slightly calmer voice, "If you don't kill them, I'll have you killed."

Leaving and closing the door to Harding's office, Monk turned to Turk and said, in earshot of Harding's secretary, "He's fuckin' crazy. We'd better talk this over."

Turk walked ahead of him and then turned and stopped. "Twenty grand! That's more than we'd make in ten years beating up those union guys, just for knocking off some dame and her boy friend."

"Don't fool yourself. With the unions, we had Carnegie and the cops looking out for us. With this nut, we're hanging by our balls. Is that what you want?"

Turk looked amused. "You're really worried about that lunatic?"

"Hell yes I'm worried."

CHAPTER NINE

▼

New York City

The search had been conducted by over twenty police officers and federal agents, and had taken four days. Stanton's offices revealed nothing, not even incriminating correspondence, but his home on 5ᵗʰ Avenue was different. In his large walnut-paneled study, they removed every book from his shelves. At the end of the fourth day, they found it. Looking behind a book titled *The Strenuous Life*, written by the new president, they found a Remington .38 caliber pistol. McDermott smirked with satisfaction. He had been redeemed, and now the doubts of Commissioner Neeley would be silenced. But first they had to determine that the bullet that killed McKinley had come from that gun. That wouldn't take long.

Two days later, in a large conference at police headquarters in Chicago, a meeting of ten men took place. With his arms folded, Jay Neely sat at the head of a long table. Sitting around him were members of his team and federal investigators who had just arrived from Washington. At the other end of the table was Charlie Wilcox, who sat chewing on an unlit cigar. McDermott was the first to speak, holding high for everyone to see the gun taken from Stanton's home. "The bullet matches it," he declared with a self-satisfying grin. "We have our second shooter."

Wilcox made some notes on a pad. Looking up, he asked, "Can we place Stanton in Buffalo on the day of the shooting?"

McDermott grunted. "The bastard's disappeared. When we find him, I'll guarantee he's too smart not to have an alibi."

Others around the table nodded their agreement. Wilcox flashed a smile at McDermott, saying, "Great work, Lieutenant."

McDermott then turned to confront Neeley. "Satisfied? I promised I'd find the gun. All we have to do now is find Stanton and get him in chains."

Neeley unfolded his arms, looking unimpressed. "So finding that gun in his house confirms his guilt?"

McDermott looked puzzled. "Are you questioning that? Hell yes, it does. Isn't that obvious?"

"What's obvious to me, McDermott, is that it's *too* obvious. Doesn't it strike you as a little odd that he shoots the President and then hides the gun in his study?"

There was a hushed silence around the table. Wilcox rose and then walked around the table to face Neeley. "You're thinking someone planted that gun?"

Neeley stood up. "That's exactly what I'm thinking."

"Maybe this guy's so smart," Wilcox retorted, "that he figured that's what we'd be thinking. Maybe *he* planted that gun for that very reason."

Neeley turned and walked over to the window. Stretching his neck from side to side, he spun back to face Wilcox. "You're a smart guy. It's too simple. I may be the only one in the room who thinks this, but I think finding that gun proves he's *not* guilty."

Wilcox shook his head slightly. "When we find him, and we will, we'll know, won't we? Innocent men don't run."

Neeley scanned the faces in the room and could sense his theory had little support. "Just don't shoot him on sight."

*   *   *   *

As the meeting was disbanding, Matthew Stanton departed the Illinois Central at the Union Station in Washington, D.C. Stepping onto the concourse with his luggage, he stopped to look for a porter. The biting cold wind whipped around his face as he pulled up his scarf for protection. He was well dressed and looked like many of the politicians flooding Washington at the time. A red-clad porter soon appeared and took his suitcase. A couple dozen people crisscrossed him, either hurrying to or from the train. A large number sat on wood benches or stood patiently waiting to meet departing passengers. There were several young men at the end of the concourse, smoking and shifting their heads from one direction to another. He felt quite certain who they were. They were neatly dressed in topcoats and hats, and wore highly polished shoes.

But it was not their appearance as much as their mannerisms that gave them away. They were alert, scanning the concourse with their eyes, studying the faces of people who passed by and looking everywhere . . . except at the information schedule board. They were not travelers. He was very tempted to speak to them – to test them to see if they could spot him. But his instincts warned him off.

Walking by them, he turned his head toward the porter as if to say something. The men remained where they were, but he knew there would be others inside the terminal. The magnificent interior was bustling with people, but he felt conspicuous. He immediately spotted other men in small groups, well dressed in dark overcoats and speaking quietly with each other, and a number of uniformed policemen, all studying the crowds. But as he walked past, he caught no one's attention. Exiting at the north end, the porter lifted his bag into a waiting carriage and gratefully received his tip. Stanton, surrounded with bustling activity, felt very isolated. He quickly stepped into the carriage, saying, "The Capitol Hotel, please." Resting his head against the red velour seat, he once again replayed in his mind the scenario that he had so carefully planned out. The sound of the two horses, pounding their hoofs along the cobble-stone street in rhythm with the iron wheels jarring the carriage as it passed over each brick, caused him to momentarily shift his thoughts to the shackles that would bind him if he were caught. He shuddered slightly.

He walked into the hotel at five in the afternoon and signed in as Mr. Harold Green. The desk clerk handed him a small package. Inside was four thousand dollars in small and medium size notes, enough to satisfy his current needs. He was so exhausted that he barely noticed the grand lobby, paneled with inlaid oak and furnished with new American furniture and rugs. It was probably as close as anyone could get to staying in the White House. He took the elevator to the fourth floor, and the bellman opened the door to his room, displaying a distant view of the White House. At any other time, he might have been a little in awe at the magnificent sight, but he fell onto the bed and was asleep in minutes.

Several hours later he was awakened by several hard knocks on the door. Laying in a daze, he took a full minute to rise and open it. He wished he hadn't. Standing there was a police officer. "I'm sorry to disturb you, sir, but we're checking newly arrived guests at the hotel. Could you please furnish me with some identification?"

Stanton rubbed his eyes, trying to mask his fear. "Who are you looking for?"

The officer studied him carefully, as if he had seen him before. "In these times, we're making routine checks at all hotels. I think you can understand with the murder of our president. Can you tell me why you're here in Washington?"

"Of course. I'm here to meet with our new president, Mr. Roosevelt." The officer stepped back, wide-eyed. "Could you tell me the nature of your business with him?"

"Officer, I run a construction company. The President has talked about building a canal, in Panama, and asked that I meet with him."

"Oh, yes, I've read something about that."

Pulling out a business card and handing it to the policeman, Stanton said, "If you would like to check this with President Roosevelt, please do."

Glancing down at the card, the officer noted, "Harold Green, President, Mid-West Construction, Co., 100 Olive St., St. Louis, Mo."

Returning the card, the officer nodded. "That won't be necessary, Mr. Green. Enjoy your stay."

Closing the door, he let out a deep sigh of relief. Had he been recognized? At first it seemed he had; now he didn't know. He had naively thought he could disappear in Washington; that they wouldn't be looking for McKinley's killers here. He was wrong. He wondered how difficult it would be for the police to check his story. A day was probably all he had if they did, unless the police were successful with a quick phone call. He hurriedly shaved and put on a dark blue pin-striped suit with a white high-collar shirt and silver tie. Combing his thick brown hair, he examined himself in the mirror and then left the room and went down to the lobby. Standing in front of the desk clerk, he said, "Excuse me, is there any message for room 410?"

The clerk checked his box and then turned to say, "Nothing."

Stanton thanked him and added in a low voice, "A police officer came by to see me. He must be knocking on a lot of doors."

The clerk examined him with suspicious eyes. "Not many. He seemed particularly interested in you. Came back down and asked if you had received any messages."

Stanton looked surprised. "Why me?"

The clerk shook his head slightly. "You resemble that guy in the drawing of McKinley's killer, but so do a lot of other men. Anyone who looks like that picture gets a once over."

"What did you tell them?"

"Sir, we're very protective of our guests, but being the police and all, I said no messages, just a package when you arrived. I hope you don't mind, but they were pretty insistent."

"They?"

"Yes, there were two of them. One in a uniform, the other in a suit."

Attempting to look undisturbed, Stanton said, "I'm glad they're being so thorough. We ought to stand those anarchists against a wall and shoot them all."

The clerk nodded. "I couldn't agree more. They're a threat to all of us."

An attractive couple walked up to the counter. Turning to help them, the clerk looked back at Stanton and added, "Said they'd be back tomorrow, so you'll likely see them again."

There was no way they could know me from that picture, Stanton thought to himself. Taking a deep breath to calm his nerves, he walked into the Blue Room, the hotel's restaurant. It was elegantly decorated in light blue, soft beige and coral. Removing a gold engraved watch from his pocket, he noted the time was 9:00 PM. He would be gone in the morning. The restaurant was nearly empty as he was shown to a table overlooking a small park, dimly lit by a single street lamp. The cold night mist had turned to a hazy drizzle. Ordering a Manhattan, he sat back, trying to assemble his jumbled thoughts. Unexpectedly, he was suddenly riveted in place when he saw a police officer walk up to the front desk. The waiter interrupted his trance with his Manhattan.

Gradually, he made himself look away from the desk and saw an attractive young woman sitting on the other side of the room. She was someone's wife. He searched for her husband, but she seemed alone. Her table was not in view of the hotel lobby; his was. Picking up his drink, he walked over to her. She looked up, slightly startled. "Yes?"

"I'm sorry to disturb you, but I'm very much alone. Would you mind if I joined you?"

Her silk-laced hat covered her eyes as he looked down, preventing him from guessing what she was thinking. "I'm married," she answered bluntly.

"I see that from your ring. So am I, but I would greatly enjoy your company during dinner if it's not an imposition."

"Mr. . . . ."

"Moffit. Edward Moffit, from Delaware," he said, offering his hand. She took it lightly, saying, "Mr. Moffit, it's nice to know

you, but I'm afraid it would raise questions if we dined together."
She was dressed in a light blue satin small-waist flared skirt, with a
white high-necked embroidered blouse and matching blue jacket. A
silk navy bow around her neck covered part of the high collar. His
thoughts briefly turned to how strikingly beautiful she was.

"Under normal circumstances, I'd agree. But look around – it's
only the two of us. Surely no harm would be done."

She narrowed her eyes, thinking of how nice he seemed and how
very attractive he was. "You're very persistent, Mr. Moffit. Please sit
down and join me."

Within minutes the police officer stepped into the restaurant,
his eyes shifting back and forth around the room. He saw only an
attractive married woman talking with her elegantly dressed husband
at a table in the corner. He turned and left.

Stanton saw him from the corner of his eye but kept both eyes
glued on her. "I forgot to ask your name?"

It's Elizabeth Ambridge. What do you do, Mr. Moffit?"

"I'm a banker from Delaware."

"And your wife?"

He cleared his throat. "I lied to you about that. I'm sorry, but I
thought it would make our dining together easier. I was married but
she died. You're not with your husband?"

"You didn't need to lie. I'm so sorry about your wife. My husband
is a journalist. It seems his profession and married life don't fit well
together. He works night and day as the publisher and editor of the
Baltimore Sun. While he's working, I use his money and travel."

"And he doesn't miss you?"

She removed her hat and placed it on a nearby chair, exposing
her soft golden hair. "He hasn't told me he does."

"Then I'd say he's not very bright."

"Oh, he's bright, all right, but I don't think he ever really wanted
to get married. I was a convenience to him." She paused, and then
with a tone of disillusionment, added, "And still am."

His eyes momentarily gazed around the room and settled onto
hers. "That sounds a little sad. Why are you in Washington?"

"A meeting for women's suffrage." She thought she saw him squirm in his seat, just a little. In a slightly irritated voice, she asked, "Mr. Moffit, does that make you uncomfortable?"

"Why would it?"

"You tell me."

He could see the anger rising in her eyes, and he wanted to quickly dispel it. "No, it doesn't. I strongly favor women's suffrage, as does President Roosevelt."

Her eyes softened. "I'm glad you do. Now we can be friends."

Several hours later, after ending the evening with champagne, he held her chair as she stood to leave. Picking up her hat, she asked with a faint smile, "And who are you really, Mr. Moffit?"

He stopped dead. "Why would you ask that?"

"I told you – I travel constantly. I've gotten to know a lot of people, and I have many friends who are bankers. You're not a banker, Mr. Moffit, or whatever your name is. I saw that policeman come in several hours ago and look around. You seemed very intent on his not seeing you."

He shook his head slightly, lowering it to avoid her eyes. "I'm Harold Green, from St. Louis."

She looked at him with a scowl in her eyes. "No you're not. Could you be a Matthew Stanton from New York?"

He froze.

"You are, aren't you?"

"If you think that, why haven't you called for the police?"

She looked down and brushed off her skirt. "My husband's newspaper printed an article about you several days ago. It said the Chicago police commissioner was interviewed and felt you were innocent – that you were the victim of a frame of some sort. Of course, everyone else disagreed with him, but I think he made sense. You see, Mr. Stanton, I'm not quick to judge. My father was hung as a horse thief. He had done nothing wrong; he was totally innocent. They were vigilantes. I'll never forget that, and I'll not forget the men who did it." Staring deeply into his eyes, she asked, "Did you do it?"

She sat back down and he sat next to her. "No. I would never do something like that."

"But you killed five men, twenty years ago."

His pulse began to race. How could she know that?

She leaned forward. "The article said you did. You were only fifteen. Why did you do that?"

His head began to hurt. "That's not a question; it's a conclusion."

"I know I'm making you uncomfortable. If it would help, after having dinner with you, I want you to know I believe the commissioner. I don't believe you would have ever done that. But I do think that you're a terrible liar, probably the worst I've ever encountered."

Stanton leaned his chair back, thinking this was the most intriguing woman he had ever met.

"Berg was the only friend I ever had. When I was abandoned, he picked me out of the gutter and saved my life. Those men – they were vicious. They clubbed him to death while I watched. I wasn't going to let them get away with that. Yes, I killed all of them, and I'd do it again."

She rose again from her chair. "Come with me," she said, taking his hand. In silence, they walked past the night clerk, stepped onto the elevator, and went to her room on the second floor.

Entering the large suite, he stopped to light two oil lamps. She asked, "My luggage?"

"First, go the front desk and checkout. Then bring your things to my room."

He looked at her in amazement. "Do you know the risk you're taking?"

"I do. Matthew . . . is that what they call you?"

"Yes."

"Matthew, my life has become quite boring. I don't think this is much of a risk. And it will make a great story for my husband."

"Would it? That you invited an accused assassin to spend the night with you. I want to be there when you explain *that* to him."

She sat down in a corner chair, smiling at his remark. "He'll understand. You don't know him. You're invited to stay for one night. That's it. And I am *not* going to sleep with you, if that's on your mind. You can sleep on the sofa in this room."

"That was *never* on my mind. I'll check out and be back in a few minutes."

*   *   *   *

At two in the morning, he lay on the sofa staring at the ceiling. He would have to send Longbourne a telegram in the morning, telling him of the change in plans. Would *they* know? It would be disguised, but they would see it was from Washington if they were monitoring his telegrams. Heavy with fatigue, sleep had eluded him. He closed his eyes, only to hear a soft voice behind him. "Have you decided where you'll go tomorrow?" He sat up and spun around, straining his eyes in the dark to see her faint figure across the room. She had on a white silk robe.

"Not quite. I'm relying a lot on instinct now."

"What do your instincts tell you?" She walked slowly over and sat on the edge of the sofa. He laid back and stared into her eyes, which seemed to shine in the darkness.

"My only hope is to talk to the President."

Her hand reached for her mouth. "My God, Roosevelt?"

"That's the one."

"He'll never see you. They'll have you in handcuffs before you get close."

"I'll find a way."

"He won't believe you, even if you get to see him."

"You did."

"That's different."

"Why?"

His question was met with silence. Then he felt the soft touch of her hand. "Because I wanted to."

"Help me."

"No."

"You won't do it?"

"No, because I would just get in the way."

"No, you wouldn't. They're looking for a man, by himself. With you, I wouldn't look suspicious. If you could give me just a few days."

She didn't answer. Holding his hand for several minutes in deafening silence, she finally whispered, "I've changed my mind."

He smiled, but she couldn't see it. "Then you will do it?"

"Not that. Please come to bed with me."

She leaned over, their lips meeting with a passion that left him breathless. Then she covered his body with hers while her tongue explored his mouth. His inner voices told him it was wrong, but it no longer mattered. Nothing mattered now except her.

CHAPTER TEN

▼

Washington, D.C.-The Federal Building

The next morning, they moved to a hotel across town, checking in as Mr. and Mrs. John Harrington from Philadelphia. Stanton showed a business card in that name portraying that he owned Fidelity Insurance Company. Two hours later, at 11:00 AM, Elizabeth stepped down from a carriage in front of the Federal Building, dressed in a black wool coat with fur lining the collar and sleeves. Snow had begun to fall, and she opened a dark pink umbrella to shield her from the wet flurries and the wind. Inside, she walked to the offices of the Federal Investigation Service and asked to meet with Charles Wilcox. At first she was told he was unavailable, but after explaining to the receptionist that she was Mrs. Dalton Ambridge, the wife of the publisher of the *Baltimore Sun*, she was asked to wait.

After fifteen minutes, she was taken to a large room located off the reception area. It was empty except for several wood chairs around a dark walnut table. Stacks of files sat on one end. The table was surrounded with gas lamps that cast eerie shadows on the walls. A large window offered some additional lighting, but the snow flurries, which had now turned to more heavy snow, blocked much of the outside light. Focused on the snow, she was startled when the door opened and a raspy voice said, "Mrs. Ambridge. I'm pleased to meet you." Wilcox was in shirt sleeves rolled up to his elbows, wearing a loosened green-striped tie. His left hand was twisted around his brown leather suspenders, and his right hand carried a writing pad and pen. Sitting across from her and tilting back with his legs crossed, he waited for her to speak.

She adjusted uncomfortably in her chair. "Thank you for seeing me."

"I've heard a lot about your husband; a talented man, though somewhat of a liberal. Did he send you here?"

"No, he doesn't know I'm here. You don't like liberals?"

"Not particularly," he said in an arrogant tone.

"Mr. Wilcox, I want to talk about Matthew Stanton."

His grin quickly faded and he abruptly sat up. "You know where he is?"

"No, I don't."

"Then why . . . ?"

Interrupting, she said, "I'm here because I believe he's innocent. I want to talk to you about that."

"Mrs. Ambridge, I've read your husband's columns, and I know you're, shall I say, an activist. But why Stanton? What's he to you?"

She stood up and removed her coat and hat, exposing a navy and cream dress and her long blonde hair. Sitting back down, she explained, "I've met with Mr. Stanton."

His mouth dropped open. "You what . . . ?"

"Let me finish, please. He told me about his past, and we discussed the evidence against him. He swears he's not guilty. I believe him. The evidence is false – he would never do anything like that."

Wilcox let out a low chuckle. "And you believed him! What did you expect him to say?"

"Yes, I believed him. That so-called evidence you have was manufactured. You're not conducting a thorough investigation, Mr. Wilcox, you're on a vigilante hunt. I believe you don't know if he's guilty or innocent, but you'll shoot him anyway, won't you?"

Wilcox looked insulted. "What do you take us for, Mrs. Ambridge? The evidence we have says he's guilty. If it's manufactured, as you say, let him prove it. This is America. We're not going to shoot him – a jury will hang him."

"Oh, so he has to prove he's not guilty or you'll hang him?"

"I didn't say that."

"Then what did you mean? Will you talk to him and give him a fair chance to tell you what he thinks happened?"

"If he gives himself up, we'll talk. But only when he's behind bars."

"So your mind's made up?"

"Mrs. Ambridge, your Mr. Stanton is one hell of a talker. He may be rich as hell, but he's a danger to our country. Men like that don't deserve to be called Americans. For Christ's sake, he masterminded the killing of our president. Doesn't that mean something to you?"

She was stunned. Looking at him with disgust, she said, "Tried, found guilty and ready to be hung. That's what you think? And you call yourself a detective. Why don't you try to do some detecting? You've set yourself up as judge and juror."

"No, Mrs. Ambridge, you're wrong. I've thoroughly looked at the evidence, and it points to him. I'll say it again – send him in and tell him to give himself up."

"And that's the only way? What would it take for you to believe him?"

He took in and then exhaled a deep breath. "A hell of a lot. Do you mind if I smoke?"

"No."

Removing a cigar from his shirt pocket, he struck a match on the table's leg and lit it, allowing the heavy smoke to drift in her direction.

She waved her hand to push it away. "Would you explain that to me?"

Taking another puff of his cigar, he responded, "There's very little to explain. I want to see an air-tight alibi on the day McKinley was shot. Then I want an explanation of the letters he wrote to Emma Goldman – and the gun."

"How do you know he wrote those letters, or that the gun was his?"

"Our handwriting experts have verified that. Mrs. Ambridge, he's already killed five men."

"When he was fifteen."

"Does that make a difference? Fifteen or thirty-five, he's a killer. And I'll tell you something else. He's an anarchist, a traitor to this country. Doesn't that bother you?"

"You don't know that," she angrily answered.

He sat forward, laying his cigar in a bronze ash tray on the table. "Read the letters, Mrs. Ambridge. Look at his background. He shot five men who worked for Andrew Carnegie, one of our most charitable citizens."

"And a man who exploits the poor for his own gain. Have you asked yourself how Mr. Stanton could shoot those men and not be charged with a crime?"

He opened a clenched fist in frustration. "I have a great deal of respect for you and your husband, but your activism is harmful to our country. I've given you my opinion. There's no need for us to carry this further. I'm not here to debate Stanton's guilt with you."

She stood up and put on her coat. Buttoning it to the top, she pulled on her gloves and turned to the door. He rushed to open it for her, and she turned. "You're an ass, Mr. Wilcox."

"I'm sorry you feel that way; I have a job to do."

Picking up her umbrella, she said, "And you're very poor at it. God save us from people like you."

After she had left, he returned to the room, picked up his cigar, and stared blankly out the window. Why, he thought to himself, would she take up the case of an assassin? She was very attractive, and obviously very smart. What would possess her to do that? Then another thought crossed his mind. He wondered . . . .

Taking a carriage to a small coffee shop ten blocks away, she walked over to Stanton, who sat with his arms and legs crossed, staring at her. Looking around to see they were alone, she whispered, "Do you still have your gun?"

"In my suitcase."

"You're going to need it."

CHAPTER ELEVEN

▼

Washington, D.C.

Charlie Wilcox walked out of the Federal Building at 5:30 PM to
see a carriage waiting at the curb. He thought of his two children
and lovely wife who would be waiting for him. "Driver," he asked as
he brushed snow from his head, "can you take me to Worthington
Place?"

"Get in."

Opening the door, he stopped cold to see a man sitting in the
corner of the cab, holding a revolver. "You heard the man," the voice
said, "get in."

He thought about running, but he would probably be shot. The
pistol was pointed at his face, and it was cocked. He stepped in,
sitting next to the occupant. Tapping on the window, the voice said,
"Drive," and the carriage pulled away.

Steadying his nerves, Wilcox looked at the occupant. "What do
you want?"

The man loosened the scarf around his neck. "I'm innocent."

Wilcox pursed his lips, thinking this was his moment. "You're
Matthew Stanton." The gun remained leveled at his head.

"I am."

Feeling the carriage jolt over a rough area in the street, Wilcox suddenly became fearful the gun might be discharged. "Could you put that thing down?"

"Not on your life. I want you to pay attention to me."

"If it goes off, I won't be here to do that."

Helplessly gazing out the small round window as the carriage crossed over Constitution Avenue, Wilcox protested, "I can't help you. Give yourself up."

"So you can hang me?"

"That's a possibility."

"I want you to shut up and listen. I had nothing to do with the murder of McKinley – I liked him and thought he was a good president."

"Then why the letters?"

"I told you to shut up. I didn't write those letters. Why would I do something that stupid? I've never met Emma Goldman, and I never owned that gun you found in my study. Ask yourself, Wilcox, why would I leave a trail of evidence like that? Those letters were forged."

"If all that is true, why did you pay five thousand dollars to Czolgosz? You can't deny that; we have your bank records."

Stanton stopped to notice that the carriage had slowed. "That wasn't my account. I never did business with that bank."

"We have bank officers who said you did."

The carriage stopped. Stanton yelled, "What's wrong, driver? Move on."

The driver yelled back, "It's the police. They're stopping all carriages."

His face flushed with anger, Stanton turned back to Wilcox. "If you say one damned thing, I'll kill you. You know I'm capable of that."

Wilcox seemed unconcerned. Stanton lowered the gun to conceal it under his coat, but kept it pointed at Wilcox's stomach. "Ever been gut shot, detective?"

Wilcox shook his head with little emotion.

"You don't want to be, believe me. It'll be a slow, painful death." Pausing to look out the back window, Stanton said, "The bank. Check their records. I've never had an account there. I don't go to banks to open accounts. I hire people for that. Whoever opened one wasn't me, he was an imposter made to look like me. Why would I deposit five thousand dollars in a new account, in my name, and then take the cash and pay it to Czolgosz? That's idiotic. I'm worth millions. I don't have five thousand dollars accounts! Use your head. Someone is working overtime to get me hanged." He paused to catch his breath. "One other thing – I'm not an anarchist! Try to place me at one of their meetings – you can't. I don't know them and I don't associate with them."

The door suddenly opened and a policeman was staring at the two men. "Identification, please," he asked with an outstretched hand. Stanton pulled a card from his coat pocket with his left hand and gave it to the officer. He studied it for a moment and then asked, "You two with the insurance company?"

"We are, officer." He pushed the gun harder into Wilcox's ribs. Wilcox remained silent, trying to signal with his eyes that he was being held captive.

"Your friend there is mighty quiet. Can't he speak?" The officer eyed Wilcox with suspicion.

"He's had a little too much to drink," Stanton said softly.

"Well get him home." The officer closed the door and moved to the next carriage.

Their carriage moved on for several blocks, and Stanton tapped on the window. "Stop." He paid the driver, jumped out, and stepped into a waiting carriage heading the other direction.

"You're safe." Elizabeth's fears were allayed, and she smiled as she took his hand. "What did Wilcox say?"

"Nothing that he didn't say to you." Taking the speaker hanging down in front of him, he said, "Driver, the road is blocked up ahead. Can you get us around that? We're in an awful hurry."

"No problem, sir." The driver cracked his whip over his two large horses, which ran abreast, and the carriage lurched into a sudden right turn and swept toward the Potomac. Passing though

Chinatown in the direction of Dupont Circle, the carriage made a wide arc along narrow roads that passed by manicured lawns and giant trees, barren now in winter. Elizabeth gripped Matthew's arm. The road was rugged, but the driver was bent on losing no time as they seemed to fly over it in feverish haste. As they wound on their seemingly endless way, the sun sank lower and lower behind them, the shadows of evening creeping around them. Suddenly the carriage pulled to a stop as the driver lit the two lamps on either side of him. With a jolt, the carriage resumed its journey.

There was a harsh austerity about the sprawling brick homes, iron gates, and paved walkways that seemed devoid of life on this blustery day. As the evening fell, it began to get colder, and the growing twilight seemed to merge into a dark curtain of mist, the tall firs and pines standing out against the background of the snow. The great masses of grayness that hung over the trees added to Matthew's feeling of impending doom. The driver lashed the horses unmercifully with his long whip, and with wild cries of encouragement urged them on.

Eventually, through the darkness, Matthew could see a patch of light ahead of them. Perched high on a hill overlooking the picturesque capitol, the mansion where Elizabeth Hastings lived was considered by many to be a landmark. Gas lamps illuminated the fancy pillars that Elizabeth had told the driver would mark the driveway. He pulled off the road and through the pillars that supported sculptured iron gates. Stopping at the entrance, she remembered with a pang of sad nostalgia her childhood and all the things she'd loved that seemed to have so quickly disappeared.

Suppressing the feeling of doom that was trying to steal over him, Matthew Stanton thought of his home in New York and wondered when, or if, he would see it again. What he had done in Washington now seemed insanity. The hunt was on; he wouldn't have much time. He stole a glance at Elizabeth and managed the semblance of a smile.

"I'm so sorry," she said, squeezing his hand. She reached for her gloves and purse, and then took the driver's hand as she stepped down.

He didn't move. "Elizabeth, we have to say goodbye. Your grandmother will be in danger if you take me inside, and your husband . . . ."

"My husband is consumed with his work. He doesn't need me. My grandmother doesn't judge people; she'll love you. She's eighty-nine years old. They wouldn't do anything to her."

"It's no good. If you stay with me, they'll put you in jail as an accomplice. I'm not going to let that happen." He pulled the door closed and tapped on the window, motioning the driver to move on. He then lifted the speaker and said, "The Federal Building." Elizabeth stood frozen, in a state of shock, watching the carriage move down the drive. He needed her help. Why would he leave now? Her eyes moist, she was overwhelmed with a feeling of loss. She knew she would never see him again.

CHAPTER TWELVE

▼

Washington, D.C. – The White House

It would be the trial of the century. Newspaper headlines around the country declared that the man responsible for McKinley's assassination was in federal custody. Only one paper, the *Baltimore Sun*, had printed in a sub-heading that he proclaimed his innocence.

In Washington, Theodore Roosevelt had become settled in his new home. His office was temporarily next to his residence on the second floor. Visitors could often hear his six young children boisterously at play. It was disconcerting to many, but not to him. He was only forty-two, the youngest man to ever occupy the presidency, and he loved the noise and activity. The West Wing was yet to be built, but the new president was hard at work on the plans. Those "damn glass houses" would soon disappear to make way for his grand project. It had been only several months since he renamed the Executive Mansion. In the future, it would be called the White House, and it would have the best diplomatic advantage of any government building in the world.

At his invitation, Charlie Wilcox made his first visit to the White House. A man considered to have nerves of steel, he found himself unsettled at meeting with the new president. He was shown into his office and sat across from Roosevelt, who was busy pouring over a thick file. Next to the President was a large world globe, a birthday gift from his daughter, Alice. It would be seen with him in many future photo shoots. Roosevelt was jovial, rigorous, and obsessed with his mission for America. When he was sworn in, he had promised to faithfully carry on the programs and visions of the deceased McKinley, but now that was the farthest thing from his mind. He had his own visions, and his programs would be more liberal than anyone had imagined. The "big stick" was his, and he had plans to use it.

Roosevelt was five feet ten inches tall and very overweight. He had brown hair and a heavy brown mustache. His prince-nez glasses had extremely thick lenses to correct vision that had been poor since his boyhood. They had no arms or rims and sat perilously on his nose, a thin cord hanging down on one side. He habitually gritted his teeth when smiling, and flashing them became one of his trademarks. When he spoke, his unusually high-pitched voice shocked many people who heard him for the first time. His speech was in the clipped, aristocratic cadences of a true Harvard man. But the thing that struck people the most about his personal characteristics was his enormous vitality – his nervous energy. He was always in motion, and when he entered the room to meet Wilcox, Wilcox would say later that he felt an incredible electric current.

Flashing his characteristic smile, the President said, "Thank you for coming, Mr. Wilcox." Roosevelt sat in a large leather chair behind his desk, shoving some papers to the side. Then he reached out across the desk and shook his hand. "Great work, detective. How in the hell did you get him so fast?"

"Mr. President, we had a national manhunt searching for him, but we missed him more than a few times when he was right under our noses. The short of it is that the manhunt got nowhere – he came to us. He said he wanted to talk to you, that he could clear things up. He insisted he was innocent."

"And what did you do?"

"What any officer would have done. We ignored his protests and locked him in chains. I have no idea what he was thinking, but there was no way he could refute the evidence we had."

"Is that so?" The phone standing next to Roosevelt suddenly began to ring. Grabbing the stand with his left hand and the receiver with his right, he spoke loudly, "What is it?"

Listening for a few minutes, he said, "I'm hearing it all now. Wilcox is sitting across from me. Why don't you come and join us?"

After a few moments, he said, "Elihu, I'll fill you in tomorrow. Come for lunch." He then placed the receiver back in its cradle and put the phone stand back on his desk. Giving Wilcox a very intimidating stare, he said, "I heard he kidnapped you."

Wilcox placed his hands tightly together. "He made me his prisoner, in a carriage, for almost half an hour while he held a gun to my head and protested his innocence. We had police blockades up within minutes, but he escaped. Amazingly, within several hours he walked in and gave himself up."

"How in the hell did you let him do that?"

"What?"

"Make you his prisoner?"

"Well, sir, as I was walking out of . . . ."

Holding up his hand, Roosevelt said, "I really don't have time to hear it. I thought our federal police were tougher than that. What about others?"

"We think we have them all. Czolgosz met with Emma Goldman and Stanton, and the three of them planned and carried out the assassination. We found a second gun in Stanton's home. It was the gun that fired the bullet that killed McKinley. The shot by Czolgosz only slightly wounded him. The killing shot was made by Stanton from a balcony."

"So you're telling me one of our wealthiest citizens, a Harvard graduate, shot McKinley and pulled the trigger himself from a balcony." The President tilted his chair back, resting his feet on the edge of the desk. His doubt was unmistakable.

Wilcox stuttered, "Yes, sir."

"Do you know he was there?"

"Not exactly. We're looking for witnesses."

Roosevelt rose from his chair and began to pace the room, fiddling with an unlit cigar. His mind drifted back to his year as a deputy sheriff in the Dakotas, to the three men he had tracked down as horse thieves only to have a judge declare they were innocent. He had shot one of them. And he thought about his years as New York's police commissioner, about the criminals, the politicians behind many of them, and the men who were put to death and later found innocent.

Returning to his desk chair, Roosevelt blurted out, "Detective, why does a man who shot McKinley come to Washington to tell you he didn't do it?"

Wilcox was momentarily at a loss for words. Surprised, he asked, "You don't think he's guilty?"

Roosevelt's eyes bore into Wilcox. In his high-pitch voice, he said emphatically, "That's not what I said. The courts will determine if he's innocent. But I want to hear your theory – why would he do that?"

Wilcox had come expecting a medal; now he wasn't so sure. "To throw us off."

The President gritted his teeth. "Bullshit! That's no answer. He wouldn't do that. Give me a better answer."

Wilcox rubbed his sweating hands together, trying to control his thoughts. "Mr. President, we'll get to work on that. There *is* a reason."

"When you find one, I want to hear it. Don't embarrass the White House or me in the press. I'll not be the goat of cartoons about this. Thank you, detective." He stood up and walked into the next room, and Charlie Wilcox was left to wonder about his standing with the new president.

CHAPTER THIRTEEN

▼

The Federal Courts Building, Washington, D.C.

It was not at all what he had expected. The wealthy shipping line owner had been treated to one indignity after another. The days of questioning had been relentless, but the answers had consistently been the same. He was innocent and knew nothing of a conspiracy to murder McKinley. They had been impressed by his poise and bearing, his ability to handle the barrage of questions and remain unflustered, throwing questions of doubt back at them, but no one believed him. Then he had been locked up in an eight-by-eight cell in the basement of the building, caged in a concrete room with a small window allowing very little light. He had been given an hour to talk to his lawyers, and after that days of solitary confinement.

He lay on the small cot in the chilly cell, thinking of the selfish life he had led. Berg had warned him against making close friends. Berg had been betrayed by his closest friends, and that had led to his murder. Stanton never sought out friends, none except Longbourne who had been with him after Berg was murdered. It was Longbourne who had convinced the police that Stanton had shot those men in self-defense and that they would have killed him too.

Now Stanton was aware, as he lay there in the dark, that avoiding friendships had led to the making of enemies. He had always been cordial and polite, but he refused to let anyone get close to him. It was that character flaw that had angered people who knew him, that had fueled their resentment. He had never stopped to think about it, but the admiration he had once received had quickly turned to envy and jealously.

He now had his wake-up call. His wealth and fortune meant nothing. McKinley's murder had changed him. And the country wanted to hang him for it. Why had everything come so late? An immense feeling of despair washed over him. He was trapped.

*   *   *   *

Two blocks away, an angry president stared at the latest caricature, showing him accepting money from a shackled Matthew Stanton. He was livid. In his run for governor of New York, Stanton had been one of his most ardent supporters, unknown to Roosevelt. He had learned of it for the first time in the *Times'* cartoon. Secretary of War Root was late, and that added to his furor. Sitting back, he tilted in his chair. His brown hair and thick mustache were neatly trimmed and his mouth tight with tension. Behind his thick round glasses, his eyes bristled with rage.

Theodore Roosevelt had just finished talking to the Police Commissioner of Chicago. He had been convincing. In his view, the anarchists behind the assassination were still out there, and they were a threat to the new president. Jay Neeley was sure of it, and Roosevelt trusted Neeley. They went back a long way.

Secretary Root walked in fifteen minutes late for the meeting. Roosevelt suppressed his temper. Root was fifty-five years old, precise in his speech, mannerisms and thought processes, and temperate in his views. As most men of the day, he parted his thinning dark hair in the center and had a carefully manicured mustache. He was the prototype of the early twentieth century statesman and presidential advisor. Unlike Roosevelt, he appeared very mild mannered, but beneath his soft veneer lay a very aggressive lion when challenged. Roosevelt liked that. He also liked that Root had served as defense counsel at the corruption trial of William "Boss" Tweed. Root had also represented many of the "Robber Barons", people like Jay Gould, who had made themselves public enemies. Root understood corruption and could deal with the sharks of Wall Street.

Dressed impeccably in a gray-striped vested suit with a maroon tie knotted around a high-collared stiff white shirt, he took a seat at a small oval table across from Roosevelt. Making no apologies, he asked, "Mr. President, how is your day?"

Roosevelt's anger quickly dissipated, and he shrugged with a silent laugh. "Not worth a damn." He leaned down and then tossed a newspaper cartoon across the table. Root gave it a severe look. "This will all go away when they hang him." Gazing at Roosevelt's large waistline, he added, "I know you have the stomach for this."

Roosevelt laughed out loud, and then suddenly became quiet. "What do you think about this anarchist movement? Is that something I need to worry about?"

Root leaned back, scratching his eyebrow. "They've shot two presidents, and you refuse a bodyguard. I'd be worried."

"This man Stanton. Is he one of them?"

"That's an interesting question. You wanted Wilcox to handle the investigation, and he brought quick results. But my people question what he's done. Mr. President, this is one hot potato. You don't want to be caught holding it. The public wants its revenge, and now they're going to have it. Leave this one alone."

Root could see in Roosevelt's eyes that he had a problem. The President stood and began to pace. Spinning abruptly, he declared, "Jay Neeley says he's innocent, and I agree with him. I wasn't police commissioner of New York because no one else wanted the job. The evidence they have against Stanton is a pile of horse manure." Calming slightly, he sat back down. "Let me ask you this. Could we use him?"

"Theodore, you're beginning to worry me. He's in jail and headed for a public hanging. How in the hell could we use him?"

"I need someone to ferret out these anarchists. Henry Ford and Randolph Hearst – they're involved in it. And there are many others. If we had someone on the inside, someone who knew what the hell he was doing . . . ."

Root lit a cigarette, faintly shaking his head at what he had just heard. "Ford and Hearst? You really think that? And you're thinking of using Stanton? I knew something like that was coming. You can't do it! What in the world makes you think the evidence is a pile of horse manure? I've looked at it, and it's pretty damning."

The President spoke in a high, frustrated voice. "I'll make this decision," he spat out, "but I want you on board. I talked to Neeley for an hour this morning. He took me through every accusation, every piece of paper. He doesn't miss much. There's no doubt in his mind - none – that the letters found in Emma Goldman's place are forgeries and the gun was planted. If there was another shooter, and he's beginning to doubt that, it wasn't Stanton. Neeley says he was in Boston the day of the shooting."

Root took a deep draw on his cigarette, slowly exhaling the smoke. He had witnessed Roosevelt's outbursts before. In a low, calm voice, he said, "If there wasn't another shooter, then tell me where that second bullet came from?"

Roosevelt's lack of patience was beginning to show. "That bullet wasn't examined for over a month. Anyone could have planted it. Mr. Secretary, we're spending too much time arguing this, and I'm not going to do that with you. Are you on board or not?"

Shifting uncomfortably in his chair, Root nodded that he was. "Theodore, you're taking a hell of a risk." He threw his hands up in defeat. "I'll do whatever you want."

"Get him up here. I want to talk to him."

"Then what?"

"I'll pardon him."

"No you won't! If you do, kiss your presidency goodbye. The American people will never stand for that."

Roosevelt stopped and lit a cigar. "Then *you* get him out of jail."

"What! Why Stanton, for Christ's sake. You have a choice of anyone you want for this. Why in the hell him?"

"Because I like him."

Root was dumfounded. "Have you met him?"

"I don't have to." Puffing on his cigar, Roosevelt said, "I signed on Rough Riders I'd never met. Not one let me down. Stanton's a man to ride the river with, mark my words." He stopped, momentarily deep in thought. "He's a Harvard graduate! Doesn't that mean something to you? You get him out – I'll do the rest."

Root put both hands behind his head and mumbled, "You're still a damn cowboy." In a stronger voice, he exclaimed, "You want me to build you the best navy in the world, rebuild West Point, modernize the army, and now I'm going to spend my time freeing a man accused of assassinating McKinley?"

"That's the sum of it."

"You got any ideas?"

Roosevelt grinned. "Mr. Secretary, are you asking me how to do your job?"

"That's not funny."

"Break the news to the press that Stanton was framed. Contradict that crap they call evidence - or get Neeley to do it for you. He'll turn their heads. But first get Stanton up here."

"What about Wilcox?"

"Get him here, too. And the Attorney General. I'll tell them to drop the case."

Root laughed. "I damn sure want to be here when you do that."

CHAPTER FOURTEEN

▼

Chicago, Illinois

The bitter cold and heavy rain fulfilled Chicago's promise of a harsh winter. The night sky was an impenetrable blanket, blocking from view the shimmering lights of the city. There were no strollers along the street; pockets of fog swirled overhead, evidence that the north winds traveled unchecked through the city. It was ten o'clock in the evening. She leaned against him, waiting for the carriage to arrive. He saw that she nervously twisted her hands around her handbag, attempting to mask her anxiety. The carriage pulled up, its gas lamps barely visible in the fog. A police officer was inside to accompany her to the station. She hugged him tightly with moist eyes as a final good-bye. She appeared calm, but inwardly he knew she was panic-stricken.

The telegram from the Pinkerton Agency said Harding knew she was with him. The detectives he had hired to protect her had betrayed him. Only the agency knew where she was, and he had trusted them. He was quick to learn that even they had a price. The decision had been made. Alyssa would leave, and Willingham would stay behind. If anyone came searching for her, he would warn her. Was it worth the risk? It had to be. He had loved her as a daughter. The police had been notified. They were not beholden to Harding as were the others.

He watched the carriage pull away and then turned and walked into his house to have a brandy. Thirty minutes later, he left his private bar for his bedroom on the second floor. Before he reached the second step of the winding staircase, he heard a loud knock on the door. Asking for identification through the soundly locked door, he heard, "Chicago police. We're here about Mrs. Harding." Hesitating, he unlocked the door to see two men who were not police officers.

As he attempted to close the door, a foot was placed in the doorway and the two men pushed him into the hallway. One man carried a black wool scarf in his thick hands. The other leaned against the door. "Where is she?" he demanded.

"Not here," Willingham nervously replied. "Get the hell out of my house."

The one with the scarf only smiled. "When you tell us where she went, we'll go."

Willingham turned to grab the phone. At the same instant, the black scarf was looped over his head. It caught him by the throat and yanked him back toward the door. He gagged while his fingers pulled and twisted at the scarf, but it was as tight as a noose. From the corners of his bulging eyes, he looked into his assailant's dark eyes as he was lifted off his feet. He tried to scream but a burning sensation in his throat stifled any sound. Then everything turned black. Within several minutes, he slumped to the floor, dead.

The next morning, the policemen who arrived first at the scene had an idea about what had happened. They had been briefed at headquarters that Willingham was with a woman. He had asked that they send an officer with her to the train station. The police regarded him as a friend, and it was done. They thought to themselves that it was too bad he hadn't asked for protection for himself. He had said a Philadelphia millionaire was searching for the woman, that he was insane and might try to kill her. It was a story they found hard to believe, but the chief had listened. And now *Willingham* was dead. The police found no evidence of his killers or their motive. A telegram was sent to the Boston police to watch out for the woman. It was the best they could do.

*　　　*　　　*　　　*

Alyssa sat in a private compartment on the night train to Boston. She was in a state of exhaustion. One thought reoccurred over and over - Willingham would warn her. Nestled on her lap was the latest edition of the *Times*, given to her by the porter. She was drawn immediately to the headline: *Mastermind of McKinley's Murder Behind Bars*, it read. He had given himself up! Why would he do that? Then she experienced a wave of relief. It was over! He *was* guilty. Now she could forget him.

She checked into the Parker House near Beacon Hill at ten the next morning. After she signed the register as Alyssa Coolidge, the desk clerk turned and handed her a telegram. She took it with her right hand, trying with her left to stifle the scream that welled within her when she read it. The clerk watched her grow pale, her hand now covering her eyes. Tears ran down her cheek. "Ms. Coolidge," he said quietly. "Can I help you?" She shook her head, unable to respond. He had done it, and he would kill her next.

The next thing she remembered was that she was in her room, lying on the bed. She was painfully tired, but sleep wouldn't come. She wondered if she would ever sleep again, if she could ever get the rest her body needed. Hours later, opening her eyes, she looked around the room in a daze. She had slept very little, and when she had, it had been as if she were in a coma. A brilliant bar of sunlight crossed the end of her bed. In an effort to clear her mind, she stumbled over to the wash basin in the room and splashed cold water in her face. Returning to the bed, she fell onto it and slept for several more hours, awakening late in the afternoon. One thought had haunted her dreams. She would have to kill him first. That would be her only salvation.

CHAPTER FIFTEEN

▼

Washington, D.C.

Matthew Stanton awoke in the dark, damp cell to hear a clanking of the door. A splash of light filled his eyes, temporarily blinding him. A husky voice demanded, "Get up, Stanton."

He stared back at the voice. When he stood up at the door, one of the guards who had been watching him leaned down and unlocked the leg-arm. Another guard grabbed his arm and led him down the white-washed hallway to a stairway that led to a prisoner's room. There, he was admonished to keep quiet. He angrily sat on a hard steel bench, seething at the treatment he'd received.

After thirty minutes, a well-dressed man walked up to him. "Do you have any better clothes?"

"What do I need them for?"

"I'm taking you to a meeting, but not like that." He called out, "Officer, where are this man's clothes?"

Within a few minutes, a burly uniformed policeman walked over and dropped Stanton's suitcase on the floor. "You taking this murderer?"

The well-dressed man stepped back, eyeing the officer. "I'd advise you to keep your mouth shut. Where can this man clean up and change?"

The officer indignantly pointed to a bathroom at the far end of the room. "Mr. Stanton, do your best to look presentable. I'll wait here for you."

"Not until you tell me what the hell's going on. If you're taking me to a firing squad, I'll go just as I am."

The man chuckled. "Forgive me. I should have introduced myself earlier." Extending his hand, he said, "I'm Zachary Roberts from the Attorney General's office. He wants to see you."

Stanton shook his hand with misgivings and then picked up his suitcase and walked down the hall. Thirty minutes later, he returned shaven and dressed in a dark blue vested suit and yellow tie. "Come with me," Roberts said.

"No handcuffs?"

Roberts turned. "You're not my prisoner, Mr. Stanton. Just don't try to run. You'll like what you're going to hear."

The Phaeton carriage was elaborate. The red velvet seats across from each other could seat four people, and were edged in gold to match the highly polished brass trim around the doors and windows. It reminded Stanton of the opulent carriages he had seen in Hong Kong. It travelled briskly down Pennsylvania Avenue, pulled by two black geldings. When they arrived at the side drive, the Marine on guard duty leaned down to inspect the occupants and then quickly waived them through.

He was taken to the side entrance, where they were met by another Marine, who led them past the colonnade, down a long corridor. Their missions accomplished, Roberts and the Marine left Stanton at the doorway to a large meeting room with pale yellow walls. The room had a highly-polished dark oak floor, partially covered by an exquisite coral, green and white carpet with the presidential seal embossed in the center, and was finished with elaborate molding and doors of a striking white. An American flag stood in one corner, a desk against a window, and matching divans and colonial chairs sat on the opposite wall. In the middle was a long walnut table surrounded by upholstered chairs in colonial colors. A fire, freshly lit, crackled in a massive fireplace. Above the mantel was a newly hung picture of former President William McKinley. It was very traditionally American.

Sitting around the table were Charlie Wilcox, Philander Knox, Elihu Root, Jay Neeley and Theodore Roosevelt. Knox, the Attorney General, was the only one to nod a welcome as Stanton entered the room. All men wore tall-collared white shirts with vests and high-button dark suits, except that the President's shirt collar was pulled down over a red and white paisley tie. Stanton stopped and stared in awe at the scene. Wiping his glasses, the President looked up and motioned Stanton to be seated at the end of the table. He stared at Stanton for several minutes, as if he knew him, and then let it pass. Stanton was perplexed and uncomfortable by the silence, but said nothing. Roosevelt turned to Knox and said, "You tell him."

Something was wrong. Knox looked at him, but at the same time seemed to be avoiding him. Roosevelt noticed his concern and smiled. "He's cross-eyed. The most brilliant attorney general anywhere, the personal attorney to Andrew Carnegie, but he can't make his eyes work. He can't focus them. He's not avoiding you. Listen to him."

Knox was slightly embarrassed. "He's right, Mr. Stanton. Now, the reason you're here. You've been charged with conspiracy . . . ."

Interrupting, Stanton protested, "I'm innocent!"

"Please let me finish. You're charged with plotting to kill President McKinley. We have a mixed opinion about that, around this table. Commissioner Neeley, over there," he said, pointing in Neeley's direction, "is a close friend of the White House. He and Mr. Wilcox, it seems, don't see eye to eye. But President Roosevelt seems to agree with the Commissioner. It won't do this government any good to have this thing continue, none at all."

Stanton looked dumfounded. "I . . . . ."

Holding up his palm, Knox stopped him. "We don't want a witch hunt, and we don't want to have the wrong man hanged. That could happen – it's what the American people want. Then we'll have been puppets for the anarchists. We're convinced that's what they want: to make us take our eyes off the ball. You following me so far?"

Stanton fidgeted nervously with his hands. "I'm trying. Can we get to the point. What do you want from me?"

Knox looked at the President, who motioned him with a flap of his hand to continue. "These anarchists pose an enormous threat to our society. Their goal is to destroy our government and our democracy."

Stanton could feel the stares of the men around the table. "I'm not one of them. You haven't answered my question."

Roosevelt put his hand inside his beige vest, pulling down his tie. Clearing his throat, he studied Stanton with piercing eyes. "The press says you contributed to my campaigns. Why?"

"Because I like your policies. You're a good man; you deserve my support."

"Mr. Stanton, I choose to ignore what Mr. Wilcox has in his mind determined. I know you're not guilty. And knowing that, I can do something for you and you for me."

"Will you grant me a pardon?"

"No. I'll do better – I'll have the charges dropped."

Wilcox's face became flushed. "Mr. President, with all due respect, that would be against the law. Mr. Stanton has been legally indicted by a grand jury. You can't do that."

Knox spoke up. "Surely we're not going to let the issue of legality interfere with what's right for this country."

Roosevelt grinned broadly. "My sentiments exactly. Wilcox, I want you to see to that."

Wilcox shook his head. "Mr. President, that can't . . . ."

The President interrupted. "If Mr. Stanton agrees to our terms, the Attorney General will call a press conference with Jay Neeley. Charlie, you can be there or sit it out – your call. I want them to say we made a mistake; Mr. Stanton is innocent and will be released immediately."

Stanton was speechless. Wilcox burst out, "How're you going to bury the evidence against him?" pointing at Stanton.

Roosevelt pushed back his chair. Glaring at Wilcox, he said, "You assembled that crap, now *you* disassemble it. Get with the Commissioner. If you can't work this out, maybe you're not smart enough for this job." Wilcox didn't respond but shifted uncomfortably in his chair.

Letting his gaze fall upon Stanton, Roosevelt said, "Let me give you my thoughts on this subject, and tell you why you're here."

"Thank you, sir." Stanton was almost speechless as he looked into the eyes of the most recognizable man in the world.

Roosevelt spoke clearly and succinctly in crisp, clipped high-pitched tones. "I hope you weren't too manhandled in the jail. If I could have stopped this sooner, I would have." He stood and leaned forward, resting his palms on the table. "You own Far East Shipping, is that right?"

"Yes, sir."

"They tell me you're somewhat of a recluse. You want to tell me about that?"

Stanton was surprised by the question. "That goes far back. I guess I have a hard time trusting people."

The President smiled. "So do I. When they set you free, what are your plans?"

Stanton could begin to sense where this was going. "Back to New York. But I first want to contact a woman I met several weeks ago. She was in need of help, and I'm afraid I let her down. I'd like to see what I can do for her."

"I'd ask you about that, but it's none of my business." Stopping to step away from the table, he became introspective. "That could affect what I have in mind for you. We'll talk about that. What about your business?"

"Right now it runs itself. I'm not involved in the day-to-day operations."

"Then you've got time on your hands."

"Not exactly, sir, I have other business interests I'm pursuing."

"That's good," Roosevelt said. "You'll need that."

"For what?"

The heads around the table turned back and forth, silently taking in the conversation with highly-focused interest. Roosevelt paced for a moment. "Philander, this man will do. I want him on board as quickly as you can get rid of the charges against him."

Knox looked at Roosevelt with questioning eyes. "On board for what?"

Taking the time to look at each man seated at the table, Roosevelt paused for an instant. "I want everyone to know – nothing said here goes outside this room. Is that clear?" Each one nodded.

"Mr. Stanton, I need a man like you to find these anarchists and put an end to them."

"What . . . ?"

"You heard me. That's the deal. We'll give you whatever training you need, and you'll have our total support. As far as the public is concerned, though, you'll be on your own."

"Mr. President, you've got the wrong man. That's not for me."

His voice rising, the President declared, "Then the charges stay as they are and you'll stand trial."

"You can't do that," Stanton protested.

Roosevelt flashed his characteristic smile, showing his large white teeth. "Do you want to bet?"

"Look, Mr. President, I love my country, but I know nothing about anarchists. I'm a businessman, not a spy."

Roosevelt sat back down. He surveyed his audience, briefly removing his glasses to rub his eyes. "Mr. Stanton, I want you and the others to have a clear understanding of why this is so critical to me." Gently clearing his throat, he continued, "Many of you know how close I was to President McKinley, closer than most vice-presidents. I considered him one of my dearest friends. Maybe I've lived too long, but it didn't seem possible that this particular president could be assassinated. He was hardly a man of even moderate means. He was about as well off as a railroad superintendent. He lived in a little house in Canton; he came from the typical hard-working farmer stock of this country.

"In every instinct and feeling, he was the absolute representative of the men who make up the bulk of this nation – the small merchants, clerks and farmers. His one great anxiety while president was to keep in touch with this body of Americans and to give expression to their needs and wants. He made himself accessible to anyone who needed to see him. I *never* heard him assail or denounce any man or any group of men."

The President paused to look out at the overcast day through the tall window on the side of the room. He thought of how sorely he would miss McKinley. Stanton's eyes were fixed on him; Secretary Root had reached for a cigar while Knox was scribbling on a small pad. The others were listening intently.

Continuing, he said, "This is what puzzles me the most. Under the present conditions of our national prosperity, of popular content, of democratic simplicity, and of President McKinley's absolute representative character, it's impossible for me to fathom the minds of men who would murder him."

Shifting his gaze to Stanton, he said in a lower voice, "We have to stop these anarchists, and the active and passive sympathizers who help them. We know who a few of them are, but not the great many of them. Until we root them out, our way of life, our constitution and our government, are at grave risk."

Putting both hands on the table, he leaned forward. "Mr. Stanton, I need your help. You have the wealth, the connections, the intelligence and the savvy to help us find them. You've been charged as an anarchist; they won't recognize you as one of us." Seeing the discomfort in Stanton's eyes, he added, "I'm not asking for your life – I'm asking for your time, perhaps a year, and your patriotic duty to your country. You'll work directly with me and Secretary Root. May I have your answer?"

"Could we discuss this in your office, Mr. President?"

"There's nothing we could say there that can't be said here. What's on your mind?"

"The woman I mentioned. I have to contact her."

"We'll help you do that. Is your answer yes?"

With a rush of misgivings, Stanton nodded his head in approval.

*   *   *   *

The press conference the next day was held in a large conference room in the Federal Building. Knox and Neeley conducted the meeting; Wilcox stood silently next to them. Over one hundred journalists were present, including a very attractive woman who represented the *Baltimore Sun*. Knox began the announcement. "Ladies and gentlemen, thank you for coming. As you know, my department, in conjunction with police agencies across the country, is conducting an extensive investigation into the murder of our beloved president, William McKinley." Stopping to clear his throat, he turned to look at Neeley.

"That investigation led us to charge Mr. Matthew Stanton, one of our leading entrepreneurs, with masterminding the assassination plot. We relied on evidence that, shall I say, fell into our laps. We have now determined that the evidence was erroneous, and we are at fault for not realizing that at an earlier time. We have put Mr. Stanton through a great deal, and for that we are sorry. We should have done a much better job than we did. With all of that said, we are here to announce that all charges against Mr. Stanton have been dropped, and this morning he was released from federal custody. I must say that Mr. Stanton has been very gracious throughout his ordeal. If it had been me, I would have shot the bastards." He paused while many in the room laughed.

"Mr. Stanton has asked one thing of us. He's been trying to contact a Miss Alise Collwell. Mr. Stanton can be reached at his company, Far East Shipping in New York. If you would be so kind to print that, it would help him in his efforts to locate Ms. Collwell. Now, Chicago Police Commissioner Jay Neeley, who has been invaluable to our investigation, will answer any questions you may have. Commissioner."

Neeley stepped to the podium and pointed to a reporter in the front row. "Commissioner," he said, "there was a report of a possible second shooter of President McKinley. Any leads on who that might be?"

"I would like to tell you where we are with that, but I'm afraid it might compromise our investigation. But I will say this. Leon Franz

Czolgosz did not act alone. There are others involved, and we will find them."

He turned to other reporters, and after thirty minutes, the press conference was ended. The attractive woman then made her way to the podium. She tapped Knox on the shoulder, and he spun around to hear her question. He first noticed how striking she looked in her tall-collared, cream silk blouse that reached to her chin, with a black onyx necklace hanging around her neck. His gaze roamed down to her shapely small-waisted figure, accentuated by a flowing dark green skirt that brushed the floor. In her left arm, she held an expensive fur coat. Her face was partially concealed beneath a broad-brimmed hat, layered with a mass of feathers. He doubted that she was a reporter. "Mr. Attorney General, excuse me. I'm from the *Baltimore Sun*. Could you tell me where Mr. Stanton is at the moment?"

"I'm not sure he wants to be contacted, particularly if you're a reporter. But as I said earlier, he owns Far East Shipping, based out of New York. You might try to reach him there." She thanked him and turned away.

PART II

CHAPTER SIXTEEN

▼

The White House

"Good evening, sir," he managed to say as he sat in a large leather chair across from the President.

Theodore Roosevelt looked at him with probing eyes. "I won't keep you long." There was no characteristic broad smile.

"Mr. President, I want to thank you for the kind things that were said at the press conference today. They were unexpected."

Without responding, the President reached into his desk drawer, removed a photograph, and tossed it across the desk. "Know anyone in that picture, Mr. Stanton?"

Stanton needed only several seconds to recognize it. "I do, Mr. President. You . . . . me, and quite a few others."

Roosevelt's penetrating eyes focused on Stanton. "September 15, 1898, the day we all went home. You and I shook hands. I wish you had stepped forward earlier and told me you were with me on San Juan Hill. I had a feeling about you, but I wasn't entirely sure." He stood up and reached for Stanton's hand. "It isn't often I have one of my Rough Riders sitting across from me. I'm baffled, Mr. Stanton. Why would you volunteer to ride up San Juan Hill with me? You're wealthy; you took a great risk."

Stanton smiled and shook the President's hand. "It was only for five months. You were there, and it was something I didn't want to miss. At the time, I thought I would be part of a historic moment. It turns out I was right."

Roosevelt looked puzzled. "Why didn't you tell me sooner? It would have made a difference."

Hesitating, Stanton answered, "It just didn't seem like the right thing to do."

Roosevelt nodded slightly. "I think I can understand that." He added, "I'm proud to see you again, Captain. If you *had* gotten word to me when you were arrested, I can promise you that you would never have seen the inside of that jail." Flipping open his pocket watch, he said, "It's past nine. Let's get to the point. Someone tried to frame you for the assassination. He knew a lot about you. You're the one to find him."

Stanton shook his head. "I've searched my brain. I have no idea why anyone would want to do that."

"You'll find the answer," Roosevelt said with conviction. "I'm smart enough to know facts from bullshit, and I know you are too. Mr. Wilcox doesn't seem to have that ability." Pausing to light a cigar, he said, "Mr. Stanton, some members of the press will fry me over what happened today. I need someone I can completely trust. I've got members of my cabinet on both sides of your case. I frankly don't have time for this. There's a bull's-eye on my back. I want you to get it off."

Stanton sat in silence, his eyes locked on the President.

"You've heard of William Randolph Hearst?"

"Yes."

"He's a goddamned anarchist. That son-of-a-bitch has his people working night and day against me. He's fanning the fires. He's already got his friends in *my* government putting together names and files to hurt me. Over on Constitution Avenue, they'll make every part of this a damn partisan issue. The Democrats don't like me one bit; there are members of my own party who feel the same way. They didn't want me to be president; they promoted me as vice president to get me out of New York. I was making things too messy for them." He was getting angry. Putting down his cigar, he stood and paced while he removed his glasses to clean them with his tie.

"I know what's going on in this country. Hearst's a cheat, a trouble-maker, a bastard and a goddamned liar. And he's a dangerous goddamned liar. He owns a dozen newspapers, and he'll use them to get at me. The public will listen to him. Mr. Stanton, there are a lot of screwball Americans out there with a streak of anarchism in them. What would you say if I told you Hearst had a thick file on you?"

"Me?"

"You're the only other one in this room. Yes, you. And also me. I have a feeling there's a strong sense of honesty in you. And loyalty. I need that."

Stanton didn't move, totally focused on Roosevelt. The agitation in the President's voice was unmistakable.

Pacing back and forth, he said, "There's a tide rising in America, Mr. Stanton. We're the most prosperous nation on Earth, but a lot of our people are poor as church mice and go to bed hungry. They're not going to tolerate it much longer. I've got to do something about that. I've only been in office six weeks, but those bastards on Wall Street are already calling me every name in the book, including Socialist and Communist. People in my own party are going to turn on me."

Stanton interrupted. "Mr. President, I'm not sure where you're going with this. I can't fix all your problems."

Roosevelt stopped his pacing and looked at him with displeasure. "You know damn well that's not what I'm asking. I want you to get me names and proof of who these anarchists are. I'll give you the means and whatever else you need. You run the biggest shipping company on the East Coast. You can do this. But I'm telling you something, Mr. Stanton. You report to me. You understand that?"

Sweat was forming on Stanton's palms. He rubbed his hands briskly together to dry them. "Yes, sir."

"And another thing. This is between you and me. I can deal with mistakes, but I don't want a public crucifixion. I don't want to see innocent people hurt. I know that's not in you, but things happen. Just be sure they don't happen in the wrong way. Do you get what I'm saying?"

Stanton's mind was spinning. What in the hell was he asking? He wasn't sure, but he nodded yes. Roosevelt returned to his desk and extended his hand to indicate the meeting was over. Stanton stood, shook it, and was surprised when the President picked up from his desk a small box and handed it to him. "Mr. Stanton, you may never need this, but I want you to have it. You'll find inside not only the latest Colt pocket .41, but also credentials identifying you as a government agent and allowing you to carry the gun. You rode with me; I know you're an expert shot – that's good. I want you to keep all of this strictly between the two of us and Secretary Root. All your communications to me should be directed through him. I want to be kept up to date on everything."

Stanton nodded his appreciation and turned to leave. Before reaching the door, he heard, "Oh, Mr. Stanton, thanks for volunteering to help me - again." He turned to see Roosevelt's broad smile.

He walked out, thinking, *Thanks, my ass*. But he didn't say it.

CHAPTER SEVENTEEN

▼

New York City

A bitter storm of wind, sleet and snow was lashing the entire East Coast when Stanton stepped inside his spacious office in Manhattan. It was ten in the morning, two days after his meeting with Roosevelt. On his desk was the latest edition of the *New York Morning Journal*. He closed the door, threw his coat across a chair, and sat back to see piles of files and documents that had accumulated since his last visit over two months ago. Glancing at the newspaper, his mouth fell open as he looked upon front page pictures of a woman purporting to be Alise Collwell. In a lead article, the paper said she had talked exclusively to one of its reporters and had told of secret evidence about the assassination. The article also spoke of "rumors" of an affair that she was having with Stanton. Forged letters, claiming to have been written by her, were printed to show she was now in hiding in fear of anarchists. It was yellow journalism at its best, a trademark of William Randolph Hearst, and had been completely fabricated by him.

Other newspapers owned by him were full of more wild speculation about Alise Collwell. Who was she, and why had her name been mentioned at the press conference? *The San Francisco Examiner* and *The Chicago American*, also Hearst newspapers, repeated Hearst's fabrications. The circulation of his newspapers doubled overnight.

Stanton tossed the newspaper into a nearby waste basket and turned to look out the large window behind his desk, staring at the tug boats and barges struggling to navigate the icy Hudson River. He studied the scene, both as a man under enormous strain and as one consumed by an eerie curiosity. Out there, somewhere in that vast space, was someone who wanted him hung for the assassination of William McKinley. That someone had gone to immeasurable lengths to forge his handwriting so accurately that it was difficult to tell it from his own, and had broken into his home in order to plant damning evidence of his guilt. They wanted him dead.

His curiosity shifted to Alyssa, wondering if she were alive or dead at the hands of her insane husband. The realization suddenly occurred to him that she was the most agonizing part of his thoughts. He sought clarity where little was to be found, probing through the lens of a microscope as a scientist would, peering with cold anxiety to find what his eyes couldn't see and his mind couldn't understand. The known and the unknown flashed through his brain, leaving him with a deep sense of foreboding. He searched his memory, seeking recognition of anyone who would hate him so much as to single him out for death. He had made formidable enemies, and that made the exercise a more painful one. It ended with a knock on his door. He blinked several times to clear his head, and said, "Come in."

Standing at the doorway was a surprised Robert Longbourne. "You should have wired that you were coming." Attempting a smile, he continued, "So it's now all over." Waiting for a response and hearing none, he asked, "Are you here for long?"

Rising to shake his hand, Stanton answered, "Not long. Robert, I'm once again in your eternal gratitude for what you've done for me. You risked everything, and I'll never forget it."

"You would do the same for me."

Stanton sat down and motioned Longbourne to a nearby chair. Under his breath, he replied, "Without doubt."

"So you're free to go back to your former life."

Inhaling a deep breath, Stanton shook his head. "I'm afraid not."

"You're not? That woman . . . Alise?"

"No, not her." Stanton looked away, lost in thought. "There are things I have to do." He turned back and gave Longbourne a look that meant, "Don't ask." "By the way, how's business?"

Longbourne knew the subject had been closed. "Booming. Your wealth is expanding by the hour." He could tell from Stanton's blank expression that it meant nothing to him.

"Robert, I need your help. Have a seat."

"I'm listening," he replied.

Leaning forward, Stanton said, "The person who tried to frame me for McKinley's murder - he knew me pretty well. I need you to search your memory, to talk to people who work for me. Someone knew enough to open a bank account in my name and to plant that gun in my house. He – or they – also had access to my letters. The forgeries not only were virtually identical to my handwriting, but they were written in a form that I would have used."

"What are you suggesting, Matthew?"

"We have a traitor here at the company. And maybe someone who works for me at my house. Talk to people, think of who might hate me enough to do that."

Longbourne grunted. "You haven't tried to make many friends here."

"No, I haven't."

"Let me say that another way. Try not to take this too personally, but Matthew, you've given a lot of people reasons to dislike you."

Stanton narrowed his eyes in deep thought. After several moments, he said, "Focus on the word *hate*. Robert, I'm not a poster child for human relations. I know that. Nevertheless, someone has gone to a lot of trouble to destroy me. Work on that."

Longbourne nodded. "Anything else?"

"Yes. I may be gone for a while. Use the codes and methods we set up before to contact me. I'd just as soon not have anybody know where I am or what I'm doing."

Longbourne had a puzzled look in his eyes. "Do you want to tell me?"

"I'd like to, but this isn't the time. Thanks, Robert."

*   *   *   *

The message arrived two hours later. It was delivered personally to him. He opened it to see five words and two initials. "The Savoy, at noon tomorrow. A.C." For Matthew Stanton, there had been only one decision. He was obsessed with her; he could not get her out of his thoughts. He would meet with her.

Emotionally close to tears, the next day Alyssa sat in a corner table behind a vase of pink roses in the opulent restaurant of the Savoy Hotel, with its glittering chandeliers, Grecian marble columns and antique mirrored walls. She had been waiting since eleven o'clock. Glancing at the small gold watch she had placed on the table, she saw that her wait had now been over an hour. She had said noon, but in desperation had hoped he would come before then. Closing her eyes, she said a silent prayer that he had read her message. Suddenly he was standing over her, gently whispering, "Hello, Alyssa."

She forced her eyes open and gazed into his deep brown eyes. "Oh my God, you came."

"And you knew Alise Collwell was you."

She nodded, dabbing her moist eyes with a lace handkerchief.

He leaned down to kiss her on the cheek and then sat down across from her. Noticing her watch, he said, "I'm sorry if you were waiting long. In this weather, the carriages move at a snail's pace." He couldn't help but stare at her creamy yellow dress, her gold jewelry encased in diamonds, and her blue eyes that had captured him the moment they met. "Alyssa," he said softly, "you're more beautiful than I remembered." In thoughtful silence, he saw, even in her despair, the glow that illuminated her expressive eyes and her natural elegance that Clayton Harding couldn't destroy. But she was still married to him.

"Matthew, I'm so very . . . ."

"Please don't say it," he asked, reaching out for her hand. "You had no reason to know. My life has been hell. I didn't know if he had found you, what he would do. Are you all right?"

Stopping to calm her nerves, she whispered, "He found me."

"But you're here."

"He murdered a man in Chicago, a friend who risked everything to get me away from him. He was my agent years ago. Now he's dead because of me."

"I'm sorry. What can I do to help you?"

"They set you free."

"Yes, they did."

She looked at him, consumed with guilt. "You begged me to listen to you, but I wouldn't. Can you ever forgive me?"

"Alyssa, that was a bad time for both of us. Don't think about that. Tell me what I can do."

She inhaled deeply and was still for several moments. "Help me get away."

"I have a house here, a place where no one will find you. You need to rest. Then we'll work out a plan."

An expression of intense relief came over her.

He stood up, put five dollars on the table, and took her hand. "Let's go. Where are your things?"

"In this hotel."

"I'll have them sent." They walked quickly through the restaurant and past two men who stared at her. The men then spoke quietly to themselves, wondering what Clayton Harding would pay to know that his wife was with another man. They hurriedly paid their check and left, one attempting to follow Stanton while the other went to the telegraph office.

CHAPTER EIGHTEEN

▼

New York

His 5th Avenue home had surprised her. It was a magnificent three-story gray stone structure, decorated in the lavish style of the Gilded Age, located in one of the most exclusive neighborhoods of the city. She walked slowly across the black and white Italian marble floor in the entry hall to view a painting of an English duchess astride a stunning black Arabian stallion. Below it was a Louis XVI chest with trim that appeared to be solid gold. Stepping back to study the rider, she was temporarily transfixed by the shadows drifting back and forth across the woman's soft complexion and green eyes from the lights of sixteen candles burning in a gold and crystal chandelier above her head. Hearing a movement behind her, she turned to see Matthew leaning against the soft green painted oak-paneled walls.

"You like that?"

"I do, very much. It must be very valuable."

"It is. The painter has a similar one hanging in the British Museum." He reached down to pick up her suitcase which had been deposited by the doorman. "I'll take this into your bedroom."

While he walked down the hallway, Alyssa moved quietly from room to room, viewing the fine art and antiques collected from auction houses around the world. She stopped in the library. Allowing her eyes to drift over the hundreds of books in highly polished dark walnut book cases, she noted an extensive collection of the classics, books on astronomy and the sciences, and a large number of law books. She also saw Jane Austen and *Alice's Adventures in Wonderland*. Picking up that book, she turned to see him watching her. Smiling with a sheepish grin, she held up the book and said, "You're a man of great interests. I'm impressed."

"Don't be. I haven't read half of them. But the book you're holding, I've read it a number of times. It's a book of great wisdom. If you haven't read it, you should."

She fell back into a large chair, laughing out loud. "A child's book?"

He walked over to her. "This is the first time I've heard you laugh. You should make a habit of that. And by the way, it's a lot more than a child's book."

Her laughter suddenly faded, and he could see the storm mounting in her eyes.

"Don't do that, Alyssa. You have to get him out of your mind."

"I can't, not while he's trying to kill me." Nervously, she blurted out, "Matthew, will you help me find someone who will kill him. I have some money; I sold most of my jewelry."

He was startled. "What are you thinking? That's murder. Get a divorce."

She choked bitterly. "A divorce won't matter to him. There's no other way. If I don't kill him, he'll kill me. You don't know him. He murdered Chester. The police know he did, but they can't do a thing."

"I'll talk to him."

She looked at him with eyes that bordered on disbelief. "You'll what? He'll kill you!" Then the dam of tears broke; she covered her face with her hands, and her body shook with wrenching sobs. She felt his hands close on her shoulders, and she let him pull her forward into his arms. He was painfully glad for the silent comfort he could offer her. He pressed a handkerchief into her hand, and Alyssa shuddered, struggling desperately for control. "Go ahead and say it," she told him, wiping her eyes. "I was stupid to marry him."

"You won't get any argument from me on that."

"Thank you," she said sarcastically, dabbing at her eyes.

"He'll listen to me. Believe me, I won't give him a choice."

Her spirits lifted at the confidence she heard in his voice. Alyssa looked at him, struck by his rigid determination and calm rationality in the face of the hopeless facts she had presented to him. She held her gaze, her head tipped back, unable to take her eyes off of him. What she saw was the same remarkably handsome man she had met on the train, but there was a difference that at first she couldn't quite place. He seemed tougher, his eyes more sure, and his smile a little harder. Her lips found his, and she was lost in his arms while her tongue gently explored his. Pulling slightly away, her eyes were captured by his. She breathed, "He's mad, totally stark raving mad. He'll never listen to you."

"He'll listen," he repeated. Watching her study him, he knew she was rating his chances at succeeding with Clayton. "There *will* be a way." Taking her hand, he led her over to a large marble fireplace that soon had a warm crackling fire. Sitting beside him on a deep blue velvet sofa, Alyssa stared at the shadows that danced off the walls from the fire. When she asked him what he would do, he turned sullen, looking into the fire. Under his breath, he said, "I'm going to get him out of your life."

She stole a sideways glance at him, wondering what would happen after that. They'd known each other for such a short time, and now more than ever she was beginning to realize what a burden she was to him. She tried to gauge his mood, but couldn't.

"What were you thinking about?" she asked abruptly.

A slight frown crossed his face. "Private things."

Her uneasiness escalated quickly. She understood with sudden clarity her strong reaction. Her first impulse was to let it go, but she went with her second and decided to ask him what he meant.

"That's not an answer."

"No, it's not. I was trying to figure out how to rid you of your husband while at the same time dealing with some other very difficult problems that seem to have fallen upon me."

She expelled a deep breath. "I can relieve you of that burden by leaving now."

"Let me be the judge of that. Alyssa, I'm drowning in guilt. I've led a thoroughly selfish life, rarely thinking of anyone other than myself, and now I've met you. I haven't yet figured out how to handle that."

"Handle that or handle me?" she asked, stepping closer to him.

He held out his arms to her, and she walked into them. Feeling the warmth of her body against his, he whispered, "That's not what I meant." She raised her face to his and kissed him, her lips sensuously caressing his in what seemed to be an eternity.

Breathless, she slowly pulled away, barely controlling her desire. "Whatever happens, I'm going to divorce Clayton. I don't know what your expectations are for the future, but I know mine."

He shook his head.

"What is it?"

Rubbing his eyes, he said, "To tell you the truth, I don't know that I've ever liked anything about my life. Not until now."

Leaning back into his arms, she said, "I've hated mine."

Pulling her close, he said, "I may have to leave for a while. Not long, but several months."

She said nothing. "It's after midnight." He released her and stood up. Taking her hand, he said, "Let's go to bed."

He left her to walk through the first floor, putting out the gas lamps. Returning, he took her to a bedroom at the end of the hallway on the second floor. When they approached the door, she took control and said, "Good night, Matthew." Stepping into the room, she turned to smile shakily and gently closed the door. He knew perfectly well that he might convince her to come to bed with him, but he was adamantly unwilling to do that. He walked down to his bedroom, leaving his door ajar.

Clad only in boxer shorts, he lay back in bed, turning over in his mind how his life had changed and thinking of the woman down the hall. Tonight he had come to realize that she was totally without affectation, that there was an unmistakable gentility in her, a natural elegance that was as appealing to him as her gorgeous face. His thoughts then shifted to Roosevelt and his commitment to find the anarchists who had murdered McKinley. The obstacles he faced were enormous. Weariness finally took over and his eyes closed.

Down the hall, Alyssa took off her layers of clothing, unbelted her corset, and put on a silk nightgown given to her by Clayton. Reaching up, she removed the combs that held her hair in a bun above her head and allowed her hair to fall down around her shoulders. She was torn in her yearning to be in bed with Matthew, yet silently grieved for what might happen to him because of her. Why hadn't he tried to talk her into sleeping with him? She wondered if his feelings for her were out of pity or as deep as she had begun to feel for him. She knew she had become wildly attracted to him. Her heart beating rapidly, she opened the door to her room and walked softly down to his. Peering through the half-closed door, she saw that he was asleep and turned to leave.

"Don't, Alyssa." She froze and turned to see him pull the covers back on his bed. She hesitated, and then walked over and lay next to him. His arms engulfed her and he pulled her to him. Her cheek against his, she put a leg across him and closed her eyes. He was intoxicated by her perfume, her soft hair and the warmth of her body against him. After a few minutes, he found her lips and captured them with his. "Oh, Matthew," was the last thing she remembered saying as his tongue entered her parted lips and she felt his hand move to caress her beneath her gown. Later, as she lay in his arms, drifting in and out of sleep, the fears that had taken control of her life seemed to fade away.

CHAPTER NINETEEN

▼

New York

The next morning, while she was half asleep, he put a breakfast tray on the nightstand and sat on the bed next to her. She looked at him through partially closed eyes, thinking of nothing except that she was falling in love. "Thank you for the best night of my life."

He gave her a boyish grin.

"Why are you smiling?"

"That, my darling, was a pointed reminder to me to fight off my temptation to make love to you again."

She sat up against her pillow, her hair loose across her eyes. "You don't have to do that."

He frowned. "Don't make it easy. We have plans to make."

She looked over at the tray. "Please take it so that we can have breakfast together. I would like to look a little more presentable."

Reaching for the tray, he said, "You couldn't be more beautiful to me. Take your time. I'll meet you in the breakfast room."

She walked downstairs twenty minutes later. Dressed in a flowing satin robe, she saw that he had prepared for them a breakfast of soft-boiled eggs, grapefruit, and coffee. The bright orange sun was rising, promising a brisk but beautiful day. Sitting across from him, she wondered if he knew how she felt about him.

"Alyssa," he said softly, "you are the most exquisite woman I've ever known."

"Exquisite? In the morning, here in my robe?"

He laughed. "Don't try to be humble. You walked in here looking as if you had just posed for a magazine cover." Unable to take his eyes off of her, he said softly, "My God, you are gorgeous." Reaching across the table for her hand, his gaze was drawn to her sparkling blue eyes. "I'm mad about you."

She closed her eyes and squeezed his hand. "And I'm mad about you."

*   *   *   *

Thirty minutes later, two men walked up to his front door. Knocking several times, they waited.

Alyssa had gone upstairs to her bedroom and was in the bath. Matthew walked into the kitchen, poured himself another cup of coffee, and headed toward his bedroom. His thoughts were interrupted by the knocking on the door. He froze. No one knew she was here. The knocking became a pounding on the door. He heard a muted voice say, "Police."

Matthew yelled, "One minute," and rushed to the library. There, he opened a desk drawer and removed the Colt given to him by Roosevelt. It wasn't loaded. He nervously grabbed a box of cartridges and had loaded three shells when the door was crashed in. He heard a scrambling of feet and voices whispering. There were two of them. Then another voice from the top of the stairs. "Matthew, is everything all right?"

He screamed, "Stay where you are. Lock your door." Without thinking, he ran into the hallway to see the two men, guns in their hands, rushing toward the staircase. He shifted his stance and yelled, "Stop." Both men spun around, raising their guns. Matthew pulled the trigger, the crack of the shot surprising the shorter one as he looked at Matthew in amazement. The shot hit him between the eyes. His surprised expression quickly turned to one of fear, and then death. The taller man fired twice, one of the bullets striking Matthew in the chest.

His movement slowed from the wound, Matthew found the strength to level his gun at the second assailant and fire once. Struggling to remain standing, he cocked the gun and fired again. The first shot pierced the gunman's cheek and the second hit him in the stomach. Thrown violently back against the wall, the assailant's gun fell from his grip. Slipping down the wall to the floor, he tried desperately to reach the gun only to see Matthew's foot kick it away. Weakened by the shot but shaking with anger, Matthew grabbed his hair, jerked his head up and demanded, "Who sent you?" The blood filled eyes stared back at him with no response. He slammed his fist into the dying man's head and screamed again, "Who – was it Harding?" The man smiled, let out a painful moan, and died.

Trying desperately to catch his breath, his vision blurred and his mind went blank. Losing all mobility, he sank to the floor. When the pounding of his heart finally slowed, he heard the hysterical sobbing of Alyssa. Attempting to stand to help her, he was overwhelmed with nausea and fell headlong back onto the floor. Then everything went dark.

*   *   *   *

For more than three days, he lay in the hospital bed. Slowly consciousness returned, and with it, pain – a heavy thudding in his skull and a stabbing in his chest. He lay still, aware only of the pain. Could he move? Through the murkiness of his brain, he tried to figure out where he was. He could hear soft sounds near him. He was in bad shape, but how bad? His head continued to throb and his chest was hot with agony. He worked his fingers and opened his eyes to the smallest slits. His memories were filled with the faces of his attackers and the explosion of their guns.

A door opened. He could see through the haze in his eyes a woman, wearing a broad feathered hat and a light blue skirt, a jacket with shoulder pads, and a white silk blouse. He could feel her hand in his and her cheek against his face. "You're going to get well," she whispered. "Don't try to move."

"Where . . . am I?"

"The New York General Hospital."

He tried to raise himself up, but got only several inches before his strength gave way. "How . . . ?"

"Matthew, you were shot."

The door opened and a doctor in a white jacket walked in. "Mr. Stanton, I'm Dr. Broderick. How are you feeling today?"

Shaking his head slightly, he said, "Terrible. When can I leave?"

"Not for a while. You were shot through the chest. The bullet passed through your right side, barely missing vital arteries and your lung. You were very lucky. Within several weeks, you should be recovered enough to leave. The President has personally asked about you. Believe me, you will have the best of care here. Miss Coolidge here has been with you every day. You're fortunate to have such good friends as she and the President."

Alyssa was astonished. "The President?"

The doctor looked at her and smiled. "My thoughts exactly. Yes, Theodore Roosevelt."

She looked back at Matthew, and his eyes told her to leave it alone.

CHAPTER TWENTY

▼

Long Island, New York

The day was pleasantly cold and sunny, with just enough breeze to make small waves across the surface of the water. The men were among the most distinguished in New York. They wore dark, high-button suits with vests and expensive silk ties from the Orient, draped with heavy fur-lined wool overcoats. They were some of America's wealthiest. The shiny black carriages, with their Eisenglass windows and velvet interiors, would take them down the tree lined streets of Glen Cove to their appointed destination. The road twisted along the North Shore of Long Island, from Great Neck to Huntington – the "Gold Coast" of the rich and famous. From the Astors to the Vanderbilts, the North Shore was home to the who's who of American high society.

The carriages passed by enormous French renaissance, English, and Gilded-Age American mansions in the hundreds. They were hidden far behind massive stone gates and pines trees that formed a perfect line down the parkway. The residences with the most enviable views overlooked the harbor and the ocean. They had enormously high ceilings, interiors of the finest polished wood, and antiques collected from around the world, and were surrounded by reinforced windows made to withstand the winds and winter storms.

One such house, in the Belmont district, was different from the others. Not in size or elegance, or in the gardens that surrounded it, or in the impressiveness of its front gate and the height of the stone wall bordering its grounds, but in its sense of isolation. Especially at night, the few gas lamps that lit the interior gave the impression that it was unoccupied. But what dramatically set it apart from the others were the unseen men, heavily armed with shotguns and revolvers, who patrolled its grounds.

After being stopped for inspection at the gates, the carriages made their way down a long drive over the one hundred acre estate to the sixty-room mansion. There, the men were taken through the huge entry hall, with its massive winding staircase, down a corridor until they reached a pair of large double doors. The gray-haired, impeccably dressed man there to meet them had a lined, elongated face with a salt and pepper beard that gave witness to his sixty-five years. His hand extended, he said in a low, gravelly voice, "Gentlemen, how good of you to come."

"It's a pleasure to see you again, Mr. Pratt." The speaker was Edmund Morris, owner of the Northeastern Railway and a member of the Beltline Trust.

"Mr. Pratt," added Anthony Waldrop, a somewhat obese man with red hair and eyes that hid behind dark glasses rimmed in steel that did not convey geniality, "there are things to be said here, things that no one should hear but the six of us. Is this a safe place for our meeting?"

"Follow me," said Pratt as he led them across the room to a door in the far corner that opened to a private drawing room. Motioning to a dark walnut table with chairs covered in brown leather, he said, "Please be seated." At five feet, eleven inches, Thaddeus Pratt was taller than many men of the day. He was heavy around the waist, weighing in at two hundred pounds, not solid but a little chubby, the result of a good appetite and the rich foods served at the private clubs to which he belonged. His mouth turned upward slightly, deceptively giving the effect of a permanent slight smile. Many thought him handsome. Outwardly, he appeared as threatening as his gardener.

Pratt did not have the appearance of a corrupt and depraved sociopath, but inwardly he had no reservations about bribing public officials, extorting money, and cheating his adversaries when it led to more wealth. Severely beating or even clubbing to death union protesters and others who would do harm to his businesses was to him a necessary way of life. More than anything about his appearance, though, were his eyes. No one who met him could forget his eyes. They were almost the purest black and revealed a dark personality that belied what appeared to be a good-tempered man. They burned with a frightening degree of malevolence and were so penetrating that men who worked for him would swear he could look into their thoughts. He was as unscrupulous and devoid of ethics and character as the worst criminals of the times. His uncanny ability for exploiting people for their money served him well; he thrived on manipulation and deceit.

Thaddeus Pratt fit well with many of the tycoons of the early twentieth century – Jay Gould, Daniel Drew, John Rockefeller and the many others who had become so well known as the "Robber Barons". With them he had formed monopolizing trusts - cartels that choked off free trade. The trusts were hugely profitable to Pratt. He had amassed more money than he could spend in several life times, but there was an unyielding determination in his sinister mind to obtain even more. There could never be enough. His insane obsession with money led him to believe he would never face a day of reckoning – he was too rich, too powerful, to ever be brought down.

McKinley was dead, and Pratt had miscalculated. The new president had vowed to destroy the trusts that had become Pratt's lifeblood, and Theodore Roosevelt had a plan to achieve his ends. Congress had passed anti-trust laws, but prior administrations had never enforced them. Roosevelt would. It was time to stop him.

"Gentlemen," Pratt began, "we have a problem. McKinley saw himself as the people's president. His policies were aimed at us, and we had to do something." Looking around the table, he saw worried looks. "We all thought Roosevelt would be our friend. He was a conservative Republican, a man we knew. He fooled us. He's a goddamned liberal Democrat, hiding in a Republican's skin."

Waldrop interrupted. "You had McKinley killed. Are you now saying you want to do something with Roosevelt?"

Intense anger filled Pratt's eyes and voice. "I didn't kill McKinley! That anarchist, Leon Czolgosz, shot him."

Edmund Morris, the most sanguine of the group, twisted his thumbs as he listened. Speaking with grim determination, he said, "Thaddeus, this is absurd! Czolgosz was insane, I'll grant you that, but you had his mind filled with garbage and you pushed him along. Emma Goldman never believed in all that crap – you used her. And then you made it worse, you decided to frame Stanton as the mastermind. That was a stupid miscalculation."

Pratt eyes were fuming. "You knew goddamned well what I was doing. Czolgosz's been executed; no one suspects us."

Waldrop was agitated. "Not yet! But if you try a hare-brained scheme to murder Roosevelt, you're fuckin' out of your mind. Then they *will* begin to look at us."

Pratt silently wondered if he should kill them all. Speaking deliberately and with little emotion, he responded, "Are you so dumb not to realize he has no vice president? If Roosevelt dies, the speaker of the house will succeed him. James Armington is the damned Speaker. He's a lily-livered idiot with no backbone. He can be bought, and I'll do it! When he's president, we'll have our man in the White House."

"And what if he turns out to be a lion in sheep's clothing? You were damn sure wrong about Roosevelt."

"I won't be wrong about Armington. If I am, I'll kill him, too."

Horrified looks were shown around the table. One person asked, "Are you mad?"

Pratt was incensed. "Get the hell out of here, all of you. I'll do this myself. And let me warn you – one word from any of you and I'll produce documents showing your involvement in the McKinley killing."

Morris was startled. "What documents?"

Pratt smiled. "Eyewitness reports, signed letters. What else do you need?"

"All manufactured, you son-of-a-bitch. Just like you did with Stanton. He beat you."

"But you won't. You're here at this meeting, and I have men listening to everything you've said. Keep your damned mouths shut! When it's done, you'll thank me." Standing, he mumbled, "Thank God we've got anarchists."

The silence was deafening. Slowly the others stood, one by one, and filed out of the room, all except Samuel Dutton. One thought occupied each person's mind: he would do it, and there was nothing anyone could do to stop him.

Pratt stared at Dutton. Dutton owned one of the largest brokerage houses in the country and had, with his competitors, formed an alliance to control and manipulate transactions completed over the New York Stock Exchange. The alliance was solidified as an old-fashioned cartel, the Exchange Trust. "You were silent throughout the meeting. Why?" Pratt asked.

"You knew you had my support. Their phony indignation pissed me off. They'll come around. I stayed to let you know I'm in."

Pratt walked over to him and shook his hand. "Let's make plans to kill that son-of-a-bitch."

CHAPTER TWENTY-ONE

▼

New York

Someone was following her. For the first week of her daily visits to the hospital, nothing seemed out of place; she felt safe. She had moved to the Madison Hotel because Clayton knew about Stanton's home on 5th Avenue. A private carriage driver with a guard was hired by Stanton to wait for her each night outside the hospital and take her to the hotel. Then, suddenly, things began to change.

She started to notice a man who stood in the shadows away from her, watching as she stepped into her carriage. If she'd stop at a café or a shop in the hotel, she'd see him hiding behind a newspaper or magazine, but always watching her. She tried to calm her panicky feeling, telling herself that no one could know where she was, but fear was beginning to take hold.

For two days, he just watched. On the third day, as she walked out of the hospital at 8:00 PM., he was there. She avoided his eyes and looked for her guard and carriage – they weren't there! Terrified, she ran back into the hospital lobby and waited. The wait was interminable. After thirty minutes, she walked to the door and looked out on the street. He was still there, but he was now standing on the opposite side. The hospital had closed to visitors; she was told she had to leave. Looking back down the hallway, she saw a fire-exit. She walked quickly to the exit and opened the door a little. Peering out and seeing no one, she nervously pushed the door all the way open and started running, silently praying for a police officer or a hansom. Her left shoe suddenly caught on a brick in the street and was ripped off. Out of breath, she stopped, leaning down to retrieve it. Looking up, she saw him standing twenty steps away, glaring at her. She was cornered, trapped.

There was nothing else to do. Alyssa screamed, again and again. "Please," the man said as he approached her, "I'm here to protect you. I was hired by Mr. Stanton." She froze. By then, several other men had appeared. Her follower defensively held up both hands, his palms facing them. One held a detective's badge.

"Help me," she pleaded. They studied the badge and the man. "It's all right," he said. "I frightened the young lady. I'm sorry. I was hired to protect her, but I failed to tell her that." They slowly began to back away. Alyssa spun around to confront him. His appearance sent a chill down her spine. He was completely bald with a dark mustache, a flattened nose and the scarred face of a boxer. Softly and without emotion, he said, "I'm a Pinkerton agent, Mrs. Harding. I was hired to help you."

First pleading with the bystanders not to leave her, she turned to him. "Matthew Stanton never hired you!"

He hesitated. Reaching for her arm, he said, "You're wrong. Please come with me."

One of the bystanders, a tall burly man, walked up and put his hand on his arm. In a coarse voice, he warned, "I'd leave this lady alone if I was you."

The follower looked at him and then at Alyssa with hatred in his eyes. "You're making a big mistake." He shook his arm loose and backed away. Pointing his finger at her, he shouted, "This isn't over. Your husband wants you back, and that's where you'll end up." He turned and walked away.

She slumped to the ground just as a police officer appeared. "What's happening here?"

After interviewing the two men, he told them to leave. "I'll take it from here," he said. "She'll be safe at the station."

*　　　　*　　　　*　　　　*

The next morning, Alyssa failed to show up at the hospital. Alarmed that something might have happened to her, Matthew had his nurse contact the police. By late in the afternoon, they reported to him that she had not returned to his home the prior night. Examining that night's police reports, they also confirmed that there was no record of any incident involving her. That evening, Matthew checked out of the hospital against his doctor's wishes. His chest heavily bandaged, he moved slowly with a burning pain that seemed to come and go. At his home, he searched for any sign of her. Nothing!

Frantic, he sent a telegram to Secretary Root asking for federal police help. The answer came back three hours later. "Mr. Stanton, I'm sympathetic to your plight," it said. "But I have no authority to dispatch federal police to help you in this matter. Suggest you hire private detectives or work with local police. Elihu Root."

A second telegram was sent to Longbourne. "Alyssa Harding disappeared. Hire three armed detectives. Have two of them meet me at Philadelphia's Union Station at noon tomorrow. The New York Central arrival gate. Send the third to her home early in the morning to tell Harding I'm coming."

CHAPTER TWENTY-TWO

▼

Philadelphia

Clayton Harding was seething. Standing before him were Turk and Monk, and seated behind them was Alyssa. "I told you to kill her," he screamed. "Not to bring her here."

Monk glared at him. "If you want her killed, you do it. You're crazy. If she's murdered, they'll know you did it. And we know you'll point the finger at us. That's not going to happen. You owe us twenty thousand dollars."

Looking at Alyssa, Harding shouted, "You'll pay for this Alyssa. No one leaves me."

She stood up, her face red with anger. "I used to be afraid of you, you bastard. Not anymore. I'm here because they said they'd kill Matthew Stanton if I didn't come. He's done nothing to you. I'm leaving!" She turned toward the door, and Harding yelled, "Stop her!"

Turk grabbed her arm and twisted it. She let out a small cry and sat back down. Calming slightly from his frenzy, Harding glared at her. "What happened to the men I sent to New York to kill you and Stanton?"

She looked at him in disgust. "They're both dead."

Monk turned to Turk and whispered, "Jesus, we weren't the only ones he hired to kill her."

Harding smiled. "Did you think I was stupid enough to trust you two morons? I would've hired twenty more if I had needed them." He reached into his desk and pulled out a pack of bills. Throwing it at Monk, he said, "Get your ass out of here." Monk motioned to Turk, and they left through the open doorway. Whispering, he said as they hurried out, "He's going to kill her."

Turk threw up his arms. "That's his business. He's loony as a March hare."

Monk stopped him. "You don't give a shit? She's a nice lady."

"No. I don't give a shit." Outside the house, he ripped open the bills and quickly counted them. There was ten thousand dollars, not twenty. Mumbling, "That son-of-a-bitch," Turk gave five thousand dollars to Monk.

Monk looked at the money. "Let's go back and get the rest."

Turk then flipped open his watch to see it was past 11:00 PM. "Forget it," he said. "That lunatic will kill us if we do. Let's get the hell out of here."

Opening the front door, the icy wind blasted them head on. They hurried through the doorway, down the long stone walk and into the black night, stopping several times to look back at the mansion. Once through the main gate, they shook hands and headed in separate directions. Their bodies were found three days later floating in the Delaware River. They had each died from gunshot wounds to the head, and neither had any identification or money.

When the two men had left, Harding walked over to where Alyssa was sitting. Looking up, she said with fury in her eyes, "I'm not afraid of you. I hate you. I'm getting a divorce." He smiled, clenched his fist, and struck her twice with massive blows to the face. She fell over, blood trickling down her face and her eyes closed. Looking at her lifeless body, Harding grinned. "That's just the beginning, Alyssa. Tomorrow you'll know what hell is really like."

*   *   *   *

At 7:00 AM. the next morning, a detective hired by Stanton pounded on the door of the Harding residence. The butler answered and said Mr. Harding was not available. When he was asked about Mrs. Harding, the butler answered with silence. "Tell Mr. Harding," the detective warned, "that Matthew Stanton will be here this afternoon with two more detectives. If anything happens to Mrs. Harding, let Harding know he'll be arrested and locked up."

It was one thirty when Matthew and two investigators stepped to the front door of the Harding mansion. The door was opened again by the butler, who said to Stanton, "Mr. Harding is waiting for you in the drawing room." Looking at the two detectives, he said, "You two will have to wait outside." One of the men moved forward to protest; Stanton stopped him with his hand. "I'll be okay. You wait here."

Following the butler, Matthew was struck by the dark colors and the suffocating atmosphere of the house. Taken to the drawing room, he saw a well-dressed man sitting behind a large leather-top desk, his arms folded and his eyes as cold as ice. Stanton allowed his eyes to roam over the fifteen foot high ceiling, the heavily paneled dark walnut walls and bookcases, and the large deep red and gold Oriental rug covering the hard-wood floors. He then focused on Harding.

Smiling, Harding said, "So you're Alyssa's protector." Without any attempt to be cordial, he pointed to a chair in front of the desk.

Stanton took several steps forward and stopped. "Where is she?"

Harding stood up and shook a finger at Stanton. "That's none of your damn business. She's my wife, and you'll stay out of her life." His eyes shifted to the right of Stanton, and he motioned to a man to shut the large double doors. Spinning around, Matthew saw two heavy-set men standing inside the room on each side of the doors. The bigger of the two caught his eye. He was huge, towering over six feet, and massively built. His face was wide and there was an old scar crossing his cheek. He looked exactly like what he was: a thug and a brawler.

Turning back, he said, "Get rid of them. This is between you and me."

"They stay! Are you going to sit down or not?"

The heavy doors were closed and locked. Moving toward the chair, Stanton said, "She *is* my business. She may be your wife, for now, but she's not your property. I want to see her."

Harding let out a soft laugh. "She's a little under the weather. You might say she's a little beaten up."

"You bastard! Either you get her in here or I'll have the police make you."

Harding's eyes glazed over, a smile creeping across his face. Picking up the phone, he held it out to Stanton. "Here, you call them. Ask for Police Chief McKinney. Tell him you're calling from my home. He's on my payroll."

Stanton pulled a revolver from his coat and pointed it at Harding. "I'll put a bullet hole through your head if you don't get her in here now."

Hesitating, Harding placed the phone back on the desk. "You're threatening to kill me in my house! The chief will enjoy that." His eyes again drifted past Stanton and to the men standing behind him. They understood the message.

Stanton half turned to see the men coming at him. A vicious punch landed in his stomach, making him drop the gun, and a heavy boot caught him in the knee. He felt a wicked stab of pain as one man grabbed his arms while the other pounded his unprotected body and face. He tried to fight back, but the incessant pounding brought him to his knees, and when he tried to stand up, they battered him down again. There was a roaring in his skull and the taste of blood in his mouth. He was on the floor, and they were pounding, beating, and kicking him. They wouldn't quit. Out of the corner of a half-closed eye, he saw Harding's wide grin. At last, he was beaten senseless and left lying in a pool of blood.

In the far distant background, he heard a muffled voice. "Dammit, you've ruined my rug. . . . Get rid of those men outside."

"Do you want us to kill them?" another voice asked.

"Hell no. I don't want the police here. Tell them Stanton no longer needs them, or whatever you can come up with. Just get rid of them. Then come back and take Stanton down to the river. Kill him."

When the doors were opened, Harding saw a beaten and bruised Alyssa staring at him. "My God, what have you done to him?"

"He's not dead – yet. Get the hell out of here!"

She hurried over to Matthew, tears running down her cheeks. Leaning down, she whispered, "Matthew, can you move?" There was no response. She stood and rushed toward Harding, hitting him in the face with her fists. "Damn you, damn you!" she screamed. He grabbed her arms and slapped her violently until she collapsed.

Somehow, Stanton knew enough to lie still. He could hear the far-off voices and the screaming. Could he move? He tried moving his fingers. They moved stiffly, but he could move them. Through the fog in his brain, he tried to think what he could do. Harding was hitting Alyssa. He suddenly remembered the gun. Raising his head slightly, he saw it off to his right, about three feet away. Alyssa was now on the floor, Harding leaning over her. Stanton slowly eased his pain-riddled body a foot across the floor, just enough to grab the gun. He would make Harding pay. Lifting himself to his knees, he held the gun tightly in his hand. Unable at first to focus his blurry vision, he aimed it in the direction of Harding and pulled the trigger, but he missed. He then pulled himself up, struggling to steady his unsure legs.

Harding froze when he heard the shot. His eyes bulging, he turned and stared at Stanton. The next bullet hit him between the eyes, and the third struck his chin. He sagged to the floor, dead. Alyssa screamed, and Stanton spun to see the other two men. Weaving with an unsteady hand, he leveled the gun at them. They hesitated, and then suddenly one pulled a gun from his coat. Stanton shot him twice in the chest. He collapsed in front of the other man, who abruptly raised his hands above his head. Looking at a terrified Alyssa, Stanton mumbled, "My men . . . the front door." Then his mind went blank and he sunk back to the floor.

CHAPTER TWENTY-THREE

▼

Washington, D.C.

The headline of the *Washington Post* was startling: *Alleged Assassin Stanton Murders Clayton Harding.* The Hearst newspapers were having a field day. Articles were published detailing illicit love affairs, the murder of one of America's wealthiest citizens, and the possible involvement of the new president.

Theodore Roosevelt was pacing back and forth in his office, his anger rising with each pace. "What in the hell is this?" he asked, holding the paper in front of Secretary Root.

"That, Mr. President, is about the man you put your trust in to find the men who killed McKinley."

Roosevelt stopped his pacing. "I'm well aware of that, Mr. Secretary. What I want to know is how in the hell did that happen?"

Root sat back in his chair. "Do you want the abbreviated version?"

Roosevelt was fuming, and Root had asked the wrong question. Clearing his throat, Root asked, "Do you remember Stanton saying he had to help some woman out of a problem?"

Roosevelt nodded. "As I recall, he got shot for his troubles."

"That woman," Root continued, "was Mrs. Clayton Harding from Philadelphia. From what we can gather, she was running from her husband. He appears to be some sort of a psychopath. During her escape, she evidently ran into your Mr. Stanton."

Roosevelt's eyes were on fire. "Our Mr. Stanton!"

Root quietly acknowledged the correction. "The short story: Harding found his wife and brought her back. He then beat her. That's when Stanton made his mistake – he went to Harding's house to find her. Harding had his men beat the hell out of Stanton. Apparently, though, they stopped too soon. Stanton pulled a gun, the one you gave to him, and shot Harding between the eyes and then killed one of his attackers."

Roosevelt's anger began to subside and a slight grin crossed his face. "A hell of a shot."

Root shook his head. "Not that good. The first one missed by a mile."

"So where is Stanton?"

"In the Philadelphia County General Hospital, handcuffed to his bed. He's been charged with murder."

Roosevelt turned and gave a slight spin to his globe. Without looking back at Root, he grumbled, "That was self-defense. Harding tried to kill him. Get the charges dropped."

"It's not that easy. The district attorney is running for governor, and he wants Stanton's hide."

Roosevelt shifted around. "Mr. Secretary, you did it before, do it again."

Root took a deep breath. "Mr. President, last time was a miracle. Frankly, I'm all out of miracles. My suggestion is we leave him alone this time. Find someone else to go after the anarchists."

"No!"

"What?"

"I said *no*, Mr. Secretary. That goddamned Hearst is trying to tie me into this mess. That's not going to happen."

Root shook his head, knowing he was fighting a losing battle. "Mr. President, if you wade into this affair, the water will quickly be over your head."

Roosevelt wasn't listening. "Get Knox and Neeley up here. We'll buy off that D.A. The only way I'll get out of this is to have him drop the charges based on self-defense."

"But . . . ."

"No 'buts', Mr. Secretary. Just do it. You know as well as I do that Stanton isn't guilty of murder. Get those charges dropped."

Root stood up to leave. Roosevelt stopped him. "Anything on McKinley's killers?"

"Our people have turned up nothing. I'll let you know if we hear anything."

Root left, and Roosevelt mumbled to himself, "That's why I need Matthew Stanton."

*   *   *   *

The offices of the district attorney of Philadelphia County were sparse. White-washed walls, scarred wood floors, and odd pieces of chairs, roll-top desks and wood file cabinets lined the rooms. Joshua Needles had just finished his second year. He was forty years old and was paid five thousand dollars a year, barely enough to support his wife, three children, and girlfriend. Needles was running for governor, as a Democrat, but he knew his chances were slim. He needed a home run, a case that would make his mark. He had a difficult time containing his elation. The case of a century had just fallen into his lap, and he wasn't about to let it go.

Needles had diverted his entire staff of five attorneys to the murder of Clayton Harding. He had personally known Harding, and down deep in his soul had hated him. It was no secret that he was a lunatic, but he was a very wealthy one. And he was known throughout the country. Now the same notoriety would fall upon Joshua Needles. The New York Times had sent its top reporters to interview him, and the Hearst papers had promised front page publicity for his governor's race in exchange for an inside track to the proceedings.

The only fly in the ointment was the new president. Through his attorney general, he had made known his wishes that the charges be dropped on the grounds of justifiable homicide. Knox had personally come to Philadelphia to outline the case for self-defense. Why did the President care? Needles would make it his mission to find out. In the meantime, he had belligerently let Knox know there would be no dismissal – Stanton would be tried in open court for murder. He had already killed five men; he was certainly capable of premeditated murder, and that's how the indictment read.

Needles needed a speedy trial and verdict for his governor's race. But the doctors said that Stanton wouldn't be well enough to stand trial for at least several months. The beating he had taken had resulted in cracked ribs, broken vertebrae, a concussion, and a broken arm. The recovery would be slow.

In Washington, Knox was reporting his meeting to the President. Roosevelt was furious. Slamming his fist on the desk, he said in a high-pitched voice that carried through the walls, "Who in the hell does he think he is? Stanton almost died from his beating, and that bastard says premeditated murder? Philander, you've got to get this thing quietly put to bed. How are you going to do that?"

The Attorney General looked stunned. "Mr. President, if we interfere any more in this case, it will be all over the papers. Do you know what that could mean to your presidency?"

Roosevelt tucked his thumbs into his vest and walked to the window. Letting several minutes go by, he said, "I'll pardon him."

"You can't do that. He hasn't been convicted of anything, not yet."

Roosevelt turned. "Give me something."

"Like what?"

"Hell if I know," blustered the President. "We can't have this trial. I need this man."

"I'll think on it," responded Knox.

Roosevelt's face tightened and then turned into a broad smile. "You do that. We'll meet at ten in the morning."

Knox was puzzled. "For what?"

"I want your solution then. Now if you'll excuse me, I have a canal to be built and a new country to be formed. How do you like the name Panama?"

"Are you joking?"

"No, I'm not joking. By this time next week, I, Theodore Roosevelt, will have formed my first country. If those damn Columbians won't permit my canal, we'll take the land away from them."

Knox was aghast. "Mr. President, this is none of my business, but you don't have the legal power to form a new country."

Roosevelt smiled again. "Tomorrow at ten, here in my office."

The next morning, precisely at 10:00 AM., Attorney General Knox and two assistants were shown into the President's office on the second floor of the White House. They could hear the laughter of his children from the residential quarters next door. The President was impeccably dressed in a dark blue suit and vest with a pink silk paisley tie. He stared at Knox impatiently as he and his assistants became seated.

"Well . . . ?" the President asked.

"A plea bargain."

"A what?"

"We'll get Stanton to plead guilty to a lesser offense, say second degree manslaughter with probation."

Roosevelt rubbed his chin and looked up at the ceiling. "Stanton will never agree to that."

"Would he rather be tried and take the risk of prison?"

Roosevelt shook his head. "You're saying we'll give this good man a criminal record. I'll lose a vote – he'll be guilty of a felony."

"Until you give him a presidential pardon," Knox answered.

"Can I do that?"

"After the court accepts his plea, you can do whatever you damn well please."

Roosevelt snapped his finger loudly and smiled. "Perfect. I can use him better with a criminal record." He paused, and then said, "Now the canal. You made a good point yesterday."

"So you're not going to form a new country?"

"No. Panama will be formed. I want you to give me a written opinion blessing it."

Knox looked at his assistants and mumbled softly, "Oh shit!"

CHAPTER TWENTY-FOUR

▼

Philadelphia

She entered his room when he was half-asleep. He opened his eyes, slightly blinded by the light. For a moment, he felt as if he were delirious. Through hazy eyes, he could see a woman wearing a high-neck white silk blouse, covered by a soft blue silk jacket, and a matching flowing skirt touching the floor. The reflection of brilliant diamonds around her neck forced him to blink several times. Then his vision began to clear as she removed her flowered hat, exposing light blonde hair brushed across her forehead which framed luminous green eyes.

"Are you surprised to see me?" she softly asked.

Attempting to sit up, he was restrained by the handcuffs. "Elizabeth."

Taking his hand, she said, "I lost track of you. I had no idea what had happened to you until I read our own newspaper. How do you manage to go from one crisis to another so smoothly?"

He smiled. "A talent I was born with. A dark cloud seems to hang over me wherever I go. You look marvelous."

She bent over and kissed him gently, slowly pulling her lips away. "We were on the verge of so many things, and then you were gone."

He laid his head back, closing his eyes. Opening them, he said, "Yes, we were. How is your husband?"

A frown crossed her face. "You could have said anything but that."

"Sorry," he mumbled.

"And how are you recovering?"

He pondered the question. "Slowly." Hesitating, he added, "It's pretty devastating, confronting people who want to kill you."

"I can imagine that it is."

He looked at her troubled face. Sitting up slightly, he said, "You seem to be about to say something. What's on your mind?"

"Why were you in Clayton Harding's home and why did you kill him?"

He coughed several times. "His wife, Alyssa Harding, needed my help. He abused her terribly. And he tried to kill me."

"Alyssa Harding? What is she to you?"

"A very close friend."

Eyes flashing, she said, "I wish I had friends like you. You were willing to risk your life for her. There's more to this than you've told me."

"More?" He was perplexed. "Are you asking me as a reporter?"

She fell silent, looking down at her hands. In a low voice, she murmured, "That was a very hurtful thing to say."

He weighed her statement and wasn't sure how to respond. "It wasn't meant to be. If you want to know more, I'll tell you. My feelings about her are very serious."

She raised her eyebrows in thought. After several moments of deafening silence, she responded, "At least you didn't say you were in love with her. Until you do, Matthew, I want you to know that I'm in love with you."

"What? That's impossible. We only spent forty-eight hours together, and you're married."

She gave him a look which mixed doubt with hope. "Alyssa Harding was also married," she replied in a soft voice. "You don't believe in love at first sight?"

He started to answer, and then stopped short.

"Matthew, I have a marriage of convenience."

He laughed. "A marriage of what? If you were married to me, it damn sure wouldn't be one of convenience. How could that have happened?"

She dismissed his laugh. "For your information, he's twice my age."

"Then why in the world . . . ?"

"Because he was there when I needed him, and . . . and I hadn't met you. We had been married for only several years when I met you at the Capitol Hotel. You know I was immensely attracted to you; my whole life, I had been searching for you, and there you were. Why do you think I slept with you? I'm not that kind of woman." She paused to take a deep breath, tenderly focusing her eyes on his. "I think you were as attracted to me as I was to you. Do you deny that?"

"You seem to know a lot," he said defensively. He was at first mystified, and then felt his emotions tearing at his insides. "Elizabeth," he said gently, "that wasn't a one-night fling for me. You are one of the loveliest women I have ever met, and you stepped in to save my life. I'll never forget that. I'll admit that you have been in my thoughts, many times. But look at me. I'm recovering from a bullet wound and a terrible beating, and I've been charged with murder. On top of that, I have to find the men who framed me for McKinley's assassination. You can't want to be part of all that."

She opened her hands as if to say "Why not?" Then in a slightly awkward voice, she said, "I'm not going to leave you. You need help; you can't do much in this hospital bed. I know you didn't murder Harding in cold blood. Look what he did to you! Let me be your . . . your assistant. I can go where you can't. I want to be part of what you do."

He struggled, Alyssa's face and smile crossing his mind. "I'll think on that." He lay back down, exhausted, and closed his eyes, not seeing Alyssa open the door momentarily and then back away.

Later that day Alyssa appeared again, dressed in light pink and yellow with a broad silk hat, looking like a high-fashion Gibson Girl. Her smile tore at his heart as she sat with him and held his hand. The bruises were beginning to disappear. "Matthew," she asked quietly, "who was that woman?"

Startled, he looked into her questioning blue eyes and silently wondered how she knew. "A friend I met in Washington," he slowly replied. "Her husband owns the *Baltimore Sun*."

He could see the relief in her eyes. "She was holding your hand."

"How did you know that?"

She suddenly felt embarrassed. "I opened the door when she was here."

"Why didn't you come in?"

She pondered his question. "I was uncomfortable, and I suppose I became jealous. I jumped to conclusions. I'm so sorry." She leaned over and kissed him passionately, her hand on his cheek.

When at last she pulled away, he moaned, "I want to hold you so much, but these damn shackles . . . ."

"You won't have them for long. I've hired a team of the best lawyers to defend you. Today I'm going to sign a sworn affidavit stating everything that happened, and that you acted in self-defense and to save my life."

"I've heard the D.A. is hell-bent on putting me in prison."

He could see the pain in her eyes. "The attorneys told me that. There has to be a way to stop him."

*   *   *   *

Philadelphia was having a heat wave. The temperature had climbed to the mid-forties. The governor's race was also heating up, and Joshua Needles felt the time was right for a press conference. Stanton had been in the hospital for over two weeks, and Needles was feeling the daily pressure from Washington to act. Attorney General Knox had hinted that there might be a place in the federal prosecutor's office for him, or even possibly on the federal judiciary. They didn't know Needles – he wouldn't be bought.

The conference was convened at 3:00 PM outside the State Court House. The reporters and others in attendance experienced the excitement of that sunny and brisk day and the sense of a carnival. Photo journalism was coming of age, and newspapers were beginning to print pictures on their front pages. It was a perfect time for political campaigning. Stopping to pose for a number of photographs, Needles began to feel, for the first time, that the governor's office was now within his reach. He stood on the second step of the court house, surveying the crowd below pushing forward to hear his announcement. He had dressed for the occasion in his favorite gray suit and vest, with a navy silk tie. His curly blond hair and long mustache were groomed to perfection. At the time he didn't realize it, but the sun reflected brilliantly off his gold-rimmed glasses like a shiny mirror, an effect that would show up in every photograph taken that day. He felt he had never looked better.

Those watching him saw a self-absorbed pompous little man who looked like the funny caricatures that portrayed him in the newspapers. He was slightly bent over from terrible posture, his skin was pock-marked from his youth, and his thick nose protruded beneath brown eyes devoid of expression.

"Ladies and gentlemen," he began, "I want to thank you for coming. I'm here today to explain to you the charges of homicide we have brought against Matthew Stanton for the premeditated murder of one of our most distinguished citizens, Clayton Harding. Mr. Harding, as you know, was a great benefactor to our city's parks and community centers, several of which are named after him. He was a genteel man, married for a number of years to one of the most beautiful women in our fair city.

"Mr. Stanton, it seems, was taken by the beauty of Mrs. Harding. He set himself up, in his twisted mind, to free her from what he perceived as cruelty imposed upon her by her husband. If you've seen Alyssa Harding and the beautiful home her husband provided for her, you would know that cruelty was hardly what he had in mind for her."

He stopped to hear several people chuckle.

"Mr. Stanton is by all appearances a solid citizen and wealthy entrepreneur of this country. But appearances are deceiving. This man started his career of violence at the early age of fifteen, when he killed in cold blood five men employed by one of the great men of our times, Andrew Carnegie. He knows how to kill.

"Two weeks ago, in the late afternoon, he entered the Harding residence armed with a Colt revolver, under the guise of wanting to *talk* (he held up two fingers of each hand illustrating quotation marks) to Mr. Harding about his wife. While there, he threatened to kill Mr. Harding, and when several employees of the deceased tried in vain to restrain him, he did in fact not only shoot Mr. Harding twice in the face, but he also shot one of the brave men trying to protect him."

There were gasps heard from the crowd. Seeing several photographers hold up their cameras for pictures, Needles smiled and struck the pose of someone running for election. Waving his hand at several friends in the audience, he continued, "I have one other thing to say. As you know, I'm a candidate for governor of this fine state – as a Democrat." Several people clapped their hands and he heard loud cheers.

"It should be no secret that I have been approached by people in Washington, tied politically to that *other* party (more laughter was heard) to either drop or lessen the charges brought against Mr. Stanton. The only conclusion I can reach for this blatant interference with justice is that he contributed significantly to their campaigns. We're looking into that."

Raising his voice to a loud crescendo, he shouted, "They thought I could be bought! Let me tell you this. There are still a few honest men left in politics. I have no price – I cannot be bought!" He stopped to gaze around the crowd, enjoying the applause. "To those who asked me for a plea deal, I have a direct answer. I'm open to a plea, but it's not a deal. Life in prison with no chance for parole; that's the deal I would make for our citizens and the justice *you* deserve." He raised both hands in a symbol of victory to the boisterously cheering crowd. He was ecstatic. Attaining the governorship of Pennsylvania was now within his grasp.

After the cheering had died down, he heard a woman's voice from the audience. "Mr. Needles," she yelled. He looked over the heads of those in the audience to see a blonde woman fashionably dressed in fur and wearing a wide-brim hat.

Pointing to her, he asked, "You have a question?"

"I do," she yelled back. "Don't you think it odd, even a serious breach of legal ethics, that you would try this man in public before he has a fair chance to defend himself in court?"

Needles cleared his throat, a look of embarrassment creeping across his face. "Ma'am," he shouted back, "by no means have I intended to try him. He will get his day in court. My actions today were merely to bring to light the true facts of this case and to remove any doubt as to my dedication to justice. You should know, after what I have said, that justice is first and foremost on my mind, and justice will be served."

Another voice rang out, "You don't want justice, Mr. Needles, you want to be governor."

Anger welled up inside of Needles. He held up his hand. "You're entitled to your opinion," he yelled back, "but it's wrong. Thank you ladies and gentlemen."

The remarks of Joshua Needles were published on the front page of many newspapers the next day, along with pictures of him wearing his reflective glasses. Only one newspaper put a different slant on what he had said. The *Baltimore Sun* printed a long article detailing the abusive character of Clayton Harding, the beatings he had given his wife and other women before her, and statements of persons who knew him attesting to their belief that he was insane.

The following day, Joshua Needles had a visit from the woman who had questioned him at the press conference. Sitting across from her in his office, Needles was on the brink of exploding. He held up a typed newspaper article that she had given him, his eyes bristling.

"What is this?" he demanded. "Blackmail? Do you have any idea of what your newspaper is getting itself into?"

"Not blackmail," she assured him. "It's journalism. And it tells the truth. Would you like to give me your side of the story?"

He threw the article across the table and then leaned his chair back against the wall. His gold-rimmed glasses slid to the end of his nose. "If this story is printed, you and your newspaper will get sued and its editors will end up in jail. I can promise you that."

"You're misreading the article," she calmly pointed out. "It's not about us – it's about you. Did you read it?"

His face appeared confused, as if torn between an urge to kill and one of self-preservation. The bluntness of what the article said left him stunned. "This would ruin me," he eventually mumbled.

"As it should," Elizabeth responded.

His hand brushed across his face several times, shaking noticeably. "Has this been released for publication?" he asked in a low voice.

"Not yet. Do you want it to be?"

He paused, trying to catch his breath. "This is an outrage."

"No, what you've done is an outrage. Publicly trying a man for murder when you know it was self-defense. Building a career on criminal convictions where you hid evidence and misled jurors. Engaging in affairs when you were married with several children."

"I never withheld evidence. And I've never had affairs."

"The people who worked for you did. As to your affairs, do you want the names of your former girlfriends? They had no hesitancy in talking to us."

He took a deep breath and turned briefly to gaze out the window. "How do you know all this?"

She let a slight smile creep across her face. "You should be more careful in whom you hire . . . and fire. I would also suggest that you be more particular in choosing those women with whom you decide to carry on your extra-marital affairs. You've made some pretty staunch enemies."

Humbled, he said slowly, "Maybe I let it go too far. Maybe that press conference was a mistake. But Stanton did murder Harding!" His icy stare turned to indignation.

Elizabeth tried to suppress her rage. "He was beaten to an inch of his life. Alyssa Harding was abused her entire marriage, and her husband was a psychopath. How can you choose to ignore those facts?"

He turned his palms upward toward her in a defeated gesture. "The governorship was mine, if I did it right. Maybe I was blinded by that."

"But you're a district attorney. You swore under oath to uphold the law. It shouldn't have happened."

"I let it get out of control; maybe I got out of control. It was an opportunity for me . . . ." He paused and looked down, in silence. Then returning his eyes to her, he asked, "What do you want me to do?"

"Drop the charges against Matthew Stanton."

He shook his head. "No! I'll let him enter a plea bargain. He'll get a parole."

"Not on your life," she exclaimed. "The charges get dropped or the article gets published."

He removed his glasses and gently rubbed his eyes. "If I agree to your terms, how will I know you won't publish it anyway?"

She stood up, giving him a contemptuous look. "You'll have to trust me."

Turning back toward the window, he mumbled, "I suppose I will."

CHAPTER TWENTY-FIVE

▼

Washington

Attorney General Philander Knox slammed down his telephone and sat rigid at his desk at the Department of Justice. He had just been told about the press conference held by Joshua Needles in Philadelphia. "Son-of-a-bitch," he cursed to himself. For several minutes he stared out the large window in his office at the cloudy day. Then he picked up a copy of the newspaper in front of him and scanned the lead story. "That goddamned two-faced bastard!" he snarled. The phone rang. Picking up the receiver and stretching the cord, he heard the President's loud voice.

Holding the receiver away from his ear, he listened to the shrill voice. After it had calmed down, he held the receiver against his ear and said, "Mr. President, I know you're as pissed off as I am. I'm trying to deal with busting up the Wall Street trusts, labor strikes and Panama, and you want me to focus my attention on this Matthew Stanton, who just killed a prominent citizen in Philadelphia? Well, sir, we've walked on coals and gotten the hell burnt out of our feet. I don't have the time for this."

Roosevelt paused to calm his temper. "He's accused us of tampering with justice. Did you read that damn article in the *Post*?"

"Yes, sir, I did. And isn't that exactly what we've done?"

Roosevelt's temper returned with a vengeance. "Hell no, we didn't do that! What we tampered with was injustice and our national security. I want you to indict Needles for a federal crime."

Knox silently laughed to himself. "And what did you have in mind, Mr. President?"

"Abuse of the justice system."

"I'm not sure that's a federal crime, particularly by a state district attorney."

The loudness of the voice in the receiver intensified. "Then make one up. No half-wit district attorney is going to make those accusations against me and get away with it. Do you hear me?"

"Yes, sir, I'll do what I can."

"You do that." He heard the phone slammed in its cradle. He replaced his phone, thinking that just over a year ago he hadn't had one, and then turned back to the window, massaging his brow with his hand. Shaking his head in disgust, he began to wonder why he took this job. The next afternoon, Knox received a call from Philadelphia. "Mr. Knox," Joshua Needles said, "I'd like to revisit with you this Stanton case. Maybe I acted a bit too hastily."

Knox was incredulous. What in the hell was this all about? "Mr. Needles, I've read about your press conference, and I've got to tell you, the President is livid. I'm not sure I can safely mention your name in his presence."

"Oh yes, that," Needles mumbled apologetically. Clearing his throat, he said, "That was poor judgment on my part. Let me ask you this. If I were to drop the charges against Mr. Stanton, on the grounds of justifiable homicide, would the President reconsider any of the appointments you indicated might come my way?"

"Mr. Needles, I indicated nothing of the sort, and you'd better get that through your head. I told you the President makes many appointments, and that he particularly favors his friends. I promised you nothing. The answer is no to your question." He paused while suspicions filled his mind. "What brought about this sudden change of heart?"

He heard a deep breath taken on the other end of the line. "I . . . . I've taken a new look at the facts. Mr. Knox, I *was* a bit hasty, and I attributed motives to you and the President that weren't there. If I could do anything . . . ."

Interrupting him, Knox said, "You can. Withdraw your statements and apologize to the President, and do it publicly. Then drop the charges against Mr. Stanton so I can get back to the pressing demands of my office."

There was silence on the other end. Then, "So you're saying there's nothing you would do to show your appreciation?"

"I told you, the answer is *no*! Good-bye, Mr. Needles."

CHAPTER TWENTY-SIX

▼

Baltimore, Maryland; Washington, D.C.

Emma Goldman was the easiest and most logical place to begin. Elizabeth had sifted through dozens of newspaper clippings and articles at the *Baltimore Sun*, searching for a connection between Czolgosz and other anarchists who would want to kill President McKinley. Occasionally, she would pull at random a thick file and superficially study its contents, but it was in the clippings and old news stories that she began to piece together odd events. She so exhausted the resources of the newspaper that its employees soon began to question her motives, as did her husband. Her answer was always the same – boredom and an interest in women's causes.

Sipping on a lukewarm cup of coffee in the copy room late one evening, she came upon a February 15, 1900, edition of the *Chicago American* that contained a vitriolic two page article about McKinley. At first, she had merely scanned the article and found nothing that caught her eye other than William Randolph Hearst's scathing hatred for the President. Meticulously going back through it, line by line, she found a quote of Emma Goldman that anarchists were being driven to action by the shameful policies of an imperialistic president who sought, by his invasion of the Philippines and Cuba, to enslave the free peoples of the world. Then she discovered another article in the *New York Journal* that the anarchists seemed to congregate at

Sach's Café in New York, and that it was there that Goldman met her lover and mentor, Alexander Berkman.

Berkman, the article said, was serving a twenty-two year sentence for the attempted murder of Henry Clay Frick. He shot Frick three times and stabbed him once, yet Frick had survived. The writer stated that Berkman and Goldman had conspired to murder Frick, a prominent industrialist, to inspire a revolt against the capitalist system. That hadn't happened. Goldman was devastated. Prosecutors were unable to tie her into the attempt, but the judge nevertheless sentenced her to one year in a federal penitentiary as a "dangerous woman".

To her profound surprise, Elizabeth later stumbled upon an article in the *Daily Business Journal* saying that several of the wealthiest men of Wall Street had expressed their sentiment with Goldman's ranting that government regulation of its citizens and control over their accumulation of wealth must be abolished. She reread the article. How could that be? Wall Street? No names were mentioned, but she was certain there were no anarchists on Wall Street. That was unthinkable.

On that same day, J. Pierpont Morgan, while at dinner in his brownstone mansion on Madison Avenue, was summoned away from his guests to an urgent phone call. He learned to his great dismay that President Roosevelt had ordered Attorney General Knox to take legal action against one of his trusts, the Northern Securities Company, for violation of the Sherman Antitrust Act, which forbade combinations in restraint of trade. He was incredulous. America had always been the land of free enterprise where there could never be a restraint to interfere with the "natural order" of business.

J. P. Morgan was the wealthiest man in America and had a tremendous physical effect on people. He was extremely large with massive shoulders, piercing eyes, stark white receding hair, and a speckled thick black mustache that extended well beyond the lines of his mouth. It was his huge deformed nose, though, that dominated his facial features. He had suffered since childhood from a rare disease known as rhinophyma, a result of the chronic skin disease rosacea. As the deformity worsened, his nose became a swollen mass of pits, nodules and fissures, which gave it a purple hue. He dared people to meet him squarely and not shrink in horror, asserting the force of his character over the ugliness of his face.

When J. P. Morgan entered a room, it was if a gale had blown through. His achievements were stunning. In 1900, he began conversations with Charles M. Schwab, president of Carnegie Co., and its owner, Andrew Carnegie, to buy Carnegie's steel business and combine it with other steel companies he would acquire to create The United States Steel Corporation. By 1901, he had completed the deal without lawyers or even a written agreement, and had formed the largest consolidation the world had ever seen. U. S. Steel was the world's first billion dollar corporation, with a capitalization of $1.4 billion. It was a monopoly that dominated not only steel but the construction of bridges, railroad cars and rails, wire, nails and a host of other products. With U. S. Steel, Morgan had captured two-thirds of the steel market.

That was only a small part of his empire. He had earlier merged Edison General Electric and Thomson-Houston Electric Company to form General Electric. In the world of finance, he formed J. P Morgan & Company in 1895, and by 1900 he controlled, through combinations and consolidations, the most powerful banking house in the world, Chase Manhattan Bank. He was also heavily involved in railroads, and reorganized several of the largest in the country to form the Great Northern Railway, a significant monopoly in rail transit. In 1896, he financed a struggling newspaper owner to purchase The New York Times Company.

Not satisfied with his massive conquests, his next goal was shipping. The International Mercantile Marine Company was formed to absorb several major American and British lines. His goal was to dominate American sea transport through interlocking directorates and combinations. Ironically, he was booked to sail on the maiden voyage of the most advanced and newest cruise ship of his company, but had to cancel at the last moment. The ship, known as the *Titanic*, led to the rare bankruptcy of a Morgan company. J. P. Morgan had become the greatest financier of the twentieth century.

Morgan was not alone. John D. Rockefeller's trust in the oil business had been justified by "God" in all his beneficence. The wire nail trust had been organized with a keg of nails priced at $1.20. A year later, the price was $25.00. The companies consolidated into U.S. Steel had engaged in so much price-fixing that steel rails were priced at twice their cost within only several months after the company's formation. To the wealthy men of Wall Street, their creed was clear. The right of a man to run his own business in his own way, with due respect *only* to the Ten Commandments and the Penal Code, was inviolate; it *was* the American way.

J.P. Morgan went to Washington a few days after learning of the suit against Northern Securities. He was a man of determination and action, and he knew a direct conversation with the man he was calling on would settle the matter, once and for all. What he didn't understand was that the President was also a man of action and had set a new course for American business. In the privacy of Roosevelt's office, Morgan lit up his favorite Havana cigar, dubbed Hercules' Clubs (he smoked dozens per day), and was direct and to the point. "Mr. President," he complained, "you owed us the decency to tell us in advance of this suit."

Unmoved, Roosevelt scrutinized his adversary with a cold stare. Standing up, he shook his head. "That's exactly what I didn't want to do."

Alarmed, Morgan began to sense something about this "Republican" president that he would grow to intensely dislike. Slowly exhaling a ring of smoke, he stared down the President. "If we've done anything wrong," he said, "send your man to my man and they can fix it up."

To Roosevelt, his brief honeymoon with Wall Street had ended. Pointing his finger at Morgan, the President said in a clipped tone, "Mr. Morgan, the time of business as usual is over. That's not going to happen."

Morgan's eyes bristling, he retreated to other grounds. "Are you going to attack my other interests?"

"Certainly not, ... unless we find out they've done something *we regard* as wrong." Morgan was suddenly aware of the rage that was gathering behind Roosevelt's rigid features. "I can promise you this," the President continued, "if your other interests are violating our anti-trust laws, they'll feel the wrath of this government. You'll get no leniency from me."

No one had *ever* talked to J. P. Morgan in that manner. Filled with anger, he stood to leave. "You regard?" Morgan said arrogantly. "Mr. President, I've been a Republican my entire life. I've contributed millions to the party. I personally stepped in and saved the American treasury in the panic of 1897. By God, this nation is indebted to me. I'm beginning to see that you and I have no basis on which to do business in the future."

Tapping a pen on his desk, the President replied disdainfully, "Mr. Morgan, you've finally said something we do agree on." With a forced smile, he added, "Good day, sir."

*   *   *   *

The new President had just begun to make his list of enemies. Within several weeks after his meeting with Morgan, he was blasted in editorials nationwide for an open letter he wrote to Cecil Springs-Rice, in which he said, "I do not see much of the big-moneyed men in New York, simply because very few of them possess the traits which would make them companionable to me, or would make me feel that it was worth dealing with them. To spend a day with them at Newport, or on one of their yachts, or even to dine with them save under exceptional circumstances, fills me with frank horror."

The San Francisco Examiner, as well as other Hearst newspapers, lashed out at him with bitter editorials predicting the destruction of the world's greatest capitalistic system by a president bent on achieving his vision of an imperialistic America. The result, they decried, would be "the ultimate enslavement of the citizens of this great nation to big government."

Emma Goldman was in agreement, but not for the same reasons. She despised the wealthy barons of Wall Street. Goldman believed that the economic system of capitalism was inimical to human liberty.

She also believed that capitalism dehumanized workers. "Wealth," she shouted to crowds across the nation, "meant the power to subdue, to crush, to degrade, to exploit and to enslave workers." In her widely read book, *Anarchism and Other Essays*, she laid out a thesis that many on Wall Street found as a common ground – people must be liberated from the shackles of government; there must be a social order based on the free grouping of individuals for the purpose of producing real social wealth. Government regulation must end.

To achieve her goals, Goldman preached to all who would listen that the use of violence against government leaders was not only appropriate but necessary to instigate change. She single-handedly instilled in the minds of sociopaths across America the idea that the murder of government leaders was a necessary evil. Widely vilified in newspapers and journals, Emma Goldman soon became known as "the most dangerous woman in America." Unknown to her, one of America's wealthiest industrialists had become her biggest fan. Her books and essays had become required reading for him, and he poured over them daily as a student of great literature would study Shakespeare.

Leon Czolgosz had found in her his inspiration to kill President McKinley. It had not taken much for Thaddeus Pratt to push the button that would cause this man, who suffered from varying degrees of mental illness, to commit the act. Goldman had unknowingly been a willing puppet, steadfastly refusing to condemn Czolgosz' action, and virtually alone in doing so. She had been immediately jailed, but throughout her detention she had defended Czolgosz, earning for herself the label in the press of High Priestess of Anarchy. In the wake of these events, newspapers nationwide declared the anarchist movement responsible for the murder. Goldman would take center stage again, and Thaddeus Pratt would again use her as the vehicle through which he could safely kill a president.

Framing Matthew Stanton had been Pratt's brainchild to divert any police investigation into who might have financed Czolosz. Stanton had earned Pratt's animosity years before, and Pratt saw it as an opportunity to destroy an old enemy. But that had been a mistake – a serious one. It would not happen again.

CHAPTER TWENTY-SEVEN

▼

Rochester, New York

The hour was late, way past eight in the evening. The windows of the small frame house were bright with light from the oil lamps inside. Elizabeth walked up the brick path as the rain, swept by fifteen mile-per-hour winds, pelted her umbrella. When she banged on the door, almost two minutes passed before there was a response. Then the door opened and the light illuminated a small, heavy-set and homely woman, barely over five feet tall. Her pudgy face and thick lips belied a woman who the press had at times referred to as a person "who craved sex continually". In an unpleasant voice, she asked, "Elizabeth Ambridge?"

"Yes. I'm here for our interview." Standing in the downpour, Elizabeth saw that Emma Goldman was unmoved by her answer. Studying her visitor, Goldman said, "You're too pretty to be a reporter. Who are you?" Her eyes were in a shadow, and Elizabeth stepped forward in an attempt to see them.

"Good evening, Miss Goldman," she said with both civility and charm. "I am who I said I was in my telegram. My husband is Dalton Ambridge, the publisher of the *Baltimore Sun* . . . . I'm getting soaked out here. May I please come in?"

Goldman recoiled rudely, stepping back two steps into a darker spot in the hallway. "Come in, but leave your umbrella." Elizabeth collapsed her umbrella, laid it against the wall, and followed her into a small sitting room. Outside, the rain continued to pound against the small windows. The home had a pungent smell of leftover food. Books and magazines were strewn over a worn rug, and Elizabeth noticed only two places to sit: a dilapidated sofa and a small velour upholstered chair. Taking off her wet coat, Elizabeth removed a tablet from her purse and sat in the chair. She couldn't help but stare at Goldman's shabby, long-sleeved dark brown dress; thick uncombed dark hair; ruddy complexion; and lack of makeup. She had the look of someone who cared nothing about her appearance. Watching her adjust her dress on the sofa, Elizabeth found her to be very repulsive.

Goldman pushed back a pair of small glasses resting near the tip of her nose. She observed Elizabeth with a look of suspicion and dislike.

Elizabeth returned the scrutiny, trying to see past the glasses into Goldman's eyes. Breaking the silence, Elizabeth said, "I'd like to hear about Leon Czolosz."

"That's not what you said you wanted to talk about," Goldman answered with condescension. "If you're smart enough to read newspapers, you know everything there is to know about Czolosz."

"But I want to hear your side of it."

Elizabeth detected a flare of anger in the eyes behind the glasses. "I told you I'd give a *short* interview on women's rights, Mrs. Ambridge. It's late, and I'm not in the mood to be cross-examined by you."

"Forgive me if I wasn't clear," Elizabeth said. "What happened to you in the Czolosz investigation is important to women everywhere. It *is* about women's rights."

Goldman sat back, her aggravated expression slowly dissipating. "The truth is, I never really knew Czolosz. In fact, until he killed the President, I thought his name was Nieman."

Surprised, Elizabeth asked, "Did you tell the police that?"

"They wouldn't listen to me and they wouldn't believe me. They gave me the 'third degree'."

"What's that?"

A pained expression crossed Goldman's face. "Deprivation of food and water, confinement in a rat hole for days on end, strip-searches, and beatings until I confessed."

"But you didn't."

"No, I didn't, because there was nothing to confess."

"I admire you for that. Tell me more about Czolosz."

"As I said, there's not much too tell."

"But publicly you defended him and what he had done."

"That doesn't mean I knew him!" she snapped. "My friend, Mary Isaak, came to me one day to tell me a young man named Nieman was in urgent need of seeing me. I told her I knew nobody by that name and that I was in a hurry to get to the train station. When she persisted, I told her I would talk to him on the way. As I left my house, I saw him. It turned out he was the blond man who had asked me to recommend reading material to him at our Cleveland meeting.

"While I was hanging onto the straps on the elevated train, Nieman told me he belonged to a Socialist local in Cleveland, that he found its members dull and boring, lacking any vision or enthusiasm. He said he couldn't bear to be with them. Then he said he had met several brother anarchists in New York who were, as he put it, 'invigorating'. They had not only instructed him in the ways of anarchism and violence, but it seems they had provided him money to live and to support his widowed mother."

Elizabeth's interest peaked. "Did he say who they were?"

"I didn't ask him and he didn't say. Oh, he did say they knew Berkman."

"Berkman, your boyfriend?"

She laughed. "Now that's a term I haven't heard in a while. Berkman the felon, my lover and my mentor. I don't know how they could have known him – he's been locked away for over ten years."

"Did you ever find out who they were?"

"I think they were a figment of his imagination. He gave their names to the Chicago police, and they said there were no such people."

Elizabeth was puzzled. "How did you find that out?"

She moved uncomfortably on the sofa. Blinking several times, she answered, "Chief O'Neill, in Chicago. He thought I was a very clever actress. It's Chief O'Neill I have to thank for my third degree treatment. He asked me if I had ever heard of them. I told him no. At the time, he didn't believe me, but I think later on he did."

"Do you remember the names he gave you?"

"No, I don't. I was being beaten."

"Then what happened?"

"Not much. At the station, I found my friends waiting for me. Max was there."

"Max?"

"Baginski. I begged Max to take care of Nieman and introduce him to the comrades. That was the last I saw of him."

"And you've heard nothing since?"

She massaged her forehead. "I did hear something. About a week later, a notice in *Free Society* had a warning against Nieman. It was written by Isaak, my friend's husband, and it said he had been around asking questions that aroused suspicion, that he was trying to get into anarchist circles. Our comrades decided he was a spy. That made me very angry. To make a charge like that on such flimsy ground! They had no evidence. They felt he was untrustworthy because he constantly talked about violence. I wrote a protest letter, and Isaak retracted his statement."

Elizabeth was astounded. "Why would you do that? You said you hardly knew him."

"Because I believe in violence to achieve our goals, and I thought he was right to encourage it."

"Violence? You were cleared in McKinley's murder."

"Yes, I was," she shot back. "I had nothing to do with that, except applauding Czolosz publicly for his courage. I'll tell you something – when I first read in the newspaper that McKinley had been shot, I had no idea who Czolosz was. Then, in one of the newspapers, I saw a picture. I was shocked. It was Nieman. Later, I found out that Czolosz told the authorities that I had inspired him. That was insane! By that time the authorities had sent out over two hundred detectives in search of me. I knew I had to go to Chicago and turn myself in."

"Do you want to tell me about your treatment in Chicago?"

She held her head low, shaking it slowly from side to side. In a subdued voice, she mumbled, "No." Slightly raising her head, she said, "If it hadn't been for Katherine Leckie of the Hearst papers, I might have died. She visited me; it was her articles that made the police back down. Then those bastards she worked for fired her, for no reason other than that she sympathized with me."

Listening intently, Elizabeth took notes on her pad.

Goldman took a deep breath. "The Chief said he only wanted a quiet talk with me. When I told him the truth, they took me to the Harrison Street Police Station and locked me in a barrel where people could see me from every side. They exhibited me like a monkey. When they finally let me out, I was beaten to the floor with fists. They knocked out two teeth and left me with my face covered in blood. I wasn't even allowed to clean up. They then moved me to the county jail, my face, waist, and skirt covered with blood. No one showed the slightest interest in me. They locked me up without water to drink or wash up. I was terrified."

"I'm sorry," Elizabeth murmured.

Without warning, Goldman stood up. With anger in her voice, she declared, "You have to leave. I've said all I'm going to say."

"Did I just do or say something that made you angry?" Elizabeth asked, mystified by her sudden mood change.

Without answering, Goldman opened the door and rudely said, "Don't come back."

Those words at first filled Elizabeth with bewilderment and then a biting rage. In disgust, she reached down, opened her umbrella and walked down the brick path through a torrent of rain mixed with sleet. Stepping into the waiting carriage, she felt a chill at the thought that someone as pathetic as Emma Goldman could have such an influence on the twisted minds of anarchists.

CHAPTER TWENTY-EIGHT

▼

Long Island, New York

Thaddeus Pratt heard of J. P. Morgan's encounter with the new president. Wall Street was in turmoil. In the streets of New York, rumors spread like wildfire. If Roosevelt were to bring down the eastern business establishment, which many thought was his goal, would America have its next financial panic? The President favored labor unions, he wanted child labor laws, and he talked of a minimum wage. A tragedy of monumental proportions was in the making.

Pratt felt he now had the allies he needed. When it was done, he would be looked upon as a savior. Carrying it out, however, was becoming more of a challenge. The attitude of the press was beginning to change. Even the Hearst newspapers, feeling the enormous public outcry over the assassination of McKinley, had changed their tune. They had toned down their editorials blasting the White House and were now harshly condemning the anarchists and their doctrines of hate. The anarchists were becoming less visible. He had to move slowly and carefully, but deliberately. And out of sight.

While Roosevelt did not want to lead the country as a president "going about guarded", he was seldom seen without a contingent of guards. Congress had not authorized the use of the Secret Service to protect the President, but it was there.

Pratt sat in a leather-bound wing chair in his paneled drawing room, staring at flocks of sea gulls navigating the harsh winds over the cold Atlantic Ocean. His eyes eventually drifted to the expressionless face of the thin balding man who had just entered the room. Dr. Frederick Seigfeld was in his late sixties, had a sparse white beard that partially covered his drawn, pasty face, and wore the standard wire-rimmed glasses that had become common in the late nineteenth century. Once nominated for a Nobel prize, Seigfeld was a noted psychiatrist and a disciple of Sigmund Freud. Seigfeld had retired from his practice in New York three years earlier.

It was Seigfeld who, as a consultant to Pratt, had profiled Leon Czolgosz. The profile had been done six months before the assassination of McKinley, and when the murder had occurred, Seigfeld had been as shocked as Pratt. Pratt had said it was needed for his detective agency. Questions arose in Seigfeld's mind, but the profile had been one of over fifty Seigfeld had been asked to complete.

Seigfeld had unique credentials. He had studied at the University of Vienna under Freud's mentor, German physiologist Ernest Wilhelm von Brücke. Freud had adopted Brücke's new "dynamic" physiology as the basis for many of his theories. Using Brucke's teachings, Freud put forward his theories of the unconscious mind and the defense mechanism of repression, and promoted the clinical practice of treating patients through direct dialogue. Freud was a prolific writer and had written numerous essays drawing on psychoanalysis to provide insight to the criminal mind.

Seigfeld carried it one step further. Applying the psychological concept of narcissism to anarchists, he observed that the political assassin avoided the self-label of being a terrorist by replacing it with an alternate identity, i.e that he was a cool, rational thinker engaged in political liberation when society offered him no other choice. From there, Seigfeld prepared a profile of the violent anarchist – the lunatic, the loner, the hater and the murderer. Convincingly, Pratt had insisted the profile was necessary for his business.

"Dr. Seigfeld," Pratt said with an outstretched finger pointing to the chair next to him, "please have a seat." Pausing for a moment, he asked in a low voice, "Do you remember Leon Czolgosz?"

Warning bells suddenly went off in Seigfeld's head. "How could I not! He murdered the President, and you asked me to specifically profile him for you *before* he committed that act."

Clearing his throat, Pratt said, "I'm aware of that. I need you to give me a different kind of profile. You talked to Czolgosz after he was arrested. He told you things, according to your report, that you had not considered earlier." Studying Seigfeld's expression, he said, "The anarchists have gone underground. With the public outrage over McKinley, they're not as recognizable as they once were. I need to be able to identify them, particularly the ones with a tendency toward violence – the future assassins."

Seigfeld was startled. "The future assassins? Why?"

"That's none of your business," Pratt said in a coarse voice.

Seigfeld was alarmed. "Mr. Pratt, you're wasting your time as well as mine. I've already told you what I think are the basic character flaws of an anarchist turned assassin."

Unyielding, Pratt demanded, "I need more. You profiled Czolgosz *after* we brought him to you. Now, I want you to tell me how to find other anarchists like him."

Shocked, Seigfeld sat up in his chair. "You what?"

"You heard me. I want to be able to walk into a room and find the next assassin."

Seigfeld was stunned. "You should know I can't do that. Without extensive psychological testing, it's impossible. They look like we do."

Pratt turned back to the window, rubbing his chin. Twisting back around, Seigfeld could feel Pratt's icy stare. "Then give me a test."

"You want a written test?"

"Yes," he insisted.

"That's never been done. I don't think it's possible. Finding a murderer among anarchists is not that simple. It would require months of one-on-one psychoanalysis."

"I can't give you that."

A disturbed look crossed Seigfeld's face. "If you can't do that, how in the world could you get a deranged person to take a test?"

Unmoved, Pratt said, "You leave that to me."

Seigfeld knew it was futile, and he needed the money. "I'll do what I can. My fee will be twenty-five dollars per hour, and I expect it will take several hundred hours."

Pratt nodded and said, "Agreed." Then in a threatening tone, he warned, "Nobody is to know about this! Do you understand?"

"Yes," Seigfeld replied slowly. Staring into Pratt's crazed eyes, Seigfeld's mind was suddenly filled with the thought that Pratt was someone to be feared. The look of apprehension in his eyes didn't go unnoticed by Pratt.

*   *   *   *

A month later, Thaddeus Pratt received a fifteen page test to be given to potential anarchists/murderers. At five o'clock in the afternoon, he sat in the stillness of his drawing room scanning the questions prepared by Dr. Seigfeld. Looking up from the document, he paused to take a drink of liqueur his butler had brought him earlier. The task was daunting. The questions were designed to elicit the social standing, educational level, reading ability, abusive or non-abusive upbringing, feelings of rage or hopelessness, employment status, violent and non-violent encounters with police or other security forces, experienced psychological traumas, motivations to kill people, physical fitness, level of idealism, arrogance, lack of feelings for others, etc., of the person taking the test. The questions were exhaustive. Pratt was tempted himself to take the test, but stopped at the fear of what it might disclose.

Attached to the package was a grading scale. According to Seigfeld, a grade of seventy or higher meant the individual taking the test was an ideal sociopath, a hostile neurotic who was intolerant, suspicious, aggressive, and extremely prone to violence for reasons of low-esteem and humiliation. He would have no reservation to committing murder if the circumstances were right. Pratt now had his challenge – to find the anarchists who would be appropriate selections to take the test.

Turning over the last page, he saw a personal note from Seigfeld. It said his bill for services was five thousand dollars. Pratt had no problem with that amount. His eyes then drifted down the note to several sentences in which Seigfeld said that after Pratt had approved the test, he intended to show it to law enforcement authorities and then submit it to a professional journal for publication. Pratt was panic-stricken; he knew immediately that wasn't what Seigfeld had in mind. Picking up a nearby telephone, he lifted the receiver from its cradle and placed a call.

*   *   *   *

Earlier that night, rain had fallen on West 53rd. The rain had passed, but the cold remained. Dr. Seigfeld pulled his collar up around his neck and walked briskly from the lecture he had just given to the New York Society of Psychiatrists. The evening had been a great success; he still felt the effects of the three glasses of wine he had been served at the reception that followed afterwards. His step was crisp along the wet street, his mind occupied by the lecture and the five thousand dollars he would soon receive from Thaddeus Pratt. That money would pay for the cruise he and Madeline would take to Europe in the fall, and a great deal more. He was content.

As he turned on West 52nd, the street seemed empty of sound and people. By the time he neared his home, it was so quiet that his steps seemed to echo back to him from the dreary, unlit brick buildings he passed. He had taken this route many times; the silence didn't bother him. The street lamps had not yet fallen prey to electricity, and they glowed from the gas flames projecting his shadow as he walked. Seeing his house down the block was reassuring; he would soon climb the dimly lit staircase to be greeted by his lovely wife of fifty years.

Without warning, he heard the sound of a crunch and felt his knees beginning to buckle. He turned his head slightly and saw a tall man standing directly behind him. The sound of the second blow resonated in his head, but strangely he felt no pain. Then something did hurt. He felt a knife cutting his throat. He gurgled, thinking, *Who could do this?* That was his last thought.

CHAPTER TWENTY-NINE

▼

Philadelphia, Pennsylvania

At five o'clock the next day, Matthew Stanton finished reading the evening news and tossed it into a nearby waste basket. His recovery from the gunshot wound and horrendous beating suffered the month before had been slow. Several ribs had been fractured. He felt little pain when lying down, but when he tried to stand, the burning pain would return. The doctors had suggested that he walk with a cane until his rehabilitation had been completed. It could take another month. He was becoming very edgy. More than that, he was angry at himself for intervening in Alyssa's domestic problems when he should have left it alone. And he silently cursed himself for not killing the third man.

Turning his thoughts to the front page article he had just read, he felt a twinge of guilt from his anger. Unlike that poor New York psychiatrist who had been viciously murdered just steps away from his home, he would eventually return to his life. Life was a crap shoot, he decided. Everyone was living on his or her own time clock.

Alyssa visited him only several times each week. She attributed her absences to the lawyers and settling the estate of the man he had killed. She was now a very wealthy single woman. He thought he loved her, but not enough to marry her. He wondered how long she would stay single.

For the past week, his principal diversion had been his business. The shipping industry was converting from the steamships of the mid to late nineteenth century to the new, more economical and faster twin-screw steam turbine ships. The cost would be enormous – Far East Shipping would need $10 million, an amount that the banks were willing to lend. His company would now have significant debt, something he had vigorously avoided in the past. Longbourne had laid it all out and had been very convincing. He had no choice.

His other diversion was Elizabeth and the anarchists. She had sent him a number of telegrams, keeping him informed of her private investigation into the assassination of McKinley. Every telegram was signed with her "devoted love and affection". He had carefully kept them out of sight from Alyssa. As much as he felt he loved Alyssa, his thoughts frequently were on Elizabeth, and that was disturbing. Deep within, when she was gone, he felt a pang of emotion. She was in Baltimore, and he was in Philadelphia. He missed her.

The last telegram she sent him had been particularly intriguing. Elizabeth reported her conversation with Emma Goldman. Matthew quickly decided he disliked "that woman" as much as she did. What had piqued his interest, though, was the possibility that two men might have been involved with Czolgosz. That had never been reported by the police or in the newspapers. Elizabeth felt they did exist, and she was determined to find them. He immediately sent a telegram back to her, warning (and then begging) her not to look for them. He would do that. His telegram brought no response.

*　　*　　*　　*

The morning after Stanton had received her last telegram, Elizabeth boarded the Illinois Central in Baltimore for a trip to Chicago. There, she had an appointment with Katherine Leckie, the former reporter for the *Chicago Times* who had been fired by Hearst because of Emma Goldman. Upon arriving late that afternoon, Elizabeth took the elevated train to the West Side building of the paper on Canal St. It was well past four o'clock when Elizabeth entered the newspaper's offices.

Several receptionists sat at a large curved desk inside the front door, one occupied with a visitor and the other working at a telephone switchboard. Approaching the switchboard operator, Elizabeth stood for several minutes as she plugged and unplugged calls. Looking around, Elizabeth saw stacks of newspapers, cartons and crates. Eventually, the woman looked up with questioning eyes. "I'm here for a meeting," Elizabeth said.

"Anyone in particular?" she asked.

"Oh, yes. Katherine Leckie."

Looking to her left, the operator said, "Go to the second floor and ask."

"Thank you." Reaching the second floor, she paused to survey the enormous room. It looked like a large warehouse with cubicles extending from one end to the other. The light was dim and was provided mainly by massive floor-to-ceiling pane windows. Elizabeth was shown to a cubicle near the center of the room where a woman with light brown shoulder-length hair was leaning down to remove items from a crate. Elizabeth was at once struck by the condition of the cubicle. Other than the packing crate, there were two hard-back wood chairs and a small desk occupying the tiny space.

Glancing up at Elizabeth, the woman said, "You must be Mrs. Ambridge." Dropping a file on her desk, she said, "I'm Katherine Liekie. I don't know whether I'll be able to help you or not, but I'll try. Pease have a seat." Elizabeth was aware of a slight British accent as she sat down. She moved slightly, attempting to get comfortable in the rigid chair.

"You're relocating?" she asked.

"In a sense," said Liekie. "I was fired from my last job and was fortunate enough to land this one only several days ago. Unpacking can be hell in a space this small." Sitting next to Elizabeth, she added, "But it doesn't take much space to listen to what you have to say. You said in your telegram that you met with Emma Goldman."

The accent was more noticeable now. Liekie seemed well spoken and educated. Her clothing was conservative yet flattering to her lithe figure. A navy blue skirt with a slim waist was hemmed to the floor, and she wore a cotton blouse with ballooned shoulders that was embroidered around her neck. Elizabeth thought how pretty she was. "How much do you know about Emma Goldman and Leon Czolgosz?"

"Enough to know that Emma's not an act and that someone pushed Czolgosz to kill McKinley."

"Pushed?"

"Yes. The police theorized there may have been a second shooter. I don't know about that. Czolgosz wasn't well educated and he had been unemployed for quite some time. Yet he was able to get himself to Buffalo, buy a gun, and intricately plan for just the right moment to shoot McKinley. He didn't do that alone."

"Emma said he told her about two men."

Liekie nodded. "She told me that, too. But if they existed, the police couldn't find them and neither could I."

"You tried to find them?"

"I tried; it would have made an incredible story. I really had very little to go on, and Emma couldn't remember any names. When I talked to Czolgosz, he gave me the same names he gave the police. As far as I could determine, they each cleverly used an alias."

"Did he describe them for you?"

Liekie reached down into the box, sifted through some papers, and pulled out a notebook. Flipping through the pages, she stopped and exclaimed, "Here it is. You're going to love this – he thought they were ordinary looking. Both were about five foot eight, had slight builds and were well-dressed. Business suits. One had a small mustache, the other a beard. According to Czolgosz, they appeared to be in their mid to late thirties. They identified themselves as avid supporters of the anarchist movement, and – get this – 'admirers' of Czolgosz. That sure must have built up his self-esteem! To top that off, they gave him a lot of money. Czolgosz said it was always in cash. When I asked how much, he just shrugged his shoulders. His eventually said he never counted it, that there was always more than he needed." Turning a page, she said, "Oh, this is interesting. I asked when was the last time he had seen them. He said it was in Buffalo, the day before the assassination."

Elizabeth was riveted to her story. "Did he tell you why they were there?"

Liekie looked down again at her notes and then turned several pages. "I did ask him that. He said they were there for support – whatever that means. They gave him the comfort in knowing that he was not alone, and somehow convinced him that he would publicly be thought of as a hero." Shaking her head, she mumbled, "You know, he really was insane. They must have been terribly persuasive."

It was beginning to feel stifling to Elizabeth. She reached up and unbuttoned the top two buttons of her blouse. Watching her, Liekie commented, "It is very hot. Even with all these windows, it can be like an oven in here. The coal furnaces put out continuous heat."

"Miss Liekie, the one thing that puzzles me is why the police seemed to dismiss so easily Czolgosz' statement that those men existed. Why do you think they did that?"

She turned her chair slightly and lifted her feet to rest them on the crate. "I don't think that's entirely correct. They did quite a search to find the men, but they had no leads and really nowhere to look other than the names Czolgosz gave them. And you must remember, they questioned him for days on end, and during that time he rambled from one thought to another. After a while, I think he just wore them down."

"So they . . . ."

Interrupting, Liekie said, "There was something else. This man, Matthew Stanton. He was the one who really grabbed their interest. When the police locked onto him, they thought they had their man. The other two men seemed to just fade away in their minds."

Elizabeth stood to stretch her cramped legs and smooth out her flared skirt. Sitting back down, she stared off into the distance.

Liekie said, "Something's on your mind. What is it?"

Snapping out of her trance, she answered, "Is there a way, any way at all, that these men might be found?"

"I don't know a way," Liekie answered, her hands raised in doubt. "I tried everything I could think of, all for nothing."

Standing to leave, Elizabeth said, "Miss Liekie, you've been so helpful. I wonder if we could talk again."

Sitting on the edge of her desk, Liekie said, "Any time you'd like. But before you leave, please tell me one thing. Why are you so interested in Czolgosz and these two men he spoke about?"

Hesitating, Elizabeth admitted, "I might as well be truthful. Matthew Stanton has become a close acquaintance of mine. I think it's awful what they did to him. I suppose I just want to know the truth."

"So it's not for a story for the *Baltimore Sun*?"

"It could be, but that's not on my mind right now."

Looking deeply into her eyes, Liekie asked, "Mrs. Ambridge, will you promise me one thing? If there is a story out of this, will you be kind enough to share it with me?"

"Of course," she said, extending her hand. "That's the least I could do. Thank you."

After shaking Liekie's hand, Elizabeth turned to leave. "Oh," she heard behind her, "one more thing." Turning, she saw Liekie's serious expression. "Be safe," she warned. "These are not Boy Scouts you're looking for."

CHAPTER THIRTY

▼

Philadelphia, Pennsylvania

Theodore Roosevelt was not known for his patience, and neither was Matthew Stanton. The President wanted action, and Stanton was determined to provide it. Checking out of the hospital against the protests of his doctors and Alyssa, Matthew hobbled with a cane and Alyssa on his arm to a waiting carriage. The burning pain returned to his stomach, and he squeezed his eyes shut in an attempt not to let it control him. Watching his tormented expression, Alyssa whispered, "Matthew, you're not at all well. Please come to my house; stay with me so I can nurse you back to health."

"For a day or two," he said. "But after that, I have to leave for a while."

"Only a day or two? What's more important than your health — and me?"

He held up a finger, motioning for her silence until they were seated in the privacy of the carriage. Once there, he said, "I'm restructuring my company. We're making major changes, and I need to be there."

"I'll go with you," she offered.

"It's not possible, not now."

"Why?" she protested.

"Alyssa, you're heir to a very complicated $60 million estate. That requires a lot of your time. I have an important business to run."

"That's not the reason," she said with a chill in her voice. "I'm sorry I couldn't be with you every day in the hospital, but you needed a lot of rest and I had things I had to do. Now I have the time." She turned and looked out the window as they passed imposing office and warehouse buildings located along the Delaware River. He remained silent. Turning back, she stunned him. "Is it *that* woman?"

His eyes flashed in surprise. "What woman?"

"Matthew, you know what I'm asking. The woman holding your hand in the hospital."

"Are you jealous?"

"I could be. Were you honest with me?"

Remorseful, he took her hand. "I've always been honest with you. 'That woman', as you describe her, is a very good friend. She saved my life, and I owe her for that. Alyssa, there's no one for me but you," he lied. "I want you to accept that."

She leaned over and kissed him gently, and then more intensely. "I have a thought about how I might help bring about your speedy recovery."

He smiled. "Do you want to tell me?"

"I'll do better than that. I'll show you – when we get home."

He rested his head against back of the seat. Mumbling under his breath, he said, "You've got yourself a deal." With that, she snuggled against him, feeling a little smug with the thought that she had that kind of control over him.

*   *   *   *

Several hours later, they sat opposite each other in the living room of her Philadelphia mansion, a silver coffee table with a glass top and a pot of hot tea separating them. His cane rested on the edge of the sofa. Next to him, a crackling fire in the marble trimmed fireplace sounded like a soothing lullaby. His hand against his forehead, he tried to distract his thoughts from the pain that would come and go.

He concentrated instead on the exquisite woman sitting across from him, dressed in a floor-length pink chiffon dress laced with red. She was breathtaking. But he knew there was trouble brewing behind her eyes.

"I think," she said, "we should talk about what happens next."

"Next?"

"Matthew, please don't play games with me. You know very well what I mean. Us."

He smiled. "I could talk better if you'd come over here."

She returned his smile with a frown. "That's precisely why I won't. Let's start at the beginning. What are you not telling me? And don't give me that innocent little boy look. I know there's something going on."

The searing pain returned to his stomach and he writhed a little.

She noticed his change of expression. "Are you all right?"

Holding his stomach while taking a deep breath, he said, "No, thanks to your deceased husband. Alyssa," he said hoarsely, "you're entitled to know everything, but this isn't a good time for me. It's late, and I'd like to go to bed - with you. Could we talk tomorrow?"

The look of aggravation in her eyes jumped out at him. "If there's something that will come between us, I'd like to hear it now. I know you're hurting, but I need you to tell me the truth."

The truth, he thought to himself. *What variation?* Answering, he said, "For now, I'll tell you this. I've made a commitment to the President that I've vowed to keep. And I will."

She wasn't pleased. "Roosevelt! Now the truth comes out, but that's hardly an answer."

"I said for now," he said faintly. "Whatever else I tell you will break my promise to him. Look, if I tell you more, it would be dangerous for you . . . and for me. I won't say this to you often, but I need you not to ask any more questions and to trust me."

"That's ridiculous. Haven't you had enough? Look at you. Matthew, you have me *now*, and I need you. I want time with you. What is it that makes you unable to accept happiness? Why are you always looking for something else?"

He hesitated. "Someday I'll tell you the whole story of my life. Right now I'm doing the best I can."

"I may not want to hear it. You have me now, but it may not last. If you continue to play your games with me, you may wake up and find me gone. Matthew, I put up with hell for almost six years. I'm through with that. You know I love you, but I also want a life. I have a lot of money and a lot of men chasing after me. You'd better make up your mind pretty soon."

"It sounds like you're threatening me."

"Take it any way you want. I know you've lived a life for yourself. That won't work with me. If that still appeals to you, my suggestion is go for it. Just don't pull me down with you."

$$*\qquad*\qquad*\qquad*$$

The light sliced across the room, crossing the bed where he rested his head. He felt the moonlight in his eyes and found it intrusive. Blinking, he opened his eyes to see someone moving in the room. For a moment, he lay silent. Focusing his eyes in the dark, he saw the figure of a nude woman standing in front of the window.

He rolled over gently, realizing he was alone in bed. He watched her as she stood there, now facing him. She suddenly realized he was not asleep but was staring at her. "Come back to bed," he said tenderly.

Reaching for a gown, she pushed her lose hair away from her face. "I was wondering," she said, "if we're really right for each other."

He pulled himself up abruptly and sat against the head-board. "In the middle of the night you're having those thoughts? My God, Alyssa, we've barely had time to know each other. You're expecting a lot for such a short time."

Tying the sash of the gown around her waist, she looked around the room. "This bedroom holds horrific memories for me. I should never have slept with you here. I woke up startled with nightmares from my past. This thing you're doing for the President – I know it's dangerous or you wouldn't be so secretive."

She stopped, unable to take her eyes off of him. In the softness of the moonlight, she saw the same remarkably handsome man whose eyes had captured hers in what seemed like an eternity ago. But something had changed. At times, he seemed to be in a different world, completely preoccupied with things other than her. There were places within him that were closed off to her. She was beginning to feel his cool courtesy.

He put on a robe lying near the bed and walked over to the window, looking down on the garden below. With his back to her, he said, "Alyssa, you've been through hell. For that matter, so have I." Turning, he put his arms around her and felt her moist cheeks. "I've never met a woman like you, but you have to understand something. I've lived with a built-in defense mechanism walling me off from close relationships. I'd like everything to just stop so that we could live happily ever after." Lifting her chin in his hand, he whispered, "It won't happen. I can't do that. The only real love I've ever experienced in my life until you was Berg, and it was the day I held his head after I had killed five men." Stopping to inhale a deep breath, he murmured, "I want you so bad it hurts."

"Then I'm yours; take me," she pleaded.

Pulling away, he said, "That would be too easy. Give me a little time."

Without answering, she returned to bed with him, putting her head on his chest and her arm around him. After a while, she said, "I may not give you that time. When are you leaving?"

"Tomorrow."

"So that's how it is. I stay and you leave." In the painful silence, she felt as though she were suffocating.

CHAPTER THIRTY-ONE

▼

New York City

Elizabeth's belief that Czolgosz' plan to kill McKinley had been initiated and set in motion by two unknown men weighed heavily on Matthew Stanton's mind. The assassination had been carried out with such surgical precision that he knew it was the mark of professionals and not a deranged killer. So had the attempt to frame him. On the morning following his return to New York, he acted on a hunch and walked into the smoke-filled den of Sach's Café at ten in the morning. Emma Goldman had met Berkman there; it was the hotbed of the anarchist movement.

The café was deceiving in its appearance. Its small exterior façade had given no indication of the large restaurant inside. Sitting at a small, round table in the rear of the café, Matthew could survey the crowd of over fifty people huddled about the room. He puffed a cigarette carefully and spoke politely with a hint of a New York accent to the few people who had walked by and bothered to speak to him. A raven-haired girl sat nearby with two female companions, frequently stealing a glance at him. He was dressed casually in dark clothes, with the beginning of a stubble beard. Sipping on a cup of coffee and reading the latest edition of *Free Society*, he barely looked up as the girl excused herself from her companions and walked over to him.

Standing several feet away, she said, "I haven't seen you here before." He looked up at her as she blurted out, "I'm an actress."

"You are? Maybe I've seen you at a theater."

She sat in a chair across from him, crossing her legs. "I don't think so," she said hesitantly. "I don't work around here."

He laid his newspaper on the floor, stubbed out his cigarette, and focused his eyes on her. She might have been attractive at another time, maybe with make-up and finer clothes, but she struck him as a woman who didn't care to be noticed. "Where do you work?"

"Around," she said evasively. "You're reading *Free Society*. Are you one of them?"

"I don't know. Who is them?"

She let out a slight grin. "*Them* is the Socialists, the anarchists who come here."

"And you're not one of them?"

"Not yet." Looking down at his ashtray, she said, "I'm Evelyn McGiver."

"Pleased to meet you, Evelyn. Can I buy you a cup of coffee."

"Yes. Thank you. You haven't given me your name."

"Henry Judson," he said. "Have you been coming here for a while?"

"About three months. Actually," she admitted, "I'm looking for work."

"Three months. Jobs must be hard to come by."

"They are. You wouldn't be looking for someone to hire, would you?"

He shook his head. "No."

A flash of disappointment crossed her face. She moved slightly, as if she were standing to leave. "Don't go," he said. "Wait for your coffee."

She settled back down, staring at him. "Why are you here?"

"I was hoping to get some information."

"About . . . ?"

"About Leon Czolgosz, the man who shot McKinley."

Her hand instinctively went to her mouth. "You're not a cop, are you?"

He smiled. "No. You can take that worried look off your face." Moving his hand in a circular gesture, he said, "I think this movement is fascinating. I'm writing a book about what makes it tick. Czolgosz is a good place to start. Did you know him?"

She sat back, alarmed. "Are you accusing me of . . . ."

"No," he interjected. "I just thought you might have met him."

"No, I never met him. But I did hear one of the waiters bragging that he had served him."

"Could you point him out to me?"

She turned and looked around the room. "He's not here."

Stopping to light a cigarette, he said, "You sure?"

"Yeah. He's a funny-looking skinny bald guy. He always seems to be bragging about something. He probably never met Czolgosz. I've heard he wasn't here much."

"Czolgosz?"

Sarcastically, she said, "Isn't that who were talking about?"

Ignoring her comment, he asked, "Do you know his name?"

"The waiter?"

Stanton just nodded.

"No, but I'll ask my friends." She got up, walked back to her table, said a few words to the women there, and returned.

"Milburn."

"Is that his first or last name?"

"Mister, I have no idea. My friends said people just call him Milburn." She turned and walked away without another word.

Signaling his waiter, Stanton asked for a check. Giving the waiter several dollars, he nonchalantly said, "When does Milburn come in?"

The waiter, a heavy-set man with suspicious eyes, asked, "Who wants to know?"

"Henry Judson, a writer. Tell him he could be the star of my next book."

"You tell him. He gets in about four."

"What's his first name?"

The waiter smiled and shook his head. "That *is* his first name. His last is Weisburg. Good luck in talking to him. That damned Russian Jew won't give me the time of day."

At four that afternoon, Stanton returned. Weisburg was taller than he had imagined, well over six feet. His cheeks were sunken and his face dotted with red blemishes. If he hadn't had an apron wrapped around his waist, his 135 pound body would have looked razor thin. He was busy arranging menus when Stanton approached. Without looking up, he said, "You wanted to talk to me?"

"How did you know that?"

Weisburg raised his blood-shot eyes to catch Stanton's look of surprise. "There aren't many secrets here," he answered in a gruff voice. "You can see I'm busy. If you've got something to say, say it."

Stanton looked around and saw they had drawn the attention of others in the restaurant. "Is there somewhere private where we could talk?"

Weisburg leaned over and whispered, "People don't want you around here. Let me tell you something – it's not safe. If I was you, I'd write my book about fly fishing or something else. You don't want to mess with these folks."

Pushing a crisp ten dollar bill into his hand, Stanton said in a louder voice, "I hate the damned government like these others do. Look at my busted up face. You see this cane," he said, holding it up high. "I don't walk with that damn thing because I'm a war hero. Those union busters beat the shit out of me. My book is about those rich bastards who are ruining our country."

Weisburg looked down at the bill, shoved it into his pocket, and thought what a poor actor Judson was. "Follow me." Dropping a stack of menus on a tray, he led Stanton through two swinging doors into the kitchen. It was empty. Rudely, Weisberg turned and said, "You've got three minutes."

"Leon Czolgosz."

"What about him? He was a crazy mixed-up lunatic. He did us all a favor, but good riddance just the same."

"I was told he met several men here, business types. Do you remember anything about that?"

Weisberg laughed. "Smith and Jones. When I heard those names, I told that little fucker he'd better be careful with them. They were phony as hell."

Stanton glanced around to be sure they were still alone. "Who were they?"

"Hell if I know. I warned him, but he said they were good guys. Helped his old lady and him out of a fix. That was his business, not mine. I dropped it. Why are you looking for them?" Weisburg asked suspiciously.

"My book."

"Oh yeah."

Walking out past the ovens, Weisburg looked back. "If you need anything else, I'm here."

Stanton followed him to the front of the café, thinking he was royally wasting his time. As he opened the door, Weisburg said, "Good luck on your book. With all the loonies in Washington, it should do well."

Stanton shrugged. Then he heard Weisburg say, "Oh, I forgot to mention. They were here yesterday."

Stanton stopped dead. "Yesterday? But Czolgosz's dead."

Weisburg stared at him. "You got that right. I think they're looking for more nuts. They were asking around about anarchists who wanted to stand up and do something about this country. They damn sure weren't running for office."

Weisburg turned to go back to his menus. Stanton walked quickly after him. "What time were they here?"

Weisburg rubbed his chin. "It was late, around nine. That's when this place really lights up."

"Thanks," Stanton said. "I'll dedicate my book to you."

With a slight grin, Weisburg said, "And I'll kiss your mother on 44th."

*   *   *   *

At nine o'clock that evening, the pianist began playing "The Maple Leaf Rag", the hit jazz tune written by Scott Joplin. It had swept the nation and was now sweeping Sach's Café. Matthew Stanton sat a table near the pianist, gently tapping his fingers in rhythm with the music. Occasionally, his eyes would search the faces for the men known as Smith and Jones. Sipping on his single malt scotch, the recurring pains he had come to know seemed to dissipate with the laughter, small talk, smoke and glittering lights from the array of gas lamps hanging from the ceiling and walls.

He was the watcher. Relaxing more with each drink, it never occurred to him that he was being studied and scrutinized by eyes in every part of the room. He was foreign to their world, an intruder, and he wasn't welcome. Milburn Weisburg was having a busy evening. The tips had already exceeded his best night at the café, and the evening was young. Serving three men sitting near the back of the room, Weisburg wondered how much money Judson would be willing to pay if he pointed out Smith and Jones. One of the men, well dressed and apparently a man of means, thanked Weisburg as he delivered their drinks and then turned to continue his conversation with the other well dressed man and a young man casually dressed. The younger man didn't fit with the other two. He was a little wild-eyed with a scruffy beard and ragged hair that were badly in need of trimming. The men had captured his attention – he was so intently wrapped up in the conversation that he barely moved when his bourbon was served.

Weisburg then walked deliberately across the room to Stanton's table, acting as though he were serving another drink. Stanton looked up as he approached, saying, "Good to see you, Milburn."

Weisburg nodded slightly and leaned over to serve the drink that hadn't been ordered. With a low voice, he asked, "How much are Smith and Jones worth to you?"

The man calling himself Judson smiled slightly. "Is anything free here?"

Weisburg raised his hands. "Hey, this is America, the land of opportunity."

Stanton pulled out a ten dollar bill, and Weisburg shook his head. "Make it fifteen this time – I'm taking a lot of risk doing this." Leaning closer, he added, "I told you you're not wanted here."

Pulling out another five dollars from his wallet, Stanton handed the fifteen to Weisburg with the comment, "That's more than a week's pay to a lot of people." Weisburg quickly shoved the money into a pocket in the front of his apron and nodded his head toward the back of the room, in the direction of the three men. "The three men in the corner," he whispered. "The two well-heeled gents are Smith and Jones." In a slightly louder tone, he said, "Thanks for the tip, buddy," and moved away.

Stanton sat back, lifted his bruised leg to the other chair at the table, and subtlety studied the men. They would have looked ordinary, like everyday businessmen, but not here, not in Sach's Café. They were engrossed in conversation with the younger man for several minutes as Stanton watched, never looking up. Then one of the men reached into his coat and removed an envelope, which he passed on to the younger man. The younger man peeked inside and nodded his thanks. Stanton guessed it contained money. The younger man then got up and left, leaving the other two to their drinks. Pulling his leg off the chair, Stanton grabbed his drink with one hand and his cane with the other, and hobbled over to their table.

"Henry Judson," he said, laying his drink down and extending his hand. Neither man attempted to be courteous. Staring at Stanton, one said, "You're the writer?" The other sat quietly assessing Stanton, letting his eyes drift down the unshaven face to the well-tailored casual clothes.

"How did you know that?"

"Word travels fast in here." Then in an aggressive tone, he said, "Is there something you want?"

Sitting down in the third chair and hanging his cane on the back, Stanton said, "Conversation. My book is about our imperialist government and their rich cronies who are destroying the working class. It's time that someone stood up and did something about it."

They seemed unimpressed. "You've found the wrong place for conversation," one said. "Why don't you go back to where you came from?"

Ignoring the offensive response, Stanton said, "You two, you don't look like the others in here. You're out of place. Are you cops?"

One laughed under his breath. "Recruiters," he murmured.

"Recruiting here? For what?"

The other man leaned forward, almost touching the oil lamp on the table. "That's none of your damn business!"

"Look," Stanton said defensively, "I'll leave. Give me your names so I can put them in my book."

"Why in the hell would you do that?" one demanded.

"Recruiters in a sea of anarchists. I think that makes good reading."

Grabbing his arm, the man with the mustache said, "I'd advise you not to do that!"

Stanton pulled away. "Are you threatening me?"

The other man put his hand on his friend's shoulder. "Calm down," he said. "Maybe we can have a little friendly conversation with Mr. Judson." Turning to Stanton, he said, "We were a little rude. My name is Jones; my friend here is Smith."

"Pleased to know you. Now, tell me, what are you recruiting for?"

The two men looked at each other and then back at Stanton. "You tell him," one said. The other warily narrowed his eyes. "Our employer is hiring patriotic Americans for his business."

"Who is he?"

"It's not a he; it's a company out in California. You wouldn't know it," he said evasively.

"Try me. What's its business?"

"Well, Mr. Judson, it has a lot of businesses. Our job is to fit our candidates into the right one, like putting a round peg in a round hole, and not a square one."

Stanton sat back, took a sip of his drink, and suspiciously eyed each man. "You haven't answered my question. What's does it do? What's so damn secret about this 'employer' you keep referring to?"

Their expressions hardened. In a low voice, one said, "You're asking too many questions for your own good. I think we've had enough of you. Goodbye, Mr. Judson." He signaled the waiter for a check.

Stanton raised his palm in a gesture of defeat. "Look," he said, "what I asked you were fair questions. I'm a writer, so I ask questions. What if I said I was looking for work?"

"You?" one questioned. "Why? You said you were writing a book."

Stanton exhaled a deep breath. "You haven't seen my name at any bookstores, have you? I need the money."

"You don't look like a man who needs work," the other said.

"How should you look to need a job?"

"Good point." He then whispered something to his friend and turned back to Stanton. "We'll think on it. What do you do other than writing?"

"I spent some time on freighters after I left the army."

"Army?" They stole a glance at each other.

"Rough Riders."

After a slight pause, one asked, "So you knew Roosevelt? What did you think of him?"

"Yeah, I knew him. Not much," Stanton said. "He's a damned imperialist. He'll destroy this country if he can."

One smiled. "So you didn't have a good time on San Juan Hill?"

"We butchered a lot of innocent women and children. You won't read about that in the newspapers."

The waiter interrupted with the check, and one of the men placed a ten dollar bill on the table. "Mr. Judson, you may hear from us. Good luck on your book." Standing to leave, he was stopped by Stanton. "How will you find me?"

"We'll be around. We may see you in here again." The other stood up and they walked away, leaving Stanton alone with his drink.

CHAPTER THIRTY-TWO

▼

Washington, D. C.

The heavy-set Marine escorted Matthew Stanton to a rear entrance of the White House. From there, he was taken down a long corridor and up to the second floor, to the President's office. When Stanton entered, Secretary of War Elihu Root stood to shake his hand. Gazing at Stanton's appearance, Root was dismayed. "Mr. Stanton," he said in a harsh voice, "do you understand you're meeting with the President of the United States, not some two-bit dictator? You look as though you haven't shaven in a week."

Slightly embarrassed, Stanton replied, "When I was asked to come to Washington, I assumed it was to meet with you."

Root said indignantly, "And I deserve less respect than the President, is that what you're saying?"

"No, not at all. Mr. Secretary, I've been hanging out in places populated by anarchists. I scarcely feel I would have much chance of penetrating their group if I were well groomed and polished."

A throat was cleared behind them, and they turned to see Roosevelt. "You were saying, Captain . . . ."

Stanton reached out and shook his hand. "How much did you hear, Mr. President?"

"Enough," Roosevelt answered. "So your best disguise is to look like you - that day we rode up San Juan Hill?"

Root's expression remained unchanged, but Stanton smiled. "That's about it, sir."

"Bully for you," Roosevelt said as he walked around his desk. Sitting down, he motioned to Stanton to do the same. "Try not to get the furniture dirty, Mr. Stanton." He then flashed his characteristic smile to Root, who saw no humor in what was said.

Glaring at Stanton through his thick glasses, Roosevelt asked, "Do you have their names for us?"

"Not yet, but I'm working on it."

Root remained silent, studying Stanton's appearance. "Ignore the Secretary. He should have been in Cuba with us. He's too damned proper. Now, tell me what you've found out."

Taking a moment for a deep breath, Stanton said, "Robert Longbourne has had a number of detectives questioning my employees and servants. They've talked to the bank officers where that five thousand dollars account was opened, and they've ransacked my house looking for any clues as to how that gun got there. Their report filled one page – they came up with nothing. Whoever got into my house was very skilled at what he did. There was no evidence of any break-in."

Roosevelt gritted his teeth. "Then why in the hell are we meeting today? And who is Robert Longbourne?"

"Longbourne runs my company."

Root cut in. "Mr. President, we're here today because Mr. Stanton told me about an encounter he had that I want you to hear first hand."

Roosevelt looked at him and then shifted his eyes to Stanton. Stanton continued, "I met two men at Sach's Café in New York, a well known meeting place for anarchists. They met with Leon Czolgosz before he shot President McKinley and, from what I was told, paid him some money."

Roosevelt leaned forward, his interest piqued. "Who were they?"

"I don't know. I was lucky enough to meet them, but they went by the names Smith and Jones."

"Did you ask them about Czolgosz?"

"No, sir. I didn't want to make them suspicious."

"Then what in the hell did you talk about?"

"I asked them what they were doing there, and they said they were recruiting."

"Recruiting? For what?"

"For an unnamed company in California. They wouldn't tell me who or what they were looking for."

Pulling out his watch, Roosevelt looked at the time and said, "What's your take on this?"

"I think they had something to do with the assassination. They're back at Sach's Café *recruiting* among anarchists. Why would they do that?"

Roosevelt stood abruptly and began to pace. "Dammit," he spat out. "If they're looking for another assassin, I want to know why. And, Mr. Stanton, we don't have a lot of time. These anarchists want to destroy my government. When do you meet with them again?"

"They wouldn't tell me."

"Bully!" Roosevelt mumbled to himself. "Mr. Secretary, I want you to send a team of your best men with Stanton to find these people."

"Mr. President," Root said, "that would be a mistake. If we do that, they'll disappear. The best we can do is give Mr. Stanton a little time."

Roosevelt stopped his pacing, opened the door and walked out. After several moments, Stanton turned to Root and asked, "What does that mean?"

"It means the meeting's over. Keep in touch," he said as he stood and followed the President.

*   *   *   *

New York City

The next afternoon, the men who called themselves Smith and Jones met with their contact in an old warehouse on 76th Street. Constricted streams of sunlight made their way through tapered windows near the ceiling, casting deep shadows across the empty cavernous room. The contact stood in those shadows, protected from the penetrating cold of an unheated building by a heavy wool overcoat and thick scarf. He lit a cigarette and took a long puff, watching the smoke slowly drift upward.

Shifting his gaze to the two men, he spoke in a deep voice that resonated throughout the building. "This man who calls himself Henry Judson, he was never with the Rough Riders. Our people at the War Department tell us there's no record that he ever served in the army. He's as phony as the two of you."

Smith and Jones remained silent, surprised by what they had heard. "This Judson, or whatever his name is, has us very worried. You made a big mistake talking to him."

Smith defensively replied, "We didn't have much choice. He came over and sat at our table."

The contact irritably stubbed out his cigarette with his foot and said, "Why in the hell didn't you leave?" The silence told him the answer. "So what are you going to do about him?"

Jones shrugged. "Do you want us to kill him?"

There were several minutes of silence as the contact lit another cigarette and more smoke drifted to the ceiling. "That would be another mistake. No, we don't want you to do that, not yet. Meet with him again. If you have to, take him through an interview process. Not ours; make one up. Find out who in the hell he is."

"What?" Jones said.

"You heard me. We want to know who he works for before we kill him."

After a pause, Smith asked, "When are you going to come out of the shadows and tell us who you are and who *you* work for?"

In an agitated voice, he answered, "You know our arrangement. You ask that again, and you won't be working for anyone." The contact tossed a thick envelope to Jones; it hit him in the chest and fell to the floor. Watching him reach down for it, the contact said, "Your monthly installment. Have you found any candidates to take the test?"

"We've got some leads, but nothing solid yet."

"Get them nailed down. I'll meet you here next week, same time. I want to know about Judson." Pointing with the burning tip of his cigarette at a back door, he said, "Go out that way."

When they had reached the back street, Jones turned to Smith with fury in his eyes. "Son-of-a-bitch!"

The next day their instructions were changed.

*   *   *   *

When Stanton walked into Sach's Café three days later, Milburn stopped him and said, "Where've you been? They're asking a lot of questions about you."

Removing his top coat, Stanton asked, "Smith and Jones?"

"Who else."

"Are they here now?"

Milburn looked around and then said under his breath, "Haven't seen them yet. Since you met them, they've been back every night looking for you. What'd you say to get them so interested?"

Stanton shook his head. "I have no idea. They didn't seem that interested when I talked to them."

Picking up a tray of plates, Milburn headed for the kitchen. Briefly pausing, he turned and said, "There's something going on."

Thirty minutes later, they walked in. Seeing Stanton, they sent a waiter over to ask him to join them. When he approached their table, Smith said, "Come join us, Mr. Judson."

"Are you ready to talk to me about a job?" Stanton asked as he sat down.

The two stared at him without answering. Then Jones said, "Do you want to tell us who you are?"

He answered unemotionally, "I'm who I said I was, Henry Judson."

"Let's cut the bullshit," the other said. "You're not Henry Judson. There is no Henry Judson."

Drawing imaginary circles on the table cloth with his finger, he wondered how they found that out. "That's my pen name."

They stole a questioning look at each other. Jones whispered something to Smith and then said, "Our employer wants to meet with you."

"Good. We're making some progress. You said your employer was a company. Who wants to meet me?"

"You'll find out tomorrow afternoon. Five o'clock. The Stafford building at Madison and 75th. Go to the second floor and ask for us. We'll meet you there at five."

"He must love intrigue. I'll think about it."

"You wanted a job, didn't you? He wants to talk to you about your writing."

"So he *can* read?"

The one with the mustache leaned into his face. "Don't get smart with us."

"Then who in the hell am I to meet with?"

"You wouldn't know him."

"Give me a name."

"You know what," said the other man, "I'm getting tired of your bullshit."

"That makes two of us," Stanton sarcastically replied.

They got up to leave. "Suit yourself," the bearded one said. "If we don't see you, then we won't see you. You're not the only one we're talking to."

They heard him mumble as they walked away, "I'll bet."

*   *   *   *

At ten minutes to five, Stanton's carriage pulled up to the Stafford building. The cloudy sky was turning dark, and the light drizzle had suddenly become a heavy downpour. He sat in the comfort of the enclosed cab, listening to the sharp cracks of thunder while he examined the Colt .41 given to him by the President. He spun the chamber to be sure it was fully loaded, and then replaced the gun in his pocket. He waited, studying the building through the small round window of the carriage. It looked like it had just been completed and was unoccupied. There wasn't a hint of any activity. Down the street, out of sight, he had arranged for two detectives to watch the building while he was inside. If he didn't return within an hour, they were to come in looking for him. He had carefully thought out the plan, not believing for a moment that Smith and Jones would introduce him to their employer. But curiosity had gotten the better of him.

What he hadn't planned for was the second carriage sitting at the opposite end of the street. Thaddeus Pratt, looking through a small pair of binoculars, was attempting to see who Stanton was through his carriage's back window. The torrent of rain, splashing against the window, interfered with his view. He slammed the binoculars down on the seat and waited. Ten minutes later, Stanton raised his umbrella and stepped out of the carriage. First looking around, he walked to the building's front entrance. Finding the door locked, he silently smiled to himself. He had expected something like this. Flashes of lightning lit up the sky. Drenched and feeling the cold, after five minutes he stepped back into the carriage and told the driver to leave.

Furious at his bad luck, Pratt had opened the door of his carriage in an attempt to see Stanton, soaking both himself and the inside of the cab. The umbrella was in the way; it was useless. Irate, he closed the door and pounded the seat with his fist. "Damn him," he roared. The man sitting opposite him raised his eyebrows. "Did you see him?"

Pratt dropped the binoculars and gazed out at the deluge. "No, that son-of-a-bitch was hidden by his umbrella." Yelling up to the driver, he screamed, "Chase down that carriage in front. Run into him if you have to." The driver cracked his whip and the carriage lurched forward in a frenzy, flying along the rain soaked street. Four blocks later, it caught up with Stanton. Pulling alongside Stanton's carriage, Pratt stared at him. He had had a hunch who he was, and he had acted on that hunch. He was rarely wrong. Stanton stared back. "Pull up, driver," Pratt screamed as Stanton's carriage moved ahead. He mumbled to himself in disbelief, "I don't know him."

Pratt decided he would go to plan B. The man who called himself Judson wouldn't stay unknown for long. He would have him followed; he *would* find out who in the hell he was! If he was a true anarchist, Pratt would use him. If he wasn't, he would have him killed. There was too much at stake. *What if Judson was too smart? What if he recognized me?* he asked himself. Judson was an enigma. Mentally drowning out the sound of the rain pummeling the top of his carriage, he thought, *If plan B fails, I'll go through the whole damned alphabet.*

CHAPTER THIRTY-THREE

▼

New York City

Mathew Stanton had been followed before. He had learned early from Berger how to know he was being watched. It was a feeling that was instinctive. That feeling was back. He walked along Madison Avenue at five in the afternoon, heading for a meeting with Longbourne. The weather was brisk and chilly; the sun was slowly setting in the west. The men following him were invisible, but he knew they were there. He stopped to look in the window of a clothing store, studying the shadowy reflections in the glass. A man across the street, wearing a black hat and coat, also stopped to look in a window. The man wasn't alone, but Stanton couldn't see any others.

His was distracted by the sounds of the steel-rimmed wheels of the carriages and the hoofs of several hundred horses hammering on the cobblestone street as they passed him by. After a moment, he looked back over his shoulder. Dozens of people crisscrossed the sidewalk. A maitre d' stood outside a restaurant, trying to attract customers. There were two rabbis talking to each other, and behind them . . . two men who had stopped to look in a window. It was a bank.

Both men were young, well dressed in dark overcoats and hats, their shoes highly shined. It was not their appearance that got his attention; it was their apparent interest in looking through a meaningless window. They were alert, taking turns in casually looking up in his direction. He thought what amateurs they were.

Who in the hell were they?

He was tempted to walk up to them, but his instincts warned him against that. Instead, he resumed his walk and then suddenly ducked into an alley separating two buildings. Standing in a side doorway, he waited. No one had followed him. He checked his watch. Ten minutes had passed. Seeing the alley was empty, he stepped out of the doorway and headed for the street. Suddenly, they were there, blocking his exit. His anger rising, he reached inside his coat and grasped the grip of his pistol and cocked the gun. Walking toward them, he felt something slam against his head. His legs collapsed and he fell hard to the ground. Then he felt their hands rifling through his pockets. One of the men was in his face. "Who are you?" he demanded.

His assailant was unprepared for the answer. Stanton squeezed the trigger of the gun inside his coat and the bullet struck the assailant in the mouth. He collapsed on top of Stanton as another assailant slammed his fist into Stanton's head.

Then everything went dark. Gradually opening his eyes, Stanton couldn't tell how long he had lain there. Eyeing the bloodied face of the dead man lying next to him, he tried to determine where he was. He was cold; they had taken his coat. Reaching for his watch, he saw that it was gone too, as was his wallet. Dragging himself up, he leaned against a wall, watching the few pedestrians remaining on the street unknowingly pass him by. Touching his swollen head, he felt a sticky crust – caked blood. He staggered out onto the street, and within moments felt the rough hands of a policeman.

"Who are you, buddy?"

Blinking several times to clear his vision, he said, "Stanton, Matthew Stanton."

The policeman turned to a companion and said, "Harry, we've found him."

Turning back to Stanton, he took his arm. "Can I help you, Mr. Stanton? We've had people out looking for you."

Feeling his knees wobble, he said, "Yes, thank you. There's a dead man in the alley. My wallet's been stolen. If you could get me home."

*   *   *   *

Baltimore, Maryland

That evening, Elizabeth Ambridge sat on the other side of a desk, engaged in a serious discussion with her husband, Dalton. In his late sixties, he had a pleasant demeanor that masked a man obsessed with his work and prone to outbursts of temper. He was short, overweight, and suffered from diabetes and skin cancer which was gradually deforming a face partially hidden by his beard. In overall appearance, though, he was considered by most to be a very elegant man, always dressed dapperly in the latest men's fashion of the day. He was a man of power and wealth, respected and feared by his peers, and unaccustomed to losing. Eyeing his wife over the rims of the glasses that sat far down on his nose, he felt a deep pang of regret for his age and physical condition, and for the platonic relationship they had shared so long.

"Elizabeth," he expelled slowly, "I want to try to understand you. You've asked a lot of me regarding this man Stanton, and I've done what you've asked. When you went to Washington to defend him, I was okay with that. But now you're saying he's in trouble again. You want to go to New York to help him, yet he hasn't asked for your help." She sat in perfect stillness listening to him, barely showing any expression.

"You are my wife, Elizabeth, and I hope you'll remain so. Without doubt, you're an extremely beautiful and intelligent woman, and I'm sure very attractive to the opposite sex. I don't know your arrangement with Mr. Stanton, but it's beginning to worry me. I love you, not in the passionate way you would like, but we both understood that when we got married." Sitting back in his chair, he removed his glasses to rub his eyes. She remained silent. "There is something very unsettling about all of this. I'm smart enough to know you have feelings for him. Would you mind telling me about them and his feelings for you?"

Quietly clearing her throat, she nervously twisted her diamond necklace between her thumb and forefinger. "Dalton, I love you, in my own way. I always have. You know that." He listened intently, unmoved. "With that said," she continued, "I'm thirty-five and you're almost seventy. I hate that, but that's just the way it is. I never intentionally sought out Mr. Stanton; we met by pure accident. I didn't want to, but I'll admit to you . . . I have fallen in love with him." Her eyes began to moisten, unable to deal with the anguish she had brought upon him. Looking down, she was overwhelmed with guilt.

In a voice betraying her misery, she admitted, "As to his feelings for me, they're not reciprocal. He's been very honest with me. He's in love with another woman."

Astonished, Dalton asked, "And you still love him?"

Wiping a tear away with her finger, she murmured, "I do."

"I'm sorry," he said leaning forward, "I didn't hear that."

Taking a deep breath in an effort to calm her emotions, she repeated, "I do. Dalton, I need to help him."

"How long will you be away?"

"I don't know."

"Elizabeth," he said tenderly, "I don't want to lose you. But putting that aside, I'm worried about your safety. From what you've told me about Stanton, trouble seems to follow him. He's dealing with anarchists, for Christ's sake! I'm not blind to the research you were doing for him, Elizabeth. These people are crazy – they're murderers."

She took a handkerchief from her pocket and dabbed her eyes. Her response was silence.

He turned away, silently wishing this wasn't happening. With shaky resignation, he said, "I can't stop you." Looking at her with woeful eyes, he whispered, "Please let me know how you are, where you are. Will you do that?"

"Of course." She walked around the desk and kissed the top of his head. He looked up to see her golden hair, her soft green eyes, and the shapely figure of the most gorgeous woman he had ever known, a woman who he wished so fervently he had met thirty-five years before.

The next day, Elizabeth checked into the Mayfair Hotel and immediately sent word to Matthew Stanton that she was in New York to help him. A deep anxiety gnawed at her, worried at what his reaction might be.

CHAPTER THIRTY-FOUR

▼

New York City

The message was slipped under his door while he lay in pain, an ice pack covering his swollen face. Reading it two hours later in the seclusion of his bedroom, he asked himself, "Why in the hell would she do that?" Lying still in the desolate silence, Matthew Stanton decided that the day after tomorrow was soon enough to deal with Elizabeth.

Thirty miles away, in the solitude of his mansion on Long Island, Thaddeus Pratt sat sifting through the contents of the wallet that had been delivered to him. He counted five hundred dollars, a large amount for any man to be carrying. Shuffling through various business cards, nothing caught his interest except two identical cards, each reading, *Far East Shipping. Matthew Stanton, Chairman.* "Son-of-a-bitch," he said to himself. Either the man he had had beaten knew Stanton . . . or he was Stanton. He now wished he had been there for the beating, then he would've known for sure. Laying the wallet down among scattered papers, he took a sip from the glass of bourbon sitting on his desk, feeling the warm sensation drift down his throat. He knew what he had to do. It was too great a risk to do nothing.

* * * *

The Mayfair Hotel was bustling with activity when Matthew Stanton walked through the lobby. Stepping into the elevator with several guests, he asked for the third floor. He had sent a message asking Elizabeth to have dinner with him at Delmonico's, and she had replied she would. He arrived ten minutes early, stopping to adjust his vest before knocking on the door. When it opened, his eyes slowly drifted from her stormy green eyes to her glittering diamond earrings and necklace, and then down to her creamy silk evening gown, with its multi-laced front, puffed sleeves and flared long skirt that made an intriguing rustling sound as she moved. "You look lovely," he admitted.

She looked at him, mesmerized. "Please come in, Matthew." Walking over to the sofa for her coat and gloves, she tried to ignore the multiple bruises on his face. Dressed in a black dinner jacket, rigid neck-high white shirt, and white bow tie, he was still the most handsome man she had ever met. Walking back from the sofa, she asked in a soft voice, "Do you want to tell me what happened?"

"Over dinner." He reached out to help her with her coat.

Locking the door behind her as they walked out, she noticed his troubled expression. "You're not happy to see me," she stated grimly.

"No, not under these circumstances. Let's talk about it later."

*   *   *   *

Delmonico's Restaurant was exquisite. The guests were greeted nightly with the glitter of crystal chandeliers, a magnificent sculptured ceiling, and men in black evening jackets and women in silk and chiffon flowing gowns wearing dazzling jewels. In the midst of the laughing conversations of the wealthy patrons and the ragtime jazz of the pianist, Matthew momentarily took his focus from Elizabeth and allowed his eyes to roam across the room, searching for familiar faces. He saw many whom he knew, but none who would now recognize his changed appearance. It was a comforting feeling.

Turning to Elizabeth as the waiter delivered their martinis in tall crystal glasses, he asked the question that had been haunting him for two days. "Why, Elizabeth?"

"Am I here?"

He nodded.

Removing the olive from her martini and placing it gently in her mouth, she stared at his injured face. "Because you're here, and because I want to help you."

With icy politeness, he said, "I appreciate that, but I don't want you here."

She smiled, and his irritated expression suddenly softened. "Thank you, but you don't have a choice. Matthew," she said in a very low voice, "you're involved with anarchists, yet I know you're not one. Tell me why?"

"I can't do that."

"Can't or won't?" she asked angrily.

Raising his glass, he said, "To one of the loveliest women I've ever know, and to her safe – and speedy – return home."

The anger in her eyes turned to amusement, and told him everything he didn't want to know. "So you're not leaving?"

"Absolutely not."

He took a long, burning sip of his martini. "I've told you about Alyssa."

She looked at him through her raised glass. "Have you asked her to marry you?"

"What has that go to do with . . . no, I haven't."

"Then I'm safe."

"Dammit, Elizabeth, I'm trying my best to make you understand that what I'm doing is too dangerous for you, and that I'm involved with another woman."

"She's not here with you?"

"No, she's in Philadelphia."

"Then she wouldn't mind."

He placed his glass down with a thump. "Yes, she would."

"Matthew, from the look of your face, I suspect someone would like to kill you. At the moment, it's not me." His expression remained taut. "You don't have to tell me, but I'll bet they now know who you are. That places limits on what you can accomplish. They don't know me. Think about that."

"I have, believe me. But what if they do this to you," he said, pointing at his face. "And what if *you're* killed?"

Without answering, she took a drink of her martini and shook her head. He had lost.

After dinner, he ordered a glass of Drambuie for each of them. It was almost midnight, and many guests had now left. The restaurant was significantly quieter. Rubbing his index finger along the top of the curved glass, he eyed her suspiciously. *Who is this gorgeous woman,* he thought to himself, *and why me?*

Looking into her questioning eyes, he said, "Now that you're going to stay, I might as well tell you what's going on."

"That would be a nice place to start," she said with a captivating smile.

Glancing around the room, he said, "Not here. My place."

Brushing back a wisp of her blonde hair, she nodded. "Your place it will be."

An hour later, at one o'clock in the morning, she sat across from him in his drawing room. Watching her remove the pins from the bun of her hair and allow it to fall to her shoulders, he undid his tie and opened the top button of his collar. "Now that we're comfy," he said, "relax and take a deep breath. I'm sworn to silence, so you never heard this from me." Her legs crossed, she casually listened. "Elizabeth, I'm working for President Roosevelt."

Her eyes bulged and she let out a slight gasp. "*The* President Roosevelt?"

"That's the one."

"But . . . you run a major shipping line. How can you work for him?"

"You haven't asked me what I'm doing for him. And by the way, I have a man who runs my company. He doesn't need me."

"I must admit, you've got my attention. What are you doing for him?"

"I'm tracking down anarchists."

Sarcastically, she said, "That sounds like fun. Are you out of your mind? Roosevelt must have an army looking for them."

"He does, but he wants me to find the man behind the murder of McKinley."

"How do you know it was one man?"

"Evidence and intuition – mine and his. He can be gruff as hell, but I've got enormous respect for him. I have no real idea why he's put his trust in me, but I'm not going to let him down."

"Unless they kill you first."

He shrugged. "That's a possibility. I've risked my life before, and I'm willing to do it again. Here's a question for you. Are you willing to die?"

She hesitated. "That's an unfair question. Of course I'm not."

"It's not unfair; it's reality. You'll slow me down because I'll be worried about you."

Crossing her legs again and sitting back, she looked at him seductively. "Let's sleep on it."

"Absolutely not. I told you that I'm in love with Alyssa."

"Well I'm not," she shot back. "You don't remember the night we spent together?"

"I remember."

"And you regret it?"

"Elizabeth, what in the hell are you doing? Of course I regret it."

With a teasing expression, she asserted, "No, you don't."

He laughed. "No. I need to get you back to your hotel. You have none of your things here."

"I don't need a thing."

"Yes you do. I have nothing for you to wear."

"Good," she said defiantly. Looking at her watch, she added, "It's almost two. I'll spend the night here."

*   *   *   *

The next morning, Elizabeth checked out of her hotel. Late that afternoon, she walked into Sach's Café and asked for Milburn. She was shown to a small table and asked to wait. Removing her coat and small brimmed hat, she glanced at the people who were now angrily staring at her. She was in a hostile environment, something she had not counted on. A slight chill ran through her body. Looking around, she saw a tall, lanky waiter strolling over to her table. "You wanted to see me?"

"Could you join me for a minute?"

"I'm not permitted to do that," he said brusquely. "What do you want?"

"Mr. Judson sent me. He wants to know if you've seen the two men you two discussed earlier."

Leaning down, he spoke in a low voice. "You don't belong here. I'd advise you to leave."

She placed a ten dollar bill in his hand. He quickly shoved it into his pocket and glanced around to see if anyone was looking. "Let me help you up," he said. Taking her arm, he whispered, "Tell Judson they're recruiting psychos."

She raised up from her chair. "They're what?"

"The two men are back. The word is they're looking for nuts to take some kind of a test."

"Nuts?"

Reaching the door, he opened it and stepped outside with her. "The anarchists who hang around here – the ones who are crazy." She looked at him with a confused expression. "Lady, I don't know how else to say it to you," he said in an annoyed voice. "The violent ones! The lunatics, for Christ's sake. Goodbye."

He left her standing alone on the sidewalk. Twisting her head to look for a cab, her eyes focused on two heavy-set men ten feet away. They were unshaven and wore dark coats and hats. One stepped quickly over to her and grabbed her arm with a vise grip. "You're coming with us, lady." She felt her other arm immobilized by the second man and was lifted off her feet. Overcome by the sour breath and the stench from their body odor, she was petrified. A rough hand

William A. Thau   193

clamped down on her mouth, and she was dragged around the corner to a waiting carriage.

A distant voice shouted out, "Hey you!" In the corner of her eye, she saw a policeman on the opposite side of the street step off the curb and walk toward them, a billy club swinging in his hand.

Taking his hand from her mouth, one man put his face in hers. "You say one word, and we'll kill you here."

The policeman reached them as they were about to shove her into the carriage. "Stand back," he demanded. "Are you all right, miss?"

"Help me," she whispered.

One of the men leaned over to the other. "Let's kill him."

In a low harsh voice, the other replied, "Are you crazy?"

They released her arms, shoved her toward the officer, and stepped into the carriage.

Elizabeth, shaken and terrified, broke into sobs. "You're all right now, miss," the soothing voice said. "I'll see you to a carriage." Trying to calm herself, she took his arm and walked to a nearby cab. Wiping her eyes, she was suddenly aware that her purse was gone. They had taken it, and they would know who she was. That thought sent a ripple down her spine.

*   *   *   *   *

Matthew demanded that she return home. "Elizabeth, dammit," he exclaimed with fury in his eyes, "they were going to kill you. I want you out of here." The next morning, he stood at the far end of the train concourse, saying goodbye to her. He looked at his watch through his burning, fatigued eyes. She boarded and the train pulled out, leaving him alone on the platform. He began the long walk back to the terminal, and then suddenly froze. Footsteps approached and he looked up to see two men. First he saw the tall, lean one, and then the shorter, stronger one, the one with the beard. *Jesus*, he thought, *don't they have anything else to do?*

"Mr. Stanton, could we have a word with you?" said the first.

Resignation settled in his eyes and he let out a deep sigh. "What do you want?"

"President Roosevelt sent us. He wants to talk to you."

"Why didn't he send a telegram?"

The short one shook his head. "Not safe. He asked us to accompany you back to Washington."

"Let me see your identification."

The tall one removed a badge from his coat. It said "U. S. Marshal." Six hours later, the New York Central arrived in Baltimore. Unknown to Stanton, Elizabeth didn't get off the train. The conductor found her beaten body an hour later, stuffed in a pull-down bed in her compartment. She died of asphyxiation; she had been strangled to death.

*   *   *   *

After packing a suitcase, Stanton walked out of the door to his house accompanied by the U. S. marshals. That evening, in the White House, he met with a reserved Theodore Roosevelt. It was eight o'clock. The President was sipping on a glass of brandy when Stanton entered his office. "Good evening, Mr. Stanton," he said, without looking up from a file on his desk.

"Mr. President," Stanton acknowledged, easing himself into a chair.

"Those damned Japanese," he muttered to himself. "Who in the hell do they think they are? They've got the most powerful fleet in the Pacific, and they're at work building more warships. My admirals tell me they want half of eastern Asia. The next thing they'll want is the Philippines." Pounding his fist on the desk, he said angrily, "Damn them! They know we can't match them in the Pacific. If I don't do something, they're going to be breathing down our necks." Looking up, he took another sip and stared through Stanton. "I've got to build a Pacific Fleet, and fast, but Congress won't allow it. They think the Japs would look at it as a threat. Well, to hell with them!"

Clearing his throat, Stanton said, "Mr. President, is this a bad time? I can come back tomorrow."

Gruffly, Roosevelt answered, "I won't be here tomorrow." He fell silent and turned to the window, staring at the bright lights of the Washington Monument. "This country is full of good, hard-working people. My job is to look after them. But out there," he said motioning to the window, "is a small group of lunatics who want me dead." Turning to face Stanton, he said, "I've got a lot of people working on this. We don't seem to have the capability to identify them or to stop them. I'm thinking of asking Congress to assign the Secret Service to protect me."

"I think that would be a good idea," Stanton said.

"I don't. What are the American people going to think about the safety of this country if their president has to go around guarded? What kind of a democracy is that?"

Stanton remained silent.

Throwing a copy of the *Washington Post* across the desk, Stanton noticed the headline, *Is This Country Safe for Any of Us*? "Our crime rate is soaring," the President said. "Unless I can make this country a good place for all of its citizens, it's going to get worse."

"You didn't ask me here for that."

"No, I didn't." He could feel the stress in the President's voice. "Lincoln, Garfield and McKinley! Being president of this great country has come to mean you've volunteered to stand in front of a shooting gallery. I don't like it, not one damn bit! Have you found out who is financing and training these assassins?"

Taking a deep breath, Stanton admitted, "No. But I'm getting close."

"What does that mean?" the President asked impatiently.

"Whoever it is, he's recruiting lunatics."

"He's what?"

"Mr. President, they're looking for sociopaths – psychopaths. They've come up with some sort of test they're giving to anarchists. They're looking for assassins."

"Jesus Christ!" Roosevelt stopped to light a cigar. "I'll send the army in if I have to, but I'll stop them."

Stanton held up his hands in frustration. "That won't help. Their own agents don't know who they are."

"How did you find this out?"

"Mr. President . . . they tried to kill me. They know who I am. I sent a woman to talk to my contact, a waiter at Sach's Café. He told her about it."

"They know you? So you're no use to me anymore." Pausing to take a puff, he let the smoke fill the room. "How's your resolve?" he asked.

"I rode with you in Cuba. I'm going to stay with this until I find them."

Rubbing his chin, Roosevelt said, "Bully for you. Use this woman again, see if she can get the names of the people taking the tests."

"She's gone."

"What?"

"I sent her home to Baltimore. They found out who she was. It wasn't safe for her."

The President fell silent, turning his chair back toward the window. After several minutes, the silence became deafening.

"Mr. President . . . ."

"Was she the wife of the publisher of the *Baltimore Sun*?"

Stanton was startled. "How in the world -"

The President interrupted in a sympathetic voice. "Read the Post article."

Stanton looked down at the article, horrified. "Elizabeth," he thought. "They did *that* to her? But why?" Speechless, he stared at the article, his mind in a trance. He heard the President's voice. "Then she is the one."

His life had suddenly evaporated within him. He looked up and nodded. Overwhelmed with grief, he struggled to hold back his emotions by clearing his throat, but he couldn't. In a choked voice, he murmured, "Excuse me, Mr. President," and stood to leave. In the background he heard, "Mr. Stanton, I'm sorry." It was only noise. He had killed her. What could he do now? It was much too late for anything.

At eight o'clock the next morning, he lay in his bed at the Capitol Hotel. Bars of light were beginning to cross the room from the rising sun. He had slept only several hours. When sleep had finally come, it had been tormented. He awoke over and over, each time shaken out of a nightmare and thinking it hadn't really happened. But it had. They had killed her. They would be coming after him next. He knew what she knew – they couldn't leave him alive. One thought dominated all others. He would be ready for them this time; they would pay for what they had done. When Berger had been killed, he had spared no one. This time would be no different.

*   *   *   *

Baltimore, Maryland

A slight drizzle was beginning to fall as the driver slowed the carriage to a halt and Matthew Stanton stepped out near the entrance to the Basilica of the National Shrine of the Assumption of the Blessed Virgin Mary. He was humbled by the enormous Roman columns and the sounds of the huge bells clanging mournfully over the hushed crowd that slowly made its way into the church. Gazing down on Baltimore Harbor, the activity of the ships was, to him, a blur. It seemed as though the world had stopped.

Waiting for the crowd to enter, he followed and sat in a pew in the back corner. He was exhausted, his weary eyes looking first to the rounded arches and pillars vaulting to the ceiling of the church, and then to the people who had gathered for the memorial service. He saw an elderly man in the front row, his head partially down and his shoulders shaking with grief. He was probably Elizabeth's husband. Matthew wanted to tell him how sorry he was, how wrong he was to get Elizabeth involved, but he knew it would be useless.

Suddenly the organ music stilled and he was drawn to a voice in the pulpit where a woman was giving the eulogy. She paused a number of times, trying to hold back the tears that eventually began to form in her eyes. Matthew couldn't remember shedding a tear, not since Berg had been murdered, but he felt his eyes grow moist now. For a brief moment, the woman's eyes met his, and they seemed to share his pain.

When the eulogy had ended, the sounds of the church became only distant noise. His head was in his hands, his mind wondering what he could have done, but it was much too late.

PART III

CHAPTER THIRTY-FIVE

▼

Washington, D. C. – The White House

It was in late February when Matthew Stanton returned to the White House. Roosevelt had requested his presence for an important meeting in the East Room with the head of psychiatry for Johns Hopkins Institute, Dr. Albert Bartow. Seated around the long table with him were Chicago Police Commissioner Jay Neeley; Attorney General Knox; Secretary of War Root; John Kilpatrick, the new head of the Secret Service; and Chief Federal Investigator Charlie Wilcox. In the middle of the table sat the President, and at the end Dr. Bartow.

Stanton's gaze, shrouded with curiosity, fixed upon the face of the President. Roosevelt's mood was sullen. Several nights before, he had invited Booker T. Washington to dine with him at the White House. The dinner had gone well; Washington had become a close friend and confidant of the President. The American press, however, was unmerciful in its bitter criticism for what he had done. *A Negro in the White House!*, the headlines screamed. On the floor of Congress, it was called "damnable". The outrage was so deep that speculation was rife that the President had destroyed his chances for re-election. A river of hate mail and death threats had descended upon him. Through it all, Roosevelt remained defiant. "I should be ashamed," he had said, "if I ever permitted the color of a man's skin to affect in any way my judgment of him."

Shaking off thoughts of that fateful dinner, the President began the meeting. "Thank you for coming," he said in a subdued voice. "I can only stay for a few minutes. Right now, I'm a little under water. Mr. Stanton, who most of you know, has discovered what appears to be a plot to kill me that has taken my interest. It seems it's not a plot devised by some crazed anarchist, but a diabolical plot by perhaps one or more of our wealthy citizens. I asked Dr. Bartow from Johns Hopkins Institute to illuminate for us the kind of people we're up against. Mr. Stanton, fill them in, if you will."

"Mr. President," he acknowledged. Turning to the others at the table, he said, "I discovered at a café in New York, a month or so ago, that several men have been interviewing anarchists to determine certain character traits. The ones selected are then asked to take tests, the purpose of which we were told is to weed out those who are psychopaths. The reason we're here - these same men were involved with McKinley's assassin, Leon Czolgosz." A look of surprise floated around the room.

Charlie Wilcox interrupted. "That's insane. If they want to kill the President, why not just shoot him?"

Stanton answered, "Why didn't *they* just kill McKinley; why use Czolgosz? This country is full of anarchists; they may believe in the violent overthrow of the government, but very few of them have the courage or the will to shoot the President to achieve their goals. They may preach it, but they wouldn't do it. The ones who have done it have all been determined to be insane – every one of them. If an insane anarchist commits the crime, the questions theoretically stop. Our newspapers have already concluded that since Czolgosz fit that category and swears he acted alone, *and* that he was convicted with no evidence to the contrary, the case is closed."

Wilcox wasn't convinced. "If there were people handling Czolgosz, why didn't he tell that to the police after days of interrogation?"

"Because he never grasped what they were doing to him. They pushed him along. His mental state was known to them; all it took was some money and prodding. He was so manipulated that, in the end, he believed it was entirely his idea to kill the President."

Wilcox shook his head. "That's nothing but speculation on your part."

"It may be, but what I've seen now makes me believe it's happening all over again. And this time we have a different president."

His patience wearing thin, Roosevelt said in an irritated voice, "Enough of this. Dr. Bartow, tell us why you think Mr. Stanton's theory has some merit."

"Mr. President," Bartow acknowledged as he rose from his chair. Surveying his audience, Bartow knew he was talking to many skeptics. His small eyes, thin frame, drawn face, and wisp of gray hair didn't give the impression of a leading medical researcher into the human mind, but his voice did. Challenging his listeners, he held up his hands. "Imagine, if you will, not having a conscience, none at all. *No feelings of guilt or remorse, whatever you do.*" He paused to see he had the full attention of everyone.

"To carry that one step further, imagine that you have no limiting sense of concern for the well-being of strangers, friends, or even family members. Imagine no struggles with shame, not a single one in your entire life, no matter what kind of selfish, lazy, harmful, or immoral action you had taken. And pretend that the concept of responsibility is unknown to you. Now add to this fantasy the ability to conceal from others that your psychological makeup is radically different from theirs. Since everyone assumes that conscience is universal among human beings, hiding the fact that you have none is effortless."

Roosevelt flipped open his pocket watch and held up a hand. "Excuse me, Dr. Bartow, but I have a meeting with the French legation. I'm sorry, gentlemen, but I'm going to leave this to you." Bartow nodded slightly as Roosevelt stood and left the room. "Does anyone else need to leave?" he asked. Hearing no response, he continued, "You may wonder where this is going. I assure you, your time is not being wasted here. What I'm laying out for you is a chilling scenario of what you may face.

"Now, back to this fantasy. In addition to what you've already imagined, consider that you're not held back from any of your desires by guilt or shame, and you are never confronted by others for your cold-bloodedness. The ice-water in your veins is so bizarre, so completely outside of their personal experience, that they cannot even guess as to your true condition. In other words, gentlemen, you're completely free of internal restraints, and your unhampered liberty to do just as you please, with no pangs of conscience, is conveniently invisible to the world. You can do anything at all, and still your strange advantage over the majority of people, who are kept in line by their consciences, will most likely remain undiscovered. Gentlemen, if you fit into these imaginings, you would be labeled in my world as a *psychopath*.

"So how will you live your life? If you are born at the right time, with some access to money, and if you have a special talent for hatred *and* a feeling of deprivation, you can arrange to kill those who you believe are the perpetrators of your misery. With the right incentives, killing would be something fulfilling, something you would feel is necessary within your twisted logic and liberating to your mind. Revenge on society would be all the impetus you would need."

Pausing for a sip of water, he held up his right index finger. "I can tell you without reservation that Leon Czolgosz fit that mold to a tee. It didn't take much encouragement for him to act out his imagined anger. Now, Mr. Stanton has mentioned a test being administered by some apparently very dangerous people. If you were to take such a test, here is the damning thing that would show up about your character, assuming for the moment that you are a certifiable psychopath. You will come out likeable, charming, intelligent, impressive, confidence-inspiring, and . . . a great success with the ladies." He stopped to notice smiles creep into the faces of several men around the table. "Before you get too carried away, you will also be labeled as irresponsible, self-destructive, a willing perpetrator of violence, and completely without a soul. You're a very efficient machine, albeit a complex one. And in the hands of a master manipulator, you're a predator, an enormous danger to society.

"Now, with all of that said, if you were to ask me if Mr. Czolgosz could have been, shall we say, handled on his way to kill the President, I would answer with an unqualified yes."

Attorney General Knox was intrigued by what he had heard. "Dr. Bartow," he asked thoughtfully, "is it possible that someone who is not a psychopath could be schooled to the degree that he would appear to be one after taking such a test?"

Bartow smiled. "Mr. Knox, I know precisely what you have in mind – to send a shill to invade their inner circles. Honestly, it's a grand idea, but if the test were well put together, as I suspect it has been, I would have to say no. Sooner or later, your shill would trap himself, and they would know."

Secretary Root let out a breath of frustration. "If they've found a psychopath who would kill the President, how in the hell do we spot him?"

"You don't. Psychopaths are the most devious and cunning of all the human race. They look like we do. Until they've done their evil deed and we catch them, if we're that lucky, you'll *never* know who they are."

"Shit," Root said under his breath.

"So they'll know us, but we won't know them," Neeley said to himself.

Looking his way, Bartow picked up on his comment. "That's the sum of it, Commissioner."

"Dr. Bartow, what I'm about to say doesn't mean we're not grateful for your time here today, and I don't want you to take it that way," Neeley responded, "but you haven't told us a damn thing. I frankly have no idea of what to do next."

Bartow placed his palms on the table and leaned forward. "I'm sorry you feel that way, Commissioner, but there is something you can do."

Neeley sat up, surprised. "What's that?"

"Find the handler; find out who's behind those tests. That's how you'll stop them."

Stanton listened intently, inhaling a deep breath. He thought he had a way.

CHAPTER THIRTY-SIX

▼

Matteawan, New York

He leaned against the iron railing near the main entrance of
the imposing Castellated Gothic building located on 246 acres
overlooking the Hudson River Valley. The nearby grounds were
impeccably manicured lawns and walkways, providing a setting for
the Fishkill Mountains that loomed in the background. The castle-
like structure, with its towers and minarets, lorded over the valley
below from the crest of the hill. To the passerby, it was as serene and
peaceful as a beautiful college campus after the students had left for
the holidays. It gave no indication of the facilities that lay beyond its
stone walls and chain-link fences.

The mist and the drizzling rain were typical of Matteawan's late
spring. The late afternoon sky was a dense haze, the edges mottled
by the lights of the gas lamps placed along the walkways. There were
no people to be seen; pockets of fog swirled overhead as evidence
that the north winds blew unencumbered across the countryside.
It was five o'clock in the afternoon. On this particular evening, the
needles of doubt kept pricking Matthew Stanton's conscience. Not
his morality; that had been replaced after Elizabeth's murder by the
practical. If what he had planned worked, it was moral; if it didn't, it
was impractical. His mind spun with a recurring question – was what

he was about to do worth the risk? On the surface, he felt the answer was yes. But if the means did not justify the ends, then what?

He touched his face, feeling the healed wounds from the beating he had suffered. The faces of the men who did it drifted in and out of his consciousness. Would he know them next time? That wasn't an option. They had taken from him a woman he had loved and who had saved his life; now they would suffer the fate they had imposed on her. The men who had brutally beaten and then killed her were sadists, indulging in their sickness until they were through with her. Stanton was not through with them. He had just begun. He made himself stop, redirecting his thoughts to the facility he would soon enter. The sheer volume of the uneven fieldstones that comprised the foundation and undergirded the façade of the building was monumental.

The facility had been given many names, but it was now officially called the Matteawan State Hospital, although to the general public it was still known as the Asylum for the Criminally Insane. Outwardly, the "madhouse" atop Asylum Road was usually quiet. Escape attempts offered occasional excitement, but they rarely succeeded.

The facility was built for 550 beds – they were not enough. It held male and female convicts who had become insane while serving their sentences and persons who had committed their crimes while insane but were never convicted. The institution's doctors described their treatment of patients as "kind and gentle"; it was the "moral treatment" developed in the early nineteenth century. The facility was designed to be a state-of-the-art institution. The indiscriminate mingling of the mild and furious, clean and filthy, convalescent and idiotic, would be not be tolerated. Patients would be divided into classes, and the "moral treatment" emphasized the human rather than the beast-like nature of the insane.

Newspapers, however, presented an entirely different view. They were filled with grim tales of madness, mistreated patients, wretched conditions, and wrongful confinement. Matteawan was described as a human rat-trap that would drive the sanest person crazy.

Convicts whose sentences had expired were discharged outright, and those others who were deemed "cured" were released at the will of the doctors into the communities. Lobotomies were performed in some cases, but treatment generally consisted of therapy and hypnosis. The treatments seldom worked, and the proportion of chronic and dangerous patients, those who could never be released, steadily rose. Patient's were doubled up, but the overcrowding continued. It was those patients, the chronic and dangerous, who had captured Stanton's interest.

The door was locked behind him after he had been granted admittance to the main lobby. Once there, he was shown down a long corridor to the office of the administrator, John Isaacs. Isaacs was a very accomplished communicator who wrote and lectured widely about his work in mental health. He felt it was his Christian duty to advocate a more humane and progressive attitude toward the mentally ill. Even so, it was beyond his capability to supervise each attendant as closely as his policies required, and patients were often abused and subjected to barbaric and ineffective treatments without his knowledge. He was often incensed at what he thought were the lies and misrepresentations perpetrated by journalists about his institution, and he was often wrong. It was a very dark period in mental health.

Isaacs stood, his hand held out, as Stanton entered. Taking it, Stanton wondered how this diminutive, gentle-looking man of sixty, with streaks of white in his dark beard and hair, could be responsible for the treatment and care of over six hundred insane inmates. With a welcoming smile, Isaacs said, "Please have a seat, Mr. Stanton."

Walking around his desk, he continued, "Mr. Stanton, I've been told of your more than generous contribution to our facility, and on behalf of everyone here, I want to thank you from the bottom of our hearts." He sat down, closely studying the benefactor who had suddenly appeared from nowhere. Isaacs knew Stanton was a man of great wealth, but he had not been told of his appearance. Stanton's clothes had the tailoring of Savile Row, and his dark thick hair, heavy eyebrows, and handsome face portrayed a man who was at home among the great industrialists of the day and accustomed to the very best of everything, but gave it little thought. He was also, Isaacs thought, a man who had a lot of power and knew how to use it.

"You're more than welcome," Stanton replied, "but you do understand why I'm here."

"I was told you needed the services of one of our patients. Honestly, that made no sense whatsoever, so I'm sure I heard it wrong."

"No, you heard it right. It is not only a need I have, but it's a condition to my gift."

A look of surprise flashed across Isaacs face. "A condition?"

"Just one man," Stanton replied.

Apprehensively, Isaacs asked, "May I know who that would be?"

"I'm expecting you to tell me that."

"What? How in the world . . . ."

"Calm down, Dr. Isaacs. Hear me out. I need a man who would fit the description of a true psychopath, and one whom you believe would be *willingly* helpful to the task I will have laid out for him."

Inhaling deeply, Isaacs said, "Do you have any idea what you're asking? You want us to release a psychopath to your custody? I couldn't assure you anything. Do you understand the nature of a psychopath?"

"That's not my biggest worry right now. I'll leave that to you. When he's released, doctor, I'll depend on you to keep him in control."

Rubbing his chin, Isaacs said, "Mr. Stanton, that's not possible for a number of reasons, the least of which is my schedule. My work occupies all my time, seven days a week. I don't have the time to help you in whatever bizarre scheme you have for this man, *if* I could even find him for you."

Stanton sat back, staring at Isaacs through narrowed eyes. Mentally, he was trying to rate his chances of success with Isaacs. "Would twenty thousand dollars free up some of you time?"

Isaacs was stunned. "Excuse me for asking, but I was under the impression that your gift would be ten thousand dollars. Is there something I misunderstood?"

"Your time, Dr. Isaacs. If you agree to my condition, the gift to your institution will be twenty thousand dollars."

"And you want me to find a psychopath from our patients, turn him over to you, and help you control him for this 'task' you have planned?"

"That's correct, doctor."

Pausing for thought, Isaacs asked, "Please tell me why you want a psychopath?"

"I want him to take a test."

"And that's all?"

"Not quite. He'll have to do more, depending on the outcome of the test."

Isaacs stood and paced the room. "Mr. Stanton, your gift will mean the world here. Nevertheless, to do what you ask, I would have to know precisely what you have in mind."

Concentrating on Isaacs eyes, he said, "I'm afraid I can't tell you that."

"Then Mr. Stanton, I'm afraid I can't help you, as much as I'd like to."

"Wait," Stanton said. "Let's go at this from another direction. Do you know the Attorney General?"

"Mr. Knox?"

"Yes."

"I don't know him personally, but I certainly know of him."

"Would you accept a letter or telegram from him asking you to do what I ask?"

Confused, Isaacs admitted, "I don't know. How would I know it was from the Attorney General?"

"I'll arrange for you to speak to him."

Returning to sit in his chair, Isaacs asked, "When will you need this psychopath?"

"Immediately."

"That won't be possible. Maybe a week." Suspiciously he added, "How much of my time will you need?"

Stanton nodded. "I'll need only part of your time for not more than several months. When you're satisfied with the Attorney General's telegram, I'll give you a list of parameters I want you to meet. When you've selected five men who fit them, I want to interview each one with you. Before those interviews, I'll need a complete personal history of each man you select."

With a severe look, Isaacs asked, "Do you understand, Mr. Stanton, how dangerous a man like that could be to you personally?"

"I'll have to take that risk." He reached into his pocket and handed Isaacs his business card. "When you're ready to proceed, send me the list of the men you've selected with their personal histories. Include the times for the interviews."

"What about the money?"

"You'll have the money when the man I approve is released to me." Reaching for the door, he turned back. "Several more things, doctor. You'll have the Attorney General's telegram in the morning. With respect to our meeting today and our dealings in the future, you *never* heard of me. Everything we do, and I mean *everything*, is to be kept strictly confidential. The Attorney General will repeat that to you. Do I have your word?"

"Yes . . . you have it."

CHAPTER THIRTY-SEVEN

▼

New York City

He had disappeared off the face of the Earth. Her telegrams had gone unanswered. A month had elapsed since she had last seen him, and the anxiety and feeling of loss were beginning to dominate her thoughts. Except for him, her life had slowly returned to normal. She now had $60 million. The house in Philadelphia had been sold, and she had decided to move to New York. Acting impulsively, she purchased a three-story home on 5th Avenue, overlooking Washington Square Park.

Alyssa had just celebrated her thirty-first birthday, alone. Her striking beauty – and her new found wealth – had attracted potential suitors by the dozens. She had no interest in any of them. Her enchanting face had been sought by a number of magazines for their covers, and had she not continued to relive in her mind the terrifying ordeal with Clayton Harding, she might have readily accepted their offers. But notoriety was the last thing she wanted. She longed for the refuge of Matthew Stanton's arms, the protection and peace he had given her. Where was he, and why had he not tried to find her? She decided she would find him.

When he walked into Annabelle's restaurant, she was sitting with her back to him. He could see her thick auburn hair under the flowered hat that was slightly tilted to one side. She lifted a glass of wine and looked to her right, as if she saw someone she knew. The movement gave him a view of her expressive blue eyes, the slightly turned-up nose, and the gentle smile he had imagined so often when his thoughts had turned to her. It now seemed like so long ago. She was as elegant and fashionable as he had remembered, but from where he stood she seemed different – a bit older and more sophisticated.

At first, his heart seemed to skip a beat, but then a sense of guilt engulfed him. He had betrayed her with Elizabeth. It had never been planned, but it had happened. Would she forgive him? Could he tell her, and if he did, would he forgive himself? The maitre d' appeared and led him to her table. She looked up to see him, her eyes suddenly moist with relief. "Hello, Alyssa," he said softly. Bending down to kiss her gently on the lips, he felt her hands circle his neck. Pulling slightly away, she breathed, "I've missed you so much, Matthew. Please sit down. I ordered you a glass of wine. I hope you don't mind."

"No, of course not. Thank you." He leaned back and regarded her, his eyes partially closed. It was her appearance that made him realize how foolish he had been. That gorgeous face of hers with those captivating blue eyes fringed with curly lashes; the proud way she held herself; her soft lips and the musical sound of her voice; and the hesitant, infectious smile. He had been such a fool to ignore her.

"I had some help finding you," she said.

"Longbourne?"

"Yes. Thanks to him, you did get the message about coming here." With quiet dignity, she added, "I wasn't certain you would come. Why, Matthew? Why did you cut me out of your life?"

To her relief, his expression softened. "I'm so sorry," he said. "I never meant to hurt you. I can't begin to explain what happened to me in the past month. I can only ask that you try to forgive me." Stopping to gaze into her intoxicating eyes, he said tenderly, "Alyssa, I'm in love with you. That has never changed." Overwhelmed with the poignancy of the moment, she watched his hand reach out for hers, felt his long fingers sliding across hers, his palm grazing her palm; and then his fingers, strong and warm, curled tightly, holding her hand.

"I love you too," she whispered, lifting her eyes to his.

As two strangers who had at first accidentally shared something more dangerous than they expected or wanted, and had later sought to withdraw onto safer ground, they were now together again. But unknown to her, he was about to face one of the most terrifying episodes of his life. And deep within himself, he was devastated by what had already happened. Reaching into the depths of his emotions, he said in a broken voice, "Alyssa, Elizabeth is dead."

"Elizabeth?"

"The woman in the hospital you saw holding my hand."

"I'm so sorry," she said. "I know you cared for her."

Inhaling deeply, he muttered, "More than you could possibly know. She saved my life."

"Matthew, how did she die?"

"She was murdered."

Her hand instinctively covered her mouth. "Oh, my God! Do you know why?"

"Because she tried to help me."

Alyssa fell silent, feeling his grief and pain. "Have they caught the man who did it?"

"No, but *I will*," he answered with grim determination.

She suddenly felt numb, realizing that he was not coming back to her. "I had hoped that you and I could . . . that we could get away from all of this. I see that's not possible."

"Not now it isn't. I would like to tell you what it is I have to do, but I can't. I told Elizabeth, and now she's dead. I need you to do something for me. I need you to go back to Philadelphia and wait for me. I *will* come for you, and we will leave all of this. I promise you that."

"I can't."

"You can't? Why?"

"I've left Philadelphia and bought a home here."

"Because of me?"

Lowering her eyes, she shook her head. "No, not you. I didn't know if I would ever see you again. I grew up here. I just wanted to come back home."

"Alyssa, you have to try to understand. Right now I'm a liability to you. It's not safe to be around me."

"And you still won't tell me why?"

"I can't."

The waiter suddenly appeared and was motioned away by Matthew. Watching her gently wipe a tear from her eyes, he was distressed by how despondent she had become. "So it's over between us?" she asked.

"No, it's not over. You didn't hear me. I need you to wait."

"For what? Forever? I can't do this, not again. Can't you understand? Please, Matthew, please stop what you're doing and be with me. Our lives are so fragile. I need you *now*, not tomorrow or next year."

He was speechless, his eyes telling her everything she didn't want to hear. She stood up to leave, choking back her emotions.

"Please," he begged, "don't leave, not now."

"I should never have come," she mumbled. "Good-bye, Matthew."

He sat in silence, watching her walk out of his life. It was what he had been programmed to do. He had learned to be alone. When anyone had tried to get too close to him, he had always conveniently pushed them away. Now he had done it to her. But this time the wind had been taken out of him. Matthew Stanton's world was crumbling, and he was helpless to stop it.

Chapter Thirty-Eight

▼

Matteawan State Hospital, New York

Gradually, his life ceased to make any sense. Life in the streets, then the private schools and Harvard, the mingling with the very rich, the speculation with other people's money that led to his own wealth, and then the shipping business that became his obsession, even though he never liked it. It was all an illusion, never reality, he thought. Was it nothing but greed that he had been programmed to enjoy? His quest for more and more money had in the end meant nothing. The more he had, it seemed the less he had. He had the disquieting thought of never having lived at all. Elizabeth had taught him there was a difference between what he thought and what was real. And Alyssa had taught him even more, that it was in him to deeply love another person. Now they were both gone. His quest for money had now become his quest for revenge.

He sat alone at a dilapidated table in a small white-washed room, waiting patiently for his interview with Milo Dance. The room was dim, lit only by two gas lamps hanging from the ceiling and a small window protected with iron bars. He began to wonder if he were no better than Dance, a career criminal who was never able to comprehend a difference between right and wrong. Dance was a psychopath. He had affectionately become known as the Dance Man by the other patients. Hearing a commotion in the hall, he stood to see an attendant enter with a manacled patient. Behind him was Dr. Isaacs.

The personal history provided by Isaacs told Stanton of a mother who deserted her family, a boy who grew up in a middle-income household and was well educated with a college degree, and grew into a man was very well-liked, charming, and had above-average intelligence. It also told of a man who had a complete lack of social responsibility and morality, and who was impulsive, manipulative, without empathy, a consummate liar, and violent. He was, Dr. Isaacs said, an excellent actor and a complete fake. Typical of psychopaths, the Dance Man was incapable of feeling concern or remorse for the consequences of his actions; he had no conscience whatsoever, and was a master at mimicking emotions like a professional actor. In Isaacs' view, it had little or nothing to do with his upbringing; it was partly genetic and partly mystery.

The most troubling part of the report, but also the part that peaked Stanton's interest the most, was that the Dance Man was fanatically driven to do one thing, and one thing alone. Unable to feel any sense of guilt, love, relationships, or fairness, the thing left for him was a relentless goal to win. And he was willing to do anything at all to win, including murder. He was incapable of identifying with or appreciating the level of physical, emotional, or mental pain he had caused his victims. Healing or trying to help him had proved to be a pointless waste of time. He was far beyond any possibility of cure.

The interview, Dr. Isaacs had said, could be nerve-wracking and totally unproductive. He warned Stanton to be aware that the Dance Man could not be swayed by appeals based on sympathy, remorse, regret or social obligation. He cautioned Stanton to practice facial expressions, body language and verbal responses that would encourage and relax him. He had to show a willingness to listen, to give the Dance Man a license to talk. The Dance Man would insist that he be the center of attention, and might attempt to shock and verbally assault Stanton. To avoid his "dark side", Isaacs instructed Stanton to understand and positively reinforce his participation in the interview with words and gestures, compliment him on his higher intelligence, never criticize him, and with respect to the task Stanton had in mind for him, ask for his slant on it. And he had to make it clear that he was very impressed with the Dance Man, and that the others he interviewed were in fact weak and lacked the courage and fortitude to carry out the assignment.

The final advice was delivered in a one-on-one meeting with a chilling warning. "Don't ever allow the Dance Man," Isaacs had said, "to believe you're the enemy. It could cost you your life. He *has* killed three men who got in his way."

Milo Dance was dressed in a shabby white uniform, his legs and arms bound with iron shackles. He was seated by the attendant in a chair opposite Stanton, and Dr. Isaacs sat at the end of the table. Dance appeared to be in his early forties, was clean shaven with close-cropped brown hair and high cheekbones, and had deep-set eyes. His face was pale, like a mask. His dark eyes darted around the room and settled on Stanton. His stare pierced through Stanton's outwardly calm demeanor, sending a chill down his spine. "Mr. Dance," he said, extending his hand, "thank you for coming." Dance reached out with his two shackled hands in a gesture of friendliness.

"I'm sorry," Stanton said, "that we're meeting under these circumstances, but perhaps that will change." He suddenly had Dance's full attention. "Mr. Dance, I'm Matthew Stanton. I own a shipping company. Dr. Isaacs has been kind enough to give me a report on you."

Interrupting, Dance said with a slight grin, "You read the part that says I'm crazy? That's bullshit, you know. They've kept me locked up here for five years. I have a college degree, had a good job, and was a good citizen, but that quack down there labels me as a nut."

Holding up his hand, Stanton said gently, "I totally understand. If they did that to me, I'd be as pissed as you. Mr. Dance, you're a hell of a bright man." He paused to watch the smile creep across Dance's face. "Top of my college class," Dance said.

"I have no doubt about that. Mr. Dance, they say you have a personality disorder. If that were a reason to lock you up, we'd all be in here with you." Narrowing his eyes, he studied Dance. "I've been interviewing some people here for a job."

"I've heard that."

"So far, no one I've talked to has the brains or the skills I'm looking for. They're weak – they have no courage to do what I'm asking."

"And what are you asking?"

"Are you familiar with anarchists?"

"I don't know any, but yeah, I know about them. They want to overthrow the government."

"How do you feel about that?'

"How do I feel?" he repeated. "I don't give a shit. I'm in here because of the government. I have no love for them."

"You'll have to make them believe you're an anarchist. Can you do that?"

Dance laughed. "I could make them think I think I'm the Tooth Fairy if I wanted to."

"As to your feelings about the government, I agree with you. But I read your case. It was a judge who put you in here, not the government."

"He works for the government," he snapped back.

"He does, but not for long. We have a new government, and they're interested in your case."

Dance rattled his shackles, angrily pounding them against his chair. "These goddamn things drive me crazy," he shouted out. Calming slightly, he asked, "Do you work for them?"

"Not exactly. The new president wants to do things differently, and I support him."

"Roosevelt."

"What do you think of him?"

"Not a thing."

Stanton glanced briefly at Isaacs, who seemed very unhappy with the way the conversation was going. "I rode up San Juan Hill with him. We won. We beat the crap out of those Spaniards. He's a good man, Mr. Dance. The reason I'm here – someone is giving tests to anarchists. Their goal, I believe, is to find willing dupes they can set up to commit murders for them. They want to manipulate them."

"Why?"

"They're smart. They don't want to be caught. Once the murder is committed, the person they set up is killed or convicted for the crime. Their involvement is never brought out."

"I can't be manipulated – not by them, and not by you."

"I understand that. I'm not here to manipulate you. I need your help."

"What kind of tests are they giving?"

"They're looking for mentally insane people who can be controlled."

Fury erupted in Dance's eyes. "You son-of-a-bitch. You think I'm insane?"

Stanton held up his hands in a gesture of truce. "Hell no, I don't! I told you that. But you've been around them for five years, and I do believe you're smart as hell. They could never manipulate you."

"So I take the test. Then what?"

"I want you to find out who's behind it."

His suspicion heightened. "Why the hell do you care who they are?"

"Because they framed me for a murder I didn't commit. I want to pay them back."

"What's in it for me?"

"A new sanity hearing. This time with a better judge – a judge I pick."

"And I go free?"

"That's my plan."

Dance shifted in his chair and mumbled to himself, "No shit!"

Isaacs was completely flustered and stood to speak. Stanton waved him down.

Dance sat forward, his eyes again darting around the room. "I'm no fool. Why don't you take the test? Why me?"

"Because I'm not that smart. You have lived around insane people; you'll know how to answer their questions. I need you to pretend you're insane and make them believe it. They're going to think they're too smart for that, but I have a hunch you're a lot smarter. Mr. Dance, I need your input on this. I need you to figure out how to find the man behind all of this. The men giving you the test may not even know who they work for, but I'm betting you can figure out how to find him."

Stanton could see that Dance had accepted the challenge. "I'll find him," he said. "When do I get out of here?"

Stanton leaned back in his chair. Looking at the end of the table, he said, "Dr. Isaacs."

"Mr. Dance," Isaacs said, "I don't have the authority to free you without a court order. Your attendant, Mr. Jenkens, will stay with you until this ordeal is over. You'll have to report to him on a schedule. At all times when you're not carrying out your duties for Mr. Stanton, you will be under his watch and control. If you violate that, you'll be sent back here permanently and there will be no new sanity hearing. Do you understand that?"

Dance nodded while warning bells went off in Isaacs' head. Back in the privacy of his office, Isaacs said, "Mr. Stanton, you may have hell to pay. This man is a cunning manipulator and a killer. He has no feelings – none. God help us all if this doesn't go as you plan."

CHAPTER THIRTY-NINE

▼

New York City

From across the street, Milo Dance approached the café. He slowed his pace and then walked to the window as if studying the people inside. He spotted two well-dressed men sitting in a corner table. Lighting a cigarette, he entered the café and walked over to the two men. "You Smith and Jones?" he asked.

"How the hell did . . . ?" one of the men started to ask.

Stopping him in mid-sentence, the Dance Man said, "You're no secret. You sit here every night. Mind if I join you?"

They said nothing as he sat down. He was new to Sach's Café. He dressed like the others and, after a while, he ranted and raved as an anarchist would. Secretly, they wondered if he was a spy. He returned for three nights, and Smith and Jones continued to study him with growing interest. He wasn't like the others. He reminded them of Leon Czolgosz. They had found four candidates, and all had taken the test. None had passed. This man was intelligent, communicative, and easily provoked. His hostility was real, as was his total lack of impulse control and empathy for anyone. On the fourth night, they decided Milo Dance would be given the test.

The next afternoon, in a small building near Sach's Café, Smith insisted, "We have to go over it again. Mr. Dance, you must answer every question or we'll have to end this."

Milo Dance was incensed. He knew what they were trying to do, and he would outsmart them. The questions were framed to make him look like an idiot. That would never happen. Holding his temper, he yanked the test from the hands of Smith and mumbled, "Your way." He then proceeded to answer the ones he had left blank, the ones they were using to trick him. An hour later, he handed the completed test to them and left. As he walked out the door, Jones yelled, "Where can we reach you?"

Looking back over his shoulder, Dance said, "Nowhere. I'll contact you." Jenkens watched him from two doors away and rose to follow Dance as he nonchalantly walked by.

Glancing at each other, Jones whispered, "That son-of-a-bitch will never pass. Our boss is going to be pissed."

The next day the news was handed down to them. Dance had scored ninety, far above the level set by Seigfeld. He would be the one.

*   *   *   *

Milo Dance groaned as he woke up the next morning. The sunlight had disappeared, and the small hotel room was filled with gray, inhospitable light. He looked across the room to see that Jenkens was still asleep. Rising slowly from the bed, he stretched to relieve the soreness in his arms and legs that plagued him from the manacles that had for so long restricted his movement. Glancing out the window, he looked at the tops of the trees, deathly still against the backdrop of the darkening sky. A sharp crack of thunder off in the distance warned him of the storm that was about to unleash its heavy rain. Flashes of lightning began to cross the room as he dressed and prepared for his first day with the handler. Jenkens, now awake, watched him dress. Admonishing Dance as he walked out the door with him, Jenkens experienced a premonition that sent a frightening chill down his spine.

An hour later, Dance stood in the downpour at the entrance to the Flatiron Building, the new architectural wonder that overlooked

Madison Square. Jenkens sat in a small café down the street. The building had been put into service just days before. Beginning a ritual that he thought would become part of his life, he walked through the lobby to a small elevator and ascended to the twenty-first floor. He smiled at the disguised guards standing outside the office and then at the ugly and overweight woman who sat at the desk. "Mr. Dance?" she asked.

He nodded. "You may go in," she said.

His eyes slowly adjusted to the dim light. Seated at a small round table, a man with a disfigured face looked up and said, "Please be seated."

Dance couldn't help but stare at the twisted mouth, the bloated cheeks, sunken forehead, and blood red eyes that sickened him. In a strangely resonant voice, he heard, "You may find my appearance somewhat disturbing, Mr. Dance. I've had to come to terms with it. There are maladies in life that we can't control. My afflictions are most rare, but they are afflictions nevertheless."

The scratchy resonant voice, the strange surroundings, and the scarlet eyes made Dance uneasy, an emotion that was foreign to him. "Is there a problem in my knowing your name?"

"You may call me the handler, which is what I am. There's no need for you to know anything else about me."

Milo told himself he would find out. Picking up the fifteen page test Milo had taken, the handler was silent for a moment. "You said here," he announced waving the test in the air, "that you killed three men. How did you feel about that?"

"Good."

"Do you want to tell me why? Was it revenge of some sort?"

Milo smiled. "Not revenge. They had pissed me off. They shouldn't have done that. I had no choice but to kill them."

"No choice?"

"Well . . . I could have let them live, but I didn't want to do that. They had to die."

Putting the test back on the table, the handler said, "You didn't just kill them, it appears you butchered them. Why did you do that?"

Milo shrugged. "No particular reason."

"I see. Would you have been satisfied with simply shooting them?"

"Yes, I could have done that." His face stiffening, Milo let his eyes drift around the room, partly out of curiosity and partly because he couldn't bear the sight of the handler. "Can we cut the bullshit? What it is you want me to do?"

The dry skin crinkled around the handler's twisted mouth. "Your test results told us you're an anarchist. Is that correct?"

"Whatever in the hell that means. I hate the goddamned government for what they've done to me."

"Mr. Dance, we want you to do only what you feel satisfies *your* needs. Whatever you decide, we're willing to help facilitate your goal. That includes the payment of a substantial sum of money."

"Why would you do that?"

"That's not a question for you to ask. Would killing someone in authority liberate you from your hatred for the government?"

Milo fell silent, thinking of the judge who had sent him to the asylum.

"Mr. Dance, I won't ask you again. Can we be of help to you or not?"

Milo felt a knot in his stomach and then the fury rise to his throat. "How much money?"

"Five thousand dollars."

"Just for killing whoever I want to?"

"Not exactly. We'll have to talk about that."

Milo sat back, thinking of his freedom. "Fifteen thousand."

"I'll have to get that approved."

"By who?"

"Mr. Dance, I'm here to ask the questions, not you."

Milo was becoming upset. He could feel the intense anger taking hold. His hands curled into tight fists. No one could talk to him like that. Then the fists relaxed and opened. He would take care of the handler later. "I'll go with you."

"No, that's not possible. I'll meet you here again tomorrow, and you'll have my answer. Tell me where I can reach you if I need to."

Milo stood up. "You can't. I'll see you tomorrow."

An hour later, the handler boarded the elevated train to Long Island. He failed to look behind him. If he had, he would have seen a man occupied with a newspaper, a man he knew too well, with Jenkens at his side. At the station in Long Island, the handler disembarked and hired a taxi. Milo Dance decided he wouldn't follow. He would wait. When the taxi returned, he would find out where the handler was dropped off.

Milo talked to Matthew Stanton the next evening and told him very little. Stanton knew he was holding something back, and warned Jenkens not to let him out of his sight. In the morning, Milo returned with Jenkens to the Flatiron Building at eleven o'clock. Jenkens waited on a park bench across the street. Walking past the ugly receptionist, Milo slowly eased himself into a chair across from the handler. The light reflecting in the unusually dim room cast a shadow across the handler's face; this time, Milo didn't find him quite so disturbing. "Where's my money?" he asked.

"First things first, Mr. Dance. You'll have your money, but not today. First, we'll have to determine what it is you want to do."

"You intend to hold out on me?"

"Who do you intend to kill?"

"A judge."

"May I ask why?"

Milo hated the waste of time conversations brought. In a fit of frustration, he said, "He means nothing to me. He deserves to die." He stopped and then added for the benefit of the handler, "He and his kind are destroying this country."

The handler wasn't satisfied. There was a lot more work he had to do. "Why a lowly judge? Why not reach higher?"

"What are you talking about?"

"I'm saying, Mr. Dance, that there are others whose killing could make you a hero. You could do something for the misery in this country."

Without responding, Milo asked, "Do you have my gun?"

"No. You'll get it, but only when we're satisfied you've made the right choice. Then I'll give you a gun."

His eyes flashing, Milo said, "No." The rage in his expression set the handler back. He wondered if they had made a mistake. "I want the gun now!"

"Mr. Dance," he said softly, "that isn't possible. I don't have it. Believe me, when the time is right, it will be given to you."

Milo twisted his hands. "When the time is right for *you*," he said in a low voice.

The next day, Milo was staring out the window at Madison Square when the handler walked in. The handler walked over to the table, sat down, and began tapping his fingers. Milo Dance was losing his patience. Looking up, the handler handed him several sheets of paper to read. Dance would be subjected to one week of propaganda and lies about the new president, and then he would be incited to kill him. If he could be persuaded, he would be provided information about the Roosevelt's schedule, and the plan would be set in motion. If he refused to kill the President, they would kill him.

Milo stared at the handler, his eyes cold and calculating. He wanted to kill him. He was breathing steadily, the muscles in his face relaxed. The handler could not know what he was thinking. "Mr. Dance," the handler said, "I want you to read the papers I've given you. They tell about the ravage our government is bringing upon its citizens. I hope you're as incensed as we are."

Milo held the papers without looking at them, his eyes glaring at the handler. They had misunderstood the degree of his intelligence. Distracted, the handler repeated his request.

"First, tell me who you work for," Milo demanded in a disturbing tone of voice.

"That's out of the question." The handler reached into his pocket for a handkerchief, using it to wipe sweat beginning to form on his forehead. A nervous twitch had developed in his thick neck. He felt something was wrong. Dance was silent, his beady eyes remaining fixed. Feeling a slight tingle in his chest, the handler nervously asked, "Is there something wrong?"

Milo smiled. It never left his thoughts that this man, and the men he worked for, thought they could win. They would lose, all of them. It was now a game. If he killed the handler first, he had thought he'd never find the others. Now he knew where someone lived on Long Island. It was a beginning. "There is something wrong," he said calmly, "it's you." Standing, he repeated, "Who do you work for?"

"Mr. Dance, I think we've gone far enough. If you'll excuse me, I have other things to do."

Milo removed a knife from his jacket. "You think you're smart enough to control me. Is that it?"

Worry turned to panic. "Mr. Dance, there . . . there's been a misunderstanding." Wiping his brow, the handler said, "Yes, that's it. Just a simple misunderstanding. We thought you harbored a hatred for the government, and that we could help you – with money and . . . ." He stopped as Milo moved closer to him. "You see," he continued, ..."

The sharp edge of the knife was placed against his throat. "Have you ever had your throat slit?" Milo asked with a frightening grin. "No, of course you haven't, or you wouldn't be here. Tell me who you work for, and you won't suffer while I cut you up."

His face flushed, the handler was panicked. He wanted to yell for the guards, but he knew that would mean certain death. "I don't know," he pleaded. "Believe me, I've never met him."

"Then you're no use to me." Grabbing the handler's hair with one hand, he used the other to trace a line with the knife along his neck. Blood began to appear along the line of the slash and slowly made its way down the handler's neck to his chest. Petrified, he begged, "Please no."

Pushing the knife deeper, Milo said, "Just a name." Struggling to pull away, the handler gagged. "He's rich," he spit out. "I don't know him. If you hurt me, he'll have you killed."

"What has he hired you to do?"

His voice shaking, tears began to show in his eyes. He mumbled, "He wants you to kill Roosevelt."

"Me?" Milo said. "I don't give a shit about Roosevelt. Sleep well," Milo said as he plunged the knife through the handler's throat. He let go of his hair, releasing him to fall into the blood that was beginning to spread across the floor. "Damn you," he said to himself, "I killed him without the name." He reached down and removed the handler's wallet, key chain and pocket watch. Opening the wallet, he saw a great deal of money. He searched for a gun. There was none. The money would buy a gun. Opening the watch, he saw the picture of a woman. He stared at it for several seconds and then dropped the watch and smashed it with his foot. The wallet had the handler's name and address. That would be helpful.

Suddenly there was a knock on the door. "Everything okay in there?"

"Fine," he answered in a muffled voice. Several minutes later, he opened the door and pushed past the guards. At the elevator, he looked back and waited for the door to close. Smiling, he thought, *I have a busy day ahead.* The day was crisp and sunny. He saw Jenkens looking the other way. Keeping his head down, he hired a taxi and headed for the train terminal, where he would buy a ticket to Long Island.

At five o'clock that afternoon, Jenkens appeared at Matthew Stanton's doorway. "He's gone." Stanton looked at him, stunned.

"Are you sure?"

"I'm sure. He never came out from his meeting, so I went into the Flatiron Building. The offices were empty, but there was blood on the floor." With a sick look on his face, he said, "He's killed someone, probably the man he was meeting with. We've got a hell of a problem."

"Oh my God!" Stanton said to himself. Isaacs had warned him, but he hadn't listened. He had learned nothing, and now he had turned a psychopath loose on the city. "Come in," he said. Walking through the foyer with Jenkens following, it occurred to him that he would now have to hunt the Dance Man down, if he could find him. What didn't occur to him was that he, Matthew Stanton, had suddenly been transformed from the hunter to the hunted.

CHAPTER FORTY

▼

Long Island, New York

Thaddeus Pratt was worried. The caller had said his man was dead – murdered by the psychopath they had chosen to kill Roosevelt. That goddamned test, he thought. Finding Leon Czolgosz had been easy. He had walked into their arms. Why had this been so difficult? He had to make other plans; there would be another way to kill Roosevelt. Lighting a cigar, he walked down the hallway of his massive home into the drawing room. Settling at his desk, he lifted his feet to rest on the top. It was only then that he saw a man sitting in the corner.

"How in the hell . . . ." he started to say, only to see a gun raised.

"Your security isn't worth a damn," Milo Dance said. "By the way, this gun is pointed directly at your head. You do or say anything I don't like, and I'll blow your head off."

"You murdered Bosley."

"If he was your handler, I'd say you'd better get another one."

With nerves of steel, Pratt took a long drag of his cigar. "Do you want to tell me what you want?"

"I haven't decided. Let's start with money."

Blowing a ring of smoke, Pratt said matter-of-factly, "I've got plenty of that."

"That's what I hear. Tell me why you want to kill Roosevelt, and why Matthew Stanton thinks you framed him."

"Matthew Stanton? How in the hell did you hear that?"

"He told me."

"How do you know him? Does he know who I am?"

Milo glanced around the room, studying the dark walnut walls, antique mahogany furniture, and priceless artwork. "You've got a hell of a lot of money," he said with a slight smile.

"Does he know who I am?" Pratt demanded.

"No. He wants me to find out you are." Milo paused to study Pratt's expression. "Did you frame him?"

"I might have . . . . but that's beside the point. What did he offer you?"

"My freedom."

"Your what?"

"I've been locked up in that nuthouse asylum for five years. If I find you, I get out."

Pratt sat back, tapping his cigar on an ashtray. "He's lying."

Milo cocked the gun. "Bullshit. He said I'd get a new sanity hearing, and he'd arrange it. Dr. Isaacs was there."

"And you believed him?"

Milo's eyes were bulging. "He didn't say dead or alive. I think I'll make it dead."

A devious smile crossed Pratt's lips. "Go ahead. Good luck at your sanity hearing. Two more murders. I'm sure that'll sit well with the judge."

Milo said nothing, holding the gun steady.

"How does one hundred thousand dollars sound to you?"

Milo stared at him, letting the words "Jesus Christ" slip from his lips.

Pratt leaned forward. "I can keep you out of the asylum and make you rich at the same time."

"I'm listening."

"All you have to do is kill Stanton and then kill Roosevelt."

Milo slowly lowered the gun. "I'll have to think on that."

"You're not smart enough to pull that off?" Pratt asked.

The gun came up again. "I'm smart enough to kill you now."

"That's not smart – that's stupid. You can get to Stanton. As far as Roosevelt, I'll set that up for you. Then you'll be on your way out of the country."

"When do I get the money?"

Pulling out his desk drawer, Pratt grabbed a bundle of thousand dollar bills. "Here's twenty-five thousand dollars," he said, tossing the bills across the room. "A down payment. I've got a place near here. You can stay there until it's done."

Milo picked up the bundle and fanned the bills. "How do I know I can trust you?"

"Look at the money you're holding. There's your trust."

Dance put the gun and the money in his pockets. Standing up, he asked, "When do you want Stanton killed?"

"Right away."

"And Roosevelt?"

"I'll tell you."

When Dance had left, Pratt lit another cigar. Putting his feet back on the desk, he was astonished at how fate had played into his hands. It occurred to him, though, that one thing was wrong. Dance knew who he was. When it was done, he would have to kill him. He smiled to himself. That would save him seventy-five thousand dollars. He was a fortunate man.

$$*\qquad *\qquad *\qquad *$$

Matteawan State Hospital, New York

Dr. Isaacs was pacing the floor when Matthew Stanton arrived in his office. In a shrill voice, he said, "Do you have any idea of what we've done?"

"I think I do," Matthew grimly responded.

"How do I explain that I've let a maniac loose in our community? I don't know what possessed me to go along with your scheme, but we'll both pay the price."

Stanton leaned against the wall, his eyes meeting those of Isaacs. "I thought I could trust him," he said in a low voice.

"A psychopath? It's I who should have known better." Rubbing his forehead, he asked, "What in the world was I thinking?"

"I've hired detectives to find him."

"And you honestly think you can? It took the police three long years to track him down before he made it into here. He's too smart for you."

Putting his palm up, Stanton said, "It's too late for second-guessing. Sit down and let's think this through."

Isaacs turned and sat at his desk while Stanton sat down across from him. A look of despair crossed Isaacs' face. The silence was deafening. Stanton broke it. "What do you think he'll do next?"

He heard nothing but Isaacs' labored breathing. Looking away to avoid his penetrating stare, Stanton asked, "Did you hear me?"

"I heard. I'll think he'll try to kill one or both of us."

"Jesus!" Stanton mumbled. "Why? Revenge?"

Shaking his head, Isaacs said, "He doesn't care about revenge. That's an emotion you and I can share. He doesn't have emotions. To him, Mr. Stanton, it's a game. He'll try because it will excite him."

"Mary Shelley's Frankenstein."

"A good description. You've created Frankenstein's monster." Turning toward the window, Isaacs said, "What I said before, about your not being able to find him. That wasn't accurate." Turning back, he looked at Stanton. "Mr. Stanton, he'll find you. I'd be prepared if I were you. As for myself, I intend to be very, very careful. I don't want to be his next victim. Now, I have many things to do. I wish you luck – and a safe passage through all of this."

Matthew Stanton stood to leave, suddenly relieved that Alyssa had cut him out of her life. Finding Milo Dance might not be so bad at all. He had a hunch Dance now knew something about the men who framed him.

CHAPTER FORTY-ONE

New York City

Early light broke over midtown Manhattan, the night rain replaced by the mist in the March morning cold. A few people, leaving their flats early, either stepped into waiting carriages or walked down the street to the trolley. The gas lamps still held their glow but were now offering little light as the sun was beginning to rise. One man, however, seemed to be in a particular hurry. Milo Dance had just stepped off a train from Long Island and was headed for a used clothing store on 3rd Avenue. He paused in front of a dirty window to review his plan for the day. The image of the man reflected in the window would soon change.

The black wool hat covered his head down to his eyebrows; the worn patched jacket was a size too large; and the dark flannel shirt, the baggy pants, and the work shoes with the heavy rubber soles were for the illiterate masses; but they were all part of who he would be today. With a flurry of construction activity in the city, he would easily blend in with the day-laborers. But he would not head for a construction site. His destination was a small park on 5th Avenue where he would sit and wait, all day if necessary.

When he reached the park, he found a bench that provided a clear view down the street. He was alone. He laid a newspaper on his lap and focused on the tall, jagged-edged gray stone house that was three doors down. Under the newspaper, he placed a .38 revolver. The windows of the house reflected light both inside and out. Maintaining his concentration, he couldn't detect any movement. He noticed the carefully manicured gardens that surrounded the house, the walls partially covered with ivy, and the expensive hand-carved wood doors that sat at the top of the brick steps.

A nagging thought occurred to him: Stanton might not be there. Maybe he had judged wrong. He would wait all day if necessary, and then the following day. And the day after that.

An hour later, Matthew Stanton stepped out of the front door of his home, hesitating as he looked up and down the street. He had made it his practice to study people, to look for odd things, things out of place. Berg had taught him that. Walking down the front steps, he had an uneasy feeling, a feeling that something was not quite right. The morning had become sunny and crisp, but windy. The bright sun was now blocking his view of the park on the corner. He shielded his eyes with his left hand, his right in his coat pocket. It was now morning rush hour, and he watched the carriages passing by, the hoofs of their horses echoing a loud thumpedy-thump on the cobblestone street.

His carriage driver had been instructed to meet him at the corner. He was in the midst of people hurrying by, but he felt someone watching him. He felt it. Stopping to scour the people around him, he saw nothing unusual.

Resuming his walk toward the corner, he noticed a man in the park. He stopped and focused his eyes on him through the traffic. Waiting for a carriage to pass, he crossed the street, never taking his eyes off the man. He steadied his nerves and walked over to the park bench. Staring down at the man, he said, "Hello, Milo."

Milo Dance looked up with insolent eyes and an ugly little smile. "How did you know?"

"Second nature. I've had to deal with people like you my whole life. You're no different than the others." He sat down next to Dance.

"I could've killed you when you walked across the street, but that would've been too easy," Milo bragged.

Unruffled, Stanton said, "Why would you want to? I thought you agreed to help me."

Milo tightened his grip on the gun and said nothing.

"In case you're thinking of doing something stupid, I've got a gun in my coat pointed at your manhood. You think you're going to kill me?" Milo jumped slightly when he heard the gun cocked. "You imbecile," Stanton said. "You told me you couldn't be controlled, and now they're doing it to you."

Blood rushed to Dance's face. He had a sudden feeling of being trapped. "Nobody controls me; not you or anyone else."

"Bullshit. Someone's controlling you right now. Put your gun away. You're not fast enough to pull the trigger before I shoot you in the gut."

Dance remained silent, a small grin coming back to his face.

"I got you out of that lunatic hospital, dammit. And now you want to kill *me*? Guess what? You're going right back in. Whatever they promised you, whatever they paid you, it'll do you no good when you're back in shackles."

"That won't happen," Dance said in a low voice.

"You know what, Mr. Dance Man, you're beginning to piss me off. I'll tell you what I'll do. I've got a feeling you know who framed me. You take me to him, and I'll hold true to my promise."

"Not interested." Dance stood up, keeping his eyes on Stanton. "I'm leaving, but I'll be back for you."

Stanton removed the gun from his pocket and aimed it at Dance's head. At the same time, Dance removed the gun from under the paper and leveled it at Stanton. Smiling, Dance said, "You don't want to die, but I don't give a shit. That's the difference between us. You're not going to shoot."

Stanton rose, lowering his gun. "You know what – you do give a shit. What brought about this change in you? Give me his name."

Pleased with himself, Dance cocked his gun and said arrogantly, "I knew you'd lose your nerve. You didn't have the guts to shoot me."

"No, I didn't. But the men behind you do."

"What . . . ." Dance spun around to see two men with guns pointed at him. One quickly took his gun away while the other grabbed his arms and slapped handcuffs on him. His cynical smile disappeared into a look of rage.

"I'm sorry this didn't work out, Milo. Maybe you'll have a change of heart back at the asylum. Call me if you do. I'll listen."

CHAPTER FORTY-TWO

▼

Long Island, New York

His plan to kill Roosevelt was beginning to unravel. Milo Dance had disappeared. Thaddeus Pratt sat at his desk, trying to reconstruct events. Looking out the floor-to-ceiling window across from his desk, he saw the day was clouding over. So was his mind. He had never been paranoid, but paranoia was beginning to set in. Dance now knew who he was. He slammed his fist on the desk. How in the hell could this have happened? Dance had been in a mental asylum. Would they believe him over Pratt? He couldn't take that chance. How could he find out what happened to him? Matthew Stanton! Dance had gone to kill Stanton. This time Pratt would be more careful.

The bar was dimly lit when he entered, presumably to give an air of intimacy. He was there for an 8:00 PM meeting. It was 7:40. He selected a table near the front, where he could watch people enter. At ten to eight, two well dressed men appeared at the door, looked around the bar, and were seated at a nearby table. After their drinks had arrived, they alternately munched on peanuts while they waited. Out of a corner of his eye, Pratt could see that they were nervous. He stood up and walked over to their table. He didn't identify himself, and neither did they. They were both young, in their mid-thirties. One had slicked-down black hair, a handle-bar mustache, and beady gray eyes. The other, who was shorter, had a thick beard, a semi-bald head, and hands that were constantly in motion.

"You're here for the situation?" Pratt asked.

"We are," said one.

Pratt reached into his coat pocket, pulled out a thick envelope, and slid it across the table. "It's all in there," he said. Without saying another word, he stood up and left.

It took three days, but they finally determined that Milo Dance was back in the New York Asylum for the Criminally Insane, the Matteawan State Hospital. He was not permitted visitors. They showed police identifications and told the attendant they were there to question him concerning two murders. After an hour, Dance was brought into a small, window-less room where he sat shackled at a small table, the attendant hovering over him. When the men entered, he sat perfectly still, taking in everything they had to say, interrupting only to ask small details. It didn't take long for him to realize they were fakes.

As the minutes elapsed, they noticed him tapping on the table with his fingers as he became agitated. The fingers tapped slowly until they got to the question that set him off. "Have you spoken to anyone," one asked, "about your contact with a wealthy industrialist?" Dance's eyes seemed to glaze over and the tapping of his fingers increased in velocity. Finally, he exploded, a cracking, raging, intemperate voice. "He set me up!" he screamed. "If he doesn't get me out of here soon, the entire fuckin' world will know about your Thaddeus Pratt."

The men looked at each other, startled, and then shifted their gaze to the attendant, who now knew what they were after and the name shouted by Dance. Taking Dance's arm, the attendant said, "Officers, I'm afraid I have to end this meeting."

Dance yelled at the attendant. "They're not officers – they're impostors!"

The attendant, wide-eyed, moved toward the door a split-second before two gunshots smashed the back of his head. Spinning around to Milo Dance, the shorter man attempted to fire but Dance leapt across the table and hit the gun with his manacled hands, causing it to discharge into the ceiling. Swinging around, he ripped his manacles across the other man's cheek, leaving a deep gash spouting blood. The man touched his cheek and screamed in agony. The door flew open and an unarmed guard rushed in, suddenly wishing he hadn't. A gun exploded in his face. Milo Dance swung his arms around again, but before he could land the chains on the other man, a bullet struck him in the neck. He fell headlong onto the floor. Stepping over him, the two men tore through the open door and disappeared down the hall, leaving a room full of blood with two men dead and one mortally wounded.

The hospital was quickly cordoned off and occupied with an army of armed guards and police officers. It was too late – the assailants had disappeared. Matthew Stanton received word from Dr. Isaacs the next morning of the carnage. Thaddeus Pratt was both relieved and furious. He wanted Dance dead – that had been accomplished. But now there would be a major investigation, and he was at the center of it. He sent the killers far away, four thousand miles to San Francisco, and waited. They had assured him that no one could connect him to the crime, but his name had been yelled out in the melee. Did anyone hear it other than the dead attendant? He would be tormented with that question. It was time to lay low.

*   *   *   *

Washington, D. C.

At the White House, Theodore Roosevelt was enraged. The only source they had to discover the men behind McKinley's murder lay in a coma and was dying. A catastrophe had occurred at one of New York's major insane asylums, and the physician in charge, a Dr. Isaacs, had talked to the press. It was now being written that he, the President, was somehow connected with this fiasco. A serial murderer had been released on the public with the blessing of his Attorney General. It made no difference that the murderer was back in custody and dying; it had led to the deaths of an innocent attendant and a guard.

Attorney General Knox and Matthew Stanton stood motionless at his doorway, waiting for the President to speak. In the deafening stillness, Knox several times stole irate glances at Stanton. When the President did speak, his voice was in an uncustomary low tone. "Mr. Stanton, I don't know all the facts, but I do know a psychopath was released into society at your insistence. I applaud you for your ingenuity, but in hindsight it was horribly conceived. As for you, Philander, I trust that your judgment in the future will not reflect as poorly on you as this affair has." Stopping to light a cigar, he took a small puff and continued, "We have not come to an end in our investigation of William McKinley's murder. I've now turned the entire matter over to Mr. Wilcox and his staff. I want each of you to be available should he need your assistance. With that, I'm releasing Mr. Stanton to return to his life and business. You may leave, Mr. Stanton. Philander, I'd like you to stay for a moment."

Stanton turned, walked down the hallway and began his descent down the tall staircase. "Oh, Mr. Stanton," he heard Knox say behind him. "Please leave your badge and gun with the attendant below." Matthew thought briefly to himself, *With pleasure.* Exiting the White House to a waiting carriage, he had another thought. *It's far from over.*

CHAPTER FORTY-THREE

―――――――――▼―――――――――

Newport, Rhode Island

It wasn't Ayssa's nature to dwell on the past or cling to sadness. She missed Matthew Stanton in every possible way, but she had now come to realize that it was never meant to be. Two months had elapsed since she saw him last, and she had met someone else for whom she had developed a great admiration. Her wealth and his stature had led her into a new circle of society. The invitation had requested her presence to the 1901 Century Ball at the summer house of Mr. and Mrs. William K. Vanderbilt in Newport, Rhode Island. William Vanderbilt was the grandson of Commodore Cornelius Vanderbilt, who established the family's fortune in steamships and the New York Central Railroad.

Marble House, as the summer house was known, was a social and architectural landmark that had set the pace for Newport's transformation from a quiet summer colony of wooden houses to the legendary resort of opulent stone palaces. Vanderbilt's wife, Alva, had envisioned Marble House as a "temple to the arts" in America. He had given it to her as a birthday present on her thirty-ninth birthday. Overlooking the breathtaking landscape and seascape of Rhode Island Sound, it was completed in 1892 at a cost of over $11 million. Seven million alone was for five hundred thousand cubic feet of marble.

On a beautiful May evening, with the ocean breezes flowing gently through the chill air, the stately carriages could be seen lined on Bellevue Avenue for what seemed miles. An extravagant social event, the five hundred guests would spend the night drinking the finest champagne and dancing the Lancers' Quadrille, the fluid and elegant flirtatious dance that had swept the nation.

The vast ballroom of the Marble House, with its gleaming gold chandeliers, shimmering black and white marble floor, and glass-domed ceiling, was magnificent. The Vanderbilts had turned it into a dazzling wonderland, filled with red roses and holly. Near the center of the room, a large white gazebo with roses trailing up its column was surrounded by the orchestra. Fountains spouted geysers of sparkling champagne while waiters, circulating among the guests, offered hors d'oeuvres to those who didn't wish to help themselves from the giant silver platters laden with food.

The gown Alyssa was wearing had been ordered from Paris. It was entirely different from the gowns of the other women. No one wore white, of course, in deference to their hostess. And they all looked lovely. But Alyssa looked more than that; she was elegant and striking – she exuded a quiet sophistication. There were no frills, ruffles or flounces. The ice blue satin gown, with its flowing skirt, seemed to ripple around her like water. It showed off her perfect figure, and the aquamarine and diamond earrings sparkled in and out of her dark auburn hair. Her dress was the color of an icy winter sky, and her skin had the color and softness of the palest creamy rose. Her lips were a bright red and caught the stares of men around her as she laughed and talked with her escort.

They drifted with the others from the reception room to the ballroom. She was perfectly at ease talking with either men or women, and there seemed to be a score of men trailing behind her every step of the way. It was a glittering evening; she enjoyed it but was very self-contained. Near the center of the room, Alyssa stood beside her date, his hand possessively around her waist, overwhelmed by the beauty of her surroundings.

Twenty feet away, Matthew Stanton paused and his companion noticed a sudden chill in his eyes. *Did Alyssa know he was going to be here?* He gasped. At the same instant, she turned and her eyes caught his. He held his breath, his gaze shifting from her to the man who accompanied her. He knew him! But where? His shock vanished as quickly as it had hit him, and he managed a drink of his champagne. Her radiance was mesmerizing, yet he had lost her. He searched for signs of the woman who walked out on him when he had last seen her, but what he saw instead was an unexpected aura of confidence and well being. Was it because of the man she was with?

What *she* saw was the man who had wanted her to leave, who refused to let her stay with him. A man who didn't offer her peace and comfort, unlike her escort, but a man who seemed to be searching for his own death. She shuddered slightly at the thought of what life would be with him. Frozen in time, she watched as he walked over to her. "Alyssa," he whispered, "I don't know quite what to say. How are you?"

"I'm fine," she answered coolly. "There's really not much to say." Turning, she said, "I'd like you to meet my date. Thaddeus Pratt, this is Matthew Stanton."

Both men turned pale. Stanton made an attempt to extend his hand, but Pratt didn't move. "You two know each other?" she asked.

Stanton ignored her question and turned to his date. "I'm so sorry," he said, "this is Mary Keyes. Mary, Alyssa Harding and Thaddeus Pratt."

Both nodded while Alyssa quickly appraised the woman he was with. Mary was very blonde and very pretty. Alyssa suddenly felt an emotion she was totally unprepared for – jealousy. Looking into his deep brown eyes, her immediate thought was that he was still the most strikingly handsome man she had ever known. Grasping for words, she was suddenly overcome with a sensation of loss. Her hard veneer slowly melting, she said, "I'm so glad to see you again, Matthew. It seems like forever."

Before Stanton could answer, Pratt pulled her away, saying, "Come, there's someone I'd like you to meet." Lost in far-away thoughts, Stanton felt a tug on his arm. "Matthew," Mary said, "you look as though you've seen a ghost. What is it?"

Feeling as though he were gasping for breath, he mumbled, "That man. I know him, but I can't place him. There's something about him that disturbs me."

She smiled, and in a gentle voice said, "Maybe the fact that he's with her? She seems to have attracted your attention."

"Oh," he answered turning to her, "I knew her once upon a time, a long while ago." He thought of her face, like a fine piece of porcelain. In his entire life, no one had been able to do this to him. He had been far too brittle for that.

*   *   *   *

He awoke in a cold sweat. The man in the carriage. He *was* Thaddeus Pratt! But why? He had done nothing to Pratt. And now Pratt was with Alyssa. It was madness. Getting out of bed to stare out the window, he noticed the time was 4:00 AM. The moon cast a hazy glow on the deserted street below, adding to his mood of regret and melancholy. Putting on a robe, he walked down to his drawing room. There, he poured a glass of sherry and sat on the sofa, watching the last embers of the fire that had burned earlier slowly lose their spark.

Pratt and Milo Dance, he thought. *Was there a connection?* Questions plagued his mind. Nothing made sense.

His thoughts slowly moved to Alyssa. He felt the pain well up inside. How could she make him feel this way, how in a ten minute encounter? He tried to fight it, but he couldn't. He was still in love with her.

CHAPTER FORTY-FOUR

▼

New York City

Alyssa also awoke in the early hours. She awoke shocked and panicked that they had killed him. The words started as a whisper in her mind, and then became a cry of warning. She was falling, spiraling into a void. "I won't let you die without me," she cried to herself. Then she was awake, abruptly sitting up in the still darkness of the room, shaking. Inhaling a deep breath, she tried to calm her jangled nerves. "It was all a nightmare," she whispered to herself.

In the morning, she took a small piece of paper and wrote three words, put it in an envelope and addressed it, and rang for her servant. She waited all day, but there was no answer. Late that evening, returning from the theater, he found it tucked to the side under his door. It was unsigned. It said, "I need you." He pulled out his watch and noted the time – 10:30. He called for his driver.

*   *   *   *

She answered the knock on the door tentatively. Opening it, she began to cry. Her tears came, washing away the final barricades she had erected to keep him away. His arms were around her, her face touching his shoulder. Her lips parted, her tears wetting his shirt. Their arms grew stronger around each other and their lips met. A faint bruise was still there, a bruise he had suffered because of her, but his strength was also there. She kissed him again, more deeply. Then the absurdity of it all struck her. Why would she ever not want to be with him? She had loved him for so long, long before they met on the train.

She closed the door and led him up the winding staircase to her bedroom. "Are you sure?" he asked tenderly. She was sure. As if they had been away from each other for years, she would not let him go. They made love again and again. At last, the rays of the sun streaked across the room. He turned to her, leaning on his elbow. "Why, Alyssa? What changed your mind?"

"The possibility that something could have happened to you tormented me, night and day. I couldn't live with it. When I saw you at the ball, my heart shattered."

"Now that you have me, what do we do?"

"I can't think that far ahead. All I want is to be with you. Move in with me."

"No," he answered.

"Tell me why . . . or don't tell me. Matthew, I don't care. I just don't want to be away from you."

"Then marry me."

She suddenly sat up straight. "Marry you?"

"Yes. Let's make it forever."

"Then will you tell me what you're involved in?"

He smiled and nodded. They made love again.

*   *   *   *

The next morning, the questioning began. Looking at her beautiful face across the rosewood table, he said, "There are things I have to know. I love you so much, but I want you to understand."

She put down her fork, puzzled. "Understand what?"

"Questions first," he said. "Alyssa, how did you get to know Thaddeus Pratt?"

She smiled. "Are you jealous?"

"It has nothing to do with that. I'll explain it to you in a moment. But tell me, how did you two get together?"

"I met him when I was settling Clayton's estate. He had a company that Clayton had invested in. At the time, I thought he was very nice. When he asked me to have dinner, you and I had broken up. I needed to get out, so I accepted. After that, I saw him several more times, and then we went to the Vanderbilts' ball together." She studied his face, looking for any change of expression. The tense muscles didn't relax. "That's all there was, I promise. You don't have to worry about Thaddeus Pratt."

Stanton shook his head. "Yes, I do."

"Why, for God's sake? He was just a friend who was kind to me when I needed it."

"Alyssa," he said reaching for her hand, "he's much more than that. In some way, he was involved with two men who were interviewing anarchists. They set up a meeting with me and failed to show up. He was there, watching me from another carriage. Then he chased me in a mad frenzy. A lot of things happened after that. I think he was involved with them."

"That sounds absurd. Why would he do that?"

"It's not absurd; it's true."

"Do me a favor. Put him out of your mind. Last night was so incredible! Matthew, we're getting married. What you've said about him is so bizarre. Can we let it be and forget about him? Let's think of our life together." She squeezed his hand with pleading eyes.

"I'm sorry I brought it up," he said. "I can forget about him. I just hope he can forget about me."

*   *   *   *

Two weeks later, the New York newspapers ran stories about the marriage of two of the city's wealthiest citizens, Alyssa Harding and Matthew Stanton. The articles told of the wedding attended by only several friends, and of the honeymoon in Europe planned on the American Lines' newest and fastest ocean liner, *The City of New*

York. Upon hearing of it, President Roosevelt sent his heartiest best wishes to the bride and groom.

CHAPTER FORTY-FIVE

▼

The Hudson River Pier, New York City

A cold rain had begun to fall, causing the blurred street lamps to look ghastly in the mist. The public houses were just closing, and men and women were clustering in broken groups around the doors. Lying back in his carriage, his hat pulled over his forehead, Thaddeus Pratt watched with listless eyes the sordid shame of a great city. Now and then, he repeated to himself the name that had turned his stomach for so long - Matthew Stanton.

His irrational thoughts then turned to the opium den where he had just bought oblivion, where the memory of his old sins was destroyed. Looking out through the foggy window of his carriage, he watched the moon drift low in the sky, hidden at times by misshapen clouds. The gas lamps grew fewer and the streets more narrow and gloomy. Steam seemed to rise from the two horses as they splashed their way through the puddles. The side windows of the carriage were now almost completely fogged over with the gray mist. A dull rage was in his heart.

The carriage plodded on and on, the lash of the driver's whip echoing in his ears. They passed by dark houses and vacant lots, dogs barking as the horses galloped by. As they turned a corner, her face floated across his mind, and then that of Matthew Stanton. He had only begun to know her, but again Stanton had taken away what was his. It was a torment that would not go away. Suddenly, the carriage drew up with a jerk at the top of a dark lane. Over the row of low roofs he could see the raked funnels of large steamships. "This will do," he said. He quickly got out and walked down a hill in the direction of the ships.

Near the bottom, he stopped at a small house and knocked. The door opened quietly, and he went in without saying a word to the man who stood in the shadow of the doorway. The floor was covered with sawdust, in some places trampled into mud.

The sailor motioned to a chair and looked at him in a hesitating manner. Pratt studied the man. "*The City of New York* sails in two weeks."

"It does, Mr. Johnson," came a hushed reply.

"And you'll be on it?"

"That I will, sir, as second mate."

"You understand what I want."

"Yes, sir, I do. You want the lady and the gentleman to disappear."

"And you can do that."

"For the sum you've offered, I can do that. It won't be easy, the ship being closed quarters and all that, but for one thousand dollars I can make it happen."

"How will you do it?"

"Is that any care of yours? Let's just say they'll not be aboard when we dock. Passengers fall overboard, you know."

"There'll be an investigation," he warned.

"Being second mate and all, I'll be very obliging. They won't suspect me."

Pratt reached into his coat and removed a wad of bills. Holding them out, he placed them in the sailor's hands. "Payment in advance," he said.

He heard the bills being fanned as he stood and walked through the doorway and stepped into his carriage. What he didn't hear was the scratchy, high-pitched voice of the woman who stepped out of the bedroom. "Here, give that to me," she demanded.

CHAPTER FORTY-SIX

---▼---

SS The City of New York

Their carriage arrived at the East River Pier shortly before noon. Matthew helped Alyssa out of the relative quiet of the Phaeton cab, into the noise and bustle of the throng of passengers. It was sunny but very windy. A couple hurried by, the man wearing a long black frock coat and a high hat, a cane in his hand and a cigar between his lips; the woman wearing a long blue dress with a matching feather-covered bonnet. They smiled in passing, and the man crimped the brim of his hat and said, "We're looking forward to our journey with you." Matthew smiled and tipped his hat in appreciation.

Their luggage was given to a stevedore who followed others with trunks and crates on their shoulders swarming up and down the gangplank, loading cargo and preparing for *The City of New York's* voyage to England. Winches creaked overhead as overflowing cargo nets were raised to the luggage hold. A man dressed in a captain's outfit, his square jaw set with hardened determination, slapped his white gloves against his thigh, yelling instructions to crew members. Alyssa took Matthew's hand as they wove among the anxious crowds to the stairway that would take them to the deck of the ship. He glanced at her lustrous eyes and intoxicating smile. Among this melee, he thought to himself, she still managed to portray an image of amazing elegance. Her floor-length dress of yellow brocade trimmed with blue, mutton sleeves made of blue chiffon, and auburn hair partially covered by a flowered straw hat, was to him the embodiment of beauty. He looked back and smiled as several men stopped to stare at her as they climbed the high stairs onto the ship.

The City of New York was distinguished as one of the first twin-screw steamships to cross the Atlantic. Its luxurious accommodations made it one of the most pretentious steamships in service carrying the American flag. It was designed to carry five-hundred first-class passengers with several suites of rooms on the first deck, all arranged with private bathrooms. For other passengers, bathrooms outside of their rooms were distributed about the ship so that each class of passengers was furnished with its own bathrooms, smoking room, saloon and dining room. The steerage was divided so that third class passengers were in the front and rear of the great ship, allowing them "glimpses" of ocean views.

Unlike the great ships that had come before it, *The City of New York* was lighted with electricity in every quarter, including even the steerage. The ship was designed for one thousand passengers. Her quarters had hot and cold running water, electric ventilation, and first class public rooms, including a library and smoking room, all fitted with walnut paneling. The dining salon for first class passengers came with a massive dome that provided natural lighting.

While Alyssa and Matthew had been accustomed to the very best of everything, when they entered their suite they felt as though they were introduced for the first time to royal splendor. It was paneled in dark walnut with an inlaid ceiling and thick Oriental carpeting on the floors. A richly upholstered sofa and matching chairs, with great puffy pillows, occupied the parlor, all in princely shades of gold and green. Ship lamps sat on gimbals, designed to burn erect whatever the sway of the ship. Beyond the parlor were a private sitting room and the bedroom, having an ornate quality that was almost stifling.

Alyssa held her hand up to her mouth to suppress a giggle. He looked at her and questioned, "A bit overdone?"

She took off her hat and removed the tortoise shell combs that held her hair in a bun, letting it flow down to her shoulders. Smiling, she said, "No, I would say it's you who's a bit overdone."

He laughed. "After what you've put me through the last two weeks, I'd have to say you're right."

She put her arms around his neck. "With everything that's happened," she whispered, "here we are, married and safe, *and* on our honeymoon. One whole month with you! How could I be so lucky?"

*   *   *   *

The bells rang at six o'clock. An hour later, the great ship picked up steam and departed on its five-day voyage for Southampton, England. At eight o'clock, Alyssa and Matthew left their suite for the grand dining salon where they were seated at the captain's table. They were treated to beef Wellington, an assortment of fresh vegetables and fruit, and a lobster salad. Throughout the exquisite meal, they were served multiple glasses of champagne. They sat with two other wealthy couples from New York and the captain. The conversation wandered from the Spanish-American War to the Wright brothers to Wall Street. The captain then excused himself while many of the women in the salon were packed off to bed, allowing their husbands to enjoy a final cigar before turning in.

Matthew took Alyssa's hand and led her out to the top deck, where they stood in silence, staring at the full moon that cast its glow on the glassy surface of the water below. It was a heavenly evening, one that Alyssa would not forget. After thirty minutes, he whispered, "I have an idea."

She pressed her head against his chest. "Are you going to keep me in suspense?"

Leaning down, he said, "I'll show you in bed."

She drew back, her lovely face smiling at him.

Returning to their suite, her lips immediately found his. "I love you, I love you," she repeated. He picked her up and carried her to the bed. He removed her combs, one by one, so that her auburn hair cascaded down her back and across her shoulders. She looked at him in silence as he began to kiss her cheeks, lips, and eyes while undoing the back of her dress. She said nothing, only breathing heavily and letting tiny, pleading noises escape her lips. The sight of the red marks on her soft skin as he undid her corset made him gasp. "Please don't wear this again," he pleaded. "You're so beautiful without it."

Then he quickly undressed. Within moments, they were lying together on the bed, their arms and legs tightly entwined. Her smile of love was radiant as she looked up at him. His hands gently caressed her breasts while his tongue explored her lips and mouth. Then he felt himself inside her, sharing her groans and exploding with an ecstasy that was almost more than either could endure. He was experiencing heaven with her. The next two days seemed to whirl by as a flash of light in a dark sky.

Late in the evening on the night before they were to reach Southampton, they stood on the deck, holding each other and staring at the stars. "I never thought," she said tenderly, "that love could be so exquisite, that I could ever love a man as much as you."

He took her chin in his hand, lifted it, and sighed. His lips traced hers with a gentle passion and then with more demand as his mouth covered hers. Taking in the scent of her perfume, he was lost.

At the same moment, the quartermaster was standing on the after bridge. For him, it was an uneventful night – just the sea, the stars and the wind that whistled through the rigging as the ship raced across the calm ocean. As he paced the deck, he heard a curious sound. He saw something below, darker than the darkness.

Finally pulling his lips away from hers, Matthew heard someone behind them say, "Very nice."

He abruptly turned to see a ship's officer not more than fifteen feet away. "Excuse me," he said indignantly. Alyssa grabbed his arm.

"If you will," the voice said, "please step over to the railing."

"What in the hell are you talking about?" Matthew exploded.

"This," the ship's officer said, raising a gun. "Either move to the railing or I'll shoot your wife here."

Matthew felt as if he were frozen in time. Alyssa was petrified. On the after bridge, the quartermaster lifted the phone and called the main bridge. At the same time, Matthew took Alyssa and pushed her behind him. With a strained voice, he asked, "Who are you?"

Waiving the gun, the voice said, "Do as I say or I'll kill you now."

"No you won't. Someone will hear the gun and you'll be caught."

"No one's here. Look around. If they hear anything, they'll find you two dead and the gun in your hand. As a ship's officer, I'll swear you shot her and then yourself."

In an angry voice, Stanton said, "On our honeymoon? You're crazy. I don't know who's paying you to do this, but I'll double it right now." His left arm held Alyssa while he started to reach into his coat with his right.

"Stop right there," the voice said. Matthew withdrew his hand. "The price is two thousand dollars. Now you can reach in and throw the money over here."

Stanton pulled out a wad of bills. "Here," he said, "you count it." He tossed the bills onto deck near the voice.

Distracted, the officer looked down momentarily and picked up the bills. "I'll count it when the two of you are in the water." Stepping forward, he saw a brief flash and then felt something impact his head. He tried to identify the sharp sound that was suddenly ringing in his ears. Reaching up with his hand, he felt something sticky and then was overcome with dizziness. Attempting to utter something, he fell backwards and collapsed on the deck, dead.

A door behind him opened and the captain stepped forward. "Mr. Stanton, please put down the gun."

Alyssa broke into violent sobs; Matthew turned to hold her, dropping the gun.

The captain walked over. "I heard some of what was said. I'm so sorry I didn't get here sooner."

When she had calmed down, Matthew took her to their cabin. Lying on the bed, she mumbled, "You had a gun?"

"Yes, I did. When you asked me to forget about Pratt, I said I would, but I remembered my gun. I decided to start carrying it again."

She closed her eyes. "I'm so glad you did."

*   *   *   *

Three weeks later they returned home. Traveling to London, Paris, Rome and Istanbul, the honeymoon wasn't what either of them had wanted or expected. Throughout Europe, they were never out of sight of four Pinkerton men hired by Stanton to protect them. The lack of privacy was painful.

More Pinkerton guards awaited them as they disembarked in a late July evening at the East River Pier. The weather was hot and humid but the skies were heavily overcast, promising a severe thunderstorm. After his driver had deposited their luggage in her entry hall, she closed the door and stared at him, exhausted. Collapsing into a chair, she looked up and said, "Is this how it's going to be? A life with guards around the clock? Matthew," she exhaled, "I couldn't live a life like that."

He walked over and took her hand. "Darling, you won't have to. I'll end this."

She shook her head in fear. "What can you do? I don't know who your enemies are, and neither do you. Someone is trying to kill you!" she said in a muffled scream. "Do you understand that? Now they want to kill me too!"

He remained silent while she stood up and climbed the staircase to their bedroom. Within thirty minutes, she was asleep on the bed, fully clothed. He sat in the drawing room, studying a thick report delivered to him by the Pinkerton Detective Agency several days before they arrived home.

Flipping through the report, he came across the investigation of the ship's officer he had killed on *The City of New York*. At one time, he had been a petty criminal, involved in larceny, prostitutes, and drugs. He wasn't married, but there was a woman, Tillie Longstreet. She had lived with him near the Hudson River Pier. She was uncommunicative, refusing to talk to the investigators. He tapped his finger on the page and then stood up and walked to the liquor cabinet, where he poured himself a glass of Courvoisier brandy.

Tillie Longstreet was not at home when he called on her the next day. He talked to several neighbors who had little to say except that she sometimes hung out at a tavern near the wharf. That evening, he left his hansom in front of a ramshackle building whose open basement door, under brown stone steps, let noise and lights out onto a dark street. He went through the basement doorway into a narrow room where a single bartender served a dozen men and women at a twenty-foot bar. Two waiters moved among tables where a number of other people sat engaged in loud conversations.

The lights from the gas lamps hanging from the ceiling were dim in the heavy cloud of smoke that hung stagnantly in the air. They flickered back and forth on a medium built bartender in his forties, with ragged gray hair, bushy eyebrows and a thick mustache that exaggerated the ruddiness of his hard-muscled face. Their eyes met, and the bartender said, "What'll you have, mate?"

"Tillie Longstreet – do you know her?" Stanton asked.

"We sell drinks, not information. If it's information you want, I suggest you look elsewhere." The bartender sourly turned away.

Over the noise, Stanton shouted, "A double scotch, on the rocks."

Delivering the drink, the bartender said, "One dollar."

Laying a ten on the bar, their eyes met again. Leaning across the bar, the bartender scooped up the bill and pointed. "In the corner, the one in the red dress. You didn't hear it from me."

The thin girl in red sitting with a bearded man looked at Stanton with weary dark eyes as he approached. He smiled politely at the man and asked, "Mind if I join you?"

"We do," he said with a scowl on his face. "Aren't you a little out of place here?"

Stanton looked down at his suit and tie and grinned slightly. "I suppose I should have worn a disguise. I need a moment of your time."

"About what?" said the man.

"About her," he answered, nodding at the woman. He pushed a five dollar bill into the man's hand. "Go have a drink at the bar. Give us a few minutes."

"What the hell . . . ." He looked down at the five and stood up. "You mind, Tillie?"

She shook her head. "Go on." When he had left, she leveled a hostile stare at Stanton. "You've got five minutes. What do you want?"

"Ned Beaumont," he said. "You lived with him."

"Not anymore. He's dead, that stupid bastard."

"He tried to kill me."

"So you're the one, on the boat."

"You know about that?"

Lighting a cigarette, she exhaled a puff of smoke. "I know."

"Why would he do that?"

"Listen, mister, I wouldn't talk to the police and I'm not gonna talk to you."

"I'll make it worth your while."

She leaned over, the cigarette dangling from her mouth. "How much?"

"They paid Ned one thousand dollars. I'll pay you the same if you can tell me who hired him."

The cigarette dropped from her lips. "How in the hell did you know that?"

"Ned told me."

"That goes to show how stupid he was."

"So you know about the one thousand dollars?"

"I know."

She stopped to look around the room. "Ned's dead. I don't want the same to happen to me."

"It won't. No one will know. Just tell me who paid him."

"When do I get the thousand?"

"When you've told me who paid him."

With frightened eyes, she whispered, "Said his name was Johnson. I didn't believe that."

Stanton rolled over in his mind the name Johnson. Nothing. "Why didn't you believe that?"

"He was acting queer. Fidgeting all the time with his hands, keeping his head down. He didn't want Ned to see his face."

"Did you?"

"I peeked through the doorway. I don't think he knew I was there."

"Give me a clue, Tillie. What'd he look like?"

"He stayed in the shadows. He was big, about two-hundred pounds. About as tall as you, but he had gray hair and a speckled beard."

Stanton let out a breath of frustration. "That would describe half the men in New York."

"He had a lot of money. Came in a ritzy carriage, dressed like a million dollars."

"You still haven't told me much."

She hesitated, wetting her lips. "He wanted you and your wife dead. That's something. Not many men in New York would want that. He must've hated you pretty bad."

Stanton sat motionless for a long minute. "Could you identify him if you saw him again?"

"I don't know. Maybe."

"That's a start."

Rubbing his eyes, he gazed at her through the smoke. "I need you to try."

"When?"

"I'll get back to you. Where can I find you?"

She looked slowly around the room again. "Tell Hennessey. He'll find me."

"Hennessey?"

"You're in Hennessey's Bar. It's on the sign out front. You said I'd get my money."

He dropped one hundred dollars on the table. "When you identify him, you'll get the rest." He stood up to leave. Behind him he heard several sobs.

"I did love him, you know. At least . . . I think I did."

CHAPTER FORTY-SEVEN

▼

New York City

"I want you to make a list," he insisted.

Robert Longbourne looked at him in amusement. "Of all your enemies? Do you know what that would involve? Matthew, you haven't tried to make many friends." Studying the expression on his longtime friend's face, he let out a sigh. "How far back?"

"As far as you think you need to go."

Frustrated, Longbourne said, "We've done business with thousands of people. Before that, think of what your life was like. Think of Berg and those men you killed."

Stanton turned his chair toward the window and lit a cigar. Looking out on the East River, he lifted his head and blew smoke upward, watching it float to the ceiling. Twisting back around, he raised his index finger. "Let's narrow it down. Only the people who you think might want to kill me."

Longbourne shook his head. "You're asking me to read minds. I don't know how to identify those whose hatred runs that deep. You've cost a lot of men a lot of money."

"Robert, do your best. This is critical to me. Alyssa's scared to death."

"What about your dealings with Roosevelt and the anarchists? Anything there?"

"That's over and done with."

"Don't be too sure. Those people are nuts."

"I'll think on it. Get me a list by Friday. I'll make my own list. We'll compare notes then."

"Matthew," Longbourne said thoughtfully. "I'm puzzled. What good is a list going to do for you? You can't interrogate everyone and ask if they want to kill you."

"Robert, I have a witness."

"A what?"

"A woman who said she saw the man who hired someone to kill us on the ship."

"Have you told the police that?"

"No. They talked to her and got nothing."

"Then why would she help you?"

"Money."

"Oh, the great persuader. Don't tell me – then you'll take her to see everyone on the list."

"Look, I know you think this is crazy, but it's all I've got. No, I won't do that, but I will sift through the names and describe the people to her."

"If you can."

"Yes, if I can. Keep this to yourself. She also seems scared. I don't want anything to happen to her."

*   *   *   *

The double shot of bourbon seemed to have calmed him down, although not entirely. He sat in his hard oak chair, his gray eyes shining in the gloom. Today was a dark day. Matthew Stanton was alive; the man he had sent to kill him and Alyssa had failed. It was time to stop. He would draw too much attention to himself. Roosevelt was more important. The President had just submitted to Congress a bill forming a Federal Food and Drug Administration. It would result in the closure of a number of meat packing plants. Thaddeus Pratt owned many of those plants. He didn't care about hygiene or the safety of the public, he cared about money. That and the minimum wage bill being pushed by the new president would destroy his business. He slammed his drink on the desk. That wouldn't happen!

Roosevelt would be making a speech on Labor Day in Washington. That idiot Grover Cleveland had signed that day into law as a result of the murders during the Pullman strike. "They should have celebrated the killers, not the victims," he spat out in the empty room. The first Monday in September; it would be a perfect time to kill him. Milo Dance was dead. Staring out at the overcast sky, he mumbled to himself, "There are plenty of other nuts out there. I'll find one." Money talked, and he had a lot of it – at least for now. He called for his carriage.

*   *   *   *

Longbourne had held his list to one hundred people. Stanton's list was much shorter, but he held a different view of his business tactics than Longbourne. When they sat down to compare notes, Stanton was dismayed at his prior life. "Was I that bad?" he demurely asked.

"You weren't bad, just what I would call insensitive. You've lived with tunnel vision for so long, I just don't think you realized it. Matthew, you never thought about it until now. I don't know Alyssa well, but she's having a mighty big effect on you. She must be one hell of a lady."

Stanton smiled. "She is that. Now, the list." He sat back and looked at what reflected the past history of his life. Scanning through the multitude of names, he stopped several times to remind himself that he needed to take the time to offer apologies. Suddenly, he came across one name and froze. Stopping to catch his breath, he looked up at Longbourne.

"What's wrong?"

"Robert, why is Thaddeus Pratt on this list? I never did anything to him."

Longbourne sat back, resting his chin in his crossed hands. "You don't think you did, but it happened. Several years ago, we were hauling food products down the coast. I came to you and said our men had discovered that a number of meat packages didn't smell quite right; they had a strange odor."

"I don't remember that."

"You had other things on your mind. I asked you what you wanted to do. You told me to unload everything and leave it on the dock."

"Even the meat that didn't have an odor?"

"All of it. Over $1 million worth of meat. I think your decision was wrong, but I wasn't in the mood to argue with you."

"What happened to it?"

"It was left there to rot. It all spoiled."

"Why didn't you tell me later about that?"

"Would you have cared?"

Stanton took a deep breath. "Then . . . probably not."

"So there you are."

"Wait a minute. What does that have to do with Pratt?"

"It was his meat."

He raised his eyebrows, staring at the ceiling. "He wouldn't want to kill me over that."

Longbourne's expression hardened. "I damn sure would. The meat was probably all bad, but that wasn't our concern. You made an arbitrary decision, and it cost him dearly."

"But I've met him recently. He didn't indicate . . . ." In the middle of the sentence, he stopped dead. "Jesus! He was the man in the carriage that day, and he wouldn't shake my hand when I offered it."

"What man in a carriage?"

"Forget about that. I think I've found the man who wants me dead." *Now*, he thought to himself, *how do I find him and how do I get Tillie to identify him?*

CHAPTER FORTY-EIGHT

▼

New York City

He would draw him out. He lived on Long Island, Alyssa had said. Tormented and unable to sleep, he sat at three o'clock in the morning writing a note to Pratt. It said, "You're looking for someone to settle an old score. That's what I do. Meet me at the restaurant in the Mayflower Hotel tomorrow at noon. You won't be disappointed." He left it unsigned. Reaching for his glass of sherry, he took a long sip, wondering if it was too simple. Pratt was a very smart man; would he fall for it and go to the hotel, or would he send someone in his place?

He tore up the note and wrote another. "A thousand dollars wasn't enough. Meet me at Hennessey's Bar tomorrow night at nine." He'd go with that one. Returning to bed, he found Alyssa awake. "Where were you?"

"Writing a note."

She snuggled against him, and he wrapped her up in his arms. "Who was the note to?" she drowsily asked.

"The Devil." She smiled and fell back asleep.

The next morning, he sent the note. Then he told Alyssa. She was horrified. "If you think he tried to murder us, tell the police. Don't do this yourself," she begged. He wasn't listening.

*   *   *   *

The following evening, he sat watching from a nook in the corner. He sipped on his second dry martini. Tillie sat at the bar, talking to Hennessey, intermittently turning to look at Stanton with questioning eyes. Pratt was forty-five minutes late. Another woman, at the opposite end of the bar nearest him, also turned at times to look mischievously in his direction. He suspected she was a prostitute and did everything he could to ignore her. Distracted, he suddenly looked at the door to see a heavy-set man walk in, dressed like many others in the bar but with a hat pulled down to his eyes. In the dim light, he tried to focus his eyes on him. The man stepped next to Tillie and said a few words to the bartender. He was within five feet of her. She turned nonchalantly toward Stanton and nodded. He stood up, paid his check, and walked hurriedly out of the bar, brushing the man as he did. It was Pratt!

Stepping quickly into his carriage, he yelled at the driver to leave. Whipping the horses with a crackling lash, the carriage plunged forward into the night just as Pratt flew out the door. Stanton looked back through the small rear window to see Pratt standing in the middle of the street, his hands on his hips and his face flush with anger.

*   *   *   *

Patches of mist descended on the low-lying sections of the road into Glen Cove, casting eerie shadows from the full moon that skimmed along the tops of trees. Matthew Stanton's thoughts were elsewhere as his carriage made its winding way to Thaddeus Pratt's mansion. It was a meeting with destiny. This time Pratt had issued the invitation. It would be only the two of them. The sleek black carriage pulled through the two guard houses and made its way to the entrance, where Pratt stood waiting. "You came," he said, as Matthew stepped down. Shaking his hand, he said, "Thank you." Both men were impeccably dressed, as if they were attending a social function.

Leading Stanton into his drawing room, the butler brought him a selection of after dinner drinks. Stanton chose a thirty-year-old brandy. Holding it up, he stared at Pratt who had become seated in a deep-cushioned chair across from him. "Is it poisoned?" he asked.

Pratt showed a little amusement. "That would be too easy."

"You tried to kill Alyssa and me. Don't deny it – I know it was you. Why?"

"Mr. Stanton, I'm not here to deny anything. Let's start by being honest with one another. I'd say the world has dealt each of us some severe blows."

"Oh God. You're not going to give me a lesson on morals?"

"Not at all. Just a few obvious facts. We each fancy ourselves as quite flawless. You needn't shake your head – I know you agree with me. Life, Mr. Stanton, is a question of nerves. There are rare moments when it hits us that we have to come to terms with who we are. I've reached that moment."

"Good for you," Stanton answered sarcastically.

"I deserved that. You're well aware of that old saying, 'What does a man achieve who gains the world but loses his soul?,' or something like that. Looking back, I've lived a life I'm not particularly proud of."

Stanton let out a contemptuous laugh. "You didn't ask me here for this. What in the hell is it that you want?"

"I'll come to that in a moment. You are blessed," he continued, "with a strong mind, very good looks, great wealth, and an exquisite wife."

Matthew felt a sudden surge of blood rush to his face. "You tried to kill her, you bastard. Don't you dare mention her in my presence!" Hesitating, he was overcome with a violent urge to kill Pratt. His eyes darkened with a blazing fury.

Aware of the eruption that had consumed Stanton, Pratt raised his palms as a calming gesture. "Mr. Stanton, you misunderstand me. That wasn't my point," he said as he backed away. "Please don't take it the wrong way. I want the two of you to have a happy life, and I want no harm to come to either of you."

"Good. Now that we have that settled, what in the hell is your point?"

Pratt stood up and walked over to the liqueur tray. Pouring himself another drink, he said, "The point, Mr. Stanton, is that I was overcome by a madness that I want to put behind me. I was obsessed with you, obsessed to the point that I was irrational. You may know this, but I even contemplated assassinating President Roosevelt for what I perceived he would do to my business interests. I went so far as to interview anarchists to help me. It was total insanity on my part. What I've done and what I've thought of doing can't be justified, and I make no excuses for it. I'll only say that you have my word that I've changed. I'll do nothing further, and I ask your forgiveness for all past things I've done to you."

Stanton was incredulous. Pratt was either crazy, lying or sincere, or all of those. Stanton didn't know which to believe. "You should be locked up. Assassinating the President? What in the hell were you thinking? Mr. Pratt, you're an evil man."

Pratt slowly lowered himself back into his chair. "I couldn't agree with you more," he said in a low voice. "Now, what would you have me do?"

Stanton stood up and began pacing the room. Turning to Pratt, he said, "Issue a full and honest public confession of everything you've done and planned."

"That's the one thing I can't do."

"Then you're not sincere in what you've said."

"I'm sincere, all right, but if I do what you ask, my life's over. What good is that?"

"You're something else. I have no pity whatsoever for you. . . . But I'll say this. As despicable as I think you are, I'll give what you've said some thought. I'm also going to give you fair warning. I may take all of this to the authorities."

"I hope you don't do that. I told you I've changed. But if you do, I'll deny it all. It'll be your word against mine." Pratt stood up. "Thank you for hearing me out."

Stanton left, thinking he was just made a party to the most bizarre conversation of his life. Pratt poured himself another glass of brandy. Smiling to himself, he thought he had performed well. Now, the question was – had he managed to convince Stanton?

CHAPTER FORTY-NINE

Matteawan State Hospital, New York

"What the hell . . . . he's gone," the attendant yelled across the floor. His supervisor ran over to him. "What do you mean, he's gone?"

"Milo Dance! One minute he's in a coma, the next minute he disappears."

"That's impossible. He *was* in a coma, dammit! Someone must have been here, taken him away."

"No one was here, sir, only me. I stepped out for only five minutes, and when I came back, his bed was empty."

"Jesus Christ! Get the police up here. I'll go tell Dr. Isaacs."

Dr. Isaacs couldn't be told. He was draped over his desk, his throat slit and his body covered in blood. An attached note said, "Good-bye."

Theodore Roosevelt read the headlines the next day with detached interest. Matthew Stanton was devastated. Thaddeus Pratt was elated. Now, like Leon Czolgosz, Milo Dance would walk into Pratt's arms. He had paid Dance twenty-five thousand dollars, a down-payment. Dance would want the other seventy-five for killing Roosevelt. Then it occurred to Pratt: the seventy-five was also for killing Stanton. Life was good.

Matthew Stanton carried a Colt .38 wherever he went. He bought a small Derringer for Alyssa and taught her how to shoot, trying to assure her all the while that Milo Dance was no threat to them. Armed guards were hired to protect them; someone was with her whenever she left he house. She hated it. Three nerve-racking weeks had passed since the escape. Maybe he had left the country.

Thaddeus Pratt was also worried, but for a different reason. Labor Day was one week away. He would miss a golden opportunity to kill Roosevelt. Milo Dance wasn't worried. He had recovered the twenty-five thousand dollars that was hidden when they caught him. He had a false identity and now lived above a dress-maker in New York. No one would find him. The dress-maker, a widow named Mrs. York, was thrilled to have a new tenant, particularly one as kind and caring as Mr. Brown. All the while, America moved forward at breakneck speed. Over fifty thousand homes now had electricity, the two-story sculpture of the goddess Diana had been placed atop the newly constructed Madison Square Garden, and Henry Ford had devised a way to make automobiles not in days but in hours. Crime was rampant and police forces were expanding. The FBI had not yet been created, and little thought was given to one escaped mental patient who had disappeared.

Theodore Roosevelt loved giving speeches. It was said he was without equal when it came to stirring up a crowd. His Labor Day speech at the Washington Memorial would be one of his best. It would be his cry for a unified America, for honest unions and conservation of natural forests. He had a resounding theme *—America won't be good for any of us unless it's good for all of us.* And he believed it.

*   *   *   *

Long Island, New York

The hansom had dropped him off in front of the massive iron gates that protected the estate on Bellevue Avenue. The early morning gray mist shrouded the mansion to such an extent that it appeared to be a blur against the irregular cloud patterns that seemed to hug the ground. At the guardhouse, his hansom had been denied entry. He smiled to himself, thinking that if he had so chosen, he could have entered the house in any number of ways.

When Thaddeus Pratt received the call from his guard saying that a Mr. Brown wished to see him, he told him to turn Mr. Brown away, that he knew no one by that name. Looking at his watch, Pratt saw it was only eight o'clock in the morning. When the guard called back and clarified that it was Milo Brown, Pratt froze. "Hold him there for five minutes and then show him in," he instructed.

Wrapping himself in a silk robe, he hurried to his drawing room where he withdrew a Remington pistol from a locked cabinet and placed it in his desk drawer. Standing behind the desk, he heard a knock on the door. "Come in, please," he said.

The door opened to a well-dressed and groomed Milo Dance. Without moving, Pratt said, "Mr. Dance, how nice to see you. Please, have a seat."

Letting his eyes roam the room and then settle on Pratt, Milo said in a low, hollow, and hypnotic voice, "You're not surprised to see me?"

Pratt nervously answered, "Not at all. You and I had a deal. I expected you back so we could complete it."

Dance nodded slightly and walked over to the desk. "You seem nervous, Mr. Pratt."

Inhaling deeply, Pratt pulled out his pocket watch, flipped it open, and held it up for Dance to see. "You've been out for three weeks. Why come here this early in the morning?"

"The early bird gets the worm. Isn't that what they say?" He walked over to stand within several feet of Pratt. Starting to reach for his desk drawer, Milo warned, "Don't." He then stepped around Pratt, pulled the drawer open, and removed the gun. Holding it in Pratt's face, he said, "Is this what you were looking for?"

Pratt cleared his throat and backed away. "I promised you a gun. That's it."

Milo sat in the desk chair, holding the gun toward Pratt. Raising his palms to face forward, Pratt said, "That thing's loaded. Would you mind putting it down? We have to talk."

Dance smiled at Pratt's unsettled expression. Pointing to the chair across the desk, he said, "Please sit down. I've always wanted to see how it felt to sit in your chair." Focusing on Pratt's eyes, he said, "You know what, it's not that great. Now, what did you want to talk about?"

Pratt tightened the sash on his robe and clenched his fists. *I won't let this nut intimidate me*, he thought to himself. Calming his nerves, he stared at Dance with hard, cool eyes. "Seventy five thousand dollars. When you finish the job, the money is yours."

"I'll finish the job. But it'll cost you another twenty-five thousand dollars, now."

Pratt's expression hardened. "That wasn't our deal."

Dance raised the gun, pointing it squarely at Pratt. "It is now."

"I don't keep that kind of money around."

Fury erupted in Dance's eyes. "Like hell you don't! You want Stanton and Roosevelt killed. You pay me now."

Pratt rubbed his nose with his forefinger, his worried mind focused on the gun. "All right. Roosevelt is giving a speech on Labor Day to thousands of people. I'll give you a plan to kill him."

"I don't want your plan; I'll do it my way." He stood up, his left hand held out while the gun remained pointed at Pratt. "The goddamned money," he demanded.

"If you'll wait in the hallway, I'll have it for you in a second."

"I'll wait here."

"You can't . . . ."

Pratt was interrupted by the sound of the cocking of the gun. "Hold it, hold it," he exclaimed. Standing up, he walked over to a bookcase, pulled it away from the wall, and opened a safe. Removing a wad of bills, he tossed them to Dance. "I don't want to see you here again. Let me know where you'll be, and I'll send you the rest of the money when the job is done."

Dance stood up, shoved the gun in his belt, and walked quietly out with the money in his hand. Feeling as though he had just escaped the Devil himself, Pratt removed a handkerchief and wiped his brow. After the assassination, he decided, Dance would be killed, even if he had to do it himself.

That afternoon, a Pinkerton agent advised Matthew Stanton that Milo Dance had met with Thaddeus Pratt. Stanton hired two more men to guard Alyssa and sent a telegram to Attorney General Knox.

CHAPTER FIFTY

▼

New York City

In the far distance, Matthew Stanton heard a noise, something that jarred him from his deep sleep. It sounded like the breaking of glass, followed by a *tap tap*. He opened his eyes, blinking while he tried to focus in the dark. The noise abruptly stopped. He looked over to see Alyssa sleeping soundly, her hair tossed across the pillow. He took a deep breath and started to lay back down when the sound resumed. *What the hell?* he thought to himself.

A sense of stark terror suddenly overcame him. He had a dreadful feeling of being watched . . . or that something was about to happen. Was he being paranoid? The Pinkerton guards were outside the house. Nothing could happen with them there. He took a deep breath to calm his nerves and quietly got out of bed. Throwing on a robe, he reached into the night table and removed his gun. He walked softly to the doorway, listening intently for any noise, but everything was quiet again.

Where in the hell did the sound come from? He walked down the hallway to the balcony. Nothing! Now he was wide awake. With faint footsteps, he descended the long winding staircase and stopped at the bottom. There it was again, but this time different. It sounded like metal grinding on metal. He walked noiselessly in his bare feet into the drawing room, went over to the desk and sat in his chair. Placing the gun on the desk, he waited. His pulse began to quicken, but for no reason. *What kind of life is this?* he thought. Inhaling deeply, his mind drifted to Alyssa upstairs and the thought of the normal life he longed for with her. So much had changed, so much of the fog in his life had been blown away. Twisting around, he stared out the large window behind him. The moon was hidden behind a layer of clouds, casting deep shadows along the landscape. Where were the guards? The heavy draperies rustled slightly.

Then he heard another sound. Lifting the gun off the desk, he released the safety while his eyes searched the darkness. He *was* paranoid. Reaching into his robe, he pulled out a match and lit the gas lamp in front of him. Letting his eyes again drift around the room, he saw it was empty. Releasing a breath of pent-up air, he sat back and closed his eyes. It was then that the cord was brought over his head and forcibly tightened on his neck. Panicked, he tried to tear it loose, only to feel the circulation cut off. His head was spinning and began to ache. *It can't end this way,* he thought.

Then a gunshot erupted and he felt himself falling . . . and falling. After that, another gunshot and the sound of running footsteps. Then the soft hands and warm lips of Alyssa, hands that pulled him up from the brink of death.

An hour later, they sat talking to one of the Pinkerton guards, a cold towel wrapped around Matthew's neck. Alyssa's head was on his shoulder. "He came through a window," the guard said.

"And none of your people saw him?"

"Sir, there was a commotion across the street. We thought it was a danger to you. Two of our men went over to see what it was. It was then that he broke a window and got inside."

Stanton massaged his neck, furious at what had happened. "Why didn't you get him when he ran out of the house? Surely you heard the gunshots."

"Mr. Stanton," the guard said with his hands folded and eyes down, "it happened so fast. We ran to the front door just as he flew through it. In the darkness, he disappeared."

"And that's it?"

"No sir. There was blood on the door and steps. He was wounded."

"Did you get a good look at him?"

"No, I'm afraid we didn't."

Matthew closed his eyes momentarily. It didn't matter; he knew it was Dance. He felt Alyssa's hand take his. "What do you suggest now?"

"That you two go away until this thing is over. Believe me, we did our best to protect you, but he's like an invisible ghost. We can bring in more men if you'd like."

"No, that won't help." Turning to Alyssa, he said, "Darling, I've been asked to go to Washington. Until now, I've said no. Come with me. Let's leave in the morning."

She nodded and cuddled closer to him. She mumbled, "I want to get as far away from here as possible."

Looking up at the Pinkerton agent, Matthew said, "If you will, detective, I'd like two of your men to accompany us."

"Yes, sir. That'll be no problem. Anything else for tonight? Do you want us to contact the police?"

Stanton shook his head. "That would only be a waste of time. I was careless. It won't happen again. You can leave. But this time, stay where I can see you."

Turning to Alyssa, he whispered, "Darling, you saved my life. Did you get a good look at him?"

A chill ran down her spine. As if in a trance, her voice was shaking but in a monotone. "He was tall, about your height. He didn't look like a burglar. He had nice clothes and a face that might have been handsome if it were not all twisted. His eyes . . . they were frightening."

"Like someone who was insane?"

"Yes, like that."

*   *   *   *

Thaddeus Pratt stood near the end of the New York Central rail platform. He looked anxiously at his watch, seeing that it was ten minutes past 9:00 AM. His eyes burned from the smoke of a nearby coal-fired plant. Two trains had come and gone. He looked up and down the platform and saw nothing but men heading off to work. A morning newspaper was dropped on a bench near him. He glanced at the headlines. They spoke of the war in the Philippines. He glanced back down the track.

What was wrong? He'd been there for half an hour. The note had said he would be coming in on the express train and that he was bringing damning evidence that would send Pratt to prison. It demanded that Pratt meet the train. Where in the hell was Stanton? He wandered toward the far end of the platform. A train was approaching. Looking back, he saw a man on crutches, his head down, attempting to lift something with a bandaged hand. *Pitiful,* he thought to himself. He heard and then felt the rumble of the train as it got closer.

Did Stanton really have proof of what he had done? How could he? He couldn't take that chance. His men were nearby, watching and waiting. Everything was working out as he had planned – except maybe Stanton. Stanton wouldn't live past the day; he might not live long enough to make it off the platform. The train would fly past Pratt until it stopped at the terminal, but Stanton would get off where Pratt was standing.

He heard a sound; the man with crutches was standing next to him. If it was money he wanted, he had made a mistake. Pratt turned away and ignored him. The shrill warning horn of the train blasted through the air. Suddenly, he felt a rush of cold air. Something was pushing him. He felt his balance give way and turned as he fell headlong onto the tracks. Within seconds, his screams ended with the screeching sounds of the brakes of the train.

CHAPTER FIFTY-ONE

▼

Washington, D. C.

The President cleared his throat. Glancing around the room, he saw two members of his cabinet, Knox and Root, together with Charlie Wilcox, and a man and a woman. Sitting down at the end of the table, he nodded to the woman. "Mrs. Stanton, I've heard much about you. I'm glad to have you here." Alyssa felt everyone's eyes turn in her direction. "Thank you, Mr. President."

"Attorney General Knox here has filled me in on what the two of you have been through lately. I must say, I've always preached the strenuous life, but I believe you're overdoing it a bit." Pausing to look first at Stanton and then at her, the President thought how remarkably beautiful this woman was, dressed in a red silk dress and straw hat tilted at an angle. "I'm truly sorry for what you've been through, and I fully understand why your husband doesn't want you out of his sight." She thought how immensely she liked this new president.

"Now," he said, "will someone kindly tell me what's going on?"

Knox spoke up. "This meeting was called because of a telegram I received from Mr. Stanton. He believes, Mr. President, that an attempt on your life is imminent. Mr. Stanton, will you please explain why you believe that."

"Mr. President, I'm somewhat embarrassed to bring this up, but you may recall the psychopath who escaped recently from the New York criminal asylum." The President nodded. "He's become involved with a wealthy man, Thaddeus Pratt, who lives on Long Island. I don't believe Mr. Pratt fits in the standard mold of an anarchist, but I do believe he's been plotting for quite some time to assassinate you. I have no doubt that this psychopath is the same man who tried to kill me several days ago."

"Mr. Stanton, is this just a gut feeling you have? I can't do my job for the American people if I have to depend on gut feelings."

"No," Stanton said thoughtfully, "it's a lot more than that. I spoke to Mr. Pratt personally and he told me he thought of killing you but later abandoned the idea."

Secretary Root eyed Stanton suspiciously, taking notes as he spoke.

Roosevelt stood up, pointing a finger in Stanton's direction. "It makes no sense that an assassin would tell you that. So where in the hell does that leave us?"

"It's a bit more complicated than that. I believe he told me the truth about his desire to kill you and then lied about abandoning it." Roosevelt, joined by several others, shook his head in disbelief. "And that's why this meeting was called?"

"I hired a team of Pinkerton agents to watch his home. Last week, he met with Milo Dance, the psychopath."

"Mr. Stanton," the President said impatiently as he begun to pace, "that tells me nothing."

"This is a complicated puzzle, Mr. President. Pratt spent quite a long time interviewing anarchists. He has a deep hatred for you. He has the money and ability to pull this off, and now he has Milo Dance again."

"Give me some hard proof of what he plans to do."

"I can't. I've told you what I know. My life's been based on my instincts, and I listen to them. I think Pratt's coming after you."

Secretary Root tossed his pen on the table. Roosevelt turned to him. "You have something on your mind, Mr. Secretary?"

Glaring at Stanton, he said, "That I do. When I was asked to attend this meeting, I naturally wanted to know what it was about. When I heard Thaddeus Pratt's name, I had my department investigate him. Mr. President, this is all a bunch of hogwash."

Stanton turned pale while Roosevelt leaned back against the wall, adjusting his glasses. "Instincts have been a great part of my life, Mr. Secretary. I'm willing to listen to Mr. Stanton."

Root scowled. "I'm happy for you both, but the threat, if there ever was one, is over. Mr. Pratt died this morning."

There was a collective gasp around the room. Matthew Stanton was shocked. "How?" he asked.

"He fell under a train."

The President was perturbed. "Mr. Stanton, what do you have to say about that?"

Stanton's mind was wandering. Suddenly, everything made sense. He knew it was Pratt who had tried to kill Milo Dance. Pratt's big mistake was not succeeding. "Mr. President, I'd like to know how that happened. I don't believe for one moment he simply *fell* under a train."

"You're calling Secretary Root a liar?"

"No," Stanton said. "If he died under a train, he was pushed."

"However he died, Mr. Stanton, it's over. I'm a very busy man, and frankly I have no more time for this." He picked up some papers, turned, and left the room. Wilcox and Root quickly followed. Knox studied Stanton. "You're not convinced?" he asked.

"Not one bit. You have to understand the mind of Milo Dance. It's not over for him. He wants to win."

"Win?" Knox asked. "That's idiotic."

"It may be to you, but not to him."

"Well," the Attorney General said with a large sigh, "I'm done."

"So you'll do nothing?"

"What can I do?"

"Check the President's schedule, add extra protection, come up with a plan."

"That's ludicrous. Do you understand this man? He won't walk around with *any* protection. He wants to shake everyone's hand in sight. Unless we had an imminent threat that we could prove to him, there's no way he would allow us to change anything. Mr. Stanton, you're spinning your wheels. This has been a waste of my time. Good day, sir."

CHAPTER FIFTY-TWO

▼

Washington, D.C. – The Washington Monument

He hobbled through the historic lobby of the Willard Hotel. Then he started toward the Washington Monument. Along the way, several people passing him stopped to salute or pay their respects. He was a war veteran, and America celebrated its heroes. He stepped onto the street. It was still morning. The celebration wouldn't begin until noon. The summer heat was still moderate, but the humidity made it feel much worse. He began to sweat in the heavy uniform.

He turned, adjusted his crutches, and limped down Connecticut Avenue to 15th Street. The Washington Monument was just coming into view. The marble, sandstone, and granite obelisk near the west end of the National Mall was striking in the morning sun. Except for the Eiffel Tower, it was the tallest structure in the world. Approaching from the east, he had a grand view of the Reflecting Pool and the Lincoln Memorial.

Over a thousand chairs were lined up in front of the speaker's podium. The other ten thousand or so spectators would sit on the lawn. It was a perfect day to celebrate America's workers. He could feel the electricity in the air as he walked closer to the reviewing stand. As a war veteran, he would be given deference. People began to stand aside as he limped toward the front row chairs. The President wouldn't appear for several hours, but he could wait. He was incredibly patient.

The years locked up in a cell had taught him that time was important only if you dwelled on it. To him, time was just a flash of light. Finding a seat only twenty yards from where the President would stand, he looked back and thought of President McKinley the previous year, full of life and giving a speech to a thunderous ovation at the Pan-American Exposition. They said what happened to McKinley couldn't happen again, but they were wrong. History always repeated itself, and time never changed anything. The idea of it was so powerful that he was spellbound.

He snapped out of it when several police officers walked up. Looking down at his crutches and then his hand, one became suspicious. He whispered something to the other and then turned to him. "Can you tell me how you hurt your hand?"

Looking up, he asked, "Is there something wrong?"

"The man who shot President McKinley, his hand was bandaged. We'll have to search you."

"No problem, officer." He struggled to stand up, and was helped by one of the men. Looking closely at his bandaged hand, one asked, "How did that happen?"

"I was shot."

"Shot?"

"Yes, in the Philippines, by the guerillas."

"Mind if we search you."

"Go ahead."

The officer patted his clothing, inch by inch, and suddenly stopped at his pockets.

"Would you please empty them."

Leaning on his crutches, he removed everything and placed them in the hands of the officer. Looking up, the officer said, "I can't let you keep this knife."

"It was a gift from my commanding officer. I'd hate to lose it."

The officer studied it and saw the insignia of the U.S. Fifth Regiment. Turning to his companion, they nodded and he returned it. Completing the search, they examined his crutches. Handing them back and giving him a slight salute, the officer said, "Sorry to bother you. We can't be too careful."

"I understand. Thank you, officer."

When they walked away, he slapped his leg smugly. *I should be on the stage*, he thought.

Several hours later, above the noise of the crowd, he heard a Marine band strike up The Star Spangled Banner. The crowd hushed and the thousands of spectators stood and placed their right hands on their chests. The band next played Hail to the Chief, which brought a roar from the crowd. Suddenly before him, so close he felt he could reach out and touch him, was the President, accompanied by a number of guests and an Episcopalian priest. After the invocation and several introductions, Roosevelt was at the podium. It stood about ten feet above ground level and was draped with an American flag. With a broad smile showing his large white teeth, he looked down and waved his hat to the crowd, who reacted with delirium. After stopping to point in the direction of several friends in the audience, he put his left hand on the flag and held up his hat with his right hand for quiet.

Roosevelt was a striking figure, dressed in a three piece dark blue suit with a yellow-print tie. A gold watch chain hung across his vest. Reaching into his coat pocket, he removed his thick written speech, hesitated, and then decided he didn't need it. He replaced it and again smiled at the now silent mass of people.

"We are a nation of pioneers," he began. "The first colonists on our shores were pioneers, and it was those pioneers and their descendants who pushed forward from the old world into the wilderness of America to form our great commonwealth. Our country has been populated by pioneers, and therefore it has in it more energy, more enterprise, more expansive power than any other in the entire world."

He stopped for tumultuous applause, enjoying more than he had ever thought the role of president. "You who I am now addressing stand for the most part but one generation removed from these pioneers. You and your ancestors have shown the qualities of daring, endurance, and far-sightedness, of eager desire for victory, and a stubborn refusal to accept defeat. Above all," he said with his fists raised in the air, "it is you who have recognized in practical form the fundamental law of success in American life – the law of worthy work, the law of high, resolute endeavor."

The speech continued on for a full hour, the crowd mesmerized with the ideals of this energetic young president. Finishing his remarks, Roosevelt said, "Above all, let us shrink from no strife, moral or physical, within or without the nation, provided we are certain the strife is justified; for it is only through strife, through hard and dangerous endeavor, that we shall ultimately achieve our goal of true national greatness."

The audience jumped to its feet with thunderous applause. Milo Dance sat staring at Roosevelt, unmoved by anything he had said. His mind was focused instead on how he would kill this man. Standing up, he tried to shuffle his way toward Roosevelt, but the President was talking to someone and then turning away as if to leave. "Mr. President," Dance yelled. Roosevelt turned back, staring at Dance. Then he smiled and waved at him. Roosevelt was still ten feet above him on the podium.

Hobbling to the stairs, Dance pulled himself up, step by step, until he reached the top. Roosevelt shifted his eyes to see Dance approaching. He briefly studied the uniform Dance was wearing, sensing that something was wrong. Turning to a man next to him, the President pointed at Dance and whispered a few words. The man's eyes locked on Dance. Cursing his painful leg that still carried the bullet fired by Alyssa Stanton, Dance lunged toward Roosevelt, the knife now in his hand.

To Matthew Stanton, it seemed to happen in the flash of a second. He reached for the President to pull him out of Dance's path, but his movements seemed a blur. Raising his arms to block the knife, two shots suddenly rang out. One hit a man standing to the right of Roosevelt in the neck, the other shattered the head of Milo Dance as if it were a watermelon. A spurt of blood hit Stanton in the face and chest as he was shoving the President to the floor. Loud screams and utter pandemonium spread through the crowd as parents grabbed their children and others ran in terror from the grandstand.

At the Lincoln Memorial, over twelve-hundred yards away, a lone gunman laid down a Lee-Enfield Mark I high-powered rifle, hurriedly walked down the staircase of the Memorial, and disappeared into the melee. The first attempt to assassinate an American president with a long-range rifle had failed. The gunman walked down the block as police officers were running to the Monument. He kept his head down, his hat pulled down near his eyes. At the corner, he spotted a glistening black carriage with two black geldings waiting for him. Seeing that no one was paying attention to him, he stepped up through the open door and into the cab. The red velour seats were covered with heavy cloths. He thought that strange.

The well-dressed man who sat across from him asked, "Did you kill him?"

The assassin shook his head. "Someone else was there. He rushed Roosevelt and all hell broke loose. Both my shots missed."

The other man was suddenly distraught. "We had planned this so carefully. How in the hell . . . ." he started to say, but then stopped himself.

The carriage tore down Connecticut Avenue at high speed, just avoiding police blockades. Once clear of the melee and turning onto 13th Avenue, the assassin said, "If you'll give me my money, you can drop me off here."

The other man nodded and bent over slightly. When he came up, he had a small revolver in his hand. The gun was wrapped in heavy padding to muffle its sound.

"What . . . ?" the assassin started to say as the gun exploded and two bullets struck him in the chest. His eyes wide, he slumped over and fell onto the seat.

Over the rumbling sound of the carriage and horses pounding along on the cobblestone street, the man yelled up to the driver, "The river. Hurry!" He reached over, grabbed both ends of the heavy cloth covering the seat, and wrapped it around the dead man. Then his thoughts turned to his plan to disappear.

At the river, the dead man was pulled from the carriage by the man and his driver, tied to a sack of bricks, and dumped into the muddy waters. *It was over*, the man thought as he stood on the bank of the river watching the body slowly sink beneath the surface. Everything had gone wrong, from the murder of his friend Pratt to the failed assassination attempts. Wiping his brow, Samuel Dutton wasn't so much disappointed as he was relieved. Theodore Roosevelt couldn't be killed, and he wouldn't try again. It was finished.

He tried to steady his nerves in the strong wind. Exhaling a deep breath, he looked toward his driver. The explosion seemed to come out of nowhere. The first bullet lodged in his spine, the second removed the top of his head. He lost his balance and plummeted headlong into the water. Glancing momentarily at the dead body, the driver threw the gun into the water and whipped the horses as the carriage pulled away. Pratt and Dutton were gone, but it was far from over.

CHAPTER FIFTY-THREE

▼

Washington, D.C.

The investigation seemed to drag on for weeks. After a complete autopsy, it was concluded the man with the knife was in fact Milo Dance. The two shots were meant for the President. There was another assassin who fired from the Lincoln Memorial. Congress passed new legislation requiring that Roosevelt and all future presidents be put under twenty-four hour guard and protected by the Secret Service. Roosevelt protested and allowed the bill to sit on his desk for a month. After a visit from a congressional delegation, he reluctantly signed it, mumbling that the American people would now lose access to their president.

On a chilly September evening, a lone man stood in the colonnade on the east side of the White House. The double doors down from him opened and a weary Theodore Roosevelt walked toward him. "Thank you, Mr. Stanton, for coming this late in the evening." Inhaling a deep breath, he said, "I like it out here at night. It gets me out of my suffocating office. When I finish the new West Wing, I'll have a colonnade and rose garden located directly outside my office. That's something I look forward to with great pleasure."

"I'm sure it will be grand, Mr. President. It's always good to see you, sir. You're looking well."

"Thanks to you. I wanted to give you a medal, but Secretary Root said it wasn't appropriate, that there was no protocol for that. But I don't suppose you need another medal, do you?"

"No, sir. You wanted to see me."

Leaning against a post, Roosevelt pointed to the full moon. "It makes you think we're the only ones on earth. But it also makes you painfully aware of your own mortality." Turning to Stanton, he said, "Mr. Stanton, this country is still full of anarchists. It beats the hell out of me why they think as they do, but maybe I'm just not that smart. One thing I do know is that they still want to kill me."

Stanton looked at his tired eyes. "It's a hell of a job you took on."

"Don't feel sorry for me. I don't dwell on it – it comes with being president. Unfortunately, it's not just the nuts in our country I have to worry about. We have a war going on in the Philippines with a band of rebels who are killing thousands of our good men. The Japanese seem to regard us as an enemy and are in a massive arms buildup. Their navy is now far larger than ours. Countries I used to believe were allies are now preaching hatred against us: Japan, Germany, Spain, Russia, and even some Arab nations."

Stanton was bewildered. "We're not a threat to those countries. That makes no sense."

Roosevelt shook his head. "We're becoming too powerful, too rich, and at times too arrogant. They can't seem to figure us out. The truth is, Mr. Stanton, the world will never love us. They'll respect us, and they'll fear us. But they'll never love us. We're much too audacious."

Stanton was silent.

"I'm reorganizing my staff. As part of it, I'm creating an office for a new advisor. The man I put in that office will be my national security advisor. You and I are Harvard boys, we've been through the war together, we think alike. You said you rely a lot on your instincts. I told you I do too. My instincts, Mr. Stanton, tell me that you'd be perfect for the job. The question is, would it be perfect for you?"

"You're asking if I'd accept it?"

"Yes, I am."

Stanton took a few steps out onto the lawn. Looking up at the stars, he turned back to the President. "I'm very honored." Momentarily closing his eyes, he stopped to rub his forehead. "I've had some close run-ins with death lately. I'm also very aware of my own mortality. Right now, there are few things in life I'm sure of. The one constant I have is Alyssa. Your offer, I assume, would take me away from her quite a bit."

The President nodded. "I'm afraid it would."

"I'm not sure I could do that, not now. I've got to discuss it with her. When do you want an answer?"

"Let me know in thirty days. Until then, Mr. Stanton, I wish you well."

"And you also, Mr. President."

*   *   *   *

New York City

She looked at him sternly, full of questions and trepidation. "Why would the President want you, why now?"

He shrugged. The reasons he gave were vague. "He sort of considers us blood brothers - Harvard, the Rough Riders, all that history between us."

She turned to him, frowning, sensing something was about to happen that would dramatically change their lives. "You wouldn't be asking me if you weren't interested in the job."

"Alyssa, it's not just a job, it's working everyday with the President of the United States, a man for whom I have the highest respect. He's truly a great man."

Her face softened. "Matthew, I share your feelings for him. Sitting with you in that meeting, listening to him, is something I'll never forget. But darling, that doesn't change how I feel about your decision. I love you, more than anything. I want to have children with you. I don't want to live my life away from you. You're not the only person who could be his National Security Advisor."

"This hasn't so much to do with him," he said softly, "but who I am, what I've become. You have made such a change in me."

She raised her eyebrows and laughed a little. "You can't fool me. This has everything to do with him. He drew you into this."

He searched her face, begging for more understanding. Yet, as he did, he was captured by her elegance, her smile, the way her eyes flashed at him. She was his world.

Watching him, her eyes locked on his. "I know you more than you think I do," she said. "I know you're torn up by this decision. Matthew, I should give in, but I'm not going to make it easy for you. In fact, I'm going to make it very hard for you. I don't want to lose you again, not after what it's taken to get this far."

He lowered his head. She had challenged him. How could he tell the President no?

Anticipating his answer, she had a fleeting smile.

"I'm going to think about it," he said.

Her smile vanished. "So I'm not part of this decision?"

Three days later, he told her. "Sweetheart, I'm going to Washington. I can't let the President down. I hope you'll come with me."

"And spend my time alone with the other wives while you're in the Philippines, Japan, Russia, or who in God's heaven knows where?" She thought she could make him understand, but he wasn't listening.

"I need to pack," he mumbled.

She knew now that he would always come and go as he pleased, that she couldn't change him. And she was heartbroken. "You've given me an ultimatum. Matthew, don't you see. Our marriage, our love for each other, is like a fine piece of porcelain. If you break it, you can try as hard as you might to glue it back together . . . but the cracks will never go away. Don't you understand that?" He stared at her moist eyes, unable to say anything. Reacting to his cool silence, she said in an aching voice, "Please don't do this to us."

"I love you," he whispered. He kissed her cheek and walked upstairs.

CHAPTER FIFTY-FOUR

▼

Manhattan

The stranger arrived at ten o'clock at the three-story sandstone house on 35th Street, a district with large homes and gardens. The hansom had dropped him off two blocks away. He didn't want anyone to know where he was going. He walked slowly up the stairs of the house, built within the last ten years, and disappeared inside. No one saw him go in. The rain had come in torrents, along with the strong winds, and even the most brave hearted had decided not to venture out.

The house was heavily furnished, mahogany and gilt, expensive but ugly paintings, a massive bronze bust in the hallway. He was shown into the drawing room by a large manservant, who didn't ask his name. A man, slightly built with white hair and deep set eyes with dark circles, rose from an armchair to greet him. The eyes didn't flinch, but an unpleasant little smile said, "Good evening." They shook hands. For a moment or two, his host let him remain standing. Two other men, sitting in large overstuffed chairs in the shadows of the gas lamps, remained seated and didn't bother to show any courtesies to the visitor. The two seated men whispered something to each other while the white-haired man carefully studied his guest. After several seconds, the white-haired man asked him to be seated.

"You were careful to be sure that no one followed you?"

The visitor nodded. "You haven't told me your names," he said.

"You're not going to know that." The three men quietly appraised him. He was smaller than they had imagined, not more than five feet five or six. He had dark wavy hair, a pale face, eyes of the most vivid gray, and an ironic smile that seemed plastered to his face. He had the look of a man who thought little of life, who thought of it as a bad joke. He was wearing a black, belted raincoat. An ugly, puckered scar of a bullet wound showed across the left side of his forehead.

The white-haired man offered him a cigarette. He leaned forward for a light, coughing slightly. Drawing back, his host said in a low voice, "Let me ask you something. You're still involved in the anarchist movement?"

The man laughed. "I'm involved in any movement that pays me well."

"You've been briefed on what we're looking for?"

"Only the bare facts. I'd like to know the rest."

"You were in the army."

"I fought in the Philippines."

The white-haired man began to wheeze and cough, and then rasped. "I'm an asthmatic. You'll have to excuse me. Now," he said clearing his throat, "they tell me you were deadly with a long-range rifle."

"I was a sharpshooter."

"And you were good?"

"Your sources must have told you that. I rarely missed."

"How do you feel about a political target?"

The visitor's face hardened, the scar standing out like a glowing bulge. "If it's not a soft target, not a woman or child, I don't care who the target is. Who did you have in mind?"

"The President."

"Jesus!" The visitor paused. Looking down, he was lost in thought for several moments. "That's a hard target. It will cost you plenty."

"We're willing to pay whatever is, shall we say, reasonable." The white-haired man stood up. "What did you have in mind?"

"Twenty thousand dollars."

"That's a bit high. I'll have to think that over."

"You have five minutes. I'm not coming back."

The host turned and looked at the other two. If they allowed Roosevelt to turn 150 million acres of land into forest reserves under the National Monuments Act, in defiance of Congress, they would be financially ruined. There was no alternative. They both nodded. "Twenty thousand it is. You'll get paid when the job is done."

"No, now."

"In advance? That's out of the question."

"Then we have nothing to talk about." The visitor stood to leave.

"Wait a minute," the host said. He walked over to his two companions, and they spoke in low voices for several minutes. Returning, he said, "At the right time, we'll tell you when and where. When I have your okay, we'll send the money."

The man pulled out a slip of paper. "Send a telegram to general delivery at this address."

Six months elapsed before the telegram was sent. It said, "Hampton Roads, Virginia, 7:00 AM on December 17. The yacht *Narcissus*." The house on 35th Street had long since been abandoned, and the white hair was now black to match the newly grown thick beard.

*   *   *   *

Hampton Roads, Virginia

At seven o'clock in the morning on December 17, the small yacht appeared and dropped its anchor a half mile from the shoreline. It joined a small flotilla of other yachts that sat in the still waters awaiting the spectacle. Thirty minutes later, the presidential yacht *Mayflower* dropped its anchor in preparation for the display of American sea power that would arrive at eight o'clock.

The waters, having been buffeted into strong waves by cold west winds only several hours earlier, had settled into a sea of calm. The President stood on deck talking to his military advisors and cabinet members as the hour quickly approached. Sensing the President's desire to be seen alone by the sailors lining the decks of the warships, the advisors and members slowly drifted away, exposing the striking figure of the nation's leader in a dark suit and silk top hat.

The marksman on the nearby yacht, hidden by the ship's rigging, carefully adjusted his Lee-Enfield Mark III rifle to bring the President within its sights. At precisely 8:00 AM, the massive armada sailed into view and began its eighteen gun salute as it passed in front of the *Mayflower*. The President's yacht, formerly a naval destroyer, remained relatively still in the choppy waters now generated by the fleet. The nearby yacht began to roll side to side.

The fleet's massive guns exploded, and simultaneously the shooter squeezed the trigger of his long-range rifle just as the *Narcissus* lurched in the waves. A man instantaneously collapsed in a pool of blood on the deck of the *Mayflower*. It wasn't the President. It was "the moment", Matthew Stanton thought. The shooter realized his mistake and attempted to steady himself by leaning against a mast. Quickly re-levering the rifle, he again brought his intended victim within the sights of the gun and nervously pulled the trigger. The bullet again missed and ripped through another spectator on the *Mayflower* amid the pandemonium that had erupted. A number of other shots immediately rang out from several nearby ships, pummeling the shooter and shredding him into pieces.

Then everything seemed to drift into slow motion. The President, held down on the floor of the deck by Secret Service agents, looked up to see Secretary of War Root lying in a pool of blood twenty feet away. Behind him, the man who was his National Security Advisor had collapsed, mortally wounded from a shot to his head. The minutes slowly turned into hours. The scene was eventually cleared and all were sent home.

The *Narcissus* was seized by the Coast Guard and torn apart in the frantic search for evidence. The assassin was found dead, or what was left of him. He had no identification. The rifle had been fired twice and two spent cartridges recovered. The boat had no registration and was immaculate except for several newspapers and other materials indicating the man was an anarchist. After weeks of deliberation, the published finding was that he acted alone. Commissioner Jay Neeley didn't believe it.

The rumors at first spread wildly that the President had been shot. The entire nation was galvanized from another assassination. Then the complete facts were disclosed, and the world gradually shifted its attention from the tragedy at Hampton Roads to the Great White Fleet as it made its astounding forty-three thousand mile journey around the globe.

EPILOGUE

▼

Washington, D. C.

It was shortly before five in the afternoon that Theodore Roosevelt stepped through the double-doors of the newly constructed West Wing to the podium in the Rose Garden of the White House. The garden was thronged with reporters and photographers. There was a rush to photograph the President as reporters began shouting questions. He looked pale and tense. His press officer fended off the questions with a promise that they would all be answered at a later time.

A hushed silence came over the reporters as the President began to speak.

"Ladies and gentlemen," he said. "I'm here because Secretary Root, who would normally be my spokesman in matters such as these, lies severely wounded in the Washington Barracks Hospital. Closure to these assassination attempts is something we've all prayed for, hoped for. But I'm sorry to tell you it won't come – not today. I've lost my National Security Advisor to a bullet intended for me. He was a good and able man, a man who I regarded as a close friend. Secretary Root is suffering through a difficult recovery, but he will survive.

"With everything that's happened, you and the American people must ask yourselves this. As faithful and true servants of the people, did either of these men deserve to be shot? Is death by an assassin's bullet to be their reward for years of dedication and service to our country?

"History has proven, time and time again, that whatever we do, however we act in the interests of our great country, there are people within our shores who will wish to kill us. They will relentlessly plan our murder. It was never contemplated by our founding fathers that our leaders would be so at risk in the service of our great nation. But through that window, that indomitable window of time, we can look back to the assassinated leaders who have come before us and heed the warnings.

"We must be ever vigilant, for the anarchists never sleep. They, and those who would give them comfort, encouragement, and help, are our enemies; they are the enemies of a great and democratic society. Through our goodness, our steadfast will and determination, and our diligence, we *will* defeat them.

"The window of time teaches us one great truth – what has gone before will come again. History *will* repeat itself. We must be prepared for it.

"Thank you for coming today."

Roosevelt held up his hand to stop any questions, nodded to the reporters, and walked back through the open doors into his office. There, he walked over to a couple standing with their young daughter. Smiling warmly at the woman and the child, he remarked, "I think Alice is a fine name." Turning to the man, his said, "I will sorely miss John Wolcott; he was a good friend and a fine and able advisor. Now, Mr. Stanton, it's time that you accept my offer and become my National Security Advisor. I have but fifteen months left to my term, and it would be an honor to have you by my side. I need you."

Matthew turned to Alyssa, who was now holding Alice, and raised his eyebrows in a questioning expression. She looked at the President and then stepped forward and kissed her husband on the cheek. "It's up to you, sweetheart. This time, I think you have Alice on your side."

* * * *

After making twenty stops on six continents, the fleet returned to Hampton Roads fourteen months later to honor its Commander in Chief at the end of his term, without having experienced a single adverse incident. During its voyage, it was met by enormous flag-waving crowds at every stop. A million people waving American flags greeted the arrival of the fleet in Australia. Over twice that many were present in Japan, the country the President had feared the most in the Pacific. American naval might had come of age, and a new balance of sea power had been established in the Pacific.

A month later, Theodore Roosevelt retired from the presidency after serving seven years and was succeeded by William Howard Taft.

In 1912, Roosevelt launched his "Bull Moose" campaign to regain the presidency. During a stop in Milwaukee, he was shot at close range by John Schrank, a psychotic New York saloonkeeper. Shrank had his .38 pistol aimed at Roosevelt's head, but a bystander saw the gun and deflected Shrank's arm just as the trigger was pulled. Roosevelt was extremely lucky. He had a manuscript of his fifty-page speech in his coat pocket, folded in two, and the bullet traversed it as well as his steel spectacle case before entering his chest. It lodged in his chest and effectively stopped his campaign. The bullet was never removed. Theodore Roosevelt died a little over six years later, at the age of sixty.

Assassins' bullets played a unique role in his career. He became president when McKinley was shot, and his final campaign was ended when he was shot. Shrank, who stalked Roosevelt all over the country, said he was motivated to shoot Roosevelt by a dream: *"I saw President McKinley sit up in his coffin pointing at a man in monk's attire in whom I recognized Theodore Roosevelt. The dead president said, 'This is my murderer, avenge my death.'"*

Shrank was never tried. He was committed to an asylum for the criminally insane, where he remained until his death.

CPSIA information can be obtained at www.ICGtesting.com

228136LV00002B/25/P